Praise for *Revenge of the Tide*

'Haynes' first novel was a sensation last year
and this, her second, is just as impressive
and in much the same mould.'
Daily Mail

'Unputdownable, this thriller with a heart of gold
reads like a breath of fresh air.'
Red Magazine

'Haynes' first book was Amazon's Book of the Year last year
so it was always going to be a tough act to follow. *Revenge of
the Tide* clearly shows her initial success was no accident.'
Sunday Express

'This second novel by Elizabeth Haynes is as excellent
as her first one. It is full of suspense and intrigue and
keeps the reader hanging on its every word.
Very highly recommended.'
Eurocrime

'Fear about the loss of control is at the heart of readers'
obsession with crime. That Haynes lends Genevieve
power over fear, her body and the men for whom she
dances has enabled her to create a character with more
complexity than is usual in genre thrillers.'
Independent on Sunday

'*Revenge of the Tide* delivers everything I crave from
a murder mystery: suspense, emotion, an element of
humour, surprise, and, just when I thought I had
the answers, Haynes adds another twist.'
Pretty Litter Magazine

'A thoroughly gripping read. This is another
great book from a promising author who is
fast becoming one of my favourites.'
Crimesquad

'Everything you could possibly want from a thriller:
an intelligent and feisty heroine, a mysterious packet,
complicated relationships and a great cast of characters who
are not always as guilty or as above suspicion as they might
at first appear. Do you want to add tension and intrigue
to your everyday life? Read this novel. Now.'
Book After Book

'Haynes' first book was a runaway success so her second
had a lot to live up to. I'm happy to say that from the first
page I was engrossed in this gripping murder mystery;
so much so that I finished it in just three sittings.'
Peterborough Evening Telegraph

'This racy jeopardy thriller proves that Haynes'
much-praised first novel was no fluke.'
Morning Star

'Do you know that feeling of dread when you pick up
the second book of an author whose first book pulled you
in and wouldn't let you go? You're longing for it to be
of the same standard with hours of indulgent, satisfying
reading ahead of you, but you're equally conscious that it
might be 'the difficult second book' which tells you quite
clearly that this isn't going to be an author to follow. This one
sat on my desk for days and then I thought that it wouldn't
harm just to have a look, just to get an idea of what it was like...
I finished it in the small hours of the following morning.
It's not long before you discover that this is the difficult-
to-put-down second book. And if you haven't read
Into the Darkest Corner then you really should.'
The Bookbag

'I really enjoyed *Into the Darkest Corner* and
was looking forward to this second book. It is
every bit as engaging. The plot is excellent...
Plenty for reading groups to discuss.'
NewBooks Magazine

'It's hard to put the uniqueness of Elizabeth Haynes' writing into words. Her stories grip you by the throat and force you to acknowledge that this is what real crime and real horror look and feel like, as well as real love, hope, fear. Suddenly, much of the other crime fiction you've read seems, in comparison, rather like stories made up by writers. Haynes is the most exciting thing to happen to crime fiction in a long time.'
Sophie Hannah

'Check the locks on your doors and windows and surrender to this obsessive thriller.'
Karin Slaughter

'Utterly unputdownable. A stunning debut.'
S J Watson

'A chilling, page-turning read that charts domestic violence without flinching and portrays OCD with insight and compassion.'
Rosamund Lupton

'A powerful psychological drama and portrayal of obsession.'
Daily Mail

'Haynes' powerful account of domestic violence is disquieting, yet unsensationalist. This is a gripping book on a topic which can never be highlighted enough.'
Guardian

'Amazon UK's Book of the Year, Haynes' claustrophobic psychological thriller is a shocking portrayal of domestic abuse.'
Mslexia

'A tense and thought-provoking debut novel with dark moments. Its portrayal of obsession will send a shiver down your spine.'
Shotsmag

About the author

Elizabeth Haynes grew up in Sussex. She works as a police intelligence analyst and lives in Kent with her husband and son. Her first novel, *Into the Darkest Corner*, was Amazon's Best Book of the Year, winner of Rising Stars and a *New York Times* Bestseller as well as featuring on the Specsavers TV Book Club. Her much-anticipated second novel, *Revenge of the Tide*, was published to rave reviews in 2012. *Human Remains* is her third novel.

HUMAN REMAINS

ELIZABETH HAYNES

Myriad Editions

Published in 2013 by
Myriad Editions
59 Lansdowne Place
Brighton BN3 1FL

www.MyriadEditions.com

3 5 7 9 10 8 6 4 2

A CIP catalogue record for this book is available from the
British Library.

ISBN: 978-1-908434-18-0

Printed on FSC-accredited paper by
CPI Group (UK) Ltd, Croydon, CR0 4YY

For my best friends
Angela Wiley, Karen Aslett and Lindsay Brown
with love

Annabel

When I got home I could smell the bins on the cold air, a faint bad smell that made me wrinkle my nose.

Inside, I opened the back door, rattling the box of cat biscuits in the hope that it would bring her scurrying. It was a clear night, so she would most likely not make an appearance at the back door until I was in the bath, when she would howl and scratch to be let in. Despite the cat flap and my efforts to get her to use it – propping it open, coaxing her and bribing her and even shoving her forcefully through it – she ignored it and came in and out only when I was home to open the door for her. I'd even tried getting rid of the litter tray, but she'd just piss on the lino in the kitchen and then pull it up at the corner with her claws to try and cover her excretions. After that I gave up.

I stood in the doorway for a few minutes. 'Lucy?' I called, experimentally. 'Lucy!'

Nothing. The bloody cat could stay out there all night, I thought, knowing for a fact that I would be down here in my bath towel in a couple of hours' time, dripping wet and freezing, rattling the cat biscuits while she sat on the lawn and stared at me, punishing me for having taken too long.

I made myself a cup of peppermint tea and some cheese on toast, and ate it sitting at the kitchen table with one eye on the open door in case the cat might walk in and I could shut it and trap her inside. When I'd finished I scraped the crusts of the toast into the kitchen bin, sniffing. Something definitely smelt bad. The last time I'd smelt something this rotten, the cat had brought in a frog and I hadn't realised until I found it, half-slimy, half-dried, under the dresser in the dining room, right at the back. I'd had to get on my hands and knees with a wad of kitchen towel and rubber gloves on to get rid of it.

I stood in the doorway again, wondering if Lucy had killed a pigeon this time and left it by the bins, not trusting me to dispose of it appropriately. I put on my slippers, took my torch from the drawer and ventured down the steps into the darkness, listening to the sound of the traffic from the main road beyond the trees. In the alleyway between my house and next door I lifted the lid off each of the two bins: the black one, and the green one for compostable waste. Both smelt unpleasant, but that wasn't it. I shone the torch around the base of the bins. No pigeon, no rat – nothing dead.

The house next door was unoccupied, had been for some time, but as I stood there I realised I could see a light coming from inside. A dim golden light, as though a single bulb shone in a room somewhere inside, undisturbed.

I tried to remember when I'd last been out here. Sunday afternoon? But it had been broad daylight, sunny, and even if the light had been on next door then I wouldn't have noticed it. Maybe an estate agent had been in, or a property developer, and left it on?

When I'd first moved in, a couple had been living next door. I fought for the memory – what was she called? Shelley, that was it. She'd introduced herself to me once. It had been summer, a hot day. I was just getting home and she was working in the front garden. She stopped me for a chat even though it was the last thing I wanted. Tired, fed up as usual, all I longed for was to get inside and prise my shoes away from my hot, aching feet and have a cold drink. All I remembered from that conversation was her name, and that her 'partner' – which always sounds odd to me, not 'boyfriend' or 'husband' or 'fiancé' – was called Graham. I never met him. I think he moved out that autumn, and although I saw her coming and going a few times up until last winter I assumed she'd moved out some time after Easter because I hadn't seen her after that, and the garden she'd previously tended had grown wild and tangled.

2

At first it was just a feeling, a creeping sense of dread, and then I heard a noise from the direction of the empty house. Something was wrong. I peered across into the darkness as the cat pushed her way through the gate and trotted over to me, winding herself around my legs. She was covered in something, some mess, sticky and foul-smelling, wrapping herself round and round my skirt. My hand flew up to my nose and mouth to block out the smell.

At that point I thought about going back to my kitchen and phoning the police. Looking back, that was exactly what I should have done. But it was Friday night, and because I worked at the police station I knew that all the patrols would be busy, if not mopping the blood and puke off the streets of Briarstone town centre, then back at the station booking people into custody. I'd worked with the police for years and never once had to call them out myself. I didn't even know what to say. That there was a bad smell next door? They'd more than likely suggest phoning the council on Monday morning.

The low metal gate to the back garden hung off its hinges; beyond it the remains of what had once been a neat patch was now an untouched wilderness. The grass and weeds were waist-high in places, having outgrown their own strength and flopped over on themselves like an army midway through a battle. I stepped over the grass on to the brick path that led to the back door. The kitchen windowsill was covered in dead flies. I shone the torch into the empty room. A few flies were still crawling on the glass of the window and still fewer followed an angular flight path around the centre of the room. The door to the dining room was ajar and the light glowed through, a dim golden light from somewhere inside.

I looked down. The lower pane of the back door was missing. Dark smears marked the bottom of it, tufts of cat hair around the edge as though cats of various colours and breeds had all been in and out as many times as had taken their fancy. I tried the door. Too much to hope that it would be unlocked, of course. Then I knocked on it, the sound of my knuckles

3

rapping on the glass, which rattled in the frame. I pushed the pane gently, and then a little harder, and before I knew what had happened the glass had fallen in and smashed into pieces on the tiled floor of the kitchen inside.

'Oh, shit!' I said aloud. I was really in trouble now.

I should have turned away from the door. I should have gone back into my own house, and locked my door, and thought no more about it. It wasn't my problem, was it? But, having practically broken into the house already, I thought I might as well finish what I'd started, and see if anyone was inside.

I put my hand through the empty frame and reached around to the inside. The key was in the lock. I struggled to turn it – it was stiff, hadn't been opened in a long time – and at the back of my mind was the thought that there were probably bolts at the bottom and top of the door as well. But when I twisted the key in the lock it eventually turned, and the door opened easily enough. The smell from within was powerful, and sudden. And then it faded just as quickly, as if all the badness from inside had escaped and fled into the night.

'Hello?' I called, not expecting a reply and not knowing what the hell I would have done had one come. 'Is anyone there?'

The house felt warmer than mine, or perhaps that was just because I was coming inside from the cold of the garden. My footsteps crunched on the broken glass, echoed in the empty kitchen and I put a hand over my mouth and nose to try to muffle the smell, which was stronger again in here. I shone the torch around the room, illuminating cupboards and shelves and a cooker, which were dirty, the surfaces dulled with a sticky film of dust.

Maybe it was just food that had gone bad, I thought. Maybe whoever had lived here had departed in a hurry and left the remains of their dinner behind. But the fridge door stood open and it was unlit, nothing but black mould inside. It was obviously unplugged.

4

I pushed the kitchen door open slightly and then there was enough light for me to turn off the torch. I was in a dining room, the table and chairs in place, a tablecloth covering the table and two placemats upon it. A table lamp sat on a sideboard, a modern design but, like everything else, with a thin film of dust blurring its surface. It was lit.

I could hear a sound. Low voices, but a bit tinny – it sounded like Radio 4. The radio was on? Surely, then, someone was in here? I felt as though I was being watched, as though someone just out of my line of sight was waiting.

I told myself not to be so paranoid, and went into the hallway. It looked lived-in, the house – carpet on the floor and pictures on the walls. The only light came from the table lamp in the dining room.

'Hello?' My voice was quieter in here, my footfalls on the carpet muffled. The smell wasn't as bad, or was it just that I was getting used to it, growing accustomed to breathing through my mouth?

The radio was louder now, the sound of an interview between a male voice and a female, the woman arguing a point and the man placating her. Above that another noise, or was I imagining things now?

I felt something against my leg and jumped, a squeak of panic coming out of my mouth before I could stop it. But it was only the cat, winding herself around my ankles once before dashing off through the dining room door and into the next room. 'Lucy!' I said, urgently, not wanting to have to crawl behind someone's sofa to try and coax her out again. I pushed open the door to the living room at the front of the house. It was dark in here, the light from the dining room not penetrating this far into the gloom. The curtains were closed, the gap between them letting in only the faintest glow from the street-lights outside. I turned on the torch again and as I did so I caught a movement, a flash of white. It was Lucy again, rolling on the carpet in the middle of the room. I could hear her purring above the thudding of my heart.

The room was furnished, but sparsely: a sofa, a low coffee table in front of it. On the table, a bunch of what must have once been carnations, stiff and brown in a waterless vase.

The beam of the torch passed over an armchair. And even having felt a presence, half-expecting to find somebody in here, in this room, I gasped at the shock of seeing a person there, one horrifically distorted out of shape: black instead of white, the skin of the face stretched and split in places, the eyelids drawn back into a wide, black, hollow stare and the belly blown up like a balloon, stretching the fabric of what it was wearing – what *she* was wearing, for it was a skirt, and the hair that still clung to the skull was long, fine, lank, and maybe still fair in places, although it was coated in something – grease, some substance. And what made it worse was that there was movement in the abdomen, as though she was breathing – although surely this wasn't possible? But when I looked closer I realised that her stomach was composed of a swarming, churning mass of maggots… And despite the horror, and my deep, heaving, choking breaths, I could not tear my eyes away. One hand was resting on the arm of the chair, and the other hand, the forearm from the elbow to the hand, was *on the floor* beside the chair, as though she'd dropped it, knocked it off the edge like a misplaced remote control.

And then the purring began again – the bloody cat – and I looked down to see her rolling on the carpet beside the dark mess, as if the smell was catnip to her, and not the stench of the putrefying bodily fluids of a decomposing corpse.

Colin

I was eating cornflakes and reading jokes aloud from the back of the 1982 *Beano* annual when my father clutched his chest and dropped dead on the kitchen floor.

Looking back it almost seems comical, but I believe that this was the moment when my life took a change in direction. My father was the sort of person you could read jokes to. He would spend Sundays fixing the car and I would help him, learning where all the pieces went and what they all did. He laughed a lot and together we both laughed at my mother, who was thin, and serious, and bitter.

After he died, I couldn't bring myself to read the *Beano* any more. I didn't really laugh any more, either.

It's grim, feeling like this on a Monday morning. Other people have hangovers, people my age; or they've spent the weekend caravanning, or shagging their girlfriends. Or shagging someone else's girlfriend. I've spent my weekend writing an essay, and staying up too late with whisky and porn. As a result I'm finding it impossible to concentrate on the budgets.

The trouble is that I'm not sure I even want a girlfriend any more. I like my life the way it is, carefully ordered. I like my house the way it is. I'm not pathetically tidy – no visiting psychologist would have concerns for my sanity – but I think I would find it annoying to have to accommodate someone else's things. Clothes finding their way into my wardrobe. Books on to my bookshelf. Food into my fridge. No, I don't want that. I don't have room in my house. And I don't suppose I have room in my head, either.

Still, sex would be nice.

Garth has once again failed to bathe this weekend. He's on the far side of the office yet I still catch a sniff of him every so often. As hard as I try to concentrate on happier things, I can't help breathing in his direction, experimentally tasting the air again and again, incredulous that such a scent could possibly come from a normal, gainfully employed adult. He picks food out of his teeth, accompanying this with a sucking noise, and while this nauseates me I find myself glancing across at him, watching him rooting around the back of his molars with a probing finger and wondering what he's eaten that could possibly become that stuck. He has ink on his fingers, too, like a schoolboy, and, whilst I loathe the man, whilst every second in his presence is a form of torture to my senses, I have this dreadful fascination with him – an unquenchable curiosity about how someone so repellent can subsist in the modern world.

Martha saunters in late. New shoes, I notice – the third pair this month by my reckoning.

'Morning, Colin – good weekend?'

She doesn't really want to know, of course. It took me a while to work out that the question is rhetorical, a ritual for a Monday morning. The first few times she asked, I told her at great length what I'd done over the weekend, carefully editing the details that even I knew were not appropriate to share with a colleague. She looked vacant after a few minutes. She stopped asking, after that, and only recently – I believe when someone else asked me the same thing within earshot and got a brief response – did she recommence with the Monday ritual.

'Fine, thank you. And you?' It had certainly been eventful, especially Friday evening, but of course I wasn't about to supply her with the details.

On occasion I heard her telling one of the others all about her weekend – kite-flying or baking or hiking or going to a fête or watching football or visiting her cousin or landscaping the garden – but her reply to me was invariably the same.

'It was good, thanks.'

Vaughn sends me an email asking if I want to go to the Red Lion at lunchtime. I'm tempted to ask if he wants to go now; I doubt things are going to suddenly get more exciting here in the next three hours. It's sad that the thought of half an hour in a dark, mouldy pub next to the gasworks with Vaughn Bradstock is so cheering.

When I get to the Red Lion, twenty minutes early, not even noon, Vaughn is already there at our usual corner table, with a pint of John Smith's waiting for me. Vaughn and I worked together, many years ago. He used to be a contractor in the IT department at the council, and for some reason we developed a friendship that endured even when he moved on to other projects. He gave up contracting in favour of the security of something more permanent, and now he works for a software development company in the town centre. Handy for the Red Lion.

'Colin,' he says tonelessly in acknowledgment of my arrival.

'Vaughn,' I reply.

He wants to talk about his girlfriend again. It's usually that, or philately.

I brace myself with a couple of good swallows of the bitter, wondering whether it's too early to be thinking about a whisky chaser. Meanwhile Vaughn chunters on about whether his girlfriend is having an affair. I want to point out that she can hardly be in the first flush of youth – surely it's unlikely? But he's convinced that she is lying to him about something. He sits with his head bent low over his pint, pondering whether taking her to Weston-super-Mare in the caravan is a good idea.

My mother took me to Weston-super-Mare on holiday the summer after my father died. We stayed in a guest house three streets back from the seafront; close enough to hear the gulls, not close enough to hear the sea. I was almost thirteen years old and already I didn't fit into my own skull. I read Eliot and Kafka and watched documentaries on BBC2. Stayed up late

9

and got up early to watch the Open University programmes, back when it was all beards and flared trousers. My mother wanted me to build sandcastles and run in the sea, laughing. I don't think I laughed once the whole time I was there. I sat in the shade and read until she took my books away. After that I sat in the shade and tried not to look at the girls on the beach.

'Weston-super-Mare's probably a bad idea,' I say.

In the end I take pity on poor old Vaughn and tell him about cortico-limbic responses and non-verbal cues, poor bugger.

'What the hell's a limbic response?' he asks me. And then, before I can respond, 'Oh, don't tell me. It's that bloody course you've been doing, isn't it?'

Poor Vaughn: he likes to think he's intellectual because he reads the *Guardian* and drinks a Java blend at weekends.

'It's how you can tell if someone's lying to you,' I explain. 'You look at body language, visual cues, autonomic responses, that kind of thing. And you may scoff, but the course has been fascinating, in fact.'

He looks blank.

'Alright,' I say, 'let's try a little experiment. I'm going to ask you three questions, and I want you to deliberately lie in one of your answers. I'll see if I can tell when you're lying. If I'm right, you can buy me another pint. If I'm wrong, I'll buy your drinks for the next month. Want to have a go?'

'Oh, yes, alright, then,' he says. I get the impression he's cheering up a bit. He's smiling, but I don't always trust my instincts with Vaughn. He might be suicidal for all I know. I have been known to get it wrong. Eleanor smiled at me that night, after all, didn't she? And look how that turned out.

'Right, then,' I say, 'let's see. Have a think back to the bedroom you had when you were a teenager. Picture what it was like. Now I want you to describe it to me, just as if you're standing in the doorway looking in. What can you see?'

'Well, goodness. I guess it's the dorm I shared with Roger Hotchkiss at St Stephen's. There are two beds, one on each side

10

of the room – mine is neatly made, Hotchkiss hasn't made his, of course – a wardrobe at the foot of each bed, nearest to the door... Then the window straight in front of me which looks out over the kitchens. And a large desk underneath the window. Bookshelves above the beds. We weren't allowed posters.'

He pauses for a moment, tapping his chin thoughtfully, his gaze up and to his left. This is going to be too easy.

'That it?'

'I can't think of anything else.'

'OK, then, next question. What does your mobile phone ringtone sound like?'

'It's just the standard ring, I'm afraid. I can never be bothered with anything more elaborate.'

That one was a bit quicker, but I still pick up on the cue that tells me he is telling the truth. In fact, I know it's the truth because his answer reminds me that I've heard his phone go off in the pub before now. Maybe I'm subconsciously trying to cheat? In any case, the next question is going to be the one.

'Right, final question. Tell me about your journey home last night. Did you go straight home? What time did you get there?'

It's only a small hesitation, a brief flick of his gaze up and to the right, but it's plenty. When he speaks, he even raises his pitch – too easy, way too easy.

'I didn't go straight home, no. I stopped off at the Co-op and bought some sausages and potatoes for supper. I probably got home – ooh, at about a quarter past six.'

I sit back and polish off the last of my pint. I press my fingertips into my temples and close my eyes, taking a deep, noisy breath in through my nostrils as though some peculiar psychic process is taking place.

'Your last answer wasn't quite true,' I say at last. 'Although I think the lie was quite nicely buried. You did get home at about a quarter past six, so you probably did stop off somewhere. You did stop off at the Co-op, but whatever it was you bought, it wasn't sausages and potatoes. Am I right?'

He's shaking his head and for a moment I wonder if I've got it wrong, or if he is going to try and fudge his way out of it.

'A bottle of Zinfandel and a toffee yoghurt,' he says softly.

'Another pint of John Smith's,' I reply.

After I get home I stay up far too late again: too much whisky again, useless porn again, a fruitless wank in the end. Too much whisky, as I said. When I got back from my visit earlier, I started off reading something improving – forensic biology in this case, a topic of endless fascination – then moved on to reading something improving but possibly not in the way the original writers intended it to be, and then something that's unlikely to improve anything other than the bank balance of some seedy porn producer in Eastern Europe. Not that I pay for it, of course.

I'm still feeling rather pleased with myself. Vaughn was so impressed with my display of brilliance that he demanded to know how I'd done it. I explained about non-verbal clues, how to watch a person's eyes to establish visual construct as opposed to recollection, how to spot signs of discomfort, and how each of the little clues adds up to form an indisputable picture. I pointed out that, when he'd considered the last question, his eyes had flickered up to the right, a sure sign of visual construct, followed by a look up to the left, indicating that there were going to be some elements of recollection in what he said, too. This told me that he was planning to frame his lie around some elements of truth. Added to this, the discomfort he showed when I prepared to ask the last question, the tensing of his shoulders, the shifting in his seat – slightly away from me, I noticed – and his breathing, told me that he'd clearly told the truth in answer to the first two questions and knew that this one was going to have to contain an untruth. When he told me about his shopping, the sausages and the – what else was it? – potatoes, that was it – bangers and mash, how utterly appropriate – he moistened his lips swiftly with the tip of his tongue and then rubbed his fingers across his mouth. A natural gesture, of course, and in any other context it might have been simply an itch, a sniffle, a crumb. But it confirmed the lie.

I told him all that, and of course gave him some ideas of things to look out for the next time he and Audrey are discussing indelicate matters. I try hard not to picture Audrey because, as soon as I do, I find myself imagining her naked and from then on it's a short hop to seeing Vaughn naked too, and the pair of them fucking away, a happy missionary pairing if ever there was one. Despite my best efforts, I still end up thinking about it all the way to Vaughn suddenly tensing and crying out, shouting in a way I've never heard him shout in the office, or the pub either, for that matter.

Feel rather grubby after that little lapse in concentration and have to get up out of bed at 02:45 to have another shower.

Martha asked me once about my parents. I must have been feeling communicative on that particular occasion, or else it could have been one of those situations where to refuse to answer might have appeared rude; in any case, I told her how my father died when I was eleven.

'You poor boy,' she said. I wondered if I should be offended, but then understood she was addressing my younger self. 'It must have been incredibly traumatic to lose your father at such a difficult age.'

I did not understand what she meant by a difficult age, nor what she meant, really, by traumatic. 'Life goes on,' I said with a shrug.

'Yes, but still – such a shame.'

'The living being is only a species of the dead, and a very rare species at that.'

'That sounds like a quote, Colin. Who said that?'

'I did. Well, to be fair, I'm paraphrasing Nietzsche. I'm assuming you would prefer to hear it in English rather than the original German.'

She thinks I'm weird; they all do. This was at the beginning, when I first started working for the council – they were all very chatty back then. Now I find that they leave me alone and avoid falling into conversation with me, unless circumstances force them to do so. Even then they seem to look at me warily. I think Martha views me as something of a personal challenge.

My father's funeral was held on a Saturday to enable his work colleagues to come along. There was considerable debate about whether I should be allowed to attend. I remember overhearing a conversation between my mother and her friend a few days before.

'You know what he's like,' my mother was saying. 'He thinks about things so much.'

'But he's nearly an adult, Delia. It might help him come to terms with things.'

In the end my mother relented – although it might have also been due to the lack of available babysitters to keep an eye on me. As it ended up being such a dramatic occasion, I remain glad to this day that I got the chance to attend.

I had no appropriate outfit so I wore my school uniform, even the blazer and cap. It was a hot day, with fierce, unrelenting sunshine, and of course the assembled throng were all dressed in black. My mother even had on her black coat, the one with the mink collar he'd bought her in New York. Everyone sweltered on the way to the church, gained some relief during the service and then sweltered outside for the interment. Bored beyond bored, I roasted and sweated – my shirt was damp under my blazer. I stood next to my mother and thought about something I'd read: how King Henry VIII's body was so bloated by decomposition gases while it was being transported from Whitehall to Windsor that the coffin burst open overnight. The next morning they found dogs feeding on the remains of the king. And that was in winter! What would the body of my father look like, given that it was the height of summer? I considered that his body, held in storage for nearly three weeks pending the post mortem and the inquest, might actually still be frozen, defrosting slowly in that box like a melting choc ice. I felt compelled to touch the wood, to feel if it was cold. As the vicar warbled on, I took a step forward towards the coffin, which was on a bed of plastic green grass of the sort you see covering the tables at the greengrocer's. My mother, who must have panicked at my sudden movement, lurched forward, her hand out to grab my shoulder, and stumbled over the uneven ground. In doing so, she knocked me over too and we both ended up lying inches from the open grave. The shock of it all, or maybe the excessive heat and her ridiculous coat, or maybe even the gin she'd consumed earlier to fortify herself for the ordeal ahead, caused her to vomit as people rushed to pull her to her feet. I couldn't help laughing at them, being sprayed with vomit as my mother continued to heave. Some of the mourners started to retch themselves. The vicar's face...

It was the primary topic of conversation at the wake which followed. All conceivable options were considered: my mother had fainted and I had tried to catch her; she'd suddenly been taken unwell and had fallen against me; we were both so grief-stricken that one or both of us were trying to throw ourselves into the grave. My mother, pale and weeping, replenishing her bloodstream with more gin and fanning herself with the Order of Service, kept a close eye on me at the wake and, afterwards, it was never spoken of again.

**Dead Woman Lay Undiscovered 'For Up To A Year',
Police Report**

*The body of a woman was discovered yesterday at a house in
Laurel Crescent, Briarstone. A police spokesperson said that the
body was in an advanced state of decomposition and was found
in the bedroom to the rear of the detached property.*

*The building is one of several in Laurel Crescent scheduled
for demolition and police were called after construction workers
noticed that the building was apparently still occupied.*

*Letters found at the address indicate that the deceased
may have lain undiscovered for up to a year. The name of
the deceased has not been made public as police and the coroner
try to trace relatives or anyone who may have known the
woman.*

Judith

My name is Judith May Bingham, and when I died I was
ninety-one.

I was afraid of many things until the end, which sounds
very silly now because of course at the end nothing matters,
nothing matters at all. I was afraid of the people who lived next
door, the teenage boys who came and went whenever they felt
like it, and banged the door, and sat outside my house on the
pavement, or even once on my fence, until they broke it. They
would drive up and down the street on their motorcycles, or
sit smoking and drinking from cans and shouting and throwing
things at each other.

I was afraid of running out of money and not being able to buy food or keep the house warm.

I grew to be afraid of going out.

I was afraid of the woman who came from Social Services once to check up on me. She said she had heard I might need some extra help. I told her I did not, but she kept talking and talking until I asked her to leave. In fact I told her to fuck off. She wasn't expecting to hear that and she tried to tell me off. She said she had a right to a pleasant working environment the same as anyone else and that there was no need for me to be rude. I said there was no need for her to speak to me in my own home as though I was an imbecile, and that I had asked her to leave nicely and she had ignored me.

At that time I was brave – and when she went and I locked the door behind her I laughed for a little while. It had been a long time since I used that word, and it felt good. It felt like being young again.

Forty years ago I was running a pub by the docks. It was a rough place. We had some nights where hardly anyone came in, and other nights when a ship or two had put in to shore when the place was full and people were spilling out on to the street outside. We had working girls in, too. When my husband Stan was alive he used to try to send them on their way, but as far as I was concerned their money was as good as anyone else's. What they did to earn a crust was neither here nor there.

We had fights all the time. It was part of the plan for them when they came off a ship – get drunk, find a girl, get into a fight, sober up, back to the ship in time for the tide. If we were lucky they took their disagreements outside; if we were unlucky the odd chair and several glasses might get broken. Once a young lad was stabbed. That was terrible; he lived, though. Was fine, after. A few stitches and on his way.

Back in those days I wasn't afraid of anything. I lived every day as it came and I expected there to be bad days; I knew I would get through them just the same as I did the good days. One thing you can't stop is time passing.

As I said, I used to use that word all the time but I haven't had cause to since I retired from the pub trade. Until Miss Prim and her leaflets turned up and tried to tell me what to do.

A few hours after her visit, though, I grew afraid. I was afraid she'd come back with some official form or something to tell me I had to leave my house, go into a nursing home. I would rather have died than gone into a home. I thought about finishing things, about doing something to make sure that I wouldn't end up being taken away, but you need courage for that and by then I had none left.

I went to the Co-op at the end of the road twice a week to get my shopping, and to the doctor's to get my prescription, but apart from that I never went out. I planned ways to finish it over and over again but it felt wrong to give up, and, besides, I was afraid of getting it wrong, not doing it properly. But all through my life I'd made choices for myself, and for the first time other people were starting to make choices for me. It was this that I objected to. I was a grown woman, an old woman, and while I still had all my marbles I wanted to be able to choose to finish this life that had become so wearing, so empty. But of course that's not done, is it? If I wanted to end things, then I must be ill, or depressed, or something and therefore I needed help to cope, help to find new ways of enjoying the world. This is how the young see it, from their position of complete and utter ignorance.

I wished for someone to help me. I wished for someone I could trust who would make sure that it happened, that I wasn't left half-dead… to make sure that I couldn't change my mind.

Annabel

There was nothing more miserable than starting a Monday in the dark with cold, wet feet.

By the time I got to work the bottom of my skirt and my suede boots were wet through. Days like this, the Park and Ride was no fun. Getting to the car park early, before it was even properly light, waiting inside the steamed-up car for the bus, then swaying in my seat, still half asleep, all the way into town. I still hadn't worked out which bus stop dropped me off nearest to the police station. I opted for the war memorial stop today, but I'd forgotten about the blocked gully in Unity Street. There was no way past it, unless you crossed the road, of course, but that wasn't easy. So I waited for a break in the traffic and took my chance, crossing that bit of pavement next to the vast puddle before another van came splashing through it and soaked me.

I was never quite quick enough. Not built for running, me.

I let myself in through the back gate, letting it swing with a heavy-duty clang behind me. The rain was easing off by now – typical. My access card bleeped through five different security points – count them: the back gate, the gate from the car park, the back door, the doorway to the Intelligence Unit and finally the door to the public protection office. I hung up my coat and my long scarf, both wet, felt the radiator – cold, of course; it was Monday after all – and filled the kettle with water from the two-litre bottle that we would carry back and forth from the kitchen, which was about half a mile away.

The fridge, needless to say, had been raided. There had been at least a pint of milk left in there on Friday but the plastic bottle had been emptied and placed neatly back on the shelf, as though that made it acceptable. My half-eaten tuna sandwich from Friday was still there, though. The smell brought back sudden memories of the house I'd been in on Friday night and everything that had happened afterwards.

Holding my breath, I took the sandwich out, carried it into the corridor, down to the patrol office, and dropped it into one of their bins. They would have been the ones who nicked the milk. They could have the sandwich as well.

I made myself a tea, black, and logged on to my computer. Everything was on a go-slow. I could hear the tannoy from the hallway; in a few hours I'd be able to tune it out, concentrate on other things, but for the time being it was insistent.

DC Hollis, if you're on the station, please contact Custody. That's DC Hollis, contact Custody thank you...

Penny Butler, Penny Butler, please ring 9151. That's Penny Butler, 9151. Thank you...

Could the driver of a blue VW Golf parked in the rear car park please move it immediately.

I gave up trying to drive in about a month after I started working at Briarstone. There were only three spaces allocated for the Intel Unit, and in fairness I didn't need my car during the day as some of the others did. It cost twelve quid a week for the Park and Ride, but at least I didn't have to fart around moving my car every five minutes because I was blocking someone in.

I always got in at least an hour before everyone else. It gave me a chance to get settled, to do things quickly that needed to be done. A chance to brace myself for another week of it.

There was no telling what order they'd roll in – it depended on traffic, the sort of weekend they'd all had, the weather and, in the case of the uniforms, whether they'd been called out for any reason. But one thing was sure: Kate would always be last, pushing it as far as she could, and when she arrived she would say hello to everyone in the office except for me.

'Morning, Trigger. Kettle on, is it? Morning, Carol – good weekend? Morning, Jo, Sarah. Where did you get to on Friday?

I lost you after the pub! Did you go to Jaxx? What was it like in there?'

Eventually – a good twenty minutes after she'd taken her coat off and hung it on the back of the door – she'd turn the computer on and complain about how bloody slow the system was. And maybe twenty minutes after that, Jo or Amy or Sarah or someone from the office next door would call for her and they'd all go up to the canteen on the top floor for breakfast.

Today, it was Carol.

'You coming?' she said.

Kate was already on her feet, purse in hand. 'Absolutely. I'm chuffing ravenous.'

'Morning, Annabel,' Carol said to me, sweetly. 'Do you want anything bringing back?'

Sometimes they asked me this. They never asked me if I'd like to go with them, of course, because they were afraid I'd say yes and then they'd have to make conversation with me.

'No, thanks.'

They'd already turned away from the door and the office was blissfully quiet again. If any of them had asked about my weekend, I would have told them. If they'd bothered, they could have heard all about how I found the body next door. I could picture their faces, rapt, over their platefuls of bacon sandwich, toast and cheese scones. For once, they would listen and not interrupt. For once, my news would trump anything they could offer.

But they didn't ask, and so I kept it to myself.

I'd forgotten to ask Kate to get a pint of milk in the canteen, and there was no way she would think of it herself, so after ten minutes of enjoying the peace in the office I got up, found my purse in my bag, and took the lift up to the top floor.

They were all gathered around a table near the till, heads together. I could hear snatches of the conversation as I found a pint of semi-skimmed in the fridge and checked the sell-by date.

21

'You see, I told you, didn't I?'

'He's only just moved out, Kate, he's not even taken all of his stuff with him yet...'

So, Carol had chucked poor old Rick out of the flat, then. I waited behind two PCs in their full patrol kit: stab vests, Airwave radios bleeping. Behind the counter Lynn was adding a generous glug of vinegar from an industrial-sized plastic bottle to the poached-egg pan. It already had an ugly brownish scum of vinegar and egg-white froth floating on the surface. I looked away.

'You started talking to the walls yet, then?' Sarah was asking Carol.

'Don't laugh. It is horribly quiet without Sky Sports on every bleeding second of the day though.'

'You'll be getting a cat next...'

'Hey, don't knock it,' Kate said. 'It's only her cat that stops Annabel from going completely batty, you know.'

'Don't be mean,' Amy said. 'She's not batty.'

'She's heading that way, if you ask me.'

I stared at them, wondering if they really hadn't noticed I was standing right there or if they were being deliberately rude.

'Is that all you want, Annabel?' asked Lynn. She'd plopped eggs into the pan and was spooning brown water over them to hurry the cooking process along. I turned towards the till, opening my purse.

'Yes,' I said. My cheeks were burning.

'Oh, shit,' I heard someone say from the table behind me.

They were all silent, then. I handed over a pound coin and took the milk and hurried away, not looking at the table, not looking at Lynn even though I heard her say, 'Wait – your change!'

The Chief's Summary arrived by email at half-past nine, just as Kate came back into the office. In the twenty minutes or so since the scene upstairs in the canteen, I'd had a few private tears, washed my face in the Ladies' and decided to put it behind me. I knew they talked about me, after all. They talked about whoever wasn't currently in the room, so I couldn't consider myself special.

Kate put the kettle on behind me and cleared her throat. 'You want a tea?'

'Yes, please. I'd love one.'

She'd obviously been hoping I'd say no, but it gave me a perverse pleasure to take her up on the offer. When it was plonked on to the desk, it was very milky. I was thirsty enough for it not to matter. She was making some sort of an effort, after all.

'Thanks, Kate. Looks smashing, just how I like it.'

The summary normally contained about five or six items of note: crimes and incidents that had taken place on the previous day. Anything classed as a critical incident was included – armed robberies, sudden and suspicious deaths, suicides. Rapes and murders were the ones that were of particular interest to me, in case any of the offenders I was supposed to monitor had crossed the line. Although I could search through the overnight crimes on the system, the summary was a handy shortcut, since the most serious offences would always be included.

And there it was.

Suspicious Death

At approximately 2032hrs on Friday patrols attended an address in Newmarket Street, Briarstone. The neighbour had noticed a strong smell coming from the address and had entered the property and discovered the decomposed remains of a female in the living room. The deceased is believed to be a 43-year-old who lived at the address. Next of kin have been informed. Major Crime Department attended the scene and, although investigations are ongoing, the opinion was that there are no suspicious circumstances.

That was all. I didn't know what I'd been expecting – some sort of fanfare maybe – but it was bland description, deliberately designed to inform those who needed to know and to obscure things from those who didn't.

The house next door had been full of people for much of Saturday. The forensics van parked outside my house, and, although I'd spoken to the first patrol that turned up, I waited around all day to be interviewed properly.

My emotional state had been fragile, spinning from nausea and shock at what I'd seen and done, to annoyance that they were taking so long about it all, and guilt that I hadn't rung them straight away, instead of breaking in like some lumbering real-life Jessica Fletcher.

After I'd found the body, I'd gone back home and shut the door. Then I'd opened the door again and thrown the cat out and shut the door behind her. In putting my hand under her belly I had felt, instead of soft fur, cold, wet, slimy muck all over her.

The smell of it, on my hands, on my tights, my skirt. Black and green and brown, the colours you get when you mix together all the colours in the paintbox, combined with the odour of putrefaction. I took my clothes off, right there in the kitchen, and put them in the washing machine. I turned the temperature up to sixty degrees and was about to turn it on when I suddenly realised that I shouldn't. Maybe it was evidence.

Of what?

I washed my hands with antibacterial handwash that had a strong perfume, but even when I rinsed it off my hands still smelt bad. I got some kitchen roll and dampened it, then squirted some of the blue soap on it and rubbed at my legs, in case the substance had come through my tights on to my skin.

And all the time, I was struggling not to vomit. Every so often I'd catch the smell at the back of my throat and cough, and gag.

When I finally felt clean, I called the police.

'Kent Police, how can I help?'

'I just found a body in the house next door. It's badly decomposed.'

'Right,' said the female voice on the other end. I could hear her rattling away at her keyboard already, entering the opening code 240B for 'suspected body'. 'Can I take your name?'

'Annabel Hayer.'

I went through all the responses – address, phone number, all the details of what I'd seen (the light on) and heard (nothing) and smelt (putrescence) and seen (a body in the armchair) – until I'd convinced myself in my head that I'd imagined the whole thing.

'We're very busy tonight,' she said, 'but a patrol will come out to you as soon as one is free.'

I went upstairs, had a shower and washed my hair, and dressed in clean clothes, yet I could still smell it, fainter now but nevertheless there. I looked outside but there was still no sign of the patrol.

The cat cried to be let in, and I shut the kitchen door and ran her a makeshift bath in the kitchen sink. I'd tried to bathe cats before and this was every bit as traumatic as all my previous experiences. She scratched my arms to shreds as I sponged her back and undersides down with my best organic pH-neutral additive-free shampoo and warm water. I got most of it off. She'd been licking herself too, her fur sticking up in spikes. The thought of it, and the smell of her, even when she'd been washed and rinsed and dried off with a teatowel, was enough to make me heave. As soon as she struggled free of the towel she started hurtling about the kitchen in a panic, knocking things flying. Fearing for my crockery, I opened the back door and she shot straight out.

The patrol had arrived by then, and, having gone next door, and called in that there was indeed a body and could they please have someone else to deal with it, they had agreed that I could go off to bed.

In the cold light of day on Saturday morning, everything had looked very different. The cat was sitting on the back step, looking exceptionally pissed off. She came in when I opened the door and immediately turned her back on me, sitting in the corner of the kitchen and only moving when I filled her bowl with cat biscuits. The fur on her back and belly stood out in sticky spikes, but at least the smell had faded.

I'd never met the Major Crime DC who eventually interviewed me, and, although he showed me his warrant card when I let him in, I instantly forgot his name. He told me he'd worked at Briarstone police station for the past year, and, when he said that, I recognised him from the canteen.

'How are you?' he asked me at last, coming into the living room. 'Must have been quite a shock.'

It was late afternoon, and I'd not eaten all day. Every time I thought about it, I remembered the horrible inflated shape of the body, the colour of the skin and the puddle under the chair.

'I guess so,' I said. 'I think I was kind of expecting it, given the smell.'

'Yes, it's quite bad in there.'

'You want a tea? Coffee?'

'Coffee would be great, thanks. Two sugars. Alright if I use your loo?'

I pointed him in the direction of the toilet and then I went to the kitchen and filled the kettle, waiting for it to boil. On the windowsill of the kitchen was a little statue of an angel that I'd bought in a New Age shop in Bath. It was lit up by the sunshine, shining as though surrounded by a halo of glory.

I brought the coffees through to the living room. He was already sitting there, his pocket notebook out on his lap, writing something, head bent over the task.

'Thanks,' he said. 'You work in Intel, right?'

'Yes,' I said. 'I'm the public protection analyst. And I'm also one of the divisional analysts.'

'You're doing two jobs?'

26

'Pretty much. There were four of us and I just did public protection, and then two of the team were redeployed last year and now there's just me and another analyst. We share the stuff for the division between us.'

He wasn't remotely interested in our job descriptions but I was always hopeful that someone would eventually take note of the injustice of having to do twice as much work for no extra money. I nearly added something about how Kate just did the analysis for the North Division, and I did that *and* the public protection work too. But, as always, I bit my lip and said nothing.

'So,' he said, 'you went in through the back door, is that right?'

'Yes,' I said. 'There was a light on. I thought that was a bit odd because I didn't think anyone was living there.'

'There was a light on? Whereabouts?'

'In the dining room. There was a lamp on the table.'

He was writing. I waited for him to finish, tense. 'Let's go back a bit. You said on the phone that you broke a window?'

'No,' I said, 'not on purpose, anyway. I pushed at the door and the pane of glass was loose and fell inside the kitchen and smashed on the floor. One of the panes at the bottom of the door was broken already.'

'But the door was open?'

'No. The key was inside. I unlocked it.'

More writing.

'And you said there was a light on...'

'Yes. In the dining room.'

'Was it still on when you left?'

'Yes.'

'You didn't turn it off?'

I stared at him, baffled. Of course I hadn't turned it off – why would I do that? Stumble back out in the dark? But then I hadn't been thinking straight. Maybe I had turned it off after all.

'I don't think I turned it off,' I said doubtfully.

He made a noise that sounded like a 'hmm'.

'Am I going to get arrested for burglary dwelling?' I asked, accompanying the question with a laugh that sounded forced even to me.

'Not right now,' he said with a grin. 'I've got enough to do.'

Taking my statement seemed to take forever, even though it was less than an hour. He got me to read his scrawled handwriting and sign his notebook to say I agreed with what he'd put. He said he'd type it up and get me to sign the proper version some time at work on Monday. Then he went back to the house next door, and left me in peace.

Not long after that, there was a knock at the front door. A man I didn't recognise: an ill-fitting jacket and jeans, a full head of grey hair swept away from his face in what might once have been a quiff.

'Hello. Sorry to trouble you,' he said, and of course what I should have done was shut the door there and then. But foolishly, and because I was polite, I didn't.

'I'm a reporter with the *Briarstone Chronicle*,' he said. 'I'm here because of your next-door neighbour. I wondered if it was you who called the police?'

I bit my lip. 'I don't know who called the police,' I said. 'Sorry.'

'They told me it was a neighbour. There isn't a house on the other side, so I thought it must be you.'

'I don't know anything about it,' I said. 'Now, I'm really busy – sorry.'

'Right. Thanks for your time.'

I didn't give him a chance to say anything else. Shut the door firmly. A few hours later there was another knock. I looked out through the peephole this time, and saw another man I didn't know, definitely not someone in uniform. Youngish, casually dressed, with dark hair that needed a cut, glasses. There was a woman standing a few paces behind him, with a huge camera dangling by its strap from her wrist. I didn't open the door.

Despite three showers and washing all my clothes, I kept sniffing the air, the smell in my nostrils still. Maybe it was my imagination. The cat had curled up on the sofa, tucked into an indignant ball, her back to me and the room. It would probably be some time before she felt ready to look me in the eye again.

It was nearly ten o'clock already and I'd hardly achieved anything useful. But I still couldn't face starting the Tactical Assessment, so I opened up the despatch system and searched for my name and address. This was, strictly speaking, against the rules, but if anyone asked I could probably argue a legitimate business interest for looking.

CALLER STATES THERE IS A BODY NEXT DOOR
*

THERE IS NO ONE LIVING THERE
*

CALLER STATES THE CAT HAS COME IN SMELLING OF SOMETHING BAD AND HAS A SUBSTANCE ON HER FUR
*

CORRECTION: THIS IS INFTS CAT NOT THE NEIGHBOURS CAT
*

PATROLS: AT55 UNAVAILABLE AZ31 UNAVAILABLE AL22 IN CUSTODY
*

INFORMED INFT THAT PATROLS WILL BE SENT AS SOON AS FREE REQUEST
*

INFT STATES SHE WILL WAIT UP FOR PATROLS
*

FROM VOTERS: RESIDENT SHOWN AS SHELLEY LOUISE BURTON
*

PLEASE CALL IF FURTHER DEV

*

2032 AL22 AT PREMISES

*

NO ANSWER TO DOOR

*

REQUEST MAJ CRIME ATTENDANCE – DET INSP
PRESTON ON CALL

*

KEYHOLDER ADVICE, NO KEYHOLDER ON
RECORD FOR THIS PREMS

*

REFER TO INTEL TO ADD TO LIST

It went on beyond that for several pages. Various teams
were called out, according to the protocol. The efforts to
locate a next of kin for Shelley Burton were dutifully recorded;
eventually they found an elderly aunt in Norfolk. No mention
was made of the partner, Graham, if indeed I'd remembered his
name correctly.

'Did you see the Chief's Summary?' I said. 'There's been
another one.'

'Another what?' Kate asked, peering over the top of her
computer screen at me.

'Another decomposed corpse. Only forty-three years old.'

Kate tutted at me. She always glossed over those ones,
since technically there wasn't any crime. Bodies found in
the comfort of their own homes with no apparent suspicious
circumstances weren't our concern. If it hadn't been for the
fact that I'd found the latest one, I probably wouldn't have
given it much thought either. But there was something else
that had been nagging away at the back of my mind – that
Major Crime guy had queried what I'd said about the light
being on. Clearly, when they'd gone into the house, the light
had been off. This in itself wasn't what was worrying me
– after all, maybe I did turn it off without thinking when I

30

left, or maybe the first patrol had turned it off, or maybe the bulb had finally blown. But I remembered how I'd thought there had been someone in the house. I'd felt something – a presence – and at the time I'd put the feeling down to there being a person in the armchair, and any noises I heard as being the cat. But what if there had been someone else there all the time?

'I just think it's a shame,' I said. 'Lying there all that time, and nobody even notices you're gone.'

'Mmm,' Kate said, but she wasn't really listening.

'I wonder how many there've been this year?'

No answer at all this time. I wasn't really expecting one. Kate was pretending to be engrossed in writing the bi-weekly report that we'd have to present to the management team on Wednesday, although what she was actually doing was updating her Facebook status on her phone.

What the hell – I wasn't busy. I set up a search to look for all calls and incidents where a body had been found since the start of the year. I added the wildcard search terms: 'decomposed' or 'decomposition'. Surely there couldn't be that many, I thought.

But I was wrong.

'Twenty-four,' I announced.

'Twenty-four what?'

'Bodies. Twenty-four since January. In Briarstone borough.'

Kate sighed and put down her phone. She craned her neck round the edge of her screen and regarded me steadily. 'What bodies? What are you on about?'

'All bodies found inside a property in a state of decomposition.'

'What are you looking at that for? We're supposed to have this finished by lunchtime.'

'And,' I said, pausing for an inaudible drum roll, 'guess how many there were in the whole of last year?'

She shrugged. 'Twenty? Ten?'

'Four.'

She stared at me for a moment, her interest piqued at last, and came round to my desk to look over my shoulder. The figures were all there – the same criteria search for the two date ranges, showing a surprisingly high figure for this year so far, and a curiously low one for last year.

'What about previous years?' she asked.

'I think that's what I'm going to check next.'

'Can't see the point myself,' she said. 'Nobody's going to be interested. It's hard enough getting them to do anything when a crime's been committed, let alone when there definitely hasn't.'

'Ah,' I said, tapping one finger on the end of my nose, 'it's all about the packaging. Community Safety. Fear of Crime. Social Cohesion. Neighbourhoods, all that.'

Kate was right, unfortunately. Working as civilians in the police force was often a battle of cultures, trying to persuade senior officers that we had a worthwhile contribution to make to an investigation, to resource-planning and to strategic initiatives, just as much as officers who had real experience of going out and arresting people. The nearest I was likely to come to a criminal was living in blissful anonymity two streets away from my local serial sex offender, or passing someone in the front office as they waited to be dealt with. I was never going to have to calm down someone who was holding a knife, nor tell someone that a loved one was dead. I was never going to have to try to persuade a woman to leave her violent partner, or tell a parent that their child was being abused. Instead I looked at all the figures, all the raw data that churned in day after day after day, forming it into patterns, looking for a way in. Even then, after finding something that was potentially interesting, trying to persuade the senior management that my recommendations were worth following up was often a battle. As I'd just said to Kate, phrasing it carefully to suggest that there were added benefits in terms of achieving Home Office targets was always a good idea.

I looked at my list of incidents. Twenty-four people, all found dead, alone, some time after they'd died. Unfortunately, as the deceased weren't classed as victims of crime, there was no way to search for other parameters such as age or sex, but scanning through a couple of the incident reports it was already clear that they weren't all elderly people.

I ran the same report going back to the start of 2005 and exported the data to a spreadsheet. A quick table showed just how interesting the latest results were – just three decomposed bodies in the whole of 2005. In the seven years between 2004 and 2011, twenty-two bodies – the highest in 2010 with eleven, but then it had been a very cold winter. And in 2012 – twenty-four bodies in the first nine months of the year.

At lunchtime I went out, walked up the hill to the town centre, puffing a bit. On the other side of the road, Kate and Carol were also heading in the same direction, talking animatedly. They hadn't seen me, or had chosen to pretend I wasn't there. They were walking twice as fast as me, anyway, and in a minute or two they would be at the top of the hill and around the corner, out of sight.

On the way back to the police station I looked at the rows of terraced houses lining Great Barr Street, rows of dirty-looking steps and greying net curtains. Piles of post against the inside of one frosted glass door; a couple of dead flies, legs up, on the windowsill of another. How many more people were out there, waiting to be found?

I drove from the Park and Ride to the supermarket in the rain, the radio on, going through the list in my head of all the things I was going to do to treat myself after the trauma of the weekend. Maybe order a takeaway. Have a long soak in the bath. Read a book, or watch a film.

I had lived on my own for years, and I liked it. Besides, I had the cat. I had the angels to protect me.

My mum was becoming frail. Since she'd had a fall last year, even though she'd only been bruised, she had been too nervous to go out – so she issued me with shopping lists, instructions to collect her prescriptions and post things for her, and on the way home from work I would stop at her house two or three times a week, make her dinner and wash up. Technically she could cook for herself and do her own washing-up, but when she'd been ill with a chest infection in December I'd cooked for her, and even though she was now well again I hadn't quite managed to get out of the habit when I was over there.

Her house was an old Victorian terrace just outside the town centre. Still parked outside was her old Nissan Micra, rusting to pieces and yet she insisted on taxing and insuring it just in case she suddenly felt the urge to leave the house. I pulled in behind it and sat for a moment, savouring the feeling of being alone, being quiet.

I opened the front door with my key, which I kept on a separate key ring as a kind of message to myself that this wasn't a permanent arrangement. 'Only me, Mum!' I called. From the back room I could hear the sound of her television, loud – one of the soaps, as it always was at this time of the evening.

'Hello, dear,' she said, without looking up. 'Can you turn the thermostat up a little bit? Getting a bit chilly.'

I reached over her head and twisted the dial until I heard the 'whoomph' of the gas boiler in the kitchen firing up again.

'I got you one of those carton soups,' I said. 'Broccoli and stilton.'

She pulled a face but said, 'Alright, dear. If it needs eating up.'

It was my favourite, this one. I opened the spout and put it in the microwave, even though she always made a fuss if I didn't do it in a saucepan. The small pan was in the sink, crusted hard with what looked like scrambled egg that she'd made for her breakfast. While I was waiting for the soup I ran the hot tap into the pan and squeezed a jet of washing up liquid into it. I stopped the microwave before the telltale ping and stirred the soup into a bowl, added it to a tray with a buttered wholemeal roll on a plate, and took it through to her.

'No white rolls?' she said plaintively.

'The Co-op didn't have any,' I fibbed. 'Anyway, wholemeal's better for you. You need more fibre, Mum, especially if you're having scrambled eggs every day.'

She'd gone back to the television.

I washed up, scrubbing the pan clean and wishing she would at least leave it in to soak, and then I cleaned the kitchen surfaces. After that, I went back into the living room. She'd eaten all the soup, despite claiming not to like it.

'While you're here,' she said, 'can you have a look for my bank book?'

There was usually a 'while you're here' moment, invariably just as I had my coat on and was about to leave.

'Which one?'

'The savings one.'

I went through to the other room and opened the top drawer of the dresser, where she kept her expired passport, driving licence, guarantee certificates and instruction manuals for every electrical item she'd purchased in the last thirty years – all the documents of life she was never going to need again, and buried underneath them the ones that she would: building society passbooks, her disabled badge, family photographs.

'Mum, it's right here.'

I looked at the open drawer, at the passbook right on the top where it never was – and noticed how everything in there was neat and tidy, as though someone had had a good old clear-out. She must have done it herself, put some order into the chaos for once, and forgotten all about it.

She was getting old and forgetful, I found myself thinking as I took the book through to her. Until now she'd always been sharp as a pin even though physically she was frail. How much longer would she be able to cope in her own house, even with me coming in to check on her?

Body of Missing Rachelle Found in Baysbury Home

Police called to a flat in Baysbury village on Tuesday night were shocked to discover the decomposed remains of Rachelle Hudson, 21, who was reported missing from her Hampshire home last December.

Neighbours told of seeing a young woman moving into the property early in the New Year, but had assumed she had moved out again as they had not seen her after that. 'We went round to say hello, but she didn't invite us in,' Paula Newman, 33, told us. 'She seemed busy. We didn't knock again and when we didn't see her after a while we thought she'd gone. I can't believe she was in there the whole time.'

Miss Hudson's family reported that Rachelle left the family home in Fareham after an argument. She had been suffering from depression for some time. It is not known why she decided to move to Baysbury, nor how she died. Her body was only discovered when police were alerted by the private landlords of the property in Balham Drive, after rent payments stopped.

A police spokesperson said, 'Police were called to an address in Baysbury where the badly decomposed body of a young woman was discovered. The death is thought to have been due to natural causes.'

Rachelle

They all said in the newspapers that they didn't know why I went, or where I'd gone. They said that it was completely out of character. They said I had friends and a loving home. They said I must have been taken by somebody because I would never have left. My mother said I was doing well at college and I had a good career ahead of me. That I had my whole life to look forward to. She said I was a beautiful girl, and that I was loved by my whole family.

All of that was lies.

She appeared on the telly, I saw her, tears in her eyes, appealing for me to get in touch. And then appealing to whoever had taken me – 'Someone, somewhere must know where my Rachelle is, where my baby is…' asking them to get in touch with the police, 'put a mother's mind at rest, she's going out of her mind with worry, we can only imagine what she's going through.'

My baby. I actually heard her say those words. I was sitting on the sofa in my new flat in a state of complete shock at seeing my own mother on the television appealing for me to get in touch. I was wrapped in three jumpers, cold, too worried about money to put the heating on. I was always cold, even in summer.

Still it meant I couldn't go out, for a while, after that. I'd already seen the neighbours once and I was hoping that they wouldn't have recognised me. I'd dyed my hair black, given it a rough choppy cut – hard to see the back but better than nothing; at least my hair was thick enough for the uneven bits not to really show. With a bit of make-up smudged around the eyes I looked a proper emo. I doubt my own mother would have recognised me, in truth, but then she had a hard time looking at me even before the makeover.

I ran out of medication after two months here but I couldn't go and find a doctor. So I did without, and it was OK. I was sick of the medicated numbness anyway. At least with the black cloud you knew where you were. It was always there anyway, it was just like with the pills it was hidden out of sight. I liked to know it was there. Even if it was bad, at least it was real.

After I saw my mother on the news, I couldn't go out for a few days. If I didn't go out, then I couldn't buy food. I would just have to stay in and go without. And by the time I really needed to go out and get things, maybe I would have lost – what? Four pounds? Maybe even half a stone? It had been a long time since I'd had a good weight loss like that. I would lose a pound here, half a pound there – every so often if I had a really bad day I'd put on, but usually I made sure that I lost it again, quickly. I would say to myself, by the time I go back (if I ever want to go back, that is) I'll be thin and beautiful and maybe then they'll all start listening to me and treating me better.

I like this flat. It's tiny, of course, but it's furnished and they let me have it for six months. I used the money Gran gave me. They didn't know about that. She gave me seven thousand pounds before she died, told me to put it in a bank account and not tell them. She left me some other money in her will, but she knew that they would take that away.

Gran was the only one who loved me no matter what, the only person who understood my drive towards perfection. She never once told me I was wasting away, or too thin, or needing to put a few pounds on. She never once told me I was ugly looking like this, nor did she ever tell me I was beautiful. To her, I was just Rachelle. I was the same little girl who'd played in her back garden when I was small, who'd dressed up in her cocktail gowns and high heels.

Whenever I thought of Gran, of being at Gran's house, it would make me smile. It was the only thing that made me smile.

I wanted to start running. I thought about going early in the morning before anyone was awake. When I was at school I loved running, I loved the feeling it gave me, and I got on with the gym teacher better than any of the other stupid teachers who were always banging on about coursework and deadlines and vocational qualifications. Miss Jackson didn't give a shit about any of that. She liked me because I never cried off sick, always helped her clear the equipment away. In years gone by the school had funding specifically for athletics, for taking students away for track events with other schools, but they didn't do that any more. I was the only one bothered, in any case. In the end I got so bad that I had to leave school, even though I needed to run still and who knows, I might have got better if I'd been able to run properly and do weights and spinning classes and things other schools got to do.

But the running was a mistake. I put the effort in but my legs didn't really work the way they used to. It was like my body had already died and was just waiting for my mind to catch up. And maybe that's what the black cloud is, after all. Maybe the black cloud is death and I just didn't recognise it for what it was. And so many of us are still walking around the world but we are all just dead because of the cloud inside us and outside and all around us.

I was under the cloud and there was no way out of it, no escape from it. It was like being in a maze where every path you choose is the wrong one, every path leads to a dead end. Except for one. There's one path, which is the way out. I just needed to find it.

Colin

Another mind-numbing day at work, although at least it's Tuesday again, which means it's gym night, which means I shall manage to sleep. Last week's effort is dutifully recorded on my fitness app, ready and waiting to be beaten.

I'm finding it quite disturbing the amount I'm masturbating. So far this week it's been hours every night. I think it must be a combination of boredom and too much porn, this obsession.

So I find comfort – of a sort – in my routines. Monday is study night. Tuesday I go to the gym. Wednesday is laundry and housekeeping. Thursday is college. Friday is takeaway and film night. Saturday and Sunday… well. I like to keep my weekends flexible, shall we say? And of course there are the visits I make to my friends. I like to keep up with them.

The main focus for my attention, however, is always the study. Although the last degree course I did was very interesting, I didn't find it a particular challenge. All my essays were on time, some of them were even early, and I got a First without even trying.

When that course came to an end last year I looked at the options for part-time study and there were very few left which appealed. I even considered doing biology again, as that had been the most enjoyable. But then I saw 'NLP and behavioural analysis techniques for business and social interaction'. The business bit is neither here nor there, I have no interest in furthering my career with the council – but I was intrigued by the idea that a course might grant me some insight into the thoughts and intentions of others. And it has been fascinating, if undemanding. Very few of the courses I have undertaken at the college have been taxing, and this was no exception. No, the intriguing thing for me has been the additional avenues I've been able to explore as a result: thought transference, hypnotism (as distinct from hypnotherapy, another matter entirely), neurolinguistic programming – a misnomer if ever there was one – and brainwashing. I rarely do a course without undertaking some additional study, especially if the subject captivates me, and this one in particular has opened up a whole new world of possibilities. Although it's unusual for me to continue with a subject beyond a year's study, unless it's a degree course, I have found this one particularly absorbing, and so I have moved on to the higher-level course. Quite surprising that some of the other participants have done the same; they have never struck me as being especially intelligent.

And why all this behavioural analysis results in me wanking every night, I have no idea.

When this course first started I remember lying in the darkness pondering, as I'm sure countless single men have before me, whether there might be a way, in all of this human contact bullshit, of getting a woman to sleep with me.

It's not as though I'm hideous, after all, am I? I'm over six feet tall, well built without being overweight, well-dressed, impeccably clean – what more could any self-respecting woman ask? The only thing I seem to lack is the ability to comprehend what any of them actually want me to say. So what is it that women really want? You don't have to answer that. I don't think I can even begin to guess – and I suspect your answer would be different from that of the person next to you.

It has crossed my mind that I could find a prostitute, but in all honesty I object to paying for something that countless filthy, vapid idiots up and down the country are managing to get for free. Not to mention the possibility of contracting some dreadful disease. But, despite my reluctance, going to a prostitute remains my fantasy of choice. I imagine going along the London Road, driving slowly into the darkness between the orange pools of light, seeing the shapes moving, women standing back, a woman leaning against a wall, maybe, or strolling along the pavement, impossibly high heels making her hips swing. I pull over behind a figure – I can't see her clearly, not at all in fact, but somehow I've chosen her. She comes into the light and leans through the open window of the car.

Some nights she's old, in her fifties if she's a day, with curly black hair that must surely be a wig. She smiles at me and gets into the car, and we go back to a filthy flat she thinks is tastefully decorated with pink nylon and polyester, a carpet with the same psychedelic pattern as the one my parents' living room had in the Seventies; I lie back on the bed that smells of damp and sex, and watch her undressing, laying all of that PVC and stretch nylon lace out on a frayed chintz settee. Her body is old and used, her skin slack against bone, her hair under the wig grey and coarse. I try to fuck her but I can't even feel the sides of her vast hole against me, so she ends up taking out her teeth and gumming me vigorously until I can finally orgasm. Of course the fantasy can't end until I've paid out some nauseatingly overinflated sum of money and been let out into the street, hot and smelling of her, filthy with her various bodily fluids all over my face, my hands, my body and my clothes.

Sometimes I can actually manage to change it around so that when the figure leans into my open window she's breathtakingly beautiful, an angel, soft blonde hair falling in waves over her ample breasts; she gets in and takes me to a hotel, straight to the penthouse suite, where she undresses me against plate-glass windows looking out over some city skyline. Her body is voluptuous and soft, her skin glowing as she lies back against the dazzling white bed sheets. And yet when I go to fuck her I can't. I can't do it. I can't bring myself to look at her and I can't even maintain my pathetic erection.

What is it in me that can't even imagine happiness?

So I go back to fucking the old pro in her grimy council flat, who by now is dead or maybe just asleep, and while she lies motionless beneath me, all sharp bones and loose skin, I permit myself an unhappy release, then I go and have a long wash in the shower and think about what sort of a man I am.

Last night after I got back into bed, towelled dry and smelling of shower gel, I thought about Janice. I've thought about her a lot recently, reliving the day they told us at work about her body being found.

I wonder if she would ever have let me fuck her.

I'm still thinking about Janice when I get to the gym at seven. Thirty minutes on the bike, thirty minutes rowing, thirty minutes on the treadmill. Feels like hard work this evening, but for most of the ninety minutes the thought of her keeps me occupied.

I remember when Janice first spoke to me. She must have been working at the council for years upon years, a figure who was as much a part of the scenery as the photocopier or the pile of ten-year-old telephone directories, and I'd never heard her speak.

That day she brought the mail up from the post room, and instead of just leaving it in a pile in the tray by the door she brought an envelope over to my desk, cleared her throat and said, 'This one's for you.'

I looked up in astonishment.

She would have been in her late thirties by then, the same age I am now, but she looked nearer fifty, hair scraped back into a lanky ponytail, dull brown and greying at the temples, pale eyes hooded in a lined face. She had the sort of face that would have benefited from make-up, and that's not the sort of thing I would say often. In fact I could have imagined her on one of those ghastly makeover shows, going in as a frumpy old maid and coming out as a beautiful, poised mature woman.

As if she could read my mind she smiled, and her whole face changed. She was almost beautiful – the old hag to the angel.

After that I spoke to her quite a few times. We often seemed to be in the kitchen at the same time making tea. She was never chatty, but polite and formal, and – I can't believe I'm saying this – I enjoyed her company. When she went off sick

I almost missed her. But then she was gone so long we forgot she existed, until the day when that incompetent numpty from personnel took us into the meeting room and told us that Janice's body had been found at her house. I imagined she'd had a heart attack, and was waiting to be told when we could recruit someone else, but then he went on to tell us that she'd been lying in her house rotting for some four months.

And it was just before lunch.

Janice's sad demise was the chief topic of conversation for the next few days, to the extent that I got sick of hearing about it and was on the verge of standing up and shouting some obscenity if I so much as heard her name. What was more alarming, though, was that moment when my name was suddenly brought into the conversation.

'I beg your pardon?'

It was Martha, of course.

'I just said, Colin, if you'd been listening, that you were friends with her, weren't you?'

'With whom? Janice? I was not.'

'You talked to her more than any of us did.'

'I spoke to her – that doesn't mean we were friends.'

'Nevertheless, don't you think it's just awful that she was dead for all that time and none of us checked up on her?'

'Yes, awful,' I said, through my teeth. I carried on working in the hope that they would all get the hint, and fortunately they moved on to talk about something else.

I did find myself thinking about her, though. Why had she spoken to me on that day, after so long without a word? Could it be that she'd found me attractive? I thought more about it: the way she'd smiled, the way her face had changed. I tried to imagine her in my bedroom at home, tried to imagine taking off her cardigan and that dreadful shapeless blouse she always seemed to be wearing, finding a brassiere underneath that could be generously described as sturdy. But underneath the clothes, when what I needed was something real, something solid, with hair and creases and moles, curves and the scent of sweat, all I found was the body of my angel, firm and lithe and golden and glowing, flawless and serene and untouchable, and with it my ardour faded, as it always does when faced with perfection.

The gym is emptying and I head to the changing rooms, a quick shower to rinse the sweat away and then thirty laps of the pool, a nice easy rhythm to cool down. Even so I've got one eye on the clock. Last week I did this in nineteen minutes. It's possible I can get it down to fifteen, which seems much more appropriate, but I will need to work up to it. Push myself.

When I moved to this gym from the one in town I was self-conscious about my workout. At the old place there had been a group of young women who always seemed to be there when I was, giggling and whispering behind their hands. And it was always packed – another reason to leave. There's nothing worse than watching someone's sweaty arse swivelling on a bike seat, waiting for them to finish.

This gym is more expensive, but to my mind it's worth the difference. It's much bigger, which means more equipment, and the cost of it means one can expect a certain standard of clientele. The women with nothing better to do with their time come during the day; the mothers come with their children after school. But later in the evening the gym is populated by other single professionals who are here to do their business and then get off home, or to the pub, or whatever else it is people do who are both like me and utterly unlike me at the same time.

It's a year ago this week that we were told that Janice had died. Perhaps that's why she has been on my mind so much recently. Something about the weather, the turning of the leaves, reminds me of decay and of her rotting corpse, slipping into liquid with nobody there to notice. I wish I'd paid more attention to her. There was so much beauty there that I could have observed, and I missed out on it.

But then again it would have just been more bother, more distraction, like that infernal woman from the nursing home.

She called again this evening before I set off for the gym, and, expecting it to be Vaughn, I answered it without looking at the caller display.

'Mr Friedland?'

I knew it was her. She has a way of pronouncing my name with the emphasis on the second syllable that is quite different from the way everyone else says it. Freed Land. The only reason I don't correct her is that she possibly uses the same pronunciation in addressing my mother. The thought of this, and of course my mother's inability to express her indignation, gives me some amusement.

'Yes, speaking,' I said, feigning ignorance.

'Mr Freed Land, it is Matron here. From the Larches.'

'Yes,' I said again.

'Your mother is quite well, there's no need to worry.'

'Oh, good,' I said.

'However she does miss you terribly.'

I doubt that very much, I thought. 'Really? Are you sure she even realises where she is?'

'On occasion she does. She has lucid moments. And in those moments she seems to feel the loss of you most acutely. You haven't been to see her in such a very long time, Mr Freed Land.'

'I've been very busy,' I said. 'Work has been hectic.'

'And at the weekends?'

'Look, I'll try to get up there on Sunday, alright? Now, if you'll excuse me, I have things to attend to.'

'Of course, of course. We will see you then.'

Damn the woman, ruining a perfectly interesting evening with her twaddle. What is the point of going to see my mother, anyway? The chances of her having a 'lucid' moment in the half-hour I happen to be there are so remote as to be negligible. And if she were lucid, the idea of it is almost too horrible to contemplate; after all this time, what would we even say to each other? Nevertheless, I will think about going on Sunday, if only to stop that dreadful woman phoning me for a while.

She calls less frequently now than she did. Last year, when my mother had the stroke that took away her ability to function as an adult human being, the nursing home was only too happy to accept her. It didn't take me long to find a loophole in the government's policy for critical illness care that meant her fees were fully funded. They didn't seem quite so happy about it then, though I've no idea why – after all, they get their payment just the same, and more reliably too, I would have thought, since that particular income flow will never run dry. I have the feeling that they want me to stay in touch so they can squeeze more money out of me, money for things that the funding doesn't quite stretch to. But what good would it do, to have a flat-screen television in her room, when there's a perfectly good set in the day room she can watch if she's so inclined? Why does she need shoes, when she's never going to set foot outside the door?

I tried to explain all this once, but the Matron's tone became decidedly brisk. After that particular conversation – which concluded with her saying something about me visiting my mother once in a while in a sarcastic tone which I could quite have done without – I started to leave the phone to ring when I saw the number for the home on the caller display. Before too long she didn't even bother to leave a message.

I'm perfectly willing to visit my mother. In fact, it's something I look forward to on occasion – a nice trip out on a sunny weekend, buying her some chocolate on the way and then eating it in her room because, after all, she can't eat it herself, can she? – but I absolutely refuse to be told by some dried-up matron when I should do so.

As I refuse to be told by anybody what I should do.

In any case, I have plans for this weekend and I expect to be particularly busy. So many of my research projects are about to come to fruition – glorious transformations, not to be missed.

Death of Pianist 'Tragic Waste'

The body of former concert pianist Noel Gardiner was dis-covered at the Catswood home he shared with his partner, vocalist Larry Scott, last Sunday. It is believed the body of Mr Gardiner had lain undiscovered for 'some time', according to police sources.

Mr Scott's death from a heart attack at the age of 59 was reported by the Chronicle *in May. Friends said yesterday that Mr Gardiner had become very withdrawn following the bereavement.*

'We tried to get him out and about,' said a friend, who did not wish to be named. 'But he missed Larry dreadfully. They were always together.'

Noel Gardiner was a talented musician who had performed with orchestras around the world. Tributes poured in following the announcement of his death and several bouquets have been laid outside the house in Lenton Lane.

Obituary: page 46.

Noel

The first time I saw him, I knew he was the one. Knew it the way they always said I would, even though I'd never believed in true love. I laughed at the people who did.

He was singing tenor in the choir and I was the last-minute replacement brought in when some old dear cried off. I played my little heart out that night, I can tell you. Looking at him when I dared to, which wasn't often, and drinking him in like wine, letting him spread through my veins like the first taste of alcohol. I wasn't brave enough to speak to him after the concert but luckily for me he'd noticed me looking at him and came strolling over to ask me to show him where the best place for a nightcap was.

I took him to the Black Bull, because I knew none of the others would be in there – I didn't want to share him. I wanted him just for myself. If he was surprised by the pub – it was a bit grim, if I'm honest – he didn't let on. He bought us a bottle of plonk to share and when we'd finished it they let us have another even though it was almost last orders. We had our heads together, gossiping and putting the world to rights as though we'd known each other our whole lives and not just for that one evening. By the time he walked me home, I was starting to panic that I'd misread the situation, that it was just another fling, another encounter that was going to be about the physical side of it and nothing else. Or maybe not even that. He was older than me, handsome, clever, and I didn't think I could possibly be that lucky.

But I was wrong. I was the luckiest boy in the world.

After that we were together all the time. Every day. Every job we got, we either did together or else the other one would turn down any other performances to be in the audience. We simply couldn't bear to be apart, not for more than a few hours. His voice electrified me; hearing him sing was sustenance enough for me to live on. And he would sit listening to me play, hour after hour; even when I'd practised enough he would make me carry on, sitting in the armchair behind me, his eyes half-closed, losing himself in the music.

I don't think anyone really understood how deep it went. We both had friends, of course, family – his more loving, more supportive than mine – but what we had together was like solid rock compared to the shifting sands of all the other relationships, people who came and went in and out of our lives, passing us by.

I found him on the floor. He'd been there for some time, even though I'd only slipped out of the house to the shops to get something nice for dinner.

I called the ambulance and while I was waiting for them to arrive I tried everything I could for him, pounding his chest, my warm mouth trying to breathe life into his cold one. I already knew it was no use. He'd gone. The light had gone from his eyes.

Three months passed after he left me but I have no recollection of them. The time after had no meaning, no purpose. I couldn't play; I didn't even try. I couldn't listen to music, couldn't look at the sky, couldn't walk in the fresh air without him because there was no reason to do it. All I could do was wait.

Annabel

I went with Kate to the tactical meeting on Wednesday, even though it was her turn to do it. She usually managed to find some way of getting out of it, but on this occasion she was surprisingly enthusiastic. She was setting up the presentation on the computer, her back to me, the set of her shoulders and the half-smile telling me in no uncertain terms that she thought I was about to make a colossal fool of myself, and she was going to enjoy the show.

DI Andrew Frost, two years away from retirement, one of my favourite people in the job, was last through the door. 'Morning, Annabel. Morning, Kate. We get two analysts for the price of one today, do we?'

'Sir,' I said. I felt an instant wash of relief that it was Frosty chairing the meeting today. A couple of the other DIs had a tendency to ask questions, lots of them, even ones which didn't make any sense. It felt as if they were trying to catch us out all the time, trying to make themselves look clever at our expense.

Around the table they all sat, uniforms on one side, civilians on the other. DI at the head of the table; DC Ellen Traynor, DC Amanda Spitz and DC Brian Jones, also known as 'Shaggy'. I had once asked Trigger how he'd got that nickname since he didn't have a chin-beard or a dog called Scooby, and it turned out that he had a habit of getting things wrong, and had once answered an accusation with the phrase, 'It wasn't me.' The nickname had stuck for ten years. I wasn't expecting much of a contribution from him. On our side of the table were Jo from the Intel Unit who was going to be taking the minutes, a woman from Social Services whose name I always managed to forget, this time with an older man wearing a cardigan, Carol, and us.

Kate did her bit first, and then began the endless discussion around the table about all the active jobs and how they were being handled, how much budget there was left to deal with them, whether the risk was being effectively managed.

I tried not to fidget, and started to worry about what I was going to say.

'Right then, any new resourcing bids? No? Alright, then. Any other business, before we wrap this up?'

I got in first, before anyone could start asking for more overtime money. 'Just one thing, sir.'

'Annabel?'

'I've been doing some research on unexplained deaths where the deceased has remained undiscovered for some time. It seems that the number of these cases so far this year is unusually high. I've done a chart...'

Dutifully Kate toggled from the tactical presentation over to the chart I'd finished earlier, nicely designed to show a huge spike.

'I should point out that the spike shows this year to date, whereas all the other years are complete. If things carry on at the average rate for this year, we can expect the figure to be over thirty. As you can see, we've never had more than eleven in a year before.'

I looked anxiously around the table. Everyone was sitting in stony silence looking at my chart.

At last, Mandy Spitz spoke. 'Sorry, Annabel, I'm not clear – are these murders?'

'No,' I said. 'They're people who have died in their own homes and not been found for a long time.'

I thought I heard a noise like someone snorting, probably Carol. Someone else was whispering something. I felt my cheeks start to grow hot.

Frosty cleared his throat. 'Do you have any theories as to why there are so many? Anything linking them?'

'Well,' I said, glancing at Kate and giving her a nod, 'the next slide shows some interesting points of note...'

It was just a few bullet points to get their attention. 'There is an unusually wide age range this year. The youngest was just twenty-one – that's Rachelle Hudson, I'm sure you all remember her – and the eldest in her early nineties. But there are people in their twenties, thirties, forties, fifties and sixties as well. In all the previous years, we only ever had two people found like this who were under sixty. One of those was a likely drug overdose, and another one was believed to be a suicide. All but one of the people this year have no apparent cause of death.'

'You mean they're just so decomposed, we can't tell the cause of death?' the man in the cardigan said. His voice was deep, sonorous, as though it came from some vast cavern within him.

'Yes, partly,' I said, warming to my subject now, 'but also the majority of these people were found in normal places in their homes: lying on their beds, or sitting in their armchairs. In previous years we've had bodies found decomposed under a makeshift noose, for example, or in the bath, as though they might have drowned. Some of the incident logs aren't specific about the location of the body, but, even so, there don't seem to be many that we could put down to anything other than that they – well, that they just died.'

'Sir, I did some work with Hampshire on the Rachelle Hudson case,' Ellen Traynor said to Frosty. 'It was quite strange at the time. It wasn't just that she'd apparently chosen to withdraw from society; she seemed to have chosen to die.'

'Chosen to die?' DI Frost said. The whole room was silent.

'Yes. There was no food at all in the house. Not a crumb. She was lying on the bed in the flat, very badly decomposed. The coroner couldn't establish a cause of death but his theory was that she'd starved.'

'Nicer ways to end it all than that,' Mandy said.

'Quite.' Andrew Frost fell silent and studied the slide. I began to feel uncomfortable again.

'I'm not sure if this is the right forum for this, really,' he said at last. 'If there was anything to suggest foul play...'

'Only the unusual ages,' I said. 'And the fact that they all appear to have gone totally unmissed. You do get that sometimes with elderly people who are so afraid of being shipped off to a home that they actively avoid contact with the outside world, but not with younger people.'

'Is this just our borough?' Ellen asked then. 'What about other parts of the county?'

I'd forgotten all about my last slide; I could have kicked myself. 'That's interesting too. I've got it on the next slide...'

Kate took her cue and pressed the button.

'It's a simple enough graph. As you can see, all the other areas are following similar patterns to previous years. Whatever it is that's causing this spike, it's only happening in Briarstone.'

They all stared at the slide. The woman from Social Services even had her mouth open. Frosty ran one hand through his short grey hair. 'I'll bring it up at the Force Tactical,' he said at last. 'See if anyone from Major Crime has any ideas. Can you email me your slides, Annabel?'

'Yes, sir,' I said.

'I'll do it now while I've got them open, if you like,' said Kate helpfully.

'You coming?' Trigger said to Kate, standing in the doorway with his coat on.

It was half-past three. Trigger had his own parking space owing to a slightly dodgy hip (which curiously didn't stop him fell-walking, his favourite weekend and holiday pastime), and Kate usually cadged a lift with him back up to the Park and Ride.

'I've got stuff to do, Trig,' she said. 'Thanks anyway. See you tomorrow.'

I looked at her in surprise. Normally, once the tactical presentation was over for another fortnight, she was so worn out with the effort that she'd leave extra early.

'Frosty emailed you yet?' she asked, when Trigger had gone. The station had fallen quiet; even the tannoy hadn't had anything to say for the last hour or so.

'Yes,' I said. He'd emailed me about an hour before, but I'd been too upset and frustrated to say anything.

'And?'

'He said they won't even look at it. Apparently they said they've got enough to do with all the actual crimes they're investigating.'

'Told you.'

Her response wasn't exactly helpful, but at least she was showing an interest in it, even if it was just so she could be smug.

'This force is too obsessed with meeting Home Office targets,' I said. 'Everything's about disposals and sanction-detection rates. If they can't clear something up, they're finding a way to pretend it didn't happen or wasn't a crime after all. They just completely ignore the fact that they're dealing with actual people, real people. Everything's been distilled down to crime figures and taking the easy way out. Drives me mad.'

Half an hour later, we were walking together up the hill towards the bus stop. She'd never walked anywhere with me before, even if we were going in the same direction at the same time. At four, I'd turned off the workstation and gone to wash up my mug. By the time I was back, Kate had her coat on and we ended up walking out of the station together, as if this was normal.

'I mean,' I said, puffing a bit as we went up the hill, 'it's not even as though we had a heatwave, or a particularly cold winter, or anything like that.'

'Or floods,' Kate said. Her long legs took one stride for every two of mine, effortless.

'And, as I said in the presentation, they're not all old, either. The one this morning was forty-three. Then there was that Hampshire woman, remember? The one they found in Baysbury? She was only twenty-one. And another one I just saw was thirty-nine.'

'How old are you again?' Kate asked.

'Thirty-eight.'

She smirked a little, the smirk of someone who was still – just – in her twenties, and for whom forty seemed an impossibly long way off.

'I just can't think of anything more awful than dying in your own home and being left there to rot,' I said quietly, walking past the automatic doors of the chemist and enjoying the brief blast of warm air.

'Well, you wouldn't know anything about it, you'd be dead,' Kate said.

I bit my lip. Imagine if it wasn't the end, though, I wanted to say. Imagine watching your body decomposing and knowing there was nobody around who cared enough to wonder why they hadn't seen you for a while.

'Don't you think,' I persisted, sniffing longingly at the smell coming from the pasty shop on the corner, 'that someone would notice? I mean the younger ones in particular. They'd have families, work colleagues, friends. Even if they weren't working, surely they'd be signing on or something like that? It's got to be pretty hard to just disappear.'

'I guess so. I think if I didn't appear on Facebook for a couple of days there'd be some kind of inquiry.'

We sat on the wall waiting for the Park and Ride buses. That was, Kate sat on the wall and smoked; I leaned against the wall upwind of her.

'Although there wouldn't be really, not if you'd withdrawn from it gradually,' she said a few minutes later.

'Withdrawn from what?' I asked.

'From Facebook. I mean, if you were intentionally withdrawing from society, then you'd gradually stop posting on Facebook, wouldn't you? And after a while nobody would even notice you'd gone. Or they might, and they could leave you a message, send you an email, but if you didn't reply... I mean, most of them aren't real friends, are they? Close friends, I mean. And the ones that are – well, what if you told them you were moving abroad? Or that your computer was broken, or something? How many months would it be before anyone seriously wondered where you were?'

'I'm not on Facebook,' I said.

She wasn't listening. 'I still think there's no point pursuing it, though. Twenty-four bodies or fifty-four, you're still talking about people who have just – died. People die every single day, hundreds of them. None of your decomposed ones were murdered, according to the logs, were they?'

I shook my head. 'There was one I saw where the coroner had failed to determine a cause of death, but most of them seem to be seen as natural causes.'

'Anything obvious linking them all?'

'Other than that they've all been left to decompose, and they all lived in Briarstone... not that I've seen so far.'

'Well, then. Unfortunately we're crime analysts. We're not here to look at social issues, that's what they're going to tell you. And what's worse,' she said, jumping off the wall and stubbing her cigarette out on the rubbish bin, 'if they think you're busying yourself looking into something like that, they'll find some other work for you to do.'

'Great,' I said.

Just for a change, my bus came round the corner bang on time. Kate, who parked in the other car park on the Baysbury side of town, was going to have to wait here a little longer.

When I got home there were no parking spaces anywhere near my house. I had to leave the car on the main road where all the chavs and druggies lived and walk back, double- and triple-checking that I'd locked the car and not left anything interesting or valuable in view. My car was a ten-year-old Peugeot, not new or worth nicking, but unfortunately the basic spec also made it rather easy to steal. It wouldn't have been the end of the world if it got nicked, just bloody inconvenient.

Lucy met me at the top of the road, jumping down from a low garden wall and trying to trip me up all the way back to the front door, acting as though she'd not been fed for three weeks. I tried to find the keyhole in the darkness – must get that light fixed – and when I finally pushed the door open the phone was ringing.

'Hello?' It was my mother. 'Yes, Mum, I've just got in. Can I ring you back?'

'Well, I did wait all day, since I thought you'd be too busy to speak to me at work, but if you can't talk to me now…'.

'Sorry, Mum. I'm just tired.'

'I'll only be a moment, anyway. Have you got a pen?'

I sat on the sofa with my coat on and a notepad balanced on my knee making a list of shopping she needed tomorrow, while the cat wound herself round my ankles, clawing at my skirt and my tights, and I swiped her away over and over again until I gave up, tucked the phone under my ear and went to the kitchen to find some cat food.

I cooked myself an omelette for tea, watched a programme about Africa on the telly and then went and had a bath. I sat there in the hot foamy water and listened to the silence in the house, the echoing silence.

I tried to imagine what could have happened in the months since the time I'd seen Shelley Burton. Maybe she'd been so unhappy after her partner had moved out that she'd given up on gardening, given up on life. Maybe he'd had an affair with someone, and she'd been devastated by it.

All of these things could have been happening next door and I hadn't noticed. I hadn't seen her for a long time. Maybe because of this I'd assumed that she'd gone, that the house was being sold or put up for letting, and it had turned out she was still living there, all along.

I wasn't feeling unhappy but the tears started before I even really expected them. Tears for the silence, the being alone.

Tears for the people who died in their houses and stayed there, their bodies rotting away to fluid and bone and slime, nothing left in the end but a black stain on the mattress or the chair. Buried with nobody there but some woman from the council who'd tried and failed to find someone who'd loved them.

If I died, here, now, would I be missed? Surely work would notice? Surely Mum would phone the police, if she couldn't get hold of me? Someone might call round. What if I didn't answer the door? How long would it be before someone kicked the door in? Days? Weeks? What state would I be in, by then?

Outside the bathroom door I heard a scratching sound. The cat, my support, my rock.

Colin

At work today I noticed Martha talking to Katrine, the new temp. I hardly registered her presence for the first couple of weeks, and then she smiled at me in the lift and ever since then I find myself acutely aware of her every time she's in the room.

She's Danish, apparently, although she doesn't appear to have an accent. They all talk about her when she's not there, the same way they undoubtedly talk about me the moment I leave. I hate their pettiness, their bitchiness, the way they pretend to be friends all the time and then verbally tear their prey to shreds in their absence.

They tried to get me to join in, asked me what I thought, but then realised that I didn't want to play their juvenile games. I'm there to work, not to socialise.

Actually, I'm there because it suits me. I earn the same amount of money every month and I can do the job without expending any intellectual effort. In fact, most days I can get my work done by half-past ten in the morning and after that I use my workstation to complete study assignments or research. There is no point in looking for additional work to do, after all, because that would just be setting myself up for bigger challenges in the future. No: I do what I have to do, I do it well, I do it slightly better than anyone else, and they leave me alone.

I've stopped masturbating, for now. I was disgusting myself. I'm saving it for the weekend, when I can waste time with it if I feel like it. I am, as always, in control.

Vaughn Bradstock has asked me if I would like to have dinner with him and the delightful Audrey on Saturday.

My first thought was that it would interrupt my evening of wanking and porn; then I reconsidered. It would be intriguing to meet Audrey, after having heard about every intimate detail of her life, her physique and her personality over the last few months. He has decided against Weston-super-Mare, by the way. I told him it was wise. If you were going to go somewhere with the woman of your dreams, then surely you would find somewhere more exotic than Weston-super-Mare?

'About six-thirty alright?' he'd asked.

Typical, I thought. 'Can we make it a bit later? I have a phone call to make at that time.'

There was a momentary pause. 'Oh, well, I suppose so. Can't you ring whoever it is earlier? It's just that Audrey doesn't like to eat too late. Something about the diet she's on.'

'I can be there for seven,' I said firmly. 'If that's no good, I'm afraid I shall have to decline.'

In the end he agreed to seven o'clock, and then he asked me if I had any special dietary requirements, at which I laughed.

'It's a serious question,' he asked. 'I'd hate to accidentally kill you with something you have an allergy to.'

'I'm not too keen on aubergine,' I said, in the end.

'We'll bear that in mind,' he said. 'Audrey's cooking.'

'Is she any good?' I asked, thinking that actually he must surely have told me about Audrey's culinary expertise at some point; after all, he'd told me about everything else.

'Oh, yes,' Vaughn said with enthusiasm.

But, given Vaughn's taste in women, beer and music, this was not enlightening. I will have to wait until Saturday and see for myself.

I dropped in to see my friend Maggie on the way home. She wasn't looking too bright, poor thing. Still, I sat with her for a while and chatted to her. I'm intrigued by her house, which is beautiful, along with everything in it – there must be about six bedrooms upstairs; no idea why she needs that many since she's been on her own for a good couple of years. I don't think I disturbed her too much, although she was looking very tired. I told her I'd go back and see how she was doing at the weekend, and left her to it.

I got home and cleaned the kitchen and bathroom, put on a load of laundry and ironed my work shirts whilst watching the news.

I'll have to plan my weekend carefully, with so much to fit in. Vaughn's dinner party, diverting as it sounds, is the least of my priorities at the moment.

Briarstone Man Found Dead in Flat

The badly decomposed body of a man in his 50s was found by council workers at a block of flats in Briarstone yesterday.

The housing officers called at the flat in North Lane after several official letters and phone calls had gone unanswered, it was revealed. 'The body was discovered sitting upright in the living area and the television was still on,' a council spokesperson said.

The man is believed to be Robin Downley, unemployed. Neighbours had not seen Mr Downley for some time. One woman who did not wish to be named told us: 'I kept calling the council about the smell. I must have rung up 30 times and they never came round.'

Robin

My wife left me, and that was the beginning of the end of my life.

I remember I was at home with the kids on a Sunday afternoon, washing up, when the doorbell rang. It was Elaine, my wife's best friend. She had tears in her eyes. I invited her in and faffed about making a cup of tea while she sat in the living room and sobbed unselfconsciously, making a hideous racket. Fortunately the kids were upstairs also making a hideous racket so they were none the wiser.

'Where's Beverley?' Elaine said to me when at last she could speak. I assumed she just wanted her best friend's shoulder to cry on, not mine.

'I'm not sure,' I said. 'She went out.' We weren't the sort of couple who spent every minute together. We had our own lives, our own hobbies, our own friends. It made the time we did spend together more exciting, more precious. Or so I thought.

The doorbell went again just then, and I remember feeling terrible, as if the world had suddenly shifted on its axis and I hadn't realised, as if something was wrong in the most fundamental way possible and I was the last one to know. On the doorstep was Beverley, with Mike, Elaine's husband.

They were holding hands.

I stood aside to let them in and they went through to the living room where Elaine was sitting, presumably already somehow aware of the bombshell they were about to drop into all of our lives. They were surprisingly calm, rational and emotionless as they delivered the news. They had been carrying on the affair for the past five months, and they were no longer prepared to continue to lie to everyone. Beverley told me she didn't love me any more, she loved Mike, and she wanted us to get a divorce so that they could get married.

At the time I took it all so well. I think if it had just been Bev and me having the discussion I might have ranted, thrown something, certainly raised my voice a little. But here we were, the four of us, having this civil discussion downstairs while upstairs our children played some game that involved a lot of banging and crashing and pounding of feet on the landing between the bedrooms.

They got their way, of course. There was nothing I could do to stop it, and, besides, after the initial hysteria Elaine seemed to get used to the idea and then she was fine with it. How could I kick up a fuss when she was being so reasonable?

In the days and weeks that followed, though, I found myself at the start of a downward spiral. I moved out into a rented flat, leaving Bev and the kids in the house while it was sold. But it was the wrong time to try and sell a four-bedroomed house, and it stayed on the market for month after month, while I paid the mortgage and the rent on the flat and money to Bev for child support.

Alone in my miserable little one-bedroomed flat, trying to make sense of what I'd done wrong, why it was me being punished when I wasn't the one who'd had the affair, who'd demanded a divorce, I started drinking every night and then eventually in the morning when I woke up, too.

I lost my job the following November, on the day when I came into work still partly drunk from the day before and even drunker because I'd had to have a bottle of strong cider before I could face the day.

Bev helped me out a bit. She was a good girl really, kind, one of the reasons why I married her in the first place. I think she felt guilty over the way things had ended. She told me I didn't have to pay for the kids for a while, until I got things sorted out, and as it turned out I didn't have to pay for the big mortgage any more since Mike and Elaine had sold their house, and he'd moved in with Bev and the kids.

I got a bit of money from the social, and that went on the rent for the flat. The little bit that I kept back from that, I tried to spend on food, and bills, and presents for the kids at Christmas and birthdays. But more often than not I'd go to the corner shop and buy a couple of bottles, just to keep me warm.

This was where I ended up, two years after the moment it all started, with me in blissful ignorance doing the washing-up on a Sunday afternoon while my kids played upstairs and my wife was who knew where doing who knew what.

You never realise what loneliness is until it creeps up on you – like a disease, it is, something that happens to you gradually. And of course the alcohol doesn't help: you drink it to forget about how shit it is living like that, and then when you stop drinking everything looks a hell of a lot worse. So you keep drinking to try and blot it all out.

I always thought if there was someone I could have talked to, someone who'd really listen... Not the doctor, who was always in a hurry to get me out of the surgery because I smelt of booze and worse; not the people at the day centre who heard stories like this all the time, every day. Besides, there are a lot worse tales to tell than mine.

There was nobody like that, of course. And if there had been, if some random person had come up to me in the street and said 'How are you?' and meant it, what would I even have said to them? Where would I have begun?

Sometimes I used to play a little game when I was outside, just to see if I could catch someone's eye, to see if I could get them to look at me, even just for a minute. And you know what? Nobody looks you in the eye. And I realised, it had been years and years since anyone made eye contact with me, and the last person was probably Bev. So what did that mean? What does it even mean? If people stop looking at you, do you cease to exist? Does it mean you're not a person any more? Does it mean you're already dead?

Annabel

I knew it was unusual to believe in angels.

I didn't talk about it at work because of course it would become some huge office joke. My colleagues dealt with horrific crime every day of the week, and the only way they coped was to have a laugh wherever and whenever they possibly could. They laughed about each other and they all took it, quite happily. Often they took the piss out of us, the analysts. Kate didn't mind it at all, of course, but then she had so much confidence in her own skin that you could tell her she was a butt-ugly nobody and she'd give you a grin and a wink and reply with something like, 'Sure thing, gorgeous.'

I knew I was too sensitive. I tried not to be. I tried to put on this brave, jolly face and deflect the worst of the jokes about my weight, or my lack of a social life, by getting in there first. I think they sensed that there was a line there that couldn't be crossed.

That was why I didn't tell them about the angels. How they were real, holy, beautiful and around us all the time. I would feel them when I was sad – a rainbow, a feather, a breath of a breeze against my skin. I talked to them and listened out for whatever they might say to me. I tried to act in a way that made them happy.

But at the moment I wasn't happy. I thought constantly about Shelley Burton and all the other ones, those people, those poor people, alone in their houses at the moment of death, waiting to be welcomed home by the angels and yet on earth, knowing that they would lie there and rot, unloved, untended, unrespected. The thought of it made me feel ill and ashamed. I wondered if they had really known what they were doing, or if life had treated them so badly that the need to die had become a greater force than the horrible prospect of what might happen to them afterwards.

Today three members of the Tac Team were in for a meeting with Intel, and they were all having a good old laugh about my sudden fascination with rotting corpses. Oh, ha ha, very funny, Annabel the fat old frump has a fetish for foetid meat, who'd have thought it... Kate was joining in and having a laugh. Well, to be fair, even I was laughing, but what else could I do – burst into tears? They didn't really mean it disrespectfully, even though any outsider would have been horrified at some of the things they were saying. It was just their way of coping with the things they had to see and deal with. Meanwhile I had my hand in my pocket, my fingers feeling the solid shape of the crystal angel I carried all the time, trusting, hoping for some peace from it all. Hoping that I could do my job properly and persuade someone to look into it, this alarming pattern of unloved and unwanted people.

Hoping that I could make it stop.

But they didn't seem interested. I replied to Frosty's email in the end, and copied in the DCI from Major Crime, Bill and even Media Services (why not, after all?). I suggested that this was a very worrying trend and that, even if there was no actual crime, it was a symptom of the dysfunctional communities that we were supposed to be trying to repair. The DCI deleted the email without opening it. Media Services opened it, then deleted it. Bill didn't even open his.

Bill was the senior analyst. Thanks to the last round of cutbacks we had to share him with the East Division, where he'd always been the one in charge. Although he claimed to be 'always on the end of the phone if need be', we'd only seen him once or twice in the six months since he'd been our senior. It was supposed to be a sign of our self-sufficiency, that we were left to get on with things the same way we always had – but in truth he liked the easy life, and travelling the twenty miles or so to a town centre police station where he wouldn't be able to park was a bit beyond him.

Until Thursday I didn't have a chance to work on them, the bodies. I had other work to do, a profile on another sex offender, this one about to be released after a long sentence. It was all about managing risk. I looked at his offending history, the places he'd lived, his associates, his family, his current situation, trying to find a pattern to determine if he was likely to prove a danger. No pressure, then – we're only talking about the most unimaginable hurt coming into innocent young lives.

Kate was off, too, which made things even more stressful. I was monitoring her list of tasks as well as my own.

I was so absorbed that I didn't even notice anyone was behind me until a hand landed on my shoulder and I jumped a mile.

'Sorry,' he said, laughing like a big kid. It was Andy Frost. 'Didn't mean to make you jump.'

'That's OK. Sir.'

'Stop with the "sir", Annabel. I've told you before.'

'I know. Force of habit.'

'I got your email,' he said, perching on the edge of Kate's desk. 'Do you think you could have a look at the list of bodies in a bit more detail? Do me some sort of comparative case analysis?'

'Of course. It would probably be a bit basic, though. Don't forget they're only on incident logs; they're not crime reports. Some of the ones I looked at were incredibly brief.'

'Hmm,' he said, pondering. 'I did mention it in the Force Tactical. Major Crime weren't remotely interested, of course, but then I'm not really surprised. They've got a lot on at the moment. But Alan Robson showed an interest, I said I'd get him a bit more detail.'

'Alan Robson? The head of Crime Reduction?'

Andy nodded. 'Yes – he was moved over from Tac Ops last month.'

'He's probably looking to build his promotion portfolio.'

'Even so, it's better than nothing. You might well have something here, and of course, as you said, it's a community issue, which is what's got his attention. And if we end up needing to do something with Social Services, or Age UK, or whoever, he'd be your man to sort that lot out.'

I gave him a smile. 'I'd best crack on with it, then.'

I went home via the supermarket and then Mum's house, to deliver the groceries she'd asked for yesterday. She'd already phoned again this afternoon: she had forgotten to tell me some of the things she needed, and didn't want to be without them for the weekend, even though I usually did a shop for her on Sunday morning. When I let myself into her house the telly was on, loud, as it always was, and if it hadn't been for her grunt in reply to my hello I would have assumed she hadn't realised I was there. I put her food away in the fridge and put a frozen shepherd's pie in the microwave to thaw, and turned the oven on to warm up. While the microwave was whirring away I washed and dried last night's dinner plate and this morning's cereal bowl and put them away in the cupboard.

My stomach growled at the smell of meat and gravy emanating from the microwave. When it pinged I put the plastic dish on to a baking tray and shoved it into the oven, setting the timer.

'It'll be done in twenty minutes or so,' I said. 'You want me to do some veg?'

'Peas'll do,' she said, not looking up. 'And potatoes.'

'It's got potatoes on the top,' I said. 'It's a shepherd's pie.'

She didn't answer. I sighed and put a pan of water on the hob to boil, got a big potato from the vegetable drawer of the fridge and stood there peeling it, wondering why the whole process made me want to weep.

By the time I'd cooked the potato and the peas the shepherd's pie was done, the top of it crispy and golden brown, the gravy bubbling up through the mash. I dished it up on a plate and put it on a tray with a knife and a fork and a piece of kitchen towel for a serviette, because all her napkins were put away somewhere in a box, covered with parcel tape which had lost its stickiness years before and now hung loosely around it.

She started eating without a word, blowing in short puffs across the top of her steaming fork, then cast a glance across to me, and at that I got up again and went to the kitchen to get her a drink. When I put the glass of water down on the tray she looked at me with an expression of disgust. 'What's that?'

I had no energy for this battle tonight. Sometimes I fought and won, more often than not, but tonight I gave in straight away and went back into the kitchen. In the fridge was a bottle of white wine, unopened. I unscrewed the top and brought it back with a wine glass for her. There was no point pouring just one glass. Once the top was unscrewed, she would finish it anyway. If she got drunk and fell over it would be her own fault.

That was the end of it. I said goodnight, put my coat on and went back out into the night.

The cat at least was comically pleased to see me, meowing at my feet and jumping up as though it would help, purring loudly when the bowl suddenly appeared in her line of sight. And, once she'd eaten, she cried at the door to be let out. I opened the door and she was gone, off into the night to do whatever it was that she spent hours doing after dark. And the house was quiet, and I was alone again.

Colin

I should have been reading about critical submodalities before this evening's tutorial but instead I found myself distracted by last year's biology text books. I recall learning about decay – such a beautiful, perfect process: designed by Nature, tarnished and distorted by human activity. So many variables, predictables, the whole system governed by Nature, which is beyond human control.

I went online to look up Active Decay, my favourite stage of Putrefaction. Active Decay, technically, starts after Bloat, Nature's announcement – the soft tissues reduce rapidly during this period, especially if, during the Bloat phase, the skin has stretched so far that it has ruptured. As well as activity by detritivores, internal processes (natural ones) accelerate the decomposition, including the endlessly fascinating autolysis, which is the destruction of cells by the body's own enzymes. The pancreas, which is full of digestive enzymes, is one of the first organs to go. At the end of the Active Decay phase there is very little left – not even skin. The molecules that once made up a living, breathing, sentient being, transformed into atoms to feed the soil and encourage new life. The ultimate in recycling.

Eventually I had to leave my computer behind. On the way to college I called in at a house in Catswood. Just a brief visit. Not very enlightening.

The Wilson building was grey in the rain, a concrete block that others find hideous and I find interesting. The structure of it, so uniform, but the closer you get to it the more you notice the cracks, the lichen invading, the textures changing as the weather corrodes it.

There were five at the tutorial: Darren, Lisa, Alison, Roger and I. Nigel, the tutor, was late as usual, and we hung around outside the locked tutorial room with our machine coffees, standing there in a grim sort of silence. I wondered if they were also trying to think of something intelligent to say. That's the trouble with this course – it puts you under real pressure to come up with something good when you do manage to speak to one another.

Roger came over to me and cleared his throat. He wanted to know if I had put any of the techniques into practice yet.

'Not at all,' I said, and then immediately gave him a smile and a half-hearted wink, since I knew by the nature of the study that he would be able to tell I was lying. Although he might have missed the lie and misinterpreted the wink. Such is the precarious nature of our methods of communication.

After the tutorial I waited in the classroom, asking inane questions about the potential for linked study and how many credits this course might give me towards a further degree, this time in psychology – why not, after all? – but really just delaying so that I would not have to walk back out to the car park with the gang of no-hopers.

Through the glass doors in the foyer I noticed Lisa and Roger standing outside the main entrance, chatting. She was standing at an angle to him, her hip facing him, the toe of her shoe pointing out and away from him. He was leaning in towards her, laughing, and – yes, there it was – moistening his lips with the tip of his tongue. And she laughed too and threw back her head, exposing her neck to him.

I turned my back on them and studied the noticeboard in the entrance. I looked at the advertisements for flat-shares, various social groups and sports societies, and student services including counselling. These I studied in a little more detail. A small advertisement, tucked away under a young mothers' breastfeeding support group (really? Here, of all places?) for bereavement support.

We are a group of students who have all suffered loss. We aim to come to terms with our different situations through mutual support. Tuesdays 6.30–9pm, Tutorial Room 13. All welcome.

I stared at the advertisement for a few moments, not wanting to turn round in case Lisa and Roger should notice me and wonder what on earth I was up to. Next to it was another, this time for eating disorders. Another, a bigger, more official-looking advertisement for Alcoholics Anonymous.

It's strange how Fate intervenes at times like this. I was at the noticeboard reading about alcoholics and bereavement and she was suddenly there, standing next to me, reading the same inane things I was. I glanced across and I had the feeling from her, that little buzz of excitement. She was wearing a denim jacket and had a scarf wound around her neck several times. She had pulled the frayed, chewed cuffs of the jacket down over her hands.

I looked at her and attempted a smile. She caught my eye and looked away again. She had that desperation in her face. I didn't know what had caused it, where it had come from. But she had it, nonetheless.

I put a hand on her arm and she jumped a little. 'Now,' I said, 'I think this might be what you need to be looking at.'

I indicated a random notice on the board, one for a student counselling group. Instantly she leaned closer to the board, and to me, and studied the scrap of card intently.

'I think…'

'Or do you think this might possibly be the right one?' I said, pointing.

'Yes,' she said, looking at me and smiling. 'It is. I think it is. Thank you.'

'It's all so easy, making things better,' I said.

She made a sound. I made eye contact with her just as a tear crept from the corner of her eye and dripped from her cheek.

I touched her arm again.

'What you need to think about doing is possibly coming to the pub with me; that would be very easy, wouldn't it?' I said.

There was barely a hesitation. Even I was surprised.

'Yes, alright,' she said.

Thankfully Roger and Lisa had gone. I led her out to the car park, wondering whether taking her in my car so soon was a good idea. There was a pub on the corner; it wouldn't be busy, which meant we would be more likely to be noticed, but it would have to do. I couldn't risk taking her in my car. It was an old man's pub, which made it more likely that two strangers would stand out; but on the positive side it was unlikely to have functioning CCTV.

I took her into the public bar and got her to sit down next to the empty fireplace. 'Where do you think you'd like to sit? Here looks like a good place, don't you think?' I said. She complied without hesitation. 'Do you think you'd like a Coke?'

'Yes,' she said.

I glanced across to the elderly bloke sitting with a half-pint of dark ale in front of him, the only other occupant of the bar. Across the other side I could hear the sound of pool balls clicking together and the laughter of some younger men. This was the right place to be.

The barmaid came round from the lounge. She was young, with bleached blonde hair in a rough plait over one shoulder. 'What can I get you?'

'A Coke and a pint of John Smith's, please,' I said, handing her a note.

While she was pulling the pint I glanced behind me at my new companion, sitting where I'd left her, nervously pulling at the sleeves of her jacket as though she was waiting to see the dentist, or about to have a job interview. All those years of wondering how to go about finding a woman and actually it's ridiculously straightforward. You just have to tell them what to do. It's so simple.

I took the drinks back to the table and sat opposite her.

'What's your name?' she asked.

'My name is John,' I said, picking a name at random. A different one every time, recognition of the different person I had to be for each of them.

'John,' she repeated, tasting the word.

'And you?'

'Leah.'

'Your name is Leah,' I repeated. 'That's right.'

She took hold of the glass of cola and drank from it, not questioning, not even looking perturbed at my strange choice of words. That was when I knew I had her. She's mine now, all mine, to do with as I choose. We had a lot to talk about, Leah and I. I wanted to hear her story, I wanted her to tell me all about her woes and her fears and her lack of hope. And now I know how to help her.

Annabel

'It's like fecking Bridgend,' Trigger said, slamming down his copy of the *Briarstone Chronicle* on to his cluttered desk.

'Bridgend?' I said. 'You mean the teen suicides?'

'Yeah, something like that. And before you start, I know all these are natural causes.'

I said nothing. In fact they weren't *all* natural causes; the report provided to us by the Coroner's Office had identified the death of two to be due to alcoholism, and one was believed due to an overdose of barbiturates. Several others seemed to have starved to death. It might have been natural causes of a type, but if they'd managed to eat once in a while it was likely that they'd still be here.

'Now the bloody paper's got wind of it, too. This'll turn out to be one huge pain in the arse, you mark my words. I was chatting to Dave Morris yesterday – you know Dave? Duty inspector in the Control Room. Used to work in traffic?'

I nodded as if I knew who he meant, just to stop him running through Dave Morris's entire career history.

'He says they're getting loads of calls about neighbours now, thanks to the press getting involved. Every few minutes: "not seen the old girl next door for a while", or "there's a funny smell around here, maybe someone's died". He said they keep sending out patrols just in case, but it's getting annoying now.'

I smiled at him, hoping he wasn't expecting me to apologise. It was as if this whole thing was my fault, just because I was the one who'd drawn attention to it.

Just for a change, it was sunny outside. I'd finished the comparative case analysis and handed copies to Andy Frost, Bill, Trigger and anyone else who might have been interested, just in the hope that someone would take it on. In truth, the document was sparse. There wasn't a lot of data beyond what I'd already unearthed; the charts looked impressive, but my intelligence requirement and recommendations were twice as long as the main body of the report. It had been all I could do to refrain from begging, in the conclusion.

I'd already read the newspaper. Trigger and Kate were assuming I'd tipped them off, but it wasn't me. They had their own links with the Coroner's Office; it would only have taken a passing remark about the number of decomposed bodies to spark off a journalist's interest.

When Trigger went off to the late-turn briefing, I took the paper off his desk and turned the pages until I found the column about the bodies. It took a while to find the name – buried at the end. Sam Everett. I made a note of it in my day book, then replaced the newspaper on Trigger's desk, exactly where he'd left it. And I went back to analysing burglaries for the crime series meeting tomorrow. I tried not to look at the name, but my eyes were drawn back to it again and again. It was as though the angels had linked me to it already.

After work I walked up the hill back to the Park and Ride, looking in the windows of the shops. Even though I'd left late, not having to shop for Mum tonight, I wasn't in a hurry to go home. The cat could wait a little bit longer for her dinner. I wanted to be where other people were, even if those people were all rushing somewhere. Another few hours and the town would be full again: people coming out to meet friends, go for a meal, have a few drinks, maybe on to a nightclub later on. I couldn't loiter around until then, though – and besides, how much fun would it be? They would all be getting drunk and rowdy, laughing at each other and laughing at me, the only person in the whole town out on her own. It would be like being back at school.

When I got to the stop, the back end of the bus was mocking me from the traffic lights a hundred yards further on.

It would be twenty minutes until the next one, so I carried on walking through the pedestrian precinct. There was another bus stop outside County Hall which would cut off the great big circuit of the town centre, and as long as I didn't dawdle I should get to it with about five minutes to spare. The precinct was empty, all the shops closed and shuttered, newspapers and litter chasing each other towards me, funnelled through the space by the wind.

My father worked at County Hall, years ago. Something in their accounts department, although Mum was not good with specifics. There had been a job advertised fifteen years ago that I'd wanted to apply for; at the time I was doing admin for a solicitor's office, bored with it and the petty bitchiness that went on between the women who worked there. But Mum had put me off. 'You'd hate it,' she'd said. 'Your father was never happy. All the bureaucracy. And you're no good with figures, you'd get muddled up all the time.'

The salary had not been much better than what I was earning, but the prospects were better – once you were employed by the council back then it was a job for life – but maybe that was why she wasn't keen for me to apply. I think she was worried about letting me go, even fifteen years ago.

When I saw the job advertised for the police, I didn't even tell her I'd applied until I got the letter offering me the position. She was furious.

'You'll have to wear a uniform,' she told me, 'you won't like that, will you? That's if they can find one to fit you.'

'It's a civvy job, Mum; they don't have to wear uniforms unless they're in the control room or on the front counter.'

'Still, you know what they say about policemen.'

'What?'

'They're all promiscuous. They're all cheating on their poor wives. You'll be there five minutes and they'll all be after you.'

As if! It made me laugh to think about it, now, even though when I started the job I was a little afraid. It took a while to build up my confidence – everyone seemed to know so much more than me – but I concentrated on the details and soon there were new people starting and I was the one showing them what to do.

I parked the car three streets away in the darkness, and walked briskly home. My feet were aching even though I'd been sitting down all day.

My house and next door were both in darkness, nothing to distinguish them from the street, both the front gardens full of weeds. I would have to sort that out at the weekend. I was drawn to the house next door, peered in through the window at the front, but I could see nothing – no light. The door to the hallway inside must be shut, the way it probably always had been.

I could see nothing, smell nothing.

The cat was winding herself around my ankles, no doubt wondering what on earth I was doing, standing in the overgrown flowerbed of the next-door house. You don't live here, you stupid cow, she seemed to be saying. Have you forgotten where you live, now, as well?

I left the house alone and fished in my pocket for my key. My hallway was empty, and quiet. I'd forgotten to reset the timer on the central heating again and the house was freezing, bitter. The cat tried to trip me up all the way to the kitchen, even though I grumbled at her and told her that I was no good to her lying in the hallway with a broken ankle.

I turned on the kitchen light, found the cat biscuits from the cupboard under the sink and shook a load into her bowl. She meowed at me, her voice cracking on the highest note.

The cat fed, I should have cooked myself something. I should have gone to the fridge – or the freezer, more likely – and found myself something decent to cook that involved vegetables and something healthy. But I had no appetite. I smiled at the thought that this whole business with the bodies was finally making me lose weight where diet after diet had failed.

The house was echoingly quiet as well as cold.

I turned the radio on in the hope of getting rid of the morbid shroud that seemed to be draping itself over my shoulders, hoping for something upbeat. The song, unidentifiable, was just coming to an end.

'...if you've just joined us, we're talking about the *Briarstone Chronicle*'s campaign, which is good news for all of us, really, isn't it? Sally, do you know your neighbours?'

'Yes, I do! We have been in our house for a few years, though, and we're really good friends. But the last house I lived in wasn't like that at all – I lived there for five years and I had no idea who lived next door. And I think it's a shame...'

'Mmm, yes, and there doesn't seem to be any reason for it – we just need to be friendly and make an effort to get to know people. You don't need to make friends, if that's not your thing – but you never know when you might need each other, after all – '

'And the population is ageing, isn't it? I think in a few years' time there will be many more elderly people living on their own, and having neighbours they can rely on is very important...'

'We're going to take some more calls on this, so give us a ring! Are you friends with your neighbours? Perhaps you're getting on a bit, and starting to worry about being on your own? Or maybe you're worried about your neighbours but don't want to intrude? Give us a call on the usual number and we'll talk to some people after the traffic...'

They were missing the point, I thought. Having neighbours didn't make a blind bit of difference if you chose to ignore them.

'... and on the line now is Alan from Briarstone – now, you don't know your neighbours, is that right?'

'Yeah, Rob, it's like, I've got this old couple on the one side, yeah, and they don't even talk to me. I mean, I said hello to them the other day and they nodded but nothing else, and – '

'But do you think they might be waiting for you to say more, Alan? You know sometimes elderly people can feel vulnerable, and they don't know who they can trust?'

'Yeah, I know, but everyone used to talk to each other, I mean, when I was growing up, yeah, everyone used to be out on the streets all the time, talking and that.'

'And people stayed in one place for longer, let's not forget that – these days people move around more, they change jobs or upsize or downsize all the time…'

I opened the back door to let the cat out, and gave an experimental sniff. There was a breeze tonight, stirring the branches in the trees behind the house. Beyond the trees, the main road, and, beyond that, the cemetery. I could smell nothing, and for a moment I wondered if I had imagined finding Shelley Burton next door. The odour had gone; the remains had been cleaned up, no doubt by some council workers while I'd been in the office. She was gone, completely gone, every trace, as though she'd never lived.

Local Woman 'Had Been Dead For Months'

Police officers called to a house in Newmarket Street, Briarstone last Friday were shocked to discover the body of Shelley Burton, 43, in the living room of her property. Ms Burton lived alone and had not been seen for some months.

See Comment, page 12.

Editor's Comment

The finding of the body of Shelley Burton, a 43-year-old former actress and model, is the latest in an astonishing list of people in Briarstone and the surrounding villages who have met their ends alone, at home, and have remained undiscovered for some time.

It is a sad indictment of our society that so many of our community do not know their neighbours, or choose to believe that someone else will be checking up, someone else will know where they are, someone else will take responsibility. In reality, there may be no one else.

Dying Alone – the Shame of Our Communities

The increasing number of bodies found a long time after death in the Briarstone borough has shocked us all in recent months. It has become clear that the community spirit that once made Britain proud has changed – no longer looking out for our neighbours, we have become a nation of curtain-twitchers and NIMBYs. Who do YOU know in your road? We took to the streets of Briarstone to ask.

'Time was, you knew everyone in the street,' said Stan Goodall, 64. 'You looked out for each other. You always knew when someone needed a hand.'

'I don't know my neighbours at all,' said a younger female, who asked not to be named. 'They keep themselves to themselves and that suits me fine.'

'I'm scared of dying alone, yes,' said Ethel Johns, 78. She looked frail but unbowed as we discussed the recent discoveries. 'I knew Judith Bingham, who was found back in March, and it plays on my mind that nobody noticed she wasn't around any more. I hate to think of her lying there all that time.'

Mr Alan Wilson, 47, agreed. 'It's a disgrace. Call ourselves community-spirited? It's a joke.'

Your Briarstone Chronicle is launching a new campaign to highlight the tragedies of these Unloved. Now is the time to check on neighbours who live alone. Make regular contact with people. Form support networks within communities. Look out for events in your area in the coming weeks, supported by the Chronicle, at which you can get out and meet your neighbours!

Shelley

Sometimes these things happen very slowly, so you don't notice them at the time. With me it was a moment, a single second that divided my life like a scythe, so that there was always a before and an after.

5th May, 2011. It was about three in the afternoon, a fine day, and although it had been hot for weeks, stifling, that day was cooler. There was a breeze, relief from the heat. I was going to the supermarket in the car thinking about my friend's wedding, which was the following weekend, and wondering if the weather would hold. It was also the Bank Holiday, which is relevant because of course if it had been a normal Monday I would have been at work and it might never have happened.

I was at the roundabout waiting to turn in to the super-market, and was about to go when a car came from the right at speed. So I braked. I remember having time to think something like *Glad the brakes work* when a van slammed into the back of me, propelling the car on to the roundabout and into the path of the other motorist.

I was lucky: the injuries weren't too bad. I had cuts and bruises, especially down my right leg, which was trapped by the impact. The other two drivers were alright. The whole drama happened in stages: waiting for the emergency services, while lots of people milled around and talked to me reassuringly through the smashed window; then, when the fire services arrived, the long process of cutting me out of the car. Then the hospital. Graham arriving. The police, asking me questions.

They let me out the next morning, with a prescription for some painkillers and instructions to get my GP to sign me off work. I remember thinking I'd had a lucky escape. That evening, Graham and I were enjoying a glass of wine – medicinal purposes, he said – and I was smiling despite the shock of it all, smiling with him when he said I must be made of rubber or something.

It took time to realise that we'd been laughing too soon. Something, somewhere, had happened inside my body at the moment the car struck, and I had broken.

The pain was constant after that. At times it would quieten down, like going through the eye of a storm, and I could function properly, walk to the shops, put on a load of washing – but then it would rise in a surge and on bad days I could barely move without crying out.

They said it was whiplash, since sometimes the pain would be isolated in the neck, and that it would be possibly months before it healed. The insurance company arranged for physiotherapy, eventually, which didn't seem to help at all. Besides, the pain moved: it was in the neck, then the next day it would be my shoulders, then my lower back, even sometimes in my legs. Wherever it was, it was always there, a demon that had possessed me and was subjecting me to a trial that had no apparent end.

I had medical investigations, one after another: scans, therapy, with weeks of waiting in between. Advice on how to manage the pain. Alternative therapies, too. I went to the pain clinic at the hospital though it never really helped much, other than to dull everything with medication – and the ordeal of getting there in the car cancelled all that out. My doctor kept signing me off work until in the end I decided it was easier to resign. By then I'd signed up with a proper claims company to try to get some sort of compensation from one or other of the drivers who had been responsible for ruining my life. They warned me it might take years, and I couldn't help but wonder what difference would money make anyway. Even money couldn't take the pain away. But Graham had insisted, and once I'd started the ball rolling I lacked the motivation to stop it again.

Those drivers had ruined my life, completely. Everything that had been normal for me was in that instant thrown up in the air and smashed. I had no job. I couldn't get out in the garden, which I had always loved so much. I couldn't sit comfortably in the car, even as a passenger, so I rarely went out of the house. Graham and I had been talking about having kids one day, but how could I even contemplate starting a family?

I thought sometimes that it might have been easier if the accident had just snapped my spinal cord and paralysed me, because then it would have been obvious to everyone. As it was, I looked perfectly normal. Nobody can see pain. They have no frame of reference for pain that's happening to someone else. They can only see inactivity – which they interpret as laziness. My friends and family, who called round often at first, gradually stopped coming round. They all thought I should just make more of an effort to get over it, that I wasn't helping myself by staying in bed or on the couch, that I should try a little bit at a time and that it would get better. They thought that staying still was making the problem worse. And meanwhile the pain came in waves which made me miserable, and irritable, and so I snapped at the few people who persevered with me, and eventually they stopped bothering with me too.

The thing that hurt more than any of it, though, was Graham. I was happy with him, but you never know how people are going to deal with problems until you have to face them. We never got married so he never promised all that 'sickness and health' shit. It kind of went without saying, I thought, and if the situations had been reversed I would have done everything I could to take care of him. But there you go.

The worst accident he'd ever had was a broken ankle playing rugby, and it had healed well with proper physio afterwards. He thought what had happened to me was the same thing, or maybe that the pain of my accident should, logically, be less than the pain of his, since I hadn't broken any bones. He got fed up with taking time off work to ferry me to medical appointments that were always inconclusive. Like the others, he couldn't deal with the way my moods had changed, and when the pain was particularly bad he would go. He would just walk out of the house, take his wallet and his car keys and his mobile phone and go somewhere else, to the pub or to his sister's, or just somewhere he could forget about his miserable sick partner.

When he did that, I was relieved, because it meant I could make noise then – I could cry and moan and swear about the fucking pain and my fucking back and he wouldn't have to listen.

And of course it wasn't just the misery and the extra effort of fetching and carrying, of helping me dress and getting a takeaway every other night or getting the shopping in. We had no intimacy any more. Even on good days, when the pain subsided to a dull ache, the most we could do was hold each other and kiss. He needed more, of course, and didn't like to ask or push me, because he was afraid of making it worse. And even when I felt alright and could have tried, I was afraid to start anything that I might not be able to finish.

He lasted five months after the accident. I don't know if it was a gradual build-up or if I said or did something that triggered it, but one morning I woke up and he wasn't there. He'd left a note on the downstairs table.

His sister came round at the weekend and together we packed up his things as best we could.

I thought about killing myself a lot, even before Graham left. There were times when I wanted nothing more than death, because afterwards it would be pain-free, but I couldn't do it when Graham was still with me. What if he found me? And he would hate me for giving up, when he had put so much hard work into keeping me going.

Once he had gone, though, I had no reason to carry on living, no one who cared about me enough to bother whether I lived or died, but I was afraid to do anything about it. I was afraid of getting it wrong, and ending up in even more pain than I was now. And, despite the copious amounts of medication I was prescribed, it was hard for me to save up enough tablets to be able to do the job properly. But I thought about it, I fantasised about it, I dreamed of death the way previously I'd dreamed of the pain leaving me, and the way before that I'd dreamed of gardens and children and weekends away. Death was my elusive lover, treasured and longed for and jealously guarded, and always distant. Always out of reach.

And my life, such a waste. Such a ruin of everything that was good, everything ripped from me, leaving this void, this chasm of pain and grief.

Who knew that it could all be so simple? I just needed someone to talk to, after all. Someone who understood how close I was to that point, and who told me it was OK to think of things like that. Everyone should have the right to decide when they've had enough. Why should I have spent years and years going through this hell, when leaving it was so beautifully straightforward?

Colin

I was at Vaughn's house at exactly half-past seven this evening, grasping a tissue-paper-wrapped bottle of white wine. It had been half-price in the supermarket, reduced from an amount that I would consider to be extravagant to one that was acceptable; the likelihood was that Vaughn would think I'd spent more on it than I had.

'Colin!' he said, opening the door to me. He shook me warmly by the hand, which I found very strange. I'm not used to physical contact from Vaughn Bradstock. I've known him for nearly four years and I can't remember the last time I actually had to touch him. If, indeed, I ever have.

He stood aside to let me in, and I took my coat off in the hallway and handed over the bottle. His house is surprisingly large, and decorated very much according to the current trend for laminate flooring and neutral coloured walls. What do you call that colour? Mushroom? Taupe? It's hideous, anyway, like the colour of the water once you've finished rinsing your watercolour paintbrush a hundred times. And he has one of those dreadful vases full of twigs in the corner of the room – twigs, sticking out of a perfectly functional ceramic umbrella stand. Why people wish to follow fashions in this way I shall never fully comprehend.

'Come through,' Vaughn was saying cheerfully. 'Come and meet Audrey.'

I was also surprised to see he was wearing jeans, and a shirt that I thought might have been designer. He looked so much younger than when we meet at lunchtimes, the tired old shirt and tie, the top button always undone. I've always assumed he has ten years at least on me, but now I'm not quite so sure.

The living room was open, with a high ceiling and painted in another one of those terrible contemporary colours that is going to date so badly in a few years. What was this one? Wheat? Cornbread? Double Gloucester?

I was so busy looking at the decor and at the generic artwork on the walls that I didn't even notice the woman who'd come through from the kitchen, until Vaughn gave a subtle cough and said, in words with a curious inflection that implied adoration, 'Colin – this is Audrey.'

I turned away from the abstract swirls of chocolate and mocha and held out a hand automatically to shake hers. She took my hand with a smile but also pulled herself up to my height and kissed me on both cheeks, which took me embarrassingly by surprise. I may even have flinched, pulled away a little. I'm so unused to this, this social contact. I felt ashamed to be there. And it was *Vaughn*, for Christ's sake, not even anyone of any consequence. I felt my cheeks flush and for a moment I couldn't bring myself to look at her in case she noticed my discomfort.

It mattered not in any case, for she had disappeared back into the kitchen, having said a few words I'd barely taken in – nice to see you, thank you for coming – nearly ready – dishing up… something of that nature.

'Have a seat, Colin,' Vaughn said at last.

Vaughn had leather sofas of the kind that were constantly on sale, presumably replaced by their owners whenever they redecorated. I eased myself down on to the nearest one. I noticed the music for the first time – some contemporary classical piano – was it Alexis Ffrench? Or possibly Einaudi?

'You alright, mate?' Vaughn asked. 'You look a bit – tense.'

'Ah,' I said, the first time I think I'd managed to speak. 'Yes. Got stuck in traffic, you know.'

He didn't seem perturbed in the slightest by my sudden inability to make conversation, and chatted away regardless about all manner of crap – the state of the economy, his new car, whether or not to add an extension to the back of the property – and all the while I thought about Audrey and wondered what the hell she was doing with Vaughn.

I'd always had the impression that she was older than him, and now I can't think why. She has smooth dark hair, bright blue eyes in an unlined face. She is petite, and even wearing jeans she seemed elegant, chic. I've never really considered the meaning of the word 'chic', but to Audrey no better word would apply.

While Vaughn talked, I got up and made my way to the kitchen, without thinking about what I was doing or whether it might be considered rude to walk away from my host while he was trying to engage me in conversation.

I wanted to see Audrey.

I stood in the doorway with my glass of wine, leaning against the doorway in a pose I hoped was casual, open, friendly. She didn't notice me at first, busy stirring something on the hob. I watched her move.

'Oh!' she said at last, when she saw me. 'It won't be long.'

I didn't know what to say to her – the perennial problem – and yet I didn't want to remain silent.

'How long have you known Vaughn?' I asked.

She looked at me in surprise, as though I'd asked her age or weight. What on earth was wrong with that question? Was it too late to take it back?

'Did he not tell you? I met him last year. We met on an internet dating site.'

'Really?' I asked, with genuine surprise. 'Which one?'

'Matchmakers,' she answered.

Of course – that would have to be one of the newer ones, probably one designed for people of a type I would discount as beneath consideration. I prefer ones where the selection criteria include details of educational achievement, career aspirations and salary brackets rather than cock size. Although perhaps that's where I've been going wrong. Maybe I should think about dating sites again; after all, it has been a long while since

I dipped my toe into that metaphorical pond. But my needs are a little different, now, aren't they? And besides, women don't join dating sites in the same way these days. They join and tell their friends all about it. They tell their friends and family where they're going, who they're going to be meeting, what time they expect to come home. They don't join dating sites unless they have hope for the future.

'Ah,' I said, wanting to ask a dozen questions and wondering which of them would be the least offensive.

She handed me a plate containing slices of melon with prosciutto draped over them. 'Could you take this through?'

For a moment we held eye contact. Did I imagine it, that she held on to the plate for a moment after I'd already taken hold of it? That she held my gaze for a fraction too long? That there was a challenge in her eyes, a curiosity… maybe – almost – a dare?

I smiled at her, feeling the warmth of my shame melting a little for the first time since I'd arrived, not relaxing exactly but starting to see the possibilities in the evening ahead. *Audrey, Audrey*, I thought, *you little minx. You little bundle of surprises.*

Vaughn sat her opposite me at the dining table, presumably so that he could touch her knee with his sweaty paw, but she clearly had other things in mind. I felt her foot brushing mine as we started our main course. At first she pulled it away and glanced up at me with a little smile of apology, as though she had kicked me hard and not just mistaken me for the table leg. I gave her a direct gaze in return, and left my foot where it was. And, a few moments later, her foot returned and this time gently rested against mine, whilst she listened to Vaughn rabbiting on about share prices and served him an extra spoonful of sauce. And the food was reasonable, I'll give her credit for that.

After dinner Audrey asked Vaughn to take the plates through to the kitchen and she led me into the living room with the second bottle of wine, topping my glass up as I sat on Vaughn's leather sofa. As she leaned forward I had an excellent view of her cleavage, although I tried not to make it obvious. Her breasts were well-rounded, the fabric of her top stretched across them, and I caught a trace of her perfume – or maybe it was even the soap or the shower gel she'd used earlier this evening, readying herself for my arrival. I wondered if she'd thought about the prospect of me burying my face between her breasts, if she'd considered the possibility that I might want to have sex with her.

'It's nice, this, isn't it?' she asked then. She'd seated herself on the sofa next to me, even though there was another sofa across the room from this one. She'd folded herself into a comfortable, cat-like curl, her feet towards me, neat little bare feet, with toenails painted a pale pink. How had I ever thought she might be nearly fifty? She was thirty, if that.

'What is?' I asked.

'The wine.'

'Yes,' I said, although it tasted like vinegar to me. I should have brought something decent with me after all, something we could discuss properly. I could tell she was a woman who knew what she wanted.

From the kitchen, the sound of Vaughn rattling plates and cutlery provided an encouraging percussion to the melody of our conversation.

'What do you do?' she asked. 'Vaughn's never told me.'

'I'm an executive performance analyst for the council.'

'That sounds exciting,' she said, and laughed, which was a relief to me, as it had been a clear lie. She was being ironic. A man could fall in love with a woman like this, I thought. Never mind fucking her, I wanted to marry her.

'Anyone for coffee?' called Vaughn, from the kitchen.

'Yes, please,' Audrey replied. She tilted her head back to rest on the cushions, exposing her throat to me, and more of that delectable cleavage. I wanted to run my tongue from the space behind her ear, down between her breasts, pushing the fabric out of the way.

'What about you?' I asked. 'What do you do?'

'I work with Social Services,' she said.

My usual sharp conversational skills struggled at this, most likely due to arousal: too much blood flow diverted away from the brain and down into the more vital parts of my anatomy. What, after all, was the point in a conversation such as this? Surely we wanted to do away with it; surely we should just get rid of Vaughn so that we could fuck? That was what she wanted as much as I did.

The moment the thought crossed my mind, I knew I had to do something about it.

I cleared my throat and stood up. She looked up at me in surprise.

'I – er – may I use your bathroom?'

She smiled, relaxed. 'Of course. It's at the top of the stairs. I'm afraid the downstairs one is temporarily out of action.'

I climbed the stairs awkwardly. At the top, I glanced to the left and saw inside Vaughn's bedroom – something I would prefer not to have seen, to be honest – pale grey walls, the far one decorated with dramatic monochrome wallpaper. A 'feature wall', they call it, don't they? It would give me a headache if I had to sleep in there.

And the bathroom. I had no desire to use it, of course. I was waiting for her.

I half-closed the door and stood inside, looking at the neat beige tiles and wondering how long it had been since Vaughn had grouted them – not long at all, judging by the faint smell of putty – and at the shiny chrome taps that had no doubt cost a small fortune. *Audrey, Audrey*, I thought, as though I could summon her up the stairs by thinking her name like a spell.

I looked at the toiletries lined up neatly on the windowsill. They were, without exception, male: shampoo, shower gel, a razor and some kind of hideous supermarket own-brand gel shaving foam with oxidation around the base. No expensive hairstylist-only shampoo, no perfume, no cosmetics.

I opened the door again and crossed the hallway into Vaughn's bedroom. Again, it was a resolutely masculine room.

There was even a multi-gym in the corner, which made me laugh out loud. I had a mental image of Vaughn working out here, sweating as he rowed his way to a muscular stomach. Not likely. I doubted it had ever been used.

So, the delectable Audrey had yet to move in. She didn't stay, often, either, or she would have started moving in some items of her own. There was nothing here of hers. I wondered if there were panties in Vaughn's drawer, maybe a spare pair, maybe a special pair... something she would only wear for him, would only wear if she were planning to fuck him.

'Everything alright?'

Audrey was behind me. I hadn't heard her coming up the stairs. I turned and gave her a smile. 'Fine,' I said.

'What are you doing?' Her question was direct.

'I was looking to see if you've moved in,' I said, preferring the truth. If it had been Vaughn who had come upstairs I would have made some comment on the feature wallpaper. But it was Audrey, and there was no point in pissing about. She had come up here because I had summoned her, I had told her what it was I wanted her to do. And here she was, standing next to me, standing close to me in fact, closer than she needed to.

'You could have just asked. Anyway, I haven't,' she said, her voice low. Her chest was heaving with her breathlessness.

'Why's that?' I asked, taking a small step towards her.

She stepped back. Ah, too soon, then? Too much, too soon? I would have to be careful. I would need to take it gently, so as not to startle her. She was worth the effort. She was worth the chase.

Her expression was odd. 'I have my own place,' she said.

That was no answer. What did she join a dating site for, if she didn't want a serious relationship? Surely that's what all women want, really: a partner with a house they can move into, marriage, children? Unless she wanted something else. Unless she just wanted sex.

I had her eyes again. I maintained contact, direct eye contact. She didn't move.

Ah, resistance! I liked that. I liked that she was a challenge. I smiled at her, a little smile of encouragement.

'Audrey? Where do you want this coffee?'

'Coming!' she shouted, without taking her eyes away from mine. Her voice was automatic, toneless. Her expression was difficult to read. Was she attracted to me? Did she want me to kiss her? What would she do if I did?

'You're...'

'What?' I whispered, moistening my lips with the tip of my tongue. 'What am I?'

'You're fucking strange, Colin,' she said. And turned around and went back downstairs, without looking back at me.

Ah, Vaughn. At that moment I could cheerfully have killed him. I could have put my hands about his neck and squeezed the air out of his lungs. If it hadn't been for that interruption, she would have done it, I knew. She wanted me.

I followed her down the stairs, tasting her scent on the air. She'd been so close. I wish she could have relented. But next time, maybe, she will give in. I wonder if I can get her on her own, find some excuse to visit her.

She was back in the kitchen with Vaughn. I could hear them talking in hushed whispers. I strained to listen, thinking she might say something useful, something about how compelled she felt to act out of character, how something came over her – but nothing. Just the sort of urgent, hushed tones of two people trying not to have an argument within earshot of other people.

I eased myself back on to the leather sofa and drank some more of the wine. Another ten minutes and I found an excuse to call a taxi and leave. The evening turned out to be less entertaining than I'd hoped, and now I have another dilemma: I've gone from wanting a woman, to realising I don't need a woman at all, to wanting one again. But not just any woman, this time. Only her. Only Audrey.

An hour later, alone at home now, relieving myself at last of that delicious tension that had grown unbearable, I have started to think about how I can win her over. Whether I can do it: whether I can turn her gaze from Vaughn's face to mine. And what it would take to make her want me.

In the night I wake up. I've been dreaming of Audrey, of course. She was here, in my room, and Vaughn was present, apparently for the purpose of undressing her for me. I was supine on my bed, the covers around my ankles. Vaughn brought her in, like a prize, like a virgin being offered to the Temple, and, having received a nod of permission, he set about removing her clothes piece by piece, while she stood still, the expression on her face unreadable. Boredom was the most likely name I would apply to it. She stared straight ahead, in my direction but not seeing me. She was here because she had to be, not because she wanted this; not because she was willing. The coercion did not in itself appeal to me, but there was something about her presence that was undeniably arousing.

'Audrey,' I said, in the dream. Even then she didn't cast a glance in my direction. She looked sulky now as well as bored, a petulant child who had been forced away from an enjoyable activity into a chore.

Vaughn pulled down her tights – tights, not stockings – of course not stockings; why should I imagine something so appealing to encase those lovely, slender legs? – and lifted each of her legs in turn like a farrier shoeing a horse, sliding the nylon off the foot and laying the tights to one side like a shed skin.

And she stood there in her bra and panties, functional, unmatching – the bra greying and with a hole in the lace; the panties large and black cotton. Clothed, in Vaughn's kitchen, she had been, not beautiful exactly, but undeniably sexy. She was certainly attractive, in any case – attractive enough to raise my ardour. But now, in my dream, everything was dulled. Her hair was not that lustrous shade of chestnut, falling in shiny waves around her shoulders. It was brownish, hanging in lanky threads. Her face ashen, her eyes a dirty grey-blue. Nothing about her was conventionally attractive.

Vaughn was unable to stop, even though I wanted him to. *Go no further, Vaughn*, I wanted to say – *stop now. I don't want to see the rest.* But he continued automatically, as though he was following a programme that could not be brought to an early conclusion.

And half-awake now, my hand under the sheets moving fast, I find myself pumping and grunting away watching Vaughn stripping the last fragments of grey nylon and black cotton from the skin of his indifferent, apathetic, complicit girlfriend. Naked, she's worse. Frumpy, sagging, grey hairs sprouting in patches from between her legs; even her knees are lumpy and spotted with moles. Despite this, despite the fact that she would clearly rather be anywhere on the planet than standing naked in my bedroom, I achieve an orgasm of gasping, heart-stopping, free-falling depths. Like staring into the abyss, and watching it stare right back at me.

I woke up late after my evening with Audrey and Vaughn. I lay there with the sunlight coming in through the gap in the curtains, thinking of my late nights with the bottle of whisky rapidly depleting and wondering if it was too early for me to consider counselling for my problem. And as for the masturbation – well, thanks to the dream, or was it a nightmare, of wanking over Audrey's prolonged and disappointing strip, I feel quite positively that I will be able to pursue a path of abstinence for at least a week. There is something deeply offputting about having to change your sheets and have a shower in the middle of the night because you've soiled yourself in a nightly emission like a hormonal teenager. Even my subconscious thinks it is a disgusting way to behave.

I got up eventually and made breakfast, then washed and dressed. It's a bright morning so I've taken myself off for a walk while I think about how to fill what remains of the weekend.

On the main road a badger lies on its side, its head flattened by the wheel of a car. It's relatively fresh, just starting to enter the Bloat stage, its four legs raised and straightened by the gases of Putrefaction that are distending its abdomen, the blood around its head still red. I stand and observe it for a little while. There is no pavement here, just a wide grass verge with a hedge and fields beyond.

I think about going home and getting a bag of some sort and taking it away somewhere so that I can watch the process unfold, but of course there is no point in intervening. It defeats the whole object. The decay must be allowed to take place here, where the animal died, otherwise it is not a genuine process. I leave it, reluctantly, thinking about coming back tomorrow evening after work, if there is time, and assuming that the council haven't found it by then and shovelled it on to the back of their roadkill van.

After luncheon I do some studying, looking into tag questions, embedded commands and double binds, thinking about the badger, thinking about Leah. Each of them is so different; each has such different needs.

She told me what had happened to her, eventually. It didn't take much to get her talking, and as she did so I responded appropriately, teasing out the story like pulling on an unravelling thread, and then watching her come apart. She had been working at a superstore as a management trainee, and the boss there had been flirting with her for weeks and weeks. He was older than her, and gradually she began to fall for his charms and admit to herself that she found him attractive. Eventually one night after work she agreed to meet him for a drink, and from there they went back to the store. I wanted details, of course – this was the interesting bit, after all – but to press her on that would be to distract from the main purpose of our conversation, which was to help her find the right path. Reminding her of the details of the sexual affair that followed was not going to do that. So – they had an affair which seemed to consist mainly of sex in the store after hours, or in his car parked in isolated rural locations. And then his wife discovered what was going on, and a humiliating encounter at work followed, with Leah shamed in front of all of the staff and a good few customers too. I wouldn't have believed it possible when first meeting her – such a shy, quiet girl – but she genuinely didn't realise he was married. And after that, of course, he avoided her at all costs, shunned her and excluded her from all the management training she was supposed to have. She applied for a transfer, which was blocked by head office. And despite it all, despite this man's appalling behaviour, the trigger that brought Leah to me was that she still loved him, even though it was hopeless.

There was the word: *hopeless*. The word I need to hear, to start things off.

'It's easy to make things better,' I said. 'The end of the road is easy to find, and it's a very simple road to take.'

'I'm afraid of pain,' she replied.

'Could there be any pain worse than this?'

'No. But I might – do it wrong. I might get things wrong, and that would be worse…'

'There are no wrong decisions. You can decide this, and feel better about everything. It's a decision you can make. The decision is completely in your hands. You have the power to do this, and the strength to do it.'

'I suppose so,' she said.

'There is always peace,' I said, softly. 'Peace, and quiet, and an end to all the pain. You can choose for it to be painless, and quiet, and completely on your terms. It's for you to choose.'

From a purely technical aspect, it really is that simple. The techniques I've learned – language patterns, inducing a trance state and a heightened relaxation state in people purely through conversation – were the easy part all along. It's just a case of listening closely to what they are telling you, not just with their words but far more importantly with their bodies, with their eyes, with their movements and shifts and subtle changes in tone. It isn't rocket science (an inexcusable cliché), but nor is it pseudo-science. It's reassuringly easy when you know how.

You want to know how I do it, don't you? I can imagine it, your fervent interest, your curiosity that others might describe as morbid: I can see it in the sparkle in your eyes. Well, ask me, then. Go on. I know you're dying to…

In any case, I can't and shan't reveal the details. Do you think I stumbled upon this overnight? Do you think this level of awareness is something everyone can master? It's a long, slow process, not just the learning of the techniques required but the effort involved in tailoring that same process to the individual concerned. It starts with a simple conversation, but this is just the first of many such meetings, many such conversations. The hard part is knowing if they are ready, and spotting the ones who are close enough to make it work.

I'm not sure if Leah is quite at that point, and I am thinking about leaving her for a few weeks, maybe trying to reconnect with her after a time. She will go one way, or the other. If she chooses the right path, then I will be ready for her.

Sometimes I meet people who aren't ready, and I leave them to continue on their own. If they need me later on, then I shall find them again.

It's not as if I don't have others to look out for, in any case.

Annabel

On Monday morning I got to work feeling empty. The sky was dark grey, threatening rain, like the inside of my heart.

Kate was off today, which meant it was just me and Trigger. I wasn't in the mood for him today, Trigger and his ever-changing moods, cheerful one minute and grumpy the next. But the office was deserted. As usual, the milk carton I'd bought on Friday and used once only was empty in the fridge. I needed a cup of tea, and the theft of the milk, such a petty thing, made me want to cry. It was the early turn, probably, who started work long before the shops opened, and needed a drink to keep them going through the dark hours before dawn. But that was no excuse for being too lazy or thoughtless to bring in their own milk. The fridge in the kitchen that served the management corridor actually had a padlock, and that was the reason.

I made a cup of green tea instead and logged into the system. I opened my email. Twenty-four new messages since I'd logged off last night. Where did they all come from?

I scrolled down, looking for ones that were interesting, and my eyes were drawn to one name: Sam Everett. I ignored it, working my way through all the intelligence reports and requests to log out of systems I didn't use anyway because they were going to reboot the servers. There was an email from the Force's Recreation Association asking me to join the monthly lottery, an email about a sergeant from Tactical Operations who was planning to run a marathon in Tibet and wanted sponsorship, and a request for additional copies of the bi-monthly Violence Profile from two people who had just joined the Strategic Planning Department.

That was it. I couldn't put it off any longer. Sam Everett – newsdesk, *Briarstone Chronicle*. The title of the email: 'Recent deaths'.

Dear Annabel,

I hope you don't mind me contacting you directly. I had a meeting with DI Andrew Frost recently and he told me that you might be able to provide me with some additional data with regards to the recent increase in – still not sure what to call them – undiscovered bodies? Decomposed deceased? You know what I mean, though, don't you? I realise I am supposed to be putting enquiries through the Force's Media Services department but so far I've met with a big blank every time I've called or emailed. Please get in touch and maybe we can meet to discuss.

With kind regards,
Sam Everett
Senior Reporter, Newsdesk
Briarstone Chronicle

Below that was a landline number and a mobile phone number. I closed the email and went back to the others, working my way through them methodically, before putting even that aside and starting work on the next sex offender profile.

Colin

In the kitchen at work someone has left a copy of today's *Briarstone Chronicle* on the table. It's covered in crumbs, has a smear of butter on the front page, and in normal circumstances I would lift it between finger and thumb and deposit it in the waste paper bin before wiping the surface down with disinfectant and washing my hands.

But today the side bar on the front page catches my eye. I stand over the table, reading. It's about their pathetic 'Love Thy Neighbour' campaign which they launched on Friday – and it seems to be an exhortation for everyone to knock on their next-door neighbour's door and check they are still breathing.

If I weren't within earshot of the two people sitting at desks just outside the kitchen door, I would probably have laughed out loud. What good do they think it's going to do? At the very best, all it will achieve is to find the ones who have still not been found. I don't know how many that is. I don't always see the paper, and many of them wouldn't even make the news.

And suddenly I have a bright idea. A wonderful, glistening, delicious and dangerous idea. I could ring them up, the people at the newspaper, and tell them where to look. Save them the trouble of their campaign. After all, the good people of Briarstone have better things to do with their days than to bother with checking up on their neighbours. Surely it would be a kind thing for me to do, to let them know (without troubling the police, who, let's face it, are already under tremendous pressure to solve burglaries and assaults and all manner of other horrible crimes) where the others could be found?

I find myself shuddering with excitement and, to my surprise, sporting a sudden and huge erection.

I sit down at the kitchen table, something I never usually do since you don't know which of the scutters has sat there before you, in order to disguise the disarrangement of my trousers. Could I do it? Should I do it? Why not, after all? I could do it in such a way that would not identify my involvement. And it would make everything suddenly much more interesting, much more exciting. I've enjoyed the last year very much indeed, but the last ones haven't been nearly so entertaining. It still feels like the right thing to do and I get a thrill of excitement each time I walk away from them, leaving them behind, but the stimulation I get now is not nearly the same as it was the first few times. I need to – how do the tabloids put it? – up my game.

So what, if the press then know it is being done deliberately? They will have no idea how, or why. They will quite likely not believe that such a thing is possible. The individuals concerned all died of natural causes, after all. There is no question of foul play.

The thought of ringing someone up – or, no, perhaps it would be better done by email, or by post – and the result of it! The story they would print for the next edition! It would be immense. It might even attract national attention.

The erection is growing, not diminishing. I'm past the point of decision. It's no longer about the 'if' – it's now all about the 'when' and the 'how'. It has given me a completely new way of approaching the matter. A new inspiration.

I pick up the newspaper, no longer concerned about the crumbs or the smear of butter, and fold it in half. Holding it casually against the front of my body, I leave the kitchen and hurry past the desks outside to the lobby, ducking into the disabled toilet tucked away around the corner by the lifts. I lock the door and undo my trousers, laying the newspaper out open on the grubby floor, a double page spread with pictures of them as I've never seen them, pictures of smiling faces from a different age, happy faces before I met them, before I released them from their pain, before I showed them the way to escape from it all. And looking at them again turns me on even more, rubbing myself hard enough for it to hurt, thrusting into my fist until I find relief, all over the newspaper, over their faces.

Annabel

The Park and Ride was quiet on a Tuesday lunchtime. I'd only ever seen it at seven in the morning, the buses busy but the car park still empty. Now I had to drive all the way to the far side before I found a space. Annoying to have to walk all the way to the bus stop and then all the way to the very back of the car park before I could start to drive home. And then, no doubt, to have to park three or four streets away from home.

I'd taken the morning as flexible hours because I'd woken up with a fierce headache, one that made me nauseous. I'd almost expected it to last the day, but by eleven o'clock it had subsided to a dull thudding, and I was bored at home anyway.

On the bus, my mobile phone rang. It rang so infrequently that it always gave me a jolt when I heard it. I felt for the phone, vibrating and playing a tinny rendition of Mozart at the bottom of my bag, tangled up in the rubbish I carried around with me everywhere I went and never needed. Someone sitting behind me tutted with annoyance at the noise, which got louder and louder as I held my bag open.

At last, when I was convinced the caller was going to give up and it was going to go to voicemail, I felt the trembling phone and grabbed it.

'Hello?'

There was a pause and I thought again that they must have rung off.

'Hello, is that Annabel?'

'Yes,' I said, wondering if it was a sales call and how I could get out of it. 'I'm just on a bus, I can't hear you very well.'

'This is Sam Everett,' said the voice. 'I'm a journalist with the *Briarstone Chronicle*.'

'Oh, yes. I got your email. How did you get my mobile number?'

'Ah – a lady in your office let me have it. Sorry, she said she thought you wouldn't mind.'

Of course. Kate would assume I wouldn't mind; I never minded anything, did I? I felt cross, but that wouldn't make a blind bit of difference now.

'No, I guess it doesn't matter.'

For some reason, I'd assumed Sam Everett was a woman. I had no idea why; I just suspected that a journalist interested in a human interest story like this one would be female, empathetic, kind. Maybe Sam Everett the man had a completely different take on it – maybe it was the bodies he was interested in, the decomposition, the potential for violence.

'Is it a good moment to talk?'

'Not really. I'm on the bus, on my way to work.'

'Ah. Maybe I could meet up with you later? What time do you finish?'

'Well, I'm late going in already,' I said.

'It won't take long. Look, I'm in the town centre. I could meet you off the bus and buy you a very quick coffee. What do you think?'

'Well…'

They didn't even know I was coming in, to be honest. I'd not phoned to let them know, reasoning that neither Kate nor Bill would answer their phones, and, if they did, they probably wouldn't much care.

'I'd really appreciate it,' Sam said. 'I think we could really help each other out with this, you know? Nobody's taking it seriously enough, and too many people are dying.'

'Yes,' I said. Where was this conversation heading? It was making me feel uncomfortable.

'So you'll meet me? What bus are you on?'

I told him, which he took to mean I had assented.

'If you get off at the stop before the shopping centre, I'll wait for you there, OK? See you in a few minutes, then.'

He rang off. I put the phone back into my bag and looked out of the window at the houses lining the road. Big houses, large front lawns. The bus paused in traffic, outside a house that was obviously empty: no curtains at the windows, the lawn overgrown, weeds growing up through the cracks in the paving stones. Was there someone inside, after all? Someone waiting to be found?

A few minutes later the bus turned the corner into the High Street. Four hundred yards further on, the shopping centre entrance would be the first of my two possible stops, there or the war memorial; from the shopping centre I would walk through the arcade, usually empty and cold first thing in the morning, but at this time of day it would be heaving with shoppers. And the bus was full of them now, too, about to get off. That was why he'd asked me to meet him at the earlier stop – I would be the only one. He wouldn't have to guess who I was, and he wouldn't have to risk me going off without him.

I stood and went to the front of the bus, holding on to the pole and swaying as it bumped its way through the potholes. I could see through the front windscreen a figure standing waiting at the bus stop, and as I got closer I realised this must be Sam Everett.

He was younger than I'd expected, certainly younger than me, maybe no more than twenty-five. He had dark hair that was long enough to curl over his collar, and wore neat glasses, black jeans and a black thigh-length coat over what looked like a band tour T-shirt. I thought I'd seen him somewhere before, but the memory wouldn't come. When I stepped down from the bus I saw it was a Pulp T-shirt that he was wearing and I thawed a little towards him then, because I'd loved Pulp when I'd been at university, they were my all-time favourite band. I gave him a smile.

'Annabel?' he asked, holding out his hand for me to shake. 'I'm Sam.'

'Nice to meet you,' I said.

'Shall we go in here?'

109

We headed inside a café called the Lunch Box. Once a greasy spoon that had catered for the taxi drivers and bus conductors on their breaks, it had been redecorated and refitted and now served panini and salad alongside the traditional full English breakfasts and chip butties.

I found a table near the back and, while Sam ordered for us at the counter, I watched him standing there and thought for a moment that he looked a little lost. I didn't know what I had expected a journalist to look like, but he probably wasn't it. I'd been wondering why he looked familiar, and then I realised he was the journalist who had knocked on my door on the day I'd found Shelley Burton. The one who'd come with a photographer.

'Thanks,' I said, 'how much was it?' I had my purse out ready, but he waved me away.

'Don't worry about it,' he said.

He probably got it all on expenses, anyway, so I put my purse back in my bag without further argument. It was warm in here after the chill of being outside, and I felt my cheeks glowing with it. This was probably a bad idea, I thought. I shouldn't really be here with this man.

'So,' he said, as the man behind the counter brought two coffees and set them down in front of us on the table, 'you're working on the decomposed bodies, right?'

'I wouldn't say I'm working on them, exactly. I've been trying to establish how many of them there are and looking for patterns. Look, I really think you need to be talking to Media Services, don't you, rather than me?'

'I tried Media Services; I know that's how it's supposed to be done. They had no knowledge of it at all. Either that, or they just didn't want to talk about it.'

'Really?'

'You may not realise this, but your organisation's media relations policy is pretty restrictive. They only tell you things they want you to hear. Which isn't very much.'

'Oh,' I said.

'I went to school with Ryan Frost. Andrew Frost is his dad. I see Ryan all the time – we still go out some weekends. Last Saturday I was round his house and Ryan's dad – sorry, I find it really hard to think of him as Andrew – was there, so I asked him about the bodies. I've been looking at it for a while, in fact. I did a Freedom of Information request to get the numbers, talked to the Coroner's Office as well.'

I looked at him. He was flushed, leaning across the table towards me. Excited about it all.

'How many did you find?' I asked him. 'I haven't seen today's paper.'

'Nineteen,' he said.

'I found twenty-four, including the one last week.'

'This is bad,' he said. 'Don't you think this is really bad? All those people. There has to be something linking them.'

'That's what I keep looking for, but I haven't found it yet.'

'I mean, they're all so different – different ages, different social backgrounds, family, no family. I can't find anything about them that's similar.'

'I thought it might be something medical. I wondered if they were all at the same doctor's surgery, or they'd all been seen at the hospital, or they'd – I don't know – engaged with Social Services, or something.'

'Have you heard of the *hikikomori*?'

'No, what's that?' I said.

'It's a phenomenon in Japan. A whole section of society – usually teenagers, specifically male teenagers, withdrawing. They shut themselves up in their rooms and don't come out for years.'

'Why?'

'Lots of theories, but nobody really knows. They reckon it might be a backlash against the high-pressure educational system in Japan. These kids are generally high-functioning, wealthy backgrounds, stable home life – no apparent reason why they should want to rebel. It's like they just give up on life. But there are so many of them now that they've actually given it a name. Estimates vary as to how many of them there are, but it's probably somewhere around three million. Out of a population of 127 million.'

'But they don't stay in their rooms till they die?'

'Usually their families keep feeding them, or they go out in the middle of the night to a *konbini* – a sort of convenience store. But it's the choice they make that intrigues me.' He took a drink from his coffee, which was growing cold on the table in front of him. I'd finished mine, drunk it in a couple of gulps.

'The choice to withdraw?'

'Yes. The choice to withdraw – for whatever reason. Maybe apathy, or as an act of rebellion. Maybe our cases are similar.'

'Rebellion against what, though?'

'I don't know. It might just be a side effect of the recession: economic meltdown, depression, despair. Or else it's something in our society they don't want to engage with. Which is why you might be right to look at public services, the medical system, Social Services, that type of thing.'

'I can't get access to all that,' I said. 'I've tried.'

'Isn't there anything on the case files?'

'There aren't any case files, that's the problem. These aren't murders. They aren't even, for the most part, suspicious deaths. They are just people who have died. Once they've been collected by the funeral directors they're no longer a police matter. The families, if we can find them, are informed, and that's the end of our involvement in it. Nothing is recorded – there's no point. For the people who do have families, I have next to no information at all – it's only the ones who are unclaimed that still remain of interest.'

He was leaning forward in his seat, frowning. Listening.

'You know it was me who found Shelley Burton?'

'Really? I didn't know that.'

'I live next door to her. I could smell something. I thought the house was empty, but she was in there the whole time.'

'That must have been a very traumatic thing to see,' he said.

'It was horrible. She was – '

I'd said so much, and at that moment I realised that the excitement of having someone show an interest had made me garrulous. This wasn't just anybody, either; this man was a journalist. He could even be recording our conversation! I hadn't thought of that... I'd been an idiot. This was going to cost me my job. I couldn't believe I'd been so stupid.

'What?' he asked. 'What's the matter?'

'What do you mean?'

'You look – I don't know. Worried.'

He was certainly perceptive. Probably that came with the job: the ability to spot discomfort in your companion; the ability to ask pertinent and impertinent questions; the capacity to memorise long sections of conversation and then subtly adapt them to make it seem that the person had actually said what you'd wanted them to say, without them ever actually saying it.

'I should go,' I said, heaving myself up out of the chair.

'Annabel, wait a minute.'

'No, really, thank you for the coffee, but I need to go...'

'Can I see you again?'

I stopped pulling my coat around my shoulders and stared at him. It sounded so odd, that phrase. 'What for?'

He stood up, blocking my route to the door of the café. 'I know you care about this,' he said. 'I don't want to compromise your job in any way, and I don't want you to feel uncomfortable. Whatever's going on isn't just going to stop. We need to try to get them to do something about it, and the only way we're going to do that is to find out what's going on. Will you help me?'

I bit my lip. He was standing close to me and I didn't like it. My back was against the wall in more ways than one.

'I don't know what I can do,' I said. 'I've tried every-thing.'

'I'll do all the hard stuff. I just need your data. The same data you've been looking at and dealing with every day. I can

113

put pressure on the senior officers by printing more about the people involved, and I can get that information elsewhere. I just need to get a better picture about who they are.'

'That's all covered by the Data Protection Act,' I said, lamely.

'Not if they're dead,' he said. 'The DPA doesn't apply after death.'

'I know that. It still applies while there's an active investigation, though. And in any case it still applies to their families,' I said, trying to recover. He knew the legislation better than I did. It would do me no good to try to look clever in front of him.

'I didn't think there *was* an active investigation.'

He must have noticed my discomfort then, because he stood aside to let me through. 'I'll walk you down the hill, OK?'

I mumbled something and he followed me out into the bright, crisp air on the main road. The pavement was crowded with shoppers and although he walked beside me we kept getting separated.

'Look,' he said at last, as we turned the corner into the wide pedestrian precinct leading down the hill to the river, 'I'd just really like to stay in touch. You're the only person I've spoken to who is taking this seriously. I've been trying to get my editor involved, too. She agreed to start up our campaign to get everyone to check up on their neighbours, but I'm still thinking it's a bit more sinister than a lack of public-spiritedness.'

'Sinister?'

'You know. That they are being murdered.'

I stopped dead and turned to look at him. 'I don't think they're being murdered,' I said.

'Really? You don't think that?'

'There's nothing to suggest they were murdered. No break-ins – ' Not apart from the house next door, I thought, remembering the crash of the pane of glass inside the kitchen. 'No trauma, no violent attacks. They just died.'

'Maybe it was a slow-acting poison,' he said, 'or they were gassed by their boilers, or something.'

'It's a bit far-fetched,' I said. 'And there's no evidence. What makes you think they're being murdered?'

His cheeks were flushed and he dropped his voice so I had to move closer to hear him. 'Well, alright, then, maybe not murdered. But someone else is involved with this. They haven't all just spontaneously decided to die, have they?'

'Why not? That's almost what your Japanese teenagers did.'

We carried on walking. At the bottom of the hill I would cross the road at the pedestrian crossing, and then I would be at the police station. I didn't really want to be seen talking to a journalist, and was trying to work out a way of parting company with him before getting to the main road.

He had his hands in his pockets, his shoulders hunched. He looked thoughtful, as though he was trying to come up with some conclusive argument that would put an end to the difference of opinion.

I stopped at the corner. 'I need to go this way,' I said, in a tone that suggested a firm goodbye. 'It was nice meeting you.'

'Sure,' he said.

Was that it? After all that pushing, he'd given up, then, so easily?

'Goodbye, Annabel.' He held out his hand and it was warm, his grip firm.

'Goodbye. Good luck.'

'You too.'

I watched Sam walk away, and then I turned and pressed the button for the crossing, waiting for the traffic to stop so I could cross and go in to work.

The only one in the office was Kate.

'I thought you were off sick?' she said. 'What are you doing coming in?'

'I had a headache,' I said, taking off my coat and hanging it on the rack by the door, 'but it's worn off now.'

I sat down and turned on the screen at my workstation, put in my user number and password and waited for it to go through the checks before I could start working. As usual it took an age. 'I'm just going to go and see someone,' I said to Kate, who was now gazing out of the window, deep in thought.

'Right,' she said.

Frosty was in his office, the door half-open. I knocked and pushed it a little. 'Are you mad busy?' I asked.

He looked up from the screen. 'Never too busy to see you,' he said. 'Come and sit down.'

I slid into the chair opposite his desk.

'I just met a friend of yours,' I said.

'Oh, yes?'

'Sam Everett.'

Frost laughed. 'I've known Sam since he was tiny.'

'You know he's interested in the bodies,' I said. 'He's trying to get his editor to make a bigger story out of it.'

'So what did you tell him?'

'Nothing,' I said quickly. 'There's nothing I can tell him, is there? Shouldn't he be talking to Media Services, not me?'

'It's the same old problem, though, I'm afraid. Media Services have their own agenda, and I'm sorry to say that our bodies aren't on it.'

Our bodies? Was he starting to take an interest in this now? A serious interest?

'Did you know I found the latest one?'

He sat forward then. 'No, I didn't know.'

'It was next door to my house. It was what got me started on all this.'

'Oh, Annabel. That's rough. Are you OK?'

He meant it. 'Yes,' I said. 'I think so. The smell – it stays with you, doesn't it?'

'It does,' he said. 'My first body – I was eighteen, two weeks into my initial stint on patrol as a probationer. Been trying to prepare for it, but you can never do that, not really. I went to this house and the neighbours said they'd not seen this old lady for three weeks. I could smell it before I got to the back door. When I went in – well, it was bad. She was lying on her bed, and when they finally moved the body her scalp was stuck to the headboard and came away from the skull. I threw up in the back garden.'

'I didn't throw up. Maybe it would have been better if I had. I just had lots of showers. And I had to bath the cat, she'd been rolling in it.'

'Yuck.'

'Look,' I said. 'Do you think they are going to start taking this seriously? That's the twenty-fourth. The next one will be along soon. There are lots of people out there, waiting for us to find them, you know that, don't you?'

'No,' he said. 'There's nothing to indicate that we're going to find any more.'

I bit my lip. This was so frustrating – just a moment ago I'd thought he was on my side, more than any of them. The others didn't get it, but I'd thought he did. He knew that this was a problem that wouldn't go away.

'You know that's not right,' I said, 'don't you?'

He looked me straight in the eye. 'If I get a chance today I'll have another go at talking to someone upstairs. OK?'

By 'someone upstairs' he meant someone in the management corridor – the area commander or one of the chief inspectors. They'd all seen my presentation, though, at the tactical meeting. They all had the data. If that hadn't convinced them, nothing would.

'Leave it with me,' he said, in a tone that suggested dismissal.

'Alright,' I said. 'Thanks.'

I got up to leave. He was already back at his computer and I wondered if he would even remember in five minutes' time that I'd visited.

On the bus going home I closed my eyes and leaned my head against the cold window. I'd stayed at work longer than usual, trying to make up for my missing hours this morning.

The tactical assessment was behind schedule but that wasn't completely my fault; a systems failure at headquarters had left the main database interrogation software temporarily unavailable.

It had been a long, shattering day and my headache was coming back. To make it even worse, I'd just been getting on the bus, rummaging around in my bag for the Park and Ride ticket that I seemed to have inexplicably mislaid, when my mobile phone rang. For a moment I thought that it might be Sam Everett again and I was preparing the words to make it clear that I wasn't interested – but it was my mum, of course, providing me with a list of shopping that she needed, which I wrote on my hand with a black pen that I hoped would not turn out to be permanent. Sugar, milk, frozen peas, potatoes, lemonade, double cream, teabags.

'You sound all tinny. Why do you sound all tinny?'

'I'm on the bus, Mum. I only just left work.'

'Why are you so late?'

'I had a headache this morning, I didn't feel well. I went in late.'

'You went in late? What's wrong with a couple of painkillers and a bit of stiff upper lip? You've got no staying power. And you don't eat properly either. Too much sugar and fat, that's your trouble.'

'Yes, Mum,' I said. It was easier to agree. 'Can I get this stuff for you tomorrow? You don't need it urgently, do you?'

'I'd like a nice bottle of white as well. You got me one last week, it was very nice.'

'I'll get it on the way back from work tomorrow, alright? I'll find you one in the fridge at the Co-op.'

'You need to take on board a bit of personal responsibility. What are you going to be like when the clocks go back in a couple of weeks, eh? You'll be no good to anyone.'

I could have told her that I'd been getting up in the dark since September, but it would have done no good – she wasn't listening anyway.

'You don't need the shopping tonight, though, do you?'

'Yes, I do. And I can't get to the kitchen, my knee's been playing me up today. I haven't had any lunch, I haven't had anything to eat or drink since last night. You know I need to eat with these tablets, or else I come over all funny.'

She wasn't supposed to drink alcohol with the tablets either, but that rule seemed to have passed her by. I told her I'd be with her in an hour or so, and at last that did the trick and she rang off.

I felt the headache starting to pound, tiredness making it worse. I felt for the angel I kept in the pocket of my coat, feeling the contours of those beautiful wings. Surely there was some reason why all this was happening? Surely someone somewhere had a plan, and eventually this was all going to make sense?

The bus pulled in to the car park and I heaved myself wearily to my feet. My back was killing me. I would have a nice bath when I finally got home – a drop of eucalyptus oil in it, something to soothe the aches away.

I could see my car, a lonely silver shape just about visible in the gloom. The orange street-lights glowed in the mist. Other people would be afraid to walk back to their cars in the dark, I thought. Other women would feel vulnerable. I didn't feel afraid. Just tired.

The car was cold and damp and didn't want to start. After two or three turns of the key it shuddered into life and I drove to the supermarket to get the shopping for Mum.

Colin

I spent Monday night trying to study but I was too distracted. Having thrown away the soiled copy of the *Briarstone Chronicle* in the kitchen bin at work, I purchased a fresh copy on the way home. Even seeing the folded cover of the newspaper with the top half of Rachelle's head on the counter was enough to make me hard again. Despite my self-imposed abstention rule, having started on the whisky early in the evening, I found it difficult to stop myself from spending most of the night masturbating. It was the newspaper article that did it – and the spark of an idea that would not ignite, no matter which angle I took as my approach.

This evening, I stopped at the supermarket after work to buy some bread, milk, olives and chorizo. As my items were gliding along on the conveyor belt at the checkout, I looked up and my eyes chanced upon a woman waiting at the next checkout. Overweight – fat, even; her hair tied back in an unkempt ponytail that had neither substance nor style. She was greying at the temples but, like Janice, she was probably not as old as she looked. No wedding ring, nothing in the items on the conveyor that suggested she was shopping for a family at home. As well as her general demeanour, she had that look that so many of them do – the look of defeat. She looked tired out, as though the day had been merciless to her, as though it had picked her up in the morning and left her at the end of the day wrung out like a dirty dishcloth, draped grey and wrinkled over the taps to dry.

She managed a smile for the cashier, and, as with Janice, it lit up her face – too briefly. And, like Leah, she isn't ready for me, whoever she is. But it might only be a matter of time.

I hope I will see her again. She looked as though she needs my help.

The sudden appearance of this new prospect, even if she wasn't quite ripe, gave me a startling idea. I had been trying to work out how I could contact the newspaper and yet manage to remain completely anonymous. Of course, I could send them an old-fashioned letter – impossible to trace – but then I would miss out on the excitement of hearing their reaction. The only way to do that was to be there in person, or to speak to them on the phone.

And then I realised how I could do it. Nietzsche said, 'The true man wants two things: danger and play.' I played with them whenever it took my fancy, but this was no longer enough. Now, it seemed, I wanted danger too…

I had three of them at the moment, all at different stages of readiness – awaiting their agonal moment and the start of the transformation. The one who was furthest along that path, readiest, also happened to be the closest to the supermarket. I parked in the street behind the house and cut through the alleyway at the back. Nobody was around; the streets were deserted. I saw a cat twisting its skinny body around the dustbins. Besides that, nothing moved.

I made the phone call: no reply. I wondered if this meant I was too late, but as I was so close to the house I went anyway. The back door was open when I got to it, and I went inside without knocking or calling out.

She was asleep, lying on her bed, the sound of her breathing raspy, dry. I said her name, then again, louder.

'Can you open your eyes?'

At first there was no response. Her breaths came regularly, faltered, then changed – a few deep ones, with pauses in between. She was too far gone.

I debated what to do, whether I could manage it by myself – after all, it was the location that was important, and potentially I could take the tone of my voice up to a falsetto in the name of entertainment. It was disappointing, though. From

121

the moment I'd had the idea the excitement had been building inside me, and now I was here, so close to it, I felt almost feverish with anticipation.

But then – to my surprise – she stirred. Lifted her head, slowly. 'Can you sit?' I asked, helping her, my hand under her arm. She was hot, her skin papery.

It took a while to get her ready, but I only needed her concentration for a short while. Her eyes were shining, the only moist thing about her: her lips were dry, her hair hung in dry shreds around her face.

'Here,' I said. 'Take this paper. Can you read it, do you think?'

She looked at the sheet of paper, confused. Her eyes clouded over. 'I don't understand.'

I'd expected this. She was past the point of sense.

'Have you had anything to drink today?'

She looked at me, baffled. 'I don't understand.'

Oh, lord, I thought. It was the downside to this process, of taking away whatever left of the desire to strive, their effort, their activity. Everything you needed them to do after that had to be specifically instructed, moving from one model that required vague language, metaphor, using gentle anecdotes to make a point, to one that relied on direct instruction.

I went to the kitchen and ran the tap. The water clattered into the sink with a tinny, metallic noise. Already the noise of an empty house, and she was still here. She hadn't even left, but already her presence was fading. I found a cup and half-filled it – too much and it would make her ill, would jeopardise the process – and brought it back to her.

'Now,' I said, 'drink this.'

I gave her the cup and helped her steady it. She drank a few sips obediently but messily, water spilling out of the corner of her mouth and down the front of her dress. Then she turned her face away. She's had enough, I thought. She must be close to the transition. I took the cup gently out of her hands, putting it out of her line of sight on the floor.

'Now,' I said, touching her arm. 'Look at the paper. Can you read it?'

'"I have something important to say…"' she recited.

'That's good,' I said. 'Stop now. I will phone the number, and then, when someone answers, I want you to read out what it says on the paper. Do you understand?'

She didn't answer at first. I touched her arm again and she flinched, then she said, uncertainly, 'Yes.'

'That's good,' I said. 'Do it now.'

I dialled the number for her, and held the phone up close to her face. I'd wanted it to be on loudspeaker, so I could hear their reaction, but the house was so quiet I could hear the noise of the ringing tone at the other end. Whatever they said, I would hear it.

'Hello, Newsdesk.'

I touched her arm as a prompt, but I don't think she even needed it.

'Hello,' she said, her voice beautifully measured and even. 'I want to speak to Sam Everett.'

'Speaking. How can I help?'

'I have something important to say. There are more bodies,' she said, as though she were announcing the arrival of a train on platform seven. 'There is one at – '

'Hold on,' said Sam Everett, on the other end of the phone. 'Wait. Just wait a sec. Let me write this down.'

She paused for a few seconds, and then said, in a voice unexcited by the subject matter, 'There are more bodies. There is one at 36 Hawthorn Crescent, Carnhurst. There are others.'

I could hear nothing from the other end of the phone, and leaned closer to her. He was writing, scribbling it all down. I pointed to the next line on the script and she read it out dutifully. 'Do you need me to repeat that.' It was technically a question but her voice was flat.

'Where are the others? And who is this, please? What's your name?'

'Do you need me to repeat that.'

'No, no – I just want to know who I'm talking to. What's your name?'

I pressed the button on the phone to disconnect the call. Sam Everett would be the last person, other than me, whom she would speak to. She had no concept of this at all. No problem with it. If I had told her, if I had explained it to her, she would have been no more concerned than she was right now.

'Well done,' I said, replacing the phone handset on its charging unit. 'You did well.'

She looked at me. In another time and place she might even have smiled, but now she was tired, exhausted beyond belief at the exertion of concentrating and following those few instructions. She fell back on to the bed.

'I'm tired,' she said. 'My head hurts.'

'I know,' I said. 'You can sleep, if you want to.'

'Yes,' she said.

She was beautiful on the verge of death, rooted in it, alive with it. She knew no pain, no anger, no fear. She was approaching it as everyone should, accepting, graceful, perfectly at peace. The water she'd sipped did not seem to have slowed the process as I had thought it might. She was too far down the path.

'Now,' I said, touching her arm. 'You're ready. You know what you have to do.'

'Go to sleep,' she said.

'That's right,' I said. 'You go to sleep now. It's time.'

Before I left the house I wiped any of the surfaces I might have touched, even though I'd worn latex gloves all the way through. She hadn't noticed them, hadn't even looked upon them with curiosity. I don't really know why I bothered wearing them, since technically she'd invited me in and would not have objected to me being there. Even at a time such as this.

At the back door I paused and looked back at the house. The next person through the door would be the one to find her. They would trace the call, without doubt, and, when they did, they would come here looking for her. They would find her fresh, this one, if they had any sense. It did cross my mind that they could find her too quickly, before she died. It was a risk. But it was likely they would initially go to the address she had given them, and she only had a few hours left. Whatever happened, they would find these human remains before she had the chance to transform as the others had. It is her misfortune, and it is a shame considering how she has served me so well today. And I will miss out on watching this one, too, observing and documenting the transformation. But it had to be done, and, after all, I will be enjoying other benefits this time.

With all the excitement earlier this evening I am too distracted at the gym to put in any serious effort towards my goals. Thirty minutes on each of the machines, my usual routine, but my thirty laps of the pool take nearly twenty-three minutes. In the gym I manage to tune out the thoughts with the thumping beat from the loudspeakers and the hypnotic rhythm of the woman's arse on the treadmill in front of me, but now, in the pool, all I can think about is Sam Everett and whether he has done anything with the information I've given him. It's tempting, so tempting, to detour via that dingy little two-up, two-down at the wrong end of Hawthorn Crescent, but instead I finish my swim and go home.

Before I've even unpacked the groceries I find myself overcome with it all. My hands are shaking, pulling the newspaper out of the plastic carrier bag. I've never been so aroused in my life. The thrill of leaving someone behind to transform has been completely eclipsed by the thrill of letting someone in on the secret, even if it wasn't the whole secret, even if I've not done the telling myself.

I want to shout it to the whole world, but then the secret would not thrill me any more – and I would probably be locked up. They would lock me up forever for what I've done. Or would they? I've done nothing to these people, other than help them escape from the terrible drudgery of the lives they were living up to now. If anything, my input is cathartic; it's a merciful release. They would have killed themselves sooner or later, and my method is infinitely neater, less painful and possibly less messy. I haven't harmed anyone. I merely crystallised their thoughts, prompted them into action that might otherwise have been a long time coming, during which time they would have suffered and lingered and probably taken several other people down with them. And I anaesthetised them too, so that from the moment their decision was made, they felt no pain, suffered no trauma, no anguish. It was perfect.

I take the newspaper upstairs with me, take off my trousers and fold them neatly over the same hanger from which I removed them this morning. My underwear, too, into the laundry basket. I'm shivering with the anticipation of it. I open the newspaper out on to the double page spread that I wanked over in the disabled toilets at lunchtime yesterday, smooth it out on the bed.

I turn on the television and press play on the DVD remote, sparking the thing to life with a whirr and a click. The porn I watched last weekend, some American tripe with two fat whores going at each other like starving dogs. A few seconds later I turn it off. It isn't doing it for me; it's distracting. The newspaper, on the other hand, is doing it. Those faces – all the smiling faces, happy at weddings, the other people in the pictures, the people who were there in past times, neatly clipped away from their lives, neatly put aside – and my penis is so hard it's painful, still bruised from the beating I gave it yesterday and last night and the night before and yet so delicious, such a relief to take hold of it again.

This time, when I come a few moments later, I am careful to use tissues, leaving the newspaper clean and undamaged for another day.

Annabel

I was in bed but not asleep when the phone started ringing.

I listened to it ringing in the stillness of the house, wondering who would be calling me at this time of night and whether it was worth getting up to find out. I only had one handset, downstairs, because the phone didn't ring often enough to warrant getting another one in the bedroom.

After the sixth ring I got out of bed, shoved my feet into my slippers, pulled on my towelling dressing gown and padded down the stairs. I thought it would probably stop right at the very moment that I put my hand on the receiver.

'Hello?'

'Is that Annabel? Annabel Hayer?' It was a man's voice, elderly. A bit uncertain.

'Speaking.'

'This is Len from next door. It's about your mum.'

For a moment I couldn't place him. From next door? I didn't have a Len next door. Then I realised exactly who he was – the old bloke who lived next door to my mother's house, the one who took her in the day her pipes burst. He lived with his wife – what was her name? Carol?

'Mum? What's the matter? I only saw her a few hours ago…'

'She's had a bit of a fall. The ambulance is here now; they're taking her to St Mary's. It's taken me all this time to find your number. She really should have it written down somewhere handy, honestly.'

'Is she alright?"

'I think so, love. You'd best get down to the hospital.'

'OK. Thank you.'

'I'll lock up here – she gave me a key. You don't need to worry about a thing.'

When I rang off a few moments later I sat in a stunned silence for a moment and then hot tears started to fall. I wasn't even sure why I was crying. 'Stop it,' I said out loud, 'stop it right now.' I rubbed my dressing gown sleeve across my cheeks and went back upstairs to get dressed.

Outside the main entrance of the hospital, a collection of people in wheelchairs and dressing gowns were openly defying the smoking ban with their abler-bodied companions. Inside, the shops were all closed up, the reception desk unstaffed.

I stood there for a moment, baffled. Where did you go to find someone, when the main reception was closed? Then I realised that the majority of pedestrian traffic was back and forth down the corridor to my left. A sign on the wall listed the various departments that I would find in this direction, including Accident and Emergency. Of course – that was where the ambulance would have taken her.

Despite the adrenaline, my brain didn't seem to be functioning properly. I wasn't used to being awake at this time of night, and after several nights of disturbed sleep I was beginning to feel light-headed and strange.

There were several people gathered around the reception desk that served A&E. I stood at what I thought was the back of the queue. The woman currently being served was having an argument with the receptionist, which grew louder and more unpleasant to listen to. The argument itself made no sense, going round and round in circles and I realised she was drunk, holding on to the counter with one hand while her feet struggled to maintain balance. In the end two security guards appeared and took the woman off to one side to speak to her, and the next person in the line moved forward.

I looked around desperately, half-expecting to see my mum sitting on one of the chairs in the waiting area. There was no sign of her. The place was busy, too, with plenty of people waiting. What was it like here on a Friday or a Saturday night? I wondered. Must be hell on earth.

'Can I help you?' A second receptionist had come to the desk and called me forward.

'My mum's been brought here. Iris Hayer. She had a fall.'

The receptionist tapped on her keyboard. 'Hayer? How are you spelling it?'

I spelled it out for her. I could see the reflection of the screen in her glasses as she moved the mouse and clicked the screen. 'And your name is?'

'Annabel Hayer.'

'And you're her daughter?'

I said that already, I thought crossly. 'Yes.'

'Right, here we go. If you take a seat, someone will be with you shortly. Alright?'

As I found a seat I thought of all the questions I should have asked. *How is she? Can I see her? How long will I have to wait?* But I'd been dismissed, and as I looked back to the desk I realised that there was now a queue twice as long as the one I'd joined.

I sat down next to a vending machine displaying bars of chocolate. My stomach grumbled at the sight of it, even though I would normally be fast asleep by now. I thought about getting a coffee and something to eat, but of course the minute I did that someone would emerge from one of the doors and call my name.

I checked my mobile phone, as though someone else might call me in the middle of the night. I looked at the girl sitting opposite me in a hospital-issue wheelchair, one naked foot swollen and pale, the skin stretched so tight it was shiny. Further down the row of chairs were two young men, their shirts covered in blood. One of them was holding a small towel, of the type used for mopping up slopped beer in pubs, to the top of his head. They were talking and laughing animatedly, some discussion about football that I had no desire to listen to but could not avoid.

I wondered how the girl had hurt her foot, and was on the verge of asking when a porter turned up and wheeled her away. I stood up, then, and went to a nearby table weighed down with dog-eared magazines. I chose three of the most gossipy and sat down again, wishing I'd brought a book so I could tune everything out. At the entrance a group of young men were loitering, getting increasingly loud. Security, having dealt with one awkward customer, were gathering like fluorescent vultures.

Above the noise of the shouting youths at the front, a toddler that had been grizzling now expanded to a full-on piercing scream. It was a little boy, red-faced, stretching and squirming in his mother's lap. His fine blond hair was sticking to his forehead with sweat, his eyes wide. His mother shushed and rocked him without effect, tried with the dummy which came straight back out again. There was a merciful pause and I thought I'd gone deaf, but he was only recovering his breath ready for another shriek.

I looked at the first magazine, tried to focus on the celebrity faces. I only knew who one of them was. I flicked through the magazine until I came across an eight-page photo spread which seemed to be about Elton John putting his bins out. I gave up and tossed the magazine to one side. The longer I waited, I thought, the less likely it was that Mum's condition was serious. If she was in a bad way they would have seen me quickly, wouldn't they?

And of course, at that moment a nurse came out of the curtained area.

'Annabel Hayer?'

I stood up quickly, feeling faint as I did so but trying to look as normal as possible. 'Yes,' I said.

'Hello,' she said, already walking back the way she'd come in the expectation that I was following. 'Have you been waiting long?'

'No,' I said. 'I don't think so. How's my mum? Is she alright?'

She opened a door and stood aside to let me in. I thought it was going to be a small room but it turned out that it was a corner of the A&E treatment area.

'Have a seat,' she said. 'The doctor will be in shortly.'

And before I could ask her anything more she'd gone, shutting the door to the waiting area behind her.

I stared out into the treatment area, trying not to cry. I wanted to call someone but for the life of me I couldn't think of anyone. Who would I call? My only cousin, in Scotland? What could she do, from the other end of the country? Maybe I could ring Kate. But I really didn't know her well enough, not for a crisis call like this one. She'd end up hating me even more than she did already. I had nobody. I was on my own.

The screaming toddler (or maybe it was a different one; all babies sounded identical to me) was being dealt with somewhere behind a curtain. Over the wailing I could hear soothing tones, inflections rising and falling: 'There you go! Good boy, what a brave boy you are. Soon be done. Nearly done now. Mum, can you hold his hand? Like that. Tight hold... Yep... There we are! That's that bit all over with.'

I heard footsteps, rapid, on the linoleum and a man came round the corner, dressed in a blue shirt with the sleeves rolled up to the elbows, stethoscope around his neck, ID badge clipped to the breast pocket. He looked very young and very tired, but he managed a smile. I scrambled to my feet, my bag half-falling from my lap until I clutched at it.

'Miss Hayer? Thank you for waiting. I'm Jonathan Lamb, I'm one of the doctors treating your mother this evening. Would you come this way?'

'How is she?' I said, trying to keep up with him as he stalked off. He led me down the corridor past several curtained bays, each one of them occupied. At the furthest one he stopped and waited. I was several paces behind him, breathless with the exertion even though we'd only walked a hundred yards or so.

'She had a fall at home, I understand?'

'Her neighbour rang me. I don't know what happened.'

'Just in here.' He pulled at the curtain and stood aside to let me in. Mum was on a trolley, equipment and tubes all over her.

'Oh, Mum!' I said. I couldn't help it.

Behind me, Jonathan Lamb's pager made a bleeping noise. 'I'll – er – I'll be back in one second, and we can talk further. Have a seat.'

I lifted Mum's hand, heavy, hot, from the sheet that covered her. She was wearing a hospital gown. *I should have brought her a nightie*, I thought; *she'd hate that*. It was clearly too small for her. 'Mum?'

There was no response to the squeeze I gave her fingers. Nothing.

I stood there holding her hand for what felt like a long time. My back was hurting standing like this, leaning over, and it was only when that dull ache became too much that I let go of her hand and sat on the chair next to the trolley. I tried to pull it closer but it was heavy. I found a tissue in my bag and wiped my eyes, blew my nose. I couldn't quite believe this was happening. It felt so unreal.

There was a clock on the wall above my head, and I twisted to look at it, watching the minutes tick past. It was nearly one. If it got to half-past one I'd go and find someone.

At twenty past, I stood up and stretched. Then the curtain twitched aside and Jonathan Lamb was back, this time with a nurse. She gave me a warm, sympathetic smile. 'Hello,' she said.

'Really sorry about the delay,' Jonathan Lamb said. 'Please have a seat.'

I did as I was told, and the doctor disappeared again and came back a moment later with two stacked plastic chairs. He unstacked them, scraping them noisily on the linoleum. He sat down. The nurse sat down. It felt bizarrely like an interview.

He looked at the cardboard folder, at the notes, and started talking. I heard the first words he said – 'It's very bad news,

I'm afraid…' – and didn't hear very much after that at all. A stroke – although he had a different word for it – CVA? Cerebrovascular accident, that was it. It made it sound like a mistake, as if one or other of us could have done something to stop it. The reason they had kept me waiting was that they were waiting for scan results.

'She'd had a chest infection recently?'

'What? Oh – well, it was a while ago now. She was on antibiotics.'

'It's quite common for this to happen, I'm afraid. I'm so sorry.'

I thought I'd missed the bit where he said what was going to happen to her. 'She'll get better? Is that what you're saying?'

'No, I'm afraid she won't get better. All we can do now is make her as comfortable as possible.'

I stared at him. Then I looked at the nurse.

'Annabel, is there anyone I can phone for you? Someone to be with you?'

'No,' I said.

The doctor was looking uncomfortable. I wondered briefly how many times he'd given bad news to a relative.

'But – but – she's breathing, isn't she? I don't understand.' I looked at the trolley, at my mother on it, not moving, but with the oxygen mask over her face, unquestionably still breathing. Still very definitely alive.

'She's breathing, but I'm afraid the scan shows conclusively that there is no chance of recovery. It's just a matter of time. I'm so very sorry.'

It was the nurse that spoke next, her voice quiet. 'We're arranging to get her transferred to the Stroke Unit upstairs; hopefully you won't need to wait much longer. It's much more comfortable up there.'

The doctor went. I didn't know what to say to the nurse, so I just looked at her forlornly. I wondered if she was used to people coming in here, spaced out from having been woken by some trauma in the middle of the night.

'She can probably hear you if you want to talk to her,' she said gently.

I stood up again, and pulled the plastic chair that Jonathan Lamb had vacated over to the trolley. I took hold of Mum's hand. It was so warm, joints swollen with the arthritis that plagued her. 'Mum,' I said, 'I'm sorry. I'm sorry I wasn't there.'

It sounded so silly, talking to someone who was patently completely unconscious. And even if she could hear me, what to say? What could I possibly say to her? The nurse handed me a tissue. I blew my nose.

I closed my eyes, listening to the rhythmic beeping of the machinery, trying to take myself away from here. I would have to ring work, I thought.

I heard a sound and opened my eyes, thinking Mum had woken up, said something, but she remained motionless. The nurse had gone. When the sound came again I realised it was from the bed next door, separated from us only by a curtain.

In the early hours of the morning they transferred Mum to the Stroke Unit, a complicated procedure involving a porter, the nurse, a different doctor who came and went, and finally the bed being moved, machines and all, through various corridors and into a lift, me beside her trying to keep up with the porter who seemed determined to approach each set of double doors at lightning speed.

There was a handover procedure at the reception desk, and a different nurse took me into a quiet room 'just for a moment, while we make Mum comfortable'. She asked if I'd had anything to eat or drink, and would I like a cup of tea? I said no first, and then I changed my mind. I'd been warm downstairs in A&E but now I was unaccountably cold. She left me. I closed my eyes again, sitting back in a chair that was the most well-padded of all the chairs I'd been in tonight. I could sleep here, I thought.

The door opened again. It was the nurse, a mug in her hand.

'Do you want to come with me?' she asked. 'We've got her all settled now.'

Mum was in a side room, freshly dressed in a new gown that was much looser around her chest and shoulders. She was lying still and, even though she was in exactly the same position as she had been in A&E, she did look more comfortable. She had a drip going into her arm but the oxygen mask was gone. She looked peaceful, although her breathing was loud, as if she was snoring.

'There we are,' the nurse said. 'You must be shattered. I can get you a zed bed, if you'd like to try and get some sleep.'

'No, thanks,' I said, not wanting to put her to any trouble. There was a chair like the one in the other waiting room. I could sleep in that.

'I'm waiting to see someone from Palliative Care,' she said. 'They should come along soon and explain what's going to happen.'

'Thank you,' I said.

'If you have any questions…' she said. 'Anything at all?'

I should have had a hundred questions, but for now I couldn't think of anything. She put the tea down on the cabinet that separated the comfy chair from Mum's bed.

'Are you alright?' she asked. 'I know that's a silly question, sorry.'

'Hm?' I looked up at her.

'It wasn't your fault,' she said. She put a hand on my arm. 'These things do happen, you know – awful things. It's hard to come to terms with sometimes.'

'I guess so.'

She was so kind; I felt tears starting. I ran a hand through my hair. My scalp felt itchy, my hair lank. 'Thank you,' I said.

After that the nurse left, and it was just me and Mum.

I slept for a few minutes at a time, upright in the chair. I must have slept properly at one point because when I woke up someone had put a blanket round me. I closed my eyes again and when I opened them it was almost daylight outside.

135

The blinds were drawn but there was light coming through them.

Mum hadn't moved. I stretched and moved the blanket to one side, then eased myself up out of the chair. I felt dizzy for a moment, then when it passed I hobbled stiffly over to the window and pulled the hanging blind to one side to look out, over the car park at the back. There were spaces. It was a grey day, dark clouds overhead. The trees at the far end of the car park were moving, so it must have been windy.

I went back to the chair.

At seven o'clock I went downstairs and out through Reception into the fresh air. There was still a crowd around the smoking area. I wondered if it was the same people. My phone had just enough battery left for me to leave a message for Bill and another one for Kate. Then I went back upstairs to Mum's room. Nothing had changed.

At about nine o'clock I went for a walk through the hospital. It was bustling now, people walking up and down corridors with a purpose. Trolleys, people pulling relatives backwards in those rear-wheel-drive wheelchairs, kids in pushchairs. I went to the café near the front entrance but the smell of food made me feel queasy, so I went into the shop and bought a bottle of water and a bag of boiled sweets. That would do.

I walked all the way down one corridor, past the clinics, past X-Ray, down to Oncology and the double doors at the end. Then I turned around and walked all the way back. After that I gave up and went back upstairs to the Stroke Unit.

At half-past ten a woman from Palliative Care finally came to see me. She was a nurse but dressed in smart trousers and a green jumper, a chunky necklace. By that time I think the news had sunk in that Mum was going to die. The sound of her breathing had changed too. The snoring got louder and then gradually it seemed to quieten for a while, before changing to a regular, short gasp.

'The morphine drip will make her more comfortable,' the nurse said. 'She's just in a very deep sleep right now.'

'How long will she be like this?' I asked.

'It's difficult to say,' she said. 'It might be a day or two, maybe less. But not long. Is there anyone you need to call?'

I'd forgotten about my cousin, but what would be the point of telling her now? I hadn't spoken to her in years.

'No,' I said.

Eventually she went. Another hour and a half went past. It was technically lunchtime, so I opened the bag of sweets and had one. I was contemplating a fourth sweet when there was a brief, sharp knock at the door and two nurses came in, wearing aprons and gloves.

'We're just going to change your mum,' one of them said, 'make her comfortable.'

'Oh, shall I go?'

'Might be best. We won't be long.'

I went into the waiting room where I'd been in the middle of the night. The television was on in the corner, some lunchtime chat show I'd never seen. I sat down and watched without paying any attention at all. I was thinking about work, and the cat.

Half an hour later I went back to Mum's room, and the nurses were gone. I went out to the nurses' station again. This time three of them were sitting there with cups of tea.

'I'm sorry to disturb you,' I said.

'That's alright, don't worry,' said the nearest. She was the one who'd come in to sort Mum out.

'I wondered if it's OK if I go home for a while,' I said. 'I need to feed the cat...'

'Of course!' the nurse said. 'And why don't you have a shower, get something to eat, too? I can ring you if anything happens.'

On my way out, I walked past the smokers, my head down, hoping that nobody would notice my distress. I needn't have worried. Even though there were clearly some seriously ill people in the group, the general atmosphere among them seemed to be one of hilarity.

I was concentrating so hard on the pavement that I didn't notice the man ahead of me until I walked into the back of him. He turned and caught me by the elbow as I went over on my ankle and half-fell into the ambulance bay at the front entrance. 'I'm sorry,' I said, 'I was – '

'Annabel?'

I looked up in surprise. For a moment I was lost and looked at him in confusion.

'Sam,' he said. 'We met yesterday?'

Yesterday? It felt like years ago. 'Oh, yes,' I said. 'Of course. I'm sorry. It's been – a long day.'

'Is everything OK?' he asked, nodding towards the hospital's main entrance.

'My mum – she had a fall.'

'I'm sorry to hear that,' he said. 'Is she alright?'

She's dying, I thought. I tasted the words, like bile, couldn't say them. 'She's unconscious,' I said. 'I was just going home.' I started to turn back in the direction of the car park, ignoring the sharp pain in my ankle. It was fine, I told myself; it wasn't a bad twist, I just needed to walk it off. Then I remembered my manners.

'What about you?' I asked. 'What are you doing here?'

'It's been a really, really mad couple of days. I'm just waiting for a taxi but I think it would have been quicker to walk.'

'I'll give you a lift,' I said, before I could help myself. 'Where are you going?'

'Just back into town,' he said. 'Keats Road.'

'I don't know where that is. You'll have to direct me,' I said, walking back towards the car park.

'Thanks,' he said. 'I'm really glad you ran into me now.'

I was trying not to hobble.

'Are you OK? You're limping.'

'I'm fine,' I said, gritting my teeth. 'Really. I just turned my ankle a bit.'

'Here,' he said, offering me his arm.

'Really, I'm fine.'

He gave me a 'suit yourself' shrug and shoved his hands back into his jacket pockets. I could see the car park ahead, full of cars driving around slowly waiting for someone to come out of a space so they could nip into it before someone else did.

I found my keys and opened the door, easing myself into the driver's seat. It was chilly inside. I reached across and unlocked the other side. Other than my mother, nobody had sat in the passenger seat until now.

I started the engine and put the heaters on full blast to try and get the windscreen cleared enough for me to drive off.

'So,' he said, 'did Andrew Frost tell you what happened to me yesterday?'

'No,' I said, 'what happened?'

'I had a phone call at work yesterday, just when I was about to go home. It was a woman's voice, but she sounded odd – distant – I don't know. Anyway, she told me there was another body, and then she gave me the address.'

'What did you do?'

'I checked it out.'

'And?'

'Then I called your lot.'

'You found someone?'

'Yes. Well – I got to the house, had a look through the window, and then rang the police. I've just spent the last three hours at the hospital trying to get information out of the mortuary team, but the person I usually speak to happens to be on holiday. So they're understaffed in there and none of them is that keen to talk to a reporter, of course... so I'm none the wiser.'

'What did you see? When you looked through the window?'

'Not much. I could see what looked like a leg, sticking out from behind a chair. Actually I only realised it was a leg because it had a slipper on it. It was a funny colour. The leg was, I mean. The slipper was... dark red... with a kind of white snowflake pattern...'

'Well,' I said, 'you'd make an excellent witness, anyway. I'm sure they'll be asking you what the slipper looked like.'

Sam laughed, briefly. 'I was trying not to look at the leg.'

The thought of it must have made the corners of my mouth turn up, just a little, because Sam said, 'You should smile more often.'

My face dropped, then. I shouldn't be smiling at all. What was I thinking? And what did he mean, exactly? It felt as if I was being flirted with, and the not knowing – I could never tell these things – made me uncomfortable.

He must have seen my reaction, and he fell silent. The windscreen was clearer now, so I turned on the lights and reversed out of the parking space.

'Thank you for the lift,' he said at last. 'My car's in for its MOT. I was going to get a courtesy car but that didn't happen, and since I was supposed to be in the office all day I didn't think it would matter. I got a taxi down here.'

I wasn't really listening to him. We were at the traffic lights, waiting to turn on to the main road back to town.

'What's the matter?'

'Hm? Nothing.'

'You seem distracted.'

'I'm just tired. I've been at the hospital all night.'

'It sounds serious.'

'Yes, I think it is. I'm just going home to feed the cat and get a change of clothes, then I'll be coming back.'

'I'm sorry to hear that, Annabel. You know, you really don't need to bother with the lift, I can always wait for the taxi...'

'No, it's fine. Don't worry. It's nice to have someone to talk to.'

'Having contacts makes such a difference,' he said. 'I've got some really good mates now through this job, you know – it's not all about getting the story, it's about building relationships with people so they trust you. People are suspicious when they find out you're a journo; if you're nice to them they think you're only doing it because you want to print intimate details of their lives. I don't know what sort of newspaper they think the *Chronicle* is, for heaven's sake...'

The town centre was busy, the lunchtime rush. A grey autumn day. The lights on the one-way system seemed to be taking forever to change.

'... but I don't work like that, I mean, it's nice if people do tell me things, but they don't get that the information I need is usually something really specific. Even if they give me a quote, the chances are I'm only ever going to use a few words of it. It's just a job, after all, like any other job...'

The traffic moved again and I drove through the town centre and out the other side, heading for the estate where all the roads were named after poets, my mind on other things.

'It all gets easier when you've got proper contacts, though – people who know you and trust that you're not going to make them look like an idiot in print. I just like talking to people, making new friends... you probably noticed...'

We drove along the main road, the side streets one after the other named after people I'd learned about at school about a hundred years ago. Longfellow Drive. Wordsworth Avenue. Keats Road...

'It's this next one,' he said.

I turned left. We drove along a wide road: semi-detached houses, big bay windows, neat front gardens edged with low brick walls. It was starting to rain.

'Just after this blue car,' he said. 'This one.'

I pulled in. It was a normal-looking house, bigger than mine, with a porch. For a moment I thought it was quite big and maybe journalists earned more than I thought they did, and then I realised he probably still lived with his parents, like lots of young people these days who couldn't get a foot on the housing ladder.

'Look,' he said, 'you want to come in for a coffee? You look as if you could do with one. I could make you some lunch?'

'Thanks, but I really need to go home.'

He made no signs of undoing his seatbelt or leaving my car. For a moment I had a sudden spark of fear, and wondered if he'd invited me in for something more than coffee. I was so bad at reading situations like this: my default position was always that nobody found me sexually attractive and therefore anyone who showed an interest in me was probably dangerous.

He half-turned in his seat towards me. I shrank back a little towards the door.

'Look,' he said, 'can I give you a call later? Just to see how you're doing?'

'I don't know,' I said. 'My battery's nearly out.'

'Oh, right,' he said, looking at me as if he wanted to ask if I'd ever heard of magic things called chargers. At last he unclipped his seatbelt and opened the door. 'See you soon, then,' he said, leaning in. 'And thanks for the lift.'

'Bye.'

As soon as he'd slammed the door shut I pulled away from the kerb.

There was nowhere to park, of course, anywhere near the house. I walked back from Howard Street, head down, thinking about my mum. It was all I could think about now. Whatever he'd said – Sam – it had failed to register.

I could see the cat standing at the corner, her tail flashing from side to side, in greeting or petulance, it was hard to tell. When I got closer she stood and waited for me as though she'd reached the edge of her known universe and to cross the road was beyond her, sliding her body affectionately against the greasy metal pole of the street-light, territory marked by a hundred dogs before her.

'Hello, puss-puss,' I said quietly, and she meowed in response, rubbing against my ankle as soon as she could and then running in front of me, rolling on the ground and running again, showing me the way home. As we got through the door she scampered joyously towards the kitchen.

But it turned out she'd got a takeaway. A dead mouse, neatly dissected with the most succulent innards, tail and feet left for me to enjoy.

I woke up completely disorientated. I was on my bed, fully dressed, and the cat was asleep in the crook of my knees. It was ten past three and the daylight was fading already. I sat up quickly, and checked my mobile phone, which I'd left charging by my bed. There were no missed calls.

I rang the hospital from my mobile, and when I finally got through to someone on the Stroke Unit they couldn't tell me very much beyond that my mother was 'comfortable'; there was 'no change'. I said I would come in as soon as I could, and the nurse – or whoever she was – told me to take my time.

I asked again if they would call me if anything happened. Even though she claimed to have my mobile phone number on file, I gave it to her again and she repeated it back slowly enough to be writing it down.

After that I sat still for a moment, wondering what was coming next. The central heating had gone off and the air felt chilly, a little damp. It was as though the house didn't want me to be here either, was pushing me towards the door, a phantom hand on my back trying to restore order to an environment where there was none.

Downstairs, the cat was in the hall, meowing at the kitchen door and pulling at the carpet with her claws. I creaked my way down the stairs, yawning, and when I opened the door the cat shot in ahead of me, mewling at me over her shoulder as though she hadn't eaten in weeks. For a treat I squeezed a sachet of expensive wet cat food into her clean bowl even though it wasn't technically anywhere near her usual feeding time, and boiled the kettle while she went at it delicately, licking at the gravy and then picking the morsels off one by one.

While I was waiting for the kettle I called work, using Kate's direct dial number to bypass the switchboard.

'Intel, Kate speaking.'

There was an official Media Services-sanctioned greeting to use when answering the phone, but neither of us could ever remember it when put under the pressure of a ringing phone. More often than not I was so distracted when I picked up a call that I would just say 'Hello?' and hope it wasn't someone too official on the other end of the phone.

'It's me,' I said. 'Annabel.' In case she'd forgotten who I was.

'Are you OK? How's your mum?'

'She's still unconscious.'

'Do you need me to talk to Bill?'

'No, I need to get on with stuff. They said they'd ring me if – you know, if there was any change.'

'Frosty was looking for you earlier.'

'Oh?'

'Wouldn't tell me what it was about. Said could you go and see him as soon as you get in. Want me to tell him you won't be in for a while?'

'No, I should be in... um... soon. I'll let you know.' I didn't want her to think I was slacking. I didn't want to give her any cause to complain about my work ethic, or for that matter to start taking over any of my responsibilities.

'Something's definitely going on with your rotting corpses, you know. There's been people coming in and out all day looking for you.'

'Really?'

'They don't tell me anything.'

I had a sudden memory of the reporter – Sam – telling me about a phone call he'd received, and I was about to blurt it out to Kate when I realised I wasn't supposed to have been talking to a reporter, never mind giving him a lift home. What was it he'd said? Some woman had phoned him... 'Have they found another body?'

'Well, there's one on the Chief's Summary this morning. Shall I get Frosty to ring you?'

I gave in. 'Sure. I've got the phone charged up.'

'I'll let him know.'

'Thanks, Kate. Bye for now.'

I sat staring at the cold living room for a moment after ringing off, my eyes failing to focus on anything. My mum's going to die, I thought. She won't be here for much longer. Surely there were things I was supposed to say to her, things I should be doing?

Frosty didn't call, and after half an hour of fidgeting I couldn't stand the wait. I drove in to work and because it was late afternoon I risked parking on the station. There were plenty of spaces, thankfully. I left my permit on the dashboard together with a laminated card I'd made up with my force number and mobile phone number on it, just in case someone wanted me to move.

When I got to the office, Kate was still hard at work, hammering away on her keyboard. 'Did Frosty get hold of you, then?' she asked, not looking up.

'No. Why are you still here?'

'Why d'you think?' she said, an edge to her voice. 'Tactical won't write itself, you know.'

'Sorry,' I said. *My mum is dying*, I nearly said. The only reason I didn't say it was because I couldn't have dealt with her embarrassment, and the things I knew Kate wouldn't say that I so badly needed to hear. 'Did I miss much?'

'You missed Trigger making the tea,' she said. This was a standing joke. Trigger only ever made the tea when one or other of us was out of the office. In other words, he didn't.

'How's your mum?' Trigger said, ignoring Kate's barbed comment.

'She's the same,' I said. 'Thanks for asking. I'll go back to the hospital after this; I just thought I'd come in and see Frosty.'

Kate didn't speak. I thought about logging on to the workstation but I didn't have the energy to deal with it. I went to the DI's office, but the door was open and he wasn't there.

I went next door to the main Intel office. Ellen Traynor was the only one in.

'Do you know where the DI is?' I asked.

'Probably in the MIR,' she said. 'He's been in and out of there all day.'

The Major Incident Room? What was going on? I took the lift up to the next floor even though it was only one flight. I was still tired despite the extra sleep, my limbs aching. I was going to knock on the door of the MIR but it was open, a man in a suit propping it with his foot while he shouted across to someone at one of the desks and spoke into the phone he was holding up to his ear.

I squeezed past him, having already caught sight of Frosty, perched on a chair pulled up to a desk just to the left of the door. He looked ridiculously relieved to see me.

'What's going on, sir?'

He didn't even notice the 'sir' this time, just beckoned me over. 'I'm glad you're here, Annabel. Come and have a look at this.'

I stood behind him and peered over his shoulder at the computer screen. 'What is it?'

'It's the statement made by our mutual friend. The reporter.'

'A statement? What's he made a statement for?'

He looked at me in surprise, then obviously realised that he was going to have to go back a few metaphorical pages and help me catch up.

'Yesterday, in the early evening, Sam Everett had a phone call from a female who claimed there was another body we hadn't found yet. She provided an address. He wrote it down. He went off to check it out – as journos do, of course, although it would have been nicer if he'd thought to notify us first – and at the address he realised that there was a body in there because he could see part of it through a downstairs window. Then he called us out.'

'Was it the next-door neighbour who rang him, then?'

'No – that's the interesting bit. We traced the call back to an address in Briarstone, right over the other side from Carnhurst where the body was. No reply. Broke in. Woman called Eileen Forbes lives there.'

'And?'

'Dead. Less than twenty-four hours.'

'Murdered?'

He shrugged. 'Got to wait for the PM, but, on the face of it, it looks bizarrely like all the others. No food in the house, no sign of any activity, just the woman on her own. Post neatly piled up on the dining room table, unopened. We got some phone data back already – she only made that one call to the newspaper. It's the only outgoing call for weeks. Incoming calls all unanswered. Like she was deliberately not contacting anyone. And at the moment we can't work out any connection between her and the body we found in Carnhurst.'

'So the woman who called – she starved to death?'

'Looks like it.'

'And the body – the one in Carnhurst?'

'Same.'

'So how did this Eileen know the body was there?'

His face lit up. 'Exactly,' he said.

I looked around the room, at the people buzzing about setting up desks, on the phone. There were six desks crammed in here already, a small office in the corner, enclosed by a partition with a glass panel at the top.

'So,' I said, wondering if I was just tired or if I was being incredibly stupid, 'all this…?'

'They've set up an incident room. They're going to treat it – for a while, anyway – as a proper murder enquiry.'

'Really?' I said, overwhelmed. 'You mean it?'

'They want you to be the analyst.'

'Me?'

'Who else, Annabel? You know more about this than anyone.'

'I've never worked in an MIR before.'

'Well, now's your chance.'

I shrank back in my chair, the thought of all this activity being my responsibility suddenly overwhelming.

'Hey,' Frosty said. 'It's OK. You'll be fine.'

'It's not that. I've got a lot on my plate,' I said, my voice unexpectedly quavering. 'My mum – my mother's been taken in to hospital.'

'Kate told me. I'm sorry, really. Should you even be here?'

'There's not much I can do really. She's unconscious. They said they'd ring if anything happens.'

'Andy?'

A man had entered the room, someone I knew vaguely but couldn't quite place. Smartly dressed, dark hair.

'Sir?'

'Ah, you must be Annabel. Pleased to meet you.'

'Annabel, this is DCI Paul Moscrop, Major Crime.'

He held out his hand and gripped mine firmly as I shook it.

'Hello,' I said.

'You're the one who's been monitoring all the incidents, so I've been told?'

'That's right.' *And you're the one who deleted my email*, I thought.

'I'd like to see everything you've got – it would really help bring us up to speed. Can I meet up with you in twenty minutes or so?'

'I guess so, yes.'

'That's wonderful, thank you. Top job. Andy, can I see you for a sec?'

The DCI ushered Frosty into the office in the corner and shut the door. I took myself off downstairs. Trigger had gone to a meeting and taken Kate with him. The office was silent apart from the whirr of the workstations. I closed the door behind me.

I logged on to the system and went through my documents and files until I got to the one marked, prosaically, 'Op Lonely'.

All of the stuff the police worked on had an op name, and no doubt this one would, too, now; but in the meantime I'd given it a name of my own.

Inside the folder was the document I'd prepared for the meeting: the slides, and the spreadsheets of data I'd kept on all the bodies found so far, which showed names, addresses, further information, which might contain anything linking them to each other, next of kin, approximate date of death, date of discovery, possible causes of death. And now it looked as though I had another two to add to the list.

I printed all the documents off and a basic version of the spreadsheet, gathered everything together and was just about to head out of the door again when the phone rang.

I looked at it, as though trying to work out from sight whether it was likely to be important or not.

Then I almost wished I hadn't answered it, because it turned out to be him. The journalist.

'Is that Annabel? It's Sam Everett.'

'Hello.'

'How's your mum doing?'

'Alright, thanks,' I said. 'The same.'

'I didn't think you'd be at work, to be honest.'

'Well, I've only popped in. I'm going back to the hospital in a minute.'

He hesitated for a moment, as though he'd been expecting me to say more. But what else was there to say? I wasn't about to go into detail discussing my mother's medical condition with a relative stranger.

'I wondered if you had any more news – about the investigation?'

'What investigation?'

He sighed, and at last resorted to sarcasm. 'You know, the one with all the bodies? The one where I got a weird phone call from a woman who knew where the next one was waiting for your lot?'

'There's no need for that,' I said, shuddering.

'Sorry. Look, I did my bit last night – I rang the police as soon as I knew I wouldn't be wasting anyone's time. Any chance you can give me a bit of news?'

'Like what? I don't know what it is you need,' I said.

'What about the woman who called me? Have you traced her?'

'Yes,' I said.

'And?'

'And what? She's dead.'

'Dead?'

'Apparently she'd been dead less than twenty-four hours when they found her today. Same as the others, just not decomposed.'

Silence from the other end of the phone. I shouldn't have said that, I thought; I was going to get into trouble now – and the investigation was barely a few hours old.

'Can you tell me who she is?' he asked.

'I don't know that yet,' I said. 'I don't know anything, really – I've only been in the office for about half an hour. And I'm really not supposed to talk to you about this. I know people who've been sacked for giving away details of an investigation.'

'Annabel, I'm not trying to put you in an awkward position. I'm sure I can find out her name from one of my other contacts. It's just that you're the first person who really gets what I'm trying to do with this story. I don't want you to give anything away, I just think we could help each other out. There's nobody else I can discuss this with who really cares about it. Could I meet up with you later, perhaps?'

'I need to go back to the hospital,' I said.

'Yes, of course,' he said. 'I'm sorry.'

I realised I was being inexcusably mean towards him for no good reason other than that I felt he was putting undue pressure on me to give him information.

'It's OK,' I said. 'Look, if I find anything out that I think might be useful, I'll give you a call. Alright?'

'Oh, yes!' he said, his enthusiasm reappearing. 'That would be great. Thank you, Annabel. I really appreciate it.'

When I'd put the phone down a moment later I gathered up all the paperwork again and headed upstairs to the MIR.

The hospital rang me on my mobile at a quarter to seven. I'd been so busy, my head a tangle of thoughts and proposals and considerations and recommendations, ideas to try and unravel the tangle of people and their lives, that when the phone rang and the woman on the end said the word 'hospital' I realised I hadn't thought of it since the call with Sam Everett earlier.

'Hello,' I said, expecting them to be giving me a list of things mother needed – a nightie? Pants, socks?

'Is that Annabel Hayer?'

'Yes, it is.'

'Miss Hayer, I'm so sorry to be contacting you with some bad news. Your mother passed away about ten minutes ago. I'm so very sorry.'

'Oh, God.' I sat still on the chair, mouth open and gaping with shock. I hadn't been there. I should have been there. 'Thank you,' I said, at last, as though she'd phoned up to offer me a voucher for some double glazing. 'Do I need to do anything?'

'You should come in, when you can,' the woman said. Was she a nurse? Had she told me? I couldn't remember how the conversation had started. Had she rung me, or had I called her? 'You might want to bring someone with you, so you're not on your own.'

That almost made me laugh. Who could I bring? There was nobody at all.

'I'll come in a while,' I said. 'Thank you again.'

'That's alright,' she said. 'We'll see you later. Take care.'

I replaced the phone and looked around the office. I was sitting in the MIR at one of the spare desks, and all around me conversations were going on, people were on the phone. Some man standing in the doorway was laughing about something with another person standing on the other side, out of my line of sight. None of them had the faintest idea what had happened. None of them knew.

I stood up and sat down again as my legs felt as though they might not hold me up.

'Are you OK?' said the DC who was sitting at the desk next to mine. Was his name Gary, or had I just made that up?

'My mum died,' I said.

I think he thought I was joking, at first, or maybe he thought he'd misheard, because he smiled at me. Then he must have seen from my face that I wasn't joking at all, and he said, quietly, 'Oh, God, I'm so sorry. Was that your dad on the phone?'

'No, the hospital.'

I tried to stand up and this time my legs felt better, so I mumbled something about getting my coat and said a curt, 'Excuse me,' to the two men standing in the doorway sharing jokes with each other. That was just not appropriate on a murder enquiry, and anyone would have been irritated even without the added distress of having just heard about the death of your parent – the end of your family.

The hospital had a bag with all my mum's things in it, which didn't amount to much because I hadn't had a chance to take anything in for her.

One of the uniformed women on the ward – possibly a nurse, maybe some kind of healthcare assistant or whatever they are – took me down to the Chapel of Rest. Everyone I saw spoke to me in hushed, gentle tones. I suppose that was their training, their way of avoiding me spiralling into hysteria. But, despite the tumultuous rush of events that had led up to this point, I did not feel hysterical. I felt calm, almost detached from it all. I had a job to do now, a list of things I needed to work my way through until I could get on with my life.

Number one, go and see Mum.

Collect form from someone. They'd made an appointment.

Take form to registrar to get death certificate.

Go to see Mum's solicitor and get temporary power of attorney over her effects.

Check her house is OK.

Contact funeral director.

Arrange funeral.

Pack up Mum's things.

Put the house on the market.

There were hundreds of other steps that would fall in between these ones, but focusing on the milestones ahead while I was sitting in the chair beside my mother's body in the Chapel of Rest was really the only way I could cope.

I wondered if I should talk to her. What could I even say?

I was so tired it was hard to think straight. My mind was wandering, searching around for her, for a sense of her, the way I felt for the angels when I needed them. I might ask and get an answer, feel a supportive hand on my shoulder, feel a breath or hear a whispered word of love. I closed my eyes and tried to feel her presence, even though she was next to me.

Mum, I thought, *help me. I don't know what to do. I don't know what I'm supposed to do.*

I could feel nothing, nothing at all. It felt as if she had gone.

I opened my eyes again. There was music playing in the background, something classical without being spiritual. It was probably Classic FM's Top 20 Chapel of Rest Hits, and the thought raised a smile that threatened to turn into a most inappropriate giggle. And something else struck me then. I'd nearly made it to the end of my thirties without having ever seen a dead body, and now in the space of a few days I'd seen two.

I stood up. I looked at her one more time, thinking I should touch her, I should kiss her goodbye, I should *do something…* but I could not. Instead I left her lying there with the white sheet up to her chin, turned my back on her and left the room, shutting the door firmly behind me.

I collected the form, which needed to be taken to the registrar as soon as possible. 'I could go now,' I said to the woman who'd handed it to me.

'It will be closed now,' the nurse said gently. 'I think you might need to leave it until tomorrow.'

My first thought was that I had work tomorrow, but they were probably expecting me to take some time off. I would ring Bill, find out what they wanted me to do. After all, it wasn't as if I didn't have stuff to do at work. They were finally starting the investigation I'd been pushing for – how much time was I was supposed to take off?

A few minutes later I was heading back down the corridor to the main entrance, thinking of my list of what I had to do and mentally ticking some things, rearranging others and adding more tasks to it.

'Annabel!'

I looked across the crowded reception area and to my dismay it was him again. Sam Everett. I continued walking towards the door, hoping he was here for some other reason and not because he was stalking me.

'Hey! Annabel!'

He touched my sleeve and then I supposed I could no longer ignore him.

'Sam. Hello again.'

He looked at me closely. 'Are you alright?'

I realised I must be behaving oddly. 'My mother died,' I said. 'I just came to collect her things.'

'I'm so sorry,' he said. He looked as if he meant it, and as if he had been expecting something like that. 'Come and have a drink with me.'

'No, thank you, I have lots of things I need to do.'

'Just a quick coffee. Over there,' he said, indicating the WRVS cafe which was still full of people. 'Come on.'

It was easier to give in. I followed him, still clutching the carrier bag they'd given me with my mum's possessions inside, and stood dumbly behind him while he moved a tray in a painfully slow progress towards the automatic drinks dispenser and thereafter the till.

'Coffee?' he asked, when he finally got to the till. 'Cappuccino OK?' All the other buttons on the machine were taped up with 'NOT WORKING' written on the tape in a wavering handwriting.

'Sure.'

While he paid I went and sat down, and a few moments later a woman came and cleared up the two trays overladen with dirty crockery and half-eaten bits of food that were taking up most of the space on the table. 'It's a self-clear area,' she said to me, pointing at the sign. 'You'd think people could read in this day and age, wouldn't you?'

I looked up at her and she didn't speak to me again. Did I have some mark on my face, I wondered? Some sign that said 'Recently Bereaved, Handle with Care'? I even smiled at her, but still she left me to it, taking the dirty trays with her.

Sam sat down in front of me and slid a mug of beige-coloured foam across the table in my direction, followed by a handful of sugar sachets and a KitKat.

'I don't really take sugar,' I said.

'Have you eaten anything? When did you last have something to drink? I think you could do with some sugar.'

'Are you my personal dietician now or something?'

'Yes,' he said. 'Put sugar in it and I might leave you in peace for a while.'

He made me smile, but I did as I was told. When I started eating the chocolate I realised I was hungry. My stomach growled and churned at the food. I sipped at the drink, expecting it to be boiling hot, but it was barely lukewarm.

'I think their machine's had it,' I said. The coffee tasted of UHT milk.

'Yeah.'

'Aren't you going to ask me about the case?'

'Interesting as that conversation might be, that's not what I'm here for.'

'Oh? What are you here for?'

He leaned forwards slightly. 'I rang your office again. Then I rang DI Frost. He told me you'd suffered an unexpected bereavement and that you wouldn't be in for a while.'

'So you came here…?'

'To find you.'

'Why?'

'To see if you were alright. Do you have anyone? Brothers, sisters? Other family?'

'Not that it's any of your business, but no. Anyway, as I said to you before, I'm fine. You don't need to worry about me. I can take care of things, I always have. I just have to work my way through a list…'

I gulped at the coffee, thinking that the sooner I drank it, the sooner I could get out of here and get home. Something was building up inside me, a feeling of unease, as if I was going to be sick or was coming down with something. I didn't want to be here any more. I wanted to be outside, in the fresh air, and then I wanted to go home and lock the door and not open it again.

'Look,' he said, 'I lost my mum last year. I know a bit about what it's like. I just thought I might be able to give you a bit of support.'

'Why?'

'What?'

'Why did she die? Was she ill?'

'She had cancer.'

I nodded, although I had no frame of reference for this. My mother had suffered a stroke. Yes, she was housebound. Yes, she was elderly and frail. But aside from that, and the chest infection, she hadn't been seriously ill at all. Only yesterday she'd been muttering some complaint about the prime minister while I cooked her dinner and put the shopping away.

I tried to remember the last thing she'd said to me. Had she even said goodbye? When was the last time I'd said something nice to her? Asked her how she felt, if she was happy? When was the last time I'd told her I loved her?

'I feel as if I should be crying, but I don't feel like I can,' I said.

'You don't have to do anything,' he said. 'And besides, it will take a long time for you to process all this.'

'What does that mean?' I snapped. 'I'm not a manufacturing plant, I'm a human being. I'm not going to "process" anything at all. I'm not going to come to terms with it, get over it or deal with it. I'm just going to carry on with my life because that's all I am able to do, the same as I've always done.'

He made a noise like a sigh and was about to say something, but stopped himself and drank the rest of his coffee instead.

'Sorry,' I said, a few minutes later.

He shrugged. 'No probs. Just trying to help.'

'So I guess your office went a bit mad after that phone call yesterday, right?'

'You could say that.'

'Is this the end of the Love Your Neighbour campaign?'

He laughed. 'I don't think that was ever going to go anywhere. It was turning into more of a Spy On Your Neighbour or Moan About Your Neighbour campaign anyway.'

'Well, that's more the British way of doing things, I suppose.'

There was a short silence.

'Are they going to check their computers?'

I looked at him. He was crossing a line.

'Oh, go on,' he said. 'It's a very general question. I thought maybe they'd all been accessing suicide chatrooms or something. Might be a link between them?'

'I'd be surprised if they all had computers. Some of them were quite elderly, don't forget.'

'You're including the elderly ones?'

'Well, *I* am. It's up to the Senior Investigating Officer if he takes any notice of what I have to say.'

He looked into his empty coffee mug. Mine was still half-full, but I had no desire to finish it. It was like drinking dirty water.

'I don't think they killed themselves,' I said. 'At least, not in the way we usually think of suicides. It wasn't a deliberate act. It was more of a… as if they just gave up.'

'Is that even possible?'

'It must be.'

'But surely your body would override that decision, wouldn't it? Surely hunger – thirst – aren't they primal forces? You would have to have a completely iron will to just sit down and starve yourself to death.'

'I don't know,' I said. 'Because of the phone call we can be reasonably sure now that someone or something is behind all this – I'm thinking that all these people had something done to them to force them to do this, something that has overridden their human instincts in some way.'

He sat forward in his chair. 'Now that,' he said, 'is very interesting.'

'Is it?'

'What could do that? What could override the basic human instinct?'

'I have no idea.'

'Scary, though, isn't it?' he said.

I nodded, not entirely sure what he meant.

'Scary that someone out there could do this,' he went on. 'I mean, we could all be victims, couldn't we?'

I shook my head. 'I don't think so.'

'Why not?'

'Well, although there wasn't anything obvious linking them, that doesn't mean that they don't have things in common. They all lived on their own, for a start. None of them had jobs, for one reason or another.'

'You're still talking about a very considerable slice of the population,' said Sam.

'You want to go out and warn everyone who lives on their own and doesn't have a job?'

'Why not?'

'Because you'd send them all into a panic.'

We were both picturing a hysterical mass of single people, and it raised a smile.

'The demographics are interesting,' he said, changing the subject neatly back to the bodies.

'Because they're so varied?'

'Exactly. I mean, if someone's getting some sort of kick out of this? I don't know, it's just so weird. What does he have to gain from it? Did they leave wills, or anything like that?'

'I don't have access to that sort of data,' I said. 'Maybe the investigation will get to that quite quickly.'

'I can't imagine it's something that simple.'

'No. I think – ' I stopped myself.

'What?'

I looked away for a minute, then down at the table. 'I think I should go. I have so much that I need to do.'

'That wasn't what you were going to say,' he said.

My cheeks were flushing and to cover up my discomfort I stood up. 'Thanks for the coffee.'

'It was awful, wasn't it? I'll buy you a decent cup next time.'

I wasn't going to agree to another meeting, no matter what excuse he came up with.

'I'll walk back to the car park with you,' he said, not giving me any sort of opportunity to refuse.

I walked as quickly as I could, hoping to leave him behind. But my fast walk was a similar pace to a normal person's stroll and he kept up with me easily. 'My car's over here,' I said at last, breathless, 'See you another time.'

'Annabel,' he said, 'you know I'd like to help if I can. I remember what it was like when I lost my mum. There's so much to do, you miss things. Let me know if I can help – alright?'

'You're very kind.'

'Have you still got my number?'

'Yes,' I said, but I'd hesitated for a fraction of a second before saying it and he'd whipped a business card out of his pocket and handed it over to me. 'I'll see you soon, then,' he said. 'Ring me. Yes?'

He was walking backwards through the car park, which was a stupid idea – someone hooted at him and he jumped out of the way of a 4x4 on the desperate hunt for a parking space.

Despite the misery of the last few hours, seeing him had done the unthinkable – it had cheered me up. But, in those moments after he left, I felt more alone than I had ever done before. There were people all around me, cars driving past, but I was completely and utterly alone. I felt fear, and then a wave of sorrow followed it. *I have no one,* I thought. *No purpose, nobody to take care of or strive to protect. I have nothing left.*

Colin

After the orgasm last night, I didn't sleep well.

Waking in the early hours in a state of agitation, I ran a warm bath and found myself wondering whether Mr Thomas Stearns Eliot caused, or contributed to, my own fascination with the subject of death and transformation, or whether my interest goes back to my father's death. Or maybe further back still.

Sitting back in the bath, eyes closed, attempting to relax, I recited the first two verses of 'Whispers of Immortality', lingering over the words, tasting them. I am still thinking of them now, hours later.

Sex and death, I think, so inextricably bound together. Dead limbs, lusts and luxuries. Sex, desire, decomposition. And such erotic words, so smooth on the tongue: 'tightening its lusts'... 'clings'... 'breastless'... 'lipless'... So perfect, so obvious, so beautiful. I think of Janice, who also inspired me to travel down this path... think of her buried (even though she was cremated, I imagine her interred), lovelier in her time of decay than she ever was breathing.

Annabel

On the way home I went to Mum's house. Force of habit almost diverted me to the supermarket on the way but there was no need for any of that any more, was there? I sat in the car outside for a little while. The house already looked empty. I wondered who had turned all the lights off after the ambulance had left with my mother.

Well, this wasn't achieving anything, and I had so much to do. The front garden looked neglected – when did that happen? – the weeds growing through the cracks in the cement path, the grass of the tiny front lawn high enough to be growing in unsightly tufts. I would have to bring the lawnmower over and cut it back before the winter really set in, especially if I was going to have to sell the house.

I mentally added it to the rapidly growing to-do list.

The house was warm, which I hadn't been expecting. But of course, the heating was still set to come on at the usual time. I should turn it off. But then maybe the pipes would freeze if it got unexpectedly cold. That reminded me about the freezer – I should empty it and turn it off, defrost it. And the fridge. I should turn off all the electrical appliances, in fact, because they were all just wasting money now. Maybe I should turn the electricity off at the mains? And the gas – but then the heating wouldn't come on, and maybe the pipes would freeze.

My mind started to spin in exhausted circles, so I forced myself to put those thoughts to one side. I turned the light on, put my bag down in the hallway and hung my coat up on the coat stand as I did every time I came into this house.

She'd moved here fifteen years ago when her sister, my aunt, moved to Scotland. They'd shared a house after I went away to university but, once Aunty Bet went, Mum had wanted to live nearer to me. Back then she was still active, still going out to bingo with her friends, still visiting the supermarket herself three times a week, going on the odd weekend coach trip with the Social Club. I don't think I had a real awareness of her getting older but, looking back, the signs were there. She fell out with someone at the Social Club so she stopped going there. Aunty Bet died five years ago and the death of her only sister started Mum on a downward spiral. She started worrying about money, even though she had a good pension and had never worried about it before. Not long after that she stopped going to bingo too. And then it was just me. I was the only person left for her, apart from the neighbours who popped in to check on her every so often, and even then she used to complain about them to me when I came round.

'They're always bothering me,' she would hiss, as though they might be listening with glasses pressed to their ears on the other side of the wall. 'They just turn up. I mean, it's not exactly convenient.'

'Why?' I said. 'What might you be doing?' I refused to lower my voice in these circumstances. We never heard them talking; why should they be able to hear what we were saying?

As it turned out, Len next door had almost saved her life, and had certainly given me the chance to say a kind of goodbye even if she couldn't hear me. I would have been to see her the next evening, but by then she would have been dead. If she'd been a bit more welcoming towards him, he might even have discovered her a bit sooner than he did, and then maybe she would have survived.

I went into the living room, turning the light on, and almost expecting to see her sitting in her chair. The impact of the empty chair hit me like a physical force and I took a step back from it. Every time I visited her – three or four times a week – she would be sitting there. Occasionally she would get up while I was there to go to the loo or do something in the kitchen, using her Zimmer or her sticks to get about, using my helpful hand to heave her out of the chair, but most of the time she would sit and wait for me to fetch things for her.

And the chair was empty. There was a dip in the seat cushion and the covers were both faded and grubby from years of use. The arms of the chair were grey from the constant touch of her hands. She was not there any more.

I was breathing quite fast and I felt panicky, strange. I wondered what it was that had suddenly set me off like this. The house was so silent, so still. Had I ever been in this room without the television being on? Even the air felt different without her in here.

I took a deep breath and got myself back under control. This was no good. I had things to do.

I turned my back on her chair and went to the kitchen. It was really dark there, the window facing only the empty yard and the unlit windows of the neighbouring house. I turned on the light.

It was suspiciously neat. Mum was not fond of doing the washing-up, and when I came to bring her dinner I would usually start by washing up the dishes from the previous few meals. But the sink was clear, the grey dishcloth draped over the mixer tap, a steady drip-drip splashing into the sink. I opened the fridge. Inside it looked bare – a couple of jars of jam, a bottle of salad cream, a cardboard egg box, the butter dish, an unopened pack of cheese, an unopened bottle of white wine. Had I even bought those things? I couldn't remember. Where were the vegetables I'd put in here... when was it? Sunday? She couldn't have eaten them all before she fell. What about the milk? I'd bought her a new two-pint bottle yesterday.

'Annabel, is that you?'

The sound from behind me made me jump out of my skin. Len was standing close by. I had no idea how he had managed to get in without me hearing him, given the silence of the house.

'Hello, Len,' I said. 'You made me jump.'

'Sorry, my dear. How are you?'

'My mum died this morning,' I said. I would have to start thinking of a better way of sharing the news with people.

'Yes, I know,' he said. 'I'm ever so sorry. You poor girl.'

'How do you know?'

'I rang up the 'ospickle this morning to see how she was.'

I found myself stifling another entirely inappropriate giggle. He had actually said ''ospickle'.

'How are you getting on?' he asked. 'Me and the wife were worried about you when we heard.'

'I'm alright. I just have so many things that I need to do.'

'I know, it's a bind. You know if there's anything we can do to help...'

'Thank you,' I said. I stood awkwardly with one hand on the fridge, wondering what it was he wanted. Wondering why he was still coming in here when it was now clear that my mother wasn't coming back. 'Did you clear out the fridge?'

I think I said it a bit brusquely, because he flushed a little and shifted uncomfortably on the spot. 'Yes, well, we didn't want the food to be going off. I thought it would be a lickle while before you came round – you know, with the grief... and everything.'

'Well,' I said, 'that's very kind of you. But really – I can manage.'

'Difficult times,' he said, appeased. 'Very difficult. Me and the wife, you know, we did our best to keep an eye on her, but she was getting very frail. Very difficult to get about, and then it's just a matter of time really, isn't it? Comes to us all, don't it? In the end?'

'Well...' I said again.

'Of course, it's different if you've got family close by, like your mum had. Our two boys are both grown up and gorn away, long time ago now. When they have families of their own, you know, it's hard because they get so busy and they know we're alright, we've got each other, we can take care of ourselves, so we don't really see them that much. Christmases, yes, and they came for her seventieth birthday last year, but that's about it really. And it does make you wonder, don't it, all this stuff in the paper about people being found dead and nobody taking care of them, it just makes you wonder about what might happen in the future.'

'I know,' I said.

'Anyway, I mustn't stand here gassing all day, she'll wonder what's happened to me. I'll be on my way. Do you want that stuff back?'

This last bit was thrown casually over his shoulder, a parting question so innocuous, but he turned then and fixed me with a beady eye. Oh, so he'd not thrown it out, then? Effectively he'd come in here and stolen all my mum's fresh food out of the fridge. I was surprised he'd left the eggs and butter behind.

'No, of course not,' I said.

'Righto, I'll be off. You know where we are if you need anything – give me a ring if you need us, yes? I'll check on her post and stuff if you like. Righto, then. See you.'

I heard the front door slam. It hadn't slammed when he'd come in. He must have shut the door quietly, crept through the hallway treading carefully on the bare wooden boards. I didn't want him to check her post. I didn't want him to have a key. I would call round and ask for it on the way out.

I looked back at the silent kitchen, everything in its place. Everything waiting to be used again, looking back at me expectantly. I had a sudden thought and opened the cupboard where she kept her dry goods – tea bags, cereals... right at the top was a commemorative tea caddy: the wedding of HRH Prince Charles to Lady Diana Spencer, 1981. In here she kept her housekeeping money, the money she kept by from her pension to pay for groceries and other incidentals. I'd set up direct debits on her bank account to pay all the bills, and I checked them once every few months to make sure everything was covered and being paid. When I got her shopping, I would take the money from the tin and put the receipt behind in its place. I would round it up or down, never bothering with coins because it all evened itself out in the end anyway. When I'd been here last Sunday there had been eighty pounds in here in twenty pound notes. I'd taken out a twenty and replaced it with a ten pound note from my purse, because the shopping had come to a total of twelve pounds ninety eight. When I'd come yesterday, though, I'd been so tired after working late that I'd forgotten to do it; the receipt was still at the bottom of my bag.

In the jar was a grand total of twenty pounds. A single twenty-pound note. Fifty pounds had gone since the last time I looked – a few days ago. For a moment I stood there looking at the single note, wondering if I was mistaken. Wondering what she might have spent it on.

After that I went to the bureau in the dining room, the bottom drawer of which contained all the important stuff: her passport, bank books, birth certificate. I rifled through it briefly but even at a glance I could see that it was all still there. That was a relief; so maybe I had imagined it? Perhaps there had been less in there when I'd seen it, or I was getting confused with another day? Or maybe she'd had the window cleaner round, or put some money in a charity envelope?

Fifty pounds, though?

I looked around the rest of the house, not really sure what I was looking for. Her bedroom had that quiet silence about it that suggested nobody had been in here in some time. The clothes that hung in the wardrobe were old, no longer in regular use: a sparkly cocktail top, heavy with silver beading. A long black skirt. She'd worn this outfit to my twenty-first birthday meal. Why had she even kept it? There was no way she would have worn this again. And other clothes that I remembered her wearing – a blazer that she used to wear to work sometimes, before she retired. Shoes in the bottom of the wardrobe for the woman who never went out of her front door.

The spare room was full of boxes that she'd never bothered to unpack when she moved here all those years ago. 'One day,' she'd say, as though she was waiting for all the social engagements and frivolities to die down before she could properly settle in. It all looked undisturbed.

Well. There was no delaying it – as much as I hated confrontations of any sort, this was one I could not put off any longer.

He looked surprised to see me when he opened the door. 'Everything alright?' He was chewing on something, and I wondered if it was a sandwich made with Mum's bread.

'Hello again. I just remembered, I need to get the key back from you. After all, there's no need for you to trouble with the house now Mum's gone, is there?'

'D'you not want me to check the post? Save you coming up here all the time?'

'It's fine, really. I'm not that far away.'

'What if there's an emergency?'

'If there's an emergency,' I said, firmly, wondering what on earth such an emergency could be now that Mum was dead, 'you can ring me, can't you?'

He looked suddenly crestfallen. 'Oh. I see. Righto, then. Hold on.'

He left the door ajar and went back into the hallway, leaving me on the step. A cooking smell, not a pleasant one, came through to me on a gust of warm air. The hallway was newly decorated, the wallpaper of that curious furry embossed type – what was it called? A weird name. Ana-something…

'Here you go, then,' he said, coming back up the hallway. He was unthreading a Yale door key from a key ring containing several others. I wondered if it was his normal key ring, or whether he just collected the keys to other people's houses.

I held out my hand and he pressed the key into the palm, hard enough for it to hurt.

'There's one other thing, Len,' I said, dreading this bit but knowing I had to ask. 'Do you know if the window cleaner came round this week? Or anyone else Mum might have given money to?'

'No, Ted comes round first week of the month usually. Why?'

Well, he did ask, I thought. 'Mum had some money in a tin, and most of it's gone. It was there when I visited her last. Any ideas?'

I said it casually and, as much as he was trying to pull off the 'kindly old gent next door' thing, he was eyeing me with bright, suspicious eyes.

'We did some shopping for her Monday,' he said. 'We told her we were going into town and she said she wanted some bits and pieces. She gave me cash and I gave her the receipt. Did you not find it?'

'What things?'

'Hmm. Well, let me think. She wanted a steak from the butcher. And batteries for the wireless... oh, and three books of first class stamps. There was some other stuff... I can't remember it all.'

I looked at the key in my hand and wondered if this was an argument I really needed to be having. It was only fifty quid, after all. 'Thanks, Len,' I said. 'I know she really appreciated everything you did for her.'

'S'alright,' he said. 'You know we were always happy to help. Any time, love. You sure you don't want us to keep an eye on things next door?'

'No, thanks,' I said. 'I'm going to get the post redirected anyway.' I wasn't sure if such a thing was possible when a person was deceased, but I didn't want him looking for an excuse to get back inside the house.

'You sure you want to do that? I mean, we can always...'

'No, Len. Honestly, you've done enough. Thanks.'

I turned and started to head down the path, back to the car. It was dark, and cold, and I wanted to get home now, shut the door and be on my own where nobody could see me.

Colin

Work today was distracting, and monumentally dull. I feel as though I am beyond all this now, as though I have a more entrancing destiny before me than dealing with council finances.

Patience is one of my strongest virtues, I've always thought. In the year following my father's death, I found it difficult to engage at school. It all felt so hideously pointless. I got into trouble regularly, although I was never disruptive. If the subject failed to interest me, I sat in the class and stared straight ahead, relentlessly patient and tirelessly disconsolate, regardless of what the rest of the class was tasked with doing.

'Friedland,' the master would say, 'are you not going to make an attempt?'

'No,' I'd say, if I replied at all.

'No, *sir*.'

I would stare back with what they must have thought of as insolence. To me it was indifference.

'That's it, I've had enough. You shall go to the headmaster's office.'

This happened on an almost daily basis. I was caned. These were the days when caning was not only allowed but, in the British public school system, a tradition. I didn't even feel the pain, not in any way that mattered. I didn't feel the humiliation. The punishments had no effect on me at all. The headmaster knew I wasn't stupid. At first, he was even sympathetic – having lost his own father at a young age – but his patience only lasted for a short while.

Stiff upper lip, that was the ticket. Putting the needs of your *compadres* ahead of yourself. Playing the game.

And I wasn't playing.

In the end he almost expected me; if I wasn't in his office before lunch he started to wonder where I was. My mother was called in. It was suggested that I might like to transfer to a different school, that I might be better suited elsewhere. A fresh start. My mother stared vacantly ahead, numbed by whichever benzodiazepine they were trying her on this month, while I stood behind her in the headmaster's office, hands sullenly in my pockets even though I'd been caned for just such insouciance the day before.

'She doesn't care,' I said.

'Friedland,' the headmaster said, 'you are present only at your mother's request. You are expected to hold your silence here.'

'I do care,' she said, though the tone of her voice suggested otherwise. 'I just don't know what to do about it.'

The money to send me to the school had been my father's. She had his pension, and a payout, but she was not used to having to deal with matters such as this. She had never worked, never had to pay a bill, never had to speak to anybody about anything more taxing than what to have for dinner and where to go on holiday.

The headmaster dismissed us both shortly afterwards, recognising another brick wall behind all the others I'd constructed in the past few weeks.

In the end, I made everything much easier for him. Two days after the meeting with Mother, a sixth form boy passed some comment on my father and my behaviour as our paths crossed in the corridor. Later in the evening I found him alone, took him into one of the empty classrooms and punched him until he was unconscious and bleeding.

The effort of finding another school willing to take me was beyond my mother. Additionally, as she told me on more than one occasion, since she had no intention of getting a job, she needed to save what was left of Father's life insurance payout for her living expenses.

And so I was enrolled into the nearest comprehensive for the remainder of my school years.

At lunchtime Vaughn called to invite me to the Red Lion. It was the first time we've been in contact since the dinner party, although I did send him a text thanking him for a super evening. Maybe he interpreted it as sarcastic.

We sat with our pints in front of us. The television bolted precariously over the corner of the bar was showing Sky Sports News, an endless jumble of primary colours and a man in a suit mouthing no doubt vital bits of information about teams I have no interest in.

'How's Audrey?' I asked at last.

'Alright, I think,' he said.

I drank some bitter, grimacing and thinking it would taste a whole lot better with a cheese and pickle baguette to soak it up. I looked hopefully towards the bar, but the barmaid, an appropriately barrel-shaped woman who was wearing red tights and calf-length black boots that looked alarming on one so short, was nowhere to be seen.

'It was a good meal,' I said. 'And nice to see your house.'

People say things like this. Compliment each other, comment on the decor in their respective houses, even when they think it's hideous. As I do.

'Actually,' he said, 'she's not really alright. She's gone a bit funny.'

'What do you mean?' I asked.

'She's a bit – well, distant. After the other night.'

'Oh,' I said, because I couldn't think of any more appropriate response.

'I've telephoned her a couple of times. She answered once, and she was terribly vague. When I went round to her flat she wasn't there.'

'Maybe she was just out,' I said helpfully. 'Or busy doing something else.'

Vaughn snorted. 'I can't imagine what.'

'Do you still think she's having an affair?'

He looked up from his pint, startled. 'What makes you say that?'

'Well, you were asking me about it just the other day. You were talking about taking her to Weston-super-Mare in the caravan. Do you remember?'

'Oh. Yes, I suppose so.'

'Really Vaughn,' I said. 'Your memory is going.'

'I've been a bit distracted,' he said, and to my surprise he put his head in his hands on the table and his shoulders started shaking. I stared at him with curiosity. In the Red Lion, of all places.

'Vaughn,' I said. 'What on earth's the matter?'

He sniffed and retrieved a handkerchief from his trouser pocket, dabbed viciously at his eyes and expectorated loudly into it. I shuddered at this display but it seemed to do the trick and he composed himself once again.

'I'm really very fond of Audrey,' he said at last.

'I know that,' I said, although what goes on between Vaughn's ears is as much a mystery to me as the thoughts of any other person. 'She's a lovely lady.'

'I think we're growing apart. That's all there is to it.'

'Maybe you should take things to the next level,' I said, borrowing unfamiliar vocabulary from one of the appalling television shows I happen to find myself watching on occasion. 'Maybe you should ask her to marry you, or something?'

'Really? You think so?'

'Why not?' I asked.

I've always thought of Vaughn's relationship as, in many ways, idyllic – someone living in another house, who would occasionally turn up for companionship, intelligent conversation and, far more importantly, sex. And who would then clean up after themselves and go back home again. But it doesn't appear to be fulfilling after all, at least not to Vaughn, who no doubt needs more emotional sustenance from a woman than I do. I have no need of it at all.

I was hoping Vaughn wouldn't put forward a series of reasoned counter-proposals because I am very poorly equipped to deal with them, but in the event I need not have concerned myself. He was beaming, the wide Cheshire-cat grin of the suddenly enlightened.

'That's what I'll do,' he said. 'I'll propose. Of course! How could I have been such an idiot?'

'I don't understand,' I said. Idiocy is not something I usually miss, but in Vaughn's case I prefer to think of him as merely confused.

'She's been hinting,' he said eagerly. 'Her sister got married last year and ever since then she's been making jokes about being on the shelf, being too old to worry about it, but it must be what she's wanted all along!'

He drank the last of his pint with unseemly haste, considering I had paid for it, and stood up, wrapping his scarf around his neck.

'Where are you going?'

'To get a ring, dear chap!' Only Vaughn could use the phrase 'dear chap' and not sound like a pompous oaf. 'I've half an hour left before I need to be back at work, I need to go and find a jeweller!'

Gaviston Comprehensive, Grove Road. I went there when I was thirteen, seven months away from my fourteenth birthday. Recovered by then from the initial shock of bereavement, I had settled into a phase that could best be described as sullen. I had no wish to meet anyone, talk to anyone or engage in activity of any kind, educational or social, so that environment, of course, I fitted in very well.

On my third day, two boys from another class cornered me in the cloakrooms.

'You're new,' one of them said. He was a pale kid, with one of those stupid haircuts they had back then, shaved at the sides, mouse-coloured and spiky on top, a ridiculous rat's tail plaited down his back. Next to him his companion was less muscular than corpulent, but still at least a foot taller than I was – it would be another two years until the growth spurt that took me up to six foot and a bit beyond.

'Yes,' I said, already wary of speaking too much and giving away an accent that didn't match theirs.

'Where you come from,' the other one offered. Was it supposed to be a question? It hadn't sounded like one and therefore I didn't feel the need to answer.

I went to leave but they were blocking my way. The smaller of the two said, 'You a bit weird, or summink? Bit funny in the 'ead?' The fat one snorted and moved closer, close enough to grant me the scent of his armpits.

I don't even suppose they were being particularly threatening; I certainly wasn't afraid of them. But they were in my way and I had no desire to hang around in this stinking, graffitied hole any longer.

I think the primary advantage I have over people is surprise. I move quickly, I don't hesitate, and I don't give anything away.

I kicked the fat one in the groin and he doubled over and fell to the floor, shrieking with a noise that sounded far too girlish and shrill for one so large. The smaller one looked at me, his eyes widening. He was about the same size as I was, and my guess was that he'd never been challenged, never had to get physical with anyone without the assistance of his chum.

He took a step backwards and went to let me pass. I thought about it, really I did, but the fat shit was still rolling around on the floor crying, and for the first time in months I felt something stirring inside me, something unfamiliar. It felt good. I was having fun.

And it was all too, too easy. I grabbed him by the shoulder, turned him around and slammed him into the wall. He was saying 'no, I'm sorry, we didn't mean it, you're alright, really, let me go' in a jumble, his voice rising to the same pre-pubescent wail as that of his friend, as though shock and fear had emasculated them both.

It was all just too tempting. Holding him against the wall with the weight of my body and with a fist pushing into the space between his shoulderblades, I wound the stupid rat's tail around my hand twice and with surprisingly little effort – though maybe the intent behind it fuelled my strength – ripped it off. So then there were two of them squirming in pain, and the smaller one took up the shrieking where the other one had now stilled to a shuddering whimper. For a moment I looked at them, thinking what a lot of noise was coming out of them and whether what had happened had entirely justified it, then I looked at the rat's tail in my hand. A small patch of bright white skin had come away with it. The other end still secured neatly with an elastic band.

The smaller one was clutching the back of his head with both his hands as though he was under arrest for something, eyeballing me with an expression I couldn't define, his eyebrows furrowed, tears pouring from his eyes, cheeks bright red. He was glaring at me, and I was looking casually back. Blood was seeping through his interlaced fingers, their knuckles white with effort.

I shook the stupid rat's tail from my hand and it fell to the floor. 'Goodnight, ladies,' I said, leaving them to their sobs.

I was suspended for a week, but not expelled. The two boys were notorious bullies, although of course I'd had no idea about that. When I was sent to see the head teacher (not a master, here, although male – he was a middle-aged homosexual who encouraged liberal attitudes towards teaching and hoped by doing so to have a supportive following amongst the staff) – he all but thanked me. He certainly wasn't angry.

'It's not the way we do things,' he said, 'causing injury to your fellow students; it's not the right thing to do, is it? Not the right choice to make?'

'I suppose not,' I said.

'What were they doing?'

I considered what to reply. In truth, they hadn't been doing very much at all. 'Standing in the way.'

'Did they say anything?'

'Not that I remember.'

'Were you afraid of them, is that what it was?'

'I'm not afraid of anyone.'

'That's good, Colin. That's the right way to be.'

'Aren't you going to cane me?'

'No,' he said. 'I prefer not to. And I think you're sorry for what you did, aren't you?'

I didn't answer that one. He wouldn't have liked the response and I wasn't prepared to lie: I was neither sorry, nor ashamed of myself. In fact I'd rather enjoyed the encounter; it had relieved the boredom of the day.

'Well, in any case, you realise I will have to suspend you.'

'Fair enough,' I said.

'A week?' As though he was asking me rather than telling. If I give you a week, will you promise to behave afterwards?

'Alright,' I said.

'I'll write a letter for your mother. I did speak to her on the phone earlier, I asked her to come in, but... anyway. Go and collect your bag and coat, and then come back to the office to collect the letter.'

I turned to go.

'Colin?'

'Yes?'

'Don't do it again.'

I didn't do it again, at least not on school property, because in a strange sort of way I liked the head teacher. He wasn't as weak as he appeared; he was a fair man who was trying to do the right thing in very difficult circumstances, and I wanted him to like me. Besides, by then my mother, who had been through what she later described to anyone who'd listen as 'a very trying time', was starting to recover. Whilst the head teacher seemed incapable of genuine anger, my mother was not.

My mother had spent a good couple of years in a semi-official state of mourning after my father's death. It was the sort of person she was. Eventually she'd realised that people had stopped paying attention when she had a tantrum and so she'd decided it was time to be brave and move on. She had never been a patient woman, however, and now it was just the two of us she was even less so. Her friends, my father's family, even her sister, had all reached the point of wanting nothing more to do with her, therefore I was the only person who was still available to whom she could direct her frustrations and her ire. She stopped taking the antidepressants and moved on purposefully to medicating herself with alcohol.

We hated each other with a fury that was as powerful as it was unspoken. She was violent until the point when she realised I was big enough to fight back, and then her bitterness was restricted to verbal assaults that were in many ways just as damaging.

'You killed your father,' she said one evening. 'You know that? I always knew it. It was the stress you put him under, always answering us back, never doing as you were told.'

We were both sitting in the living room, having had dinner together in silence. This happened with increasing frequency – civility giving way to hostility with no apparent warning. She'd had wine with dinner, gin before it, sherry before that, but, even so, she was not what anyone would describe as drunk. The television was on in the background, and, because we'd disagreed over what to watch, the tension in the room had risen. She blamed me utterly for my father's death, just as I blamed her. It passed the time.

'You killed him, you little piece of shit. He was so happy with me until you came along.'

I searched for a suitable weapon to use in response, and settled on Kafka.

'"To die would mean nothing else than to surrender a nothing to a nothing."'

'Kafka again?' she said. 'What a load of codswallop.'

'Kafka was a nihilist,' I said. 'And if you take his views on board, whether either of us is to blame for his death is rather beside the point.'

'I wish you'd never been born,' she answered coldly.

'So do I,' I said.

Sometimes these exchanges were even funnier. She was so easy to respond to. The more she hated me, the more amusing she was. And yet we carried on living together in the same house, even after I left school. She cooked dinner, sometimes, when she wasn't too drunk to stay upright. I did most of the washing and cleaning. She did the shopping, so that she could buy alcohol. We had a strange, symbiotic and oppositional relationship that served a purpose for both of us.

I usually find myself thinking of my mother on a Wednesday evening, and occasionally I used to wonder why this was, until I realised that of course, with Wednesday being my laundry and housekeeping evening, doing these menial tasks reminds me of our time in the house together after my father died.

The woman from the nursing home rang again half an hour ago. My mother needs a new dressing gown, apparently, and she has been asking after me. This last I know to be a lie. Why are they so keen for me to visit? I have nothing to say to her, and, if by some miracle she were to be compos mentis at the moment I chose to arrive, the chances of her having something of consequence to say to me are very slim indeed.

One of these days I will shout something down the phone at the Matron, or whatever she is. I will be driven to madness, to fury by her lack of sensitivity. *The woman abused me*, I shall cry. *She ruined my childhood and has therefore made it impossible for me to form a functioning adult relationship with a woman. I don't want to see her. May she rot quietly and stinkingly in her wing-backed armchair...*

See how quickly she rings back after that, shall we?

In the meantime, whilst I am terribly distracted at the thought of the next edition of the newspaper and what delicious details it may contain, I am also very aware of the fact that at the moment I only have two on the go, and it is becoming my custom to have three. Three is manageable, a beautiful, stylish and balanced number. When one of them finally goes, then I always find a replacement. I'm getting so good at spotting when they are close. Sadly, however, I have been a bit distracted of late and I had to hurry the last one on a bit.

So – where to next? Back to the university? That place has been especially productive; I met three of them there. Who would have thought that the foyer of a university building would attract such a high proportion of depressives? The doctor's surgery – I had several from there. But that is a dangerous place... any more and they will see the pattern. The supermarket is always a good bet, and there are so many of them that the chances are no link between them would be made. There's a trick to it, and it's the time of day. Between half-past six and nine at night is when they come out.

You can spot them too. Discard the harassed parents escaping to the shop once the partner is home from work to do the kids' bedtime – in the trolley: nappies, ready meals, colic drops. The executives, single maybe, but they will have good jobs – quality meat, small packs of exotic vegetables, stir-fry sauce, still wearing a suit and tie.

The ones you want are those who look as if they are wearing the clothes they wore to bed last night. The ones who come out at night because they can't bear the crowds. They don't shop during the daytime because they think the noise of babies yelling might burst their eardrums, and it makes them want to cry themselves. They shop at night, when it's quiet and dark and nobody will stare at them, nobody will notice them, nobody will give them a second glance. They work their way around the supermarket as if they are invisible because that's how they feel. In their trollies will be frozen food, mostly, because they'll only shop once a month, if that. They will have a list, because they don't want to have to come back if they've forgotten something. They will not make eye contact. They will not talk to anyone.

Thinking about the supermarket reminds me of the one I saw earlier in the week. She looked almost ready. I might go back there to see if I can find her. Cat food, though – that was a problem. Cats have a habit of drawing attention to themselves if they don't get fed. Dogs are worse, of course, since they will bark if they have to. But cats... they add an element of risk, and risk is something I try to eliminate at all costs.

There are plenty of them out there who do not own cats. I shall keep looking.

I need a public place where sad people go...

Annabel

I didn't know the first thing about planning a funeral, but when I went to the register office this morning to get Mum's death certificate they gave me a leaflet with a helpful checklist to work through, and another one with a list of local funeral directors. Back home, sitting at the dining table, a pad and pen next to me, I listened to answering machine messages about out-of-hours services and how much they would like to call me back. The third one I tried – Co-operative Funeralcare – had a live person on the other end of the phone.

'My mother died,' I said, by way of introduction.

The woman who answered was very professional and calm. She told me she was deeply sorry to hear that, and that the best way forward was for them to come and see me to discuss possible options for the funeral.

I looked around the living room, at the state of it. 'Can I come to your office?' I asked. 'I could do with the fresh air.'

I felt dazed by all this, the suddenness of it, and all my routines had been profoundly disturbed. I'd hardly slept, hadn't really eaten, for what must be days. Last night I had gone to bed early and after two hours of restlessness got up and watched television until four o'clock. Then I'd gone back to bed and the next time I woke up it was ten to eleven. I felt adrift, as if I lacked any sort of plan or purpose, feeding the cat – who wasn't interested – then making toast which I never got around to eating. I decided to get my act together, starting with planning Mum's funeral.

As the day dwindled I drove to the small shopping centre on the outskirts of town, a concrete walkway lined with shops, at the end of it the Co-op where I used to stop on the way home from work to get groceries for Mum. Next door to it, to my surprise although it must have been there for years upon years, was the Co-operative Funeralcare.

I stood outside for a minute as I was early, window-shopping for headstones. Most of them were sculptures of Mary, her hands out in welcome, or Jesus pointing to his heart. Or an angel looking sad. At the edge, a plain headstone made out of red granite, the only words carved upon it, in a garish gold lettering, 'In Loving Memory'. Not, as I would almost have expected, 'Your Loved One's Name Here'.

I went inside.

'Ms Hayer?' The woman behind the desk was soberly dressed in a white blouse and dark grey skirt, a bleached-blonde bob tucked neatly behind ears that sported a single diamond stud. She regarded me with sympathetic blue eyes, head tilted to one side.

I'm not going to start crying, I wanted to say. You don't need to worry. I'm not going to cave in.

'Yes,' I said, holding out my hand. 'You must be Jackie?'

She took me through into an office next door that was decorated like a living room, comfy but upright sofas, a coffee table which held several leather-bound albums and a box of tissues. On the wall, a large framed print of a woodland shrouded in mist. A big, solid-looking Swiss cheese plant dominated one corner. The window looked out over the car park at the back, people coming and going with their shopping.

Jackie talked me through the options for running a funeral. They could do the whole lot for me, she said, from the coffin to the cars, taking care of the deceased, planning the service in conjunction with the crematorium or the church of my choice. Or, if I preferred, and some people did nowadays, they could do a very nice Humanist service and arrange a natural burial in a wood specially designated for the purpose. And it could all be done for one simple cost, with interest-free payment options if need be.

I wanted to sign up, get it over with. She glanced up at the clock on the wall above my head and said I could probably do with thinking about it, and if I wanted to go ahead she could see me the next day. She gave me a brochure with the different coffin designs and wood colours in it, a brochure about woodland burials, and a sheaf of other bits of paper.

When I got back out into the shopping arcade, it was chilly and nearly dark. Most of the shops were closing. I stood there for a moment, disorientated, wondering what had happened to the day.

'Are you alright?'

I looked round, surprised, to find a man standing next to me. He was tall, in a brown jacket with a scarf around his neck, and although his head was shaved he was younger than he looked. He wasn't smiling and yet he seemed to know me.

'Yes,' I said. 'I'm OK.'

'Very well,' he said.

He hesitated next to me for a moment. Did I know him? I felt as if I should have known his name and I tried some out, experimentally, in my head. Ian? No, that wasn't it... Dave? Simon? The trouble with recognising people unexpectedly was that it was possible that I knew him from work – not as a colleague, but rather as a subject – someone I'd worked on, some nominal whose face was familiar and yet I'd never spoken to them, never would.

He put a hand on my upper arm. 'Now,' he said, gently, 'it's just that I think you look as though you might be lost.'

His hand was still there, on my arm, warm and quite firm. It felt as though I was leaning against him. As though I'd initiated the contact, not him, and it was such a curious thing. At the same time as knowing that this was strange, unwarranted, being touched like this – even with layers of clothing between his skin and mine – it was comforting. It was comfortable. I felt a little struggle inside between the part of me that thought this was unnecessary and intrusive, and the part of me that needed to be comforted.

And the word bubbled up inside me like it had been held down and suddenly released. 'No,' I said. 'Not lost. I'm not lost. I'm just…'

'What's your name?' he asked.

'Annabel,' I said. 'What's yours?'

His hand was still there and then it slipped away from me. My upper arm felt suddenly chilled, as though a draught had passed over it. All around us people were hurrying home, carrying bags of shopping, bundled up against the breeze that blew around the walkways. It felt like coming round. I could hear noises, people talking; two older ladies came out of the hairdressers next door laughing, and fitted clear plastic rain hoods over their newly set styles.

'Ed,' he said. 'I am Ed.' His eyes were dark green. I couldn't remember ever looking into a pair of eyes and being aware of their colour before. If you'd asked me what colour my mother's eyes were, Kate's, Sam Everett's, I couldn't have given you an accurate response. But his eyes were green.

'That doesn't sound right,' I said.

'What do you mean?' he asked. The tone of his voice had changed: he sounded suspicious, wary. I didn't like that at all. It was as though there had been some sort of test and I'd failed it.

'That doesn't sound like your name.'

He laughed, exposing his teeth. 'Well, I assure you that it is.'

'Ed,' I said.

'That's right,' he said. 'You need to remember that.'

'Yes,' I said. 'Well, I've got to come back here tomorrow morning.'

'Yes,' he said. 'I will meet you here tomorrow.'

'Alright,' I said.

I think he said more. There were other things he said, too, things I couldn't remember.

A few minutes after that, or maybe it was an hour, or maybe it was a whole day, I was back in my car in the car park, and the engine was running. The heater was on and it was warm in there, and I was looking out through the windscreen into the darkness and the car park was almost empty. There was nobody else around. I looked at the clock and it was gone six o'clock. What time had I left the funeral people? It felt like just a few seconds, as though I had walked away from the place and got into my car and started the engine and then waited for something to happen. It was as if time had slipped out of my reach.

'The strangest thing,' I said aloud. It was like waking up slowly. When you were lying in bed in the middle of the night and you realised you were awake, not asleep, but you'd been lying on your hand and it was numb and it felt as if it belonged to someone else and you had to lie still and wait for it to belong to you again. I felt like that. But I felt good, too, warm inside and comforted.

And I knew what it was. I'd just met an angel.

Colin

Vaughn called me at work this afternoon to tell me that Audrey was at her mother's.

Fortunately I stopped short of asking him why he thought this information might be of interest to me. I'd finished work for the day and packed up, and was almost ready to leave when he'd called. I was in a hurry to get to the Co-op before going out to the college, and so I found I was standing there with my coat on, talking into the telephone receiver and feeling mildly annoyed.

'She wasn't at home,' he said, with boyish enthusiasm. 'She wasn't ignoring me at all; she'd just gone to stay with her mother. She said she'd told me about it, but that I clearly hadn't been listening.'

'Or you'd forgotten,' I added helpfully, thinking that it was entirely possible that he really was slipping into some kind of early dementia.

'Anyway, I thought I'd give you a ring to let you know,' he said. 'I knew you'd be worried.'

I ignored the slight hint of sarcasm around this last comment. 'And did you find a ring?'

'Yes,' he said. 'I'm thinking when the best time to propose might be. What do you think?'

Of all the people to ask. As if I would have the faintest idea about such matters.

'You could take her away somewhere,' I said. 'For the weekend. Or something like that.'

'Weston-super-Mare?' he said.

'Not Weston-super-Mare. Somewhere romantic. Paris, or Bruges. Or maybe even Rome?'

'Rome?' he echoed, as if I'd suggested going to Siberia. 'Surely I should be saving somewhere that exotic for the honeymoon?'

'Vaughn,' I said, 'I've really got to go.'

'Oh, I'm sorry, dear chap. Am I holding you up?'

'Yes, you are rather.'

He rang off, and I went home via the supermarket to buy small essentials. And after that, one of those delicious coincidences happened that make me occasionally consider that some higher power is guiding my hand in my enterprise. I came out of the Co-op with the intention of waiting outside in the precinct, to see if I could see any new subjects, any looking promising among the recently bereaved. And there she was – the woman I'd seen at the checkout on Tuesday evening. And, whilst she hadn't appeared to be ready just two days ago, she certainly looked it now. Observing her, I felt a particular thrill of affection and excitement that convinced me more than anything else that she is the next one.

She had a bag, a kind of canvas satchel in a grubby shade of brown, the strap worn across her body. It looked heavy. I wondered why it suddenly gave me a jolt, the sight of that bag, and then I realised it was because Helen had had one just like it. It was her school bag – covered over with notes and signatures and drawings in felt-tip pen, a CND button badge, another, larger badge with 'Free Mandela' on it under which some wag had written 'with every purchase'.

In my last year at Gaviston Comprehensive I acquired a friend, of sorts. She had joined the school in the sixth form as her previous school had no facility for students wishing to study at A-level. For the whole of the lower sixth, I barely noticed her. She was one of the confident ones, a girl who had no problems making friends. She blended in with them all, the ones who went out every weekend and spent the rest of the week talking about it.

I survived without such complications.

I was walking home from school on a Friday, and it was already dark so it must have been winter. Helen was walking home too, about fifty yards ahead of me, and I paid her no attention. I think for part of it she was walking with another girl, and then at some point her companion took one of the side roads and they said their goodbyes. Helen carried on walking and I slowed my pace a little to allow for the brief interruption in her stride, not wishing to narrow the gap between us.

At the top of the hill she crossed the main road and then took the alleyway which ran behind the Leisure Centre and would emerge again in Newarke Street. The alley was lit by a single street-light halfway along its length.

She was slowing down, which was annoying me. I slowed my pace to avoid catching up, not just infuriated because of her pace but also that the very thought of it was taking my concentration away from what I'd previously been thinking about, namely the difficulties in maintaining resonance frequency with a minimum electrical current.

We were about a quarter of the way up the alley when I realised there was someone walking in front of her, someone who had also slowed their pace. A few moments after that, Helen stopped walking. She was about to step into the pool of light created by the street-light; in fact she was partly illuminated by it, her hair a bright orange halo around her head. She looked back, and saw me, then back the other way.

Clearly I must have seemed less threatening than what lay ahead, because she turned then and started walking in my direction, her step quickening. I tutted with annoyance, not wanting to have to stand to one side in the narrow alley to let her pass with enough room between us, not wanting to have to smile or nod or whatever one was supposed to do in situations like this one.

Despite all this, I had a jolt. That's the only way I can describe it. I don't even think it was the expression on her face

– which was strange. It was that I was looking at her properly for the first time, and she was looking at me, and her mouth was forming the word: 'HELP'.

She came up to me and behind her was another of the sixth form girls, another of those whom I preferred to have nothing whatsoever to do with. I couldn't even have told you her name. She was striding in our direction and Helen was behind me, not moving further away, just behind me as though I was expected to do something – stand in between them? Act as some kind of physical buffer so we could all continue to walk home in the same direction?

It was such a peculiar situation. I felt uncomfortable with the whole thing. Not afraid, that would be the wrong word for it.

And I was more uncomfortable with Helen sheltering behind me than with the girl striding towards us both.

She had a knife in her hand. I remember thinking, what's she got that out for? As though everyone carried knives around with them every day, but to have one out on display was somehow completely inappropriate.

'Hiding behind Creepy Colin, are you?' the girl called. 'Think he's gonna help ya?'

I had stopped walking and stood at ease, my legs hip-width apart. I felt something else now – excitement. It was the thought of a confrontation, something I usually avoided, but this one had a context that gave me permission to behave in a certain way. I was being threatened, after all. Even if the knife was meant for Helen, it was now pointed at me.

'She's got a knife, be careful!' Helen said from somewhere behind me.

'Yes, thank you, I can see it,' I said.

It took one punch to lay her out. I had no idea it was going to be that easy, and if I had realised I would have taken it a bit more steadily so I could make the most of it. I suppose she just wasn't expecting me to hit her. It wasn't done to hit girls, even girls who were coming towards you with a knife in their hand,

and of all people she probably wasn't expecting me to cause her any trouble.

Behind me, Helen squeaked with surprise.

The girl, whoever she was, had landed in a heap against the brick wall that marked the boundary with someone's garden. Somewhere nearby a dog was barking. The girl didn't move. I looked round at Helen. She was breathing fast, her chest rising and falling, her mouth open with shock. To my surprise, in the light from the street-light, there were tears on her cheeks. I nearly said, 'What are you crying for?'

But she just looked from the girl to me and then started to walk away, in the direction of home. Her steps grew faster and faster and then she was running, running fast.

I looked down at the white legs of the girl on the floor. She was stirring, making a noise as though she was winded, a kind of drawn out 'uuhhhhh' as though she was struggling to get her breath. The knife was on the dirty tarmac where she'd dropped it.

There were many options laid out before me, many. Any one of them I could have taken and it could have changed my life from that point on. But I was not ready for it, then. I often look back at that evening, the nights already drawn in ready for winter, the air chilly but not yet bitter, the sound of Helen's running feet echoing down the alleyway, the sight of the girl with her legs splayed, her head smack against the bottom of the wall, her face in the glass and litter and dog shit that lined the edges of the path.

What I did was kick her. I didn't look where the kick landed, but it was only one, and it was to make sure she was still alive. I didn't say anything to her. I just walked away, following Helen but with a gait no faster than a purposeful saunter. I didn't even look back.

When I got home I went straight upstairs to the bathroom. My mother was in the kitchen preparing dinner. I wasn't even sure if she heard me coming through the door; either way, I made it to the bathroom and locked the door. There was blood on the sleeve of my school shirt, and my knuckles were red and swollen, although they didn't hurt. I had no idea where the blood had come from. I ran the sleeve of the shirt under the tap and scrubbed at it with the nail brush until it was clean, then hung the shirt over the radiator to dry. I was aware of my own arousal, but only in an abstract way until I undressed and got in the shower. Was this what violence prompted in me? I wondered? Or was it because I'd punched a girl? And then the image of her lying there, lying in the dirt and the crap on the tarmac, barely moving – her white legs against the ground, open – and the sound of Helen's feet, Helen running away. And Helen's hair like a halo around her face, the shape of her mouth when she whispered that word to me... HELP. I had probably misinterpreted the whole situation; I had most likely got it all wrong. But none of that mattered as I relieved the arousal in the shower, thinking of all those things in combination, and the fact that it might not be what the world thought of as normal never entered my head.

Helen acted strangely towards me after the incident in the alleyway. She stared at me at school. When she was with her friends she would say hello to me and they would all dig her in the ribs and laugh at her. She would sit next to me at lunchtime and start talking to me about what she'd seen on television the night before. I fended these approaches off as best I could, but, as much as they were unsolicited, they were not unwelcome. Every time I saw her I had that same jolt, the one in the alleyway as she'd walked towards me with that word silent on her lips.

The girl I'd punched – I assumed she made a full recovery. I never heard anything more about it and I never saw her again.

Helen didn't refer to the incident in her monologues, which made her approaches to me even more odd. Her friends all seemed to think she had gone completely mad in talking to me. But it continued into the summer term, our last term, when we were all busy with the pressure of A-levels and the heat and the hay fever seemed to grow worse every day.

Helen's last exam was on the Thursday; mine was on the day after. She went to the pub with her friends straight after the exam, and by the time I finished my afternoon's cramming in the library she was walking home. I caught her up because she was walking unsteadily, smiling and singing at the world in general.

'Colin!' she said when she saw me. 'It's all over – isn't it wonderful?'

'Not for me. I have my last physics paper tomorrow.'

'Pfft, physics.'

She swung her bag around her ankles and we walked to the alley. We'd walked this way – together – most days since that incident in the winter, but no word about it had passed between us. Today, though, she seemed to hesitate as we entered the path, even though it was brightly lit by the sun overhead.

I'd never felt comfortable with a girl before Helen, and it had taken many months of her smiling at me and talking to me to get me to this place of trust. But in the last couple of weeks, just in that tense, hot summer full of study and pressure and intense concentration, I had started to wonder if she was attracted to me. Once I'd got the idea into my head it wouldn't leave again, and I started to try and interpret everything she said, all the little comments, the laughs, as maybe her way of trying to flirt with me.

It made no sense to me, the complicated system of interaction between the sexes. The way the girls stood, the way they moved. Apparently you could tell if someone liked you by the way they behaved towards you when you were near.

It was Helen's last day at school. Exams ended, she had no reason to be there any more and the rest of her summer would be filled with lazy days sunbathing and shopping, going away with her parents and going out in the evenings with her girlfriends. This would be our last walk home together. And my last chance to decide whether there was anything in it.

'You should ring me,' she said, as we walked along. 'We could meet up, you know. If you felt like it.'

'Or you could ring me,' I said, already knowing she wouldn't.

'Write your number on my bag,' she said, fishing a black marker out of her canvas satchel and pulling off the lid with her teeth. I had no choice but to comply. There was a small unadorned patch of canvas on the inside of the flap and she flattened her palm beneath it to provide support while I wrote my phone number, followed by my name in neat capitals. The ink bled into the canvas and I wondered whether she would be able to read it. Her head was close to mine, the sunlight shining on her hair. I gave her back the pen and we continued walking.

'Helen,' I said, as we got towards the end of the alley.

'Mm?' she said, stopping too. She looked sleepy, her eyes half-open, shading them against the bright sun with one hand as she tried to look at me.

There was nothing I could think of to say, so I kissed her. I pushed her gently back against the wall and kissed her. Even now I don't know what I thought it was going to be like, but I was unprepared for her to respond, and when she did I made a sound that seemed to alarm her and she pulled away from me.

'Colin? It's alright.'

So I kissed her again, and this time it was still uncomfortable. I was much taller than she was and my neck was bent at an awkward angle to facilitate the kiss.

When it was over I remember walking home feeling – not elated, not at all, but disappointed. Was that all there was to it? I remember thinking? That hot, slimy feeling of someone's tongue against yours? The taste of spearmint gum and the beer she'd been drinking… it was all I could do not to shudder.

The final paper was the one that pulled my grade down from an A to a B, and effectively lost me the chance to enjoy an Oxbridge place. I never saw Helen again. She never phoned me, of course, and possibly this came as something of a relief.

As I talked to the woman earlier this evening, standing outside the funeral place in the precinct, I looked down – just once – at the satchel she carried and wondered whether, if I lifted the flap, I would find my name printed there in felt tip pen, along with a phone number, faded into the canvas.

Anyway – Vaughn has had contact with Audrey, so all's well in his little world. I don't know if he's made the decision about proposing to her. I find it amusing, however, trying to picture them in different situations and which one he might select to do the deed... on one knee, in the cinema? Scuba-diving? Watching television with a microwaved meal on a matching set of his-and-hers fold-up tables?

I'm being unkind. The meal they served was perfectly acceptable, and I am really glad for them both, despite Audrey's flirtatious boldness with me that evening. She was, as I believe they say, a little minx.

I am looking forward to reading tomorrow's edition of the *Briarstone Chronicle*. I am planning to collect a copy on the way to work, and then hope I can make it to work after reading it in the car. I suspect I shall find it quite – diverting. After that, of course, I have my new subject to tend to. I must make sure I'm not so distracted by the newspaper that I miss out on the chance to watch this new one transform.

I do wonder, briefly, if I said something a little bit – amiss – to Audrey and she's decided to go the same way as the others. It wasn't my intention, not at all. But I wonder sometimes if I'm not just a little too good at this. Maybe I'm not fully aware of how exceptional these powers are. Or perhaps I am getting so comfortable with them that I am starting to blur the edges of what is acceptable and what is not.

In any case, as I say, I'm glad she turned up safe and well. Audrey lives to fight another day... and who knows, proposal or no proposal, I might get an opportunity to have another go at her one of these days. Maybe I should return the invitation and invite them both to dinner at mine. What would they make of it, I wonder, this big old Edwardian villa? I expect they would be surprised that I can afford a place such as this. And no mortgage on it, either, of course – all my salary is mine to do with as I please. And, when my mother finally decides to take up her place in the realm of eternal damnation, then it will be my name on the deeds, too.

Two Bodies Found Following Tip-Off: Police Hunt Killer

Briarstone police have confirmed they are launching a murder investigation following the discovery of two more bodies in the borough on Tuesday night and early Wednesday morning, a police spokesperson today revealed. Dana Viliscevina, 30, originally from Serbia but more recently living in Hawthorn Crescent, Carnhurst, was discovered after the Chronicle *received a tip-off phone call from a woman who claimed to know where more bodies were. The woman rang off without leaving her name. A police source said yesterday that a second body had been found. The second victim has been named locally as Eileen Forbes, 45, of Oak Tree Lane, Briarstone. It is understood that Ms Forbes died only hours before being found, but our source confirms that her death is being closely linked to the investigation.*

Ms Viliscevina was employed by St Margaret's Church of England Primary School, Newington, as a teaching assistant. The head teacher of St Margaret's, Bethan Davies, said yesterday that Ms Viliscevina was on long-term sick leave from her job. 'We had no idea,' she said yesterday. 'I kept in touch with her regularly and she seemed to be getting better. We were all hoping that she would come back to work. The children are all very upset today.' Counselling services have been brought in to speak to members of the class that Ms Viliscevina taught earlier this year.

The two bodies discovered this week mean that a total of twenty-six bodies have now been found in the Briarstone area since the beginning of the year. The 'Love Your Neighbour' campaign was launched by your Briarstone Chronicle *in an effort to get across the importance of taking care of the lonely and vulnerable members of our society. However, it seems clear following the tip-off phone call that the increase in decomposed bodies in Briarstone may not be a random coincidence, nor does it represent a failure on the part of our community to take good care of our neighbours. The police are now looking for an individual who may have had contact with all of the people who have been found deceased, in the hopes of discovering exactly how they met their deaths.*

Anyone with any information regarding the death of Dana Viliscevina is asked to call the Incident Room at Briarstone Police Station.

Remember too that it is not too late to check up on your neighbours!

Detective Inspector Andy Frost said: 'We all have a duty of care to look in on people we know are living on their own. There are a lot of vulnerable members of our community and the recent news means we should all be taking care of these people and not leaving it for someone else to do.'

Dana

I'd been in this country for years but I never quite thought of it as home. I came here to escape the civil war that was raging, the stories we heard about the soldiers attacking towns and villages to the north, the things they were doing. I took all the money we had saved up and I bought transport for my elderly parents and me. First we went on a ship to Sicily, landing the day before Christmas Eve. The place was chaos. Others were trying to head north into mainland Europe, catching lifts from lorry drivers, or stowing away in transport containers when they could access them.

My parents were not able to do that. My mother was sick already at that time, coughing blood and very weak. My father had very bad arthritis and found it difficult to walk. We still had money and it felt dangerous for me to have it, so I bought airline tickets for us all and two days into the New Year we landed in London.

The airport closed after we landed, due to bad weather. We were taken to an asylum centre somewhere outside of the city. My mother was taken to hospital and she died the next day. She had pneumonia and they were too late giving her the drugs which might have helped her live.

My father tried to carry on without her, but could not. He died within the month, a 'myocardial infarction', according to the death certificate. But really he had no reason to live without her. He had no will left, no strength. And so he left me, too.

That is the story of how I came to be in this country. At home, I was a primary school teacher and a well qualified member of society. Here, I was nothing. I earned money waiting at tables in London, helping in the kitchen. I worked for a while in one of the London hotels. Anything I could to pay the rent on the bedsit I shared with three other girls from Eastern Europe, all of them refugees like me from the civil wars and ethnic cleansing. They all had stories to tell about things they had seen, what they had been through to get out. All three of them had suffered more than I had.

I saved up what I could and eventually I had enough money to do a course that qualified me to be a teaching assistant in the UK. I looked for work up and down the country and eventually I got a job at a primary school in Briarstone.

I had never heard of Briarstone before, even though it was nearer to London than most of the other jobs I applied for. The school was a small one, friendly, and the staff were kind – but I had nothing in common with any of them. They did not know me and there was no point in telling them what had happened to me in the last few years.

I don't know what started the problem. I was at the school for a long time. I saw the children progress from tiny little children in reception class to the verge of puberty, and then all their younger siblings as they grew up too.

I think it might be that I had been tired for so long, fought for so long to just keep going. I found myself finally at the end, and I was so tired I closed my eyes every night and it was a struggle to open them again the next morning. I think if I had ever found someone, a friend, or a lover – someone to be with, a reason to be happy – then perhaps I would have stayed alive. There was just nothing left. No strength, no courage, no energy. And in cases like that, the only solution is to lie quietly and wait.

Eileen

there was no act of violence perpetrated against me no Act of Violence no actofviolence no Act. No violence they said they would come for me one day and they did they told me what to say when to say it what to do when to do it

it was not violence it did not hurt

it was a choice I made a choice my own free will my own destiny the distance between us like spaces like the void in my heart the voices in my heart the depths of my soul the depths of my despair

you can take this away this pain this grief you can take it from me and make it disappear

make me disappear

peace at peace in pieces

my choice my decision my desecration my will my bones my soul my path that I have chosen I did it my way and you can take nothing from me now you can take nothing

Annabel

I slept well. That was the first thing that crossed my mind when I woke up. The cat was calling me from the bottom of the stairs, and I was wide awake instantly, sitting up on the side of the bed looking at the weak sunshine lighting up the branches of the tree in my back garden. I'd slept well, and for a change I felt positive, ready to face things. Ready to do whatever needed to be done.

It was nearly eight o'clock. I got dressed quickly and went down to feed Lucy, who trotted happily in front of me to the kitchen, tail raised in a neat question mark.

By nine, I was back in the shopping centre car park. It was a much nicer day. Overhead, a bright blue sky was spotted with freshly laundered white cotton clouds, and the rain in the night had made everything look glossy. The little angel that dangled from my rear-view mirror sparkled and danced.

I felt none of it. I felt nothing but the instinctive need to carry on, to put one foot in front of the other, to carry on completing one task at a time, one day at a time, until it all came to some sort of end. I felt so tired, all of a sudden. So completely drained.

My mobile phone rang just as I was locking the car. It was Andy Frost. He hesitated after the initial condolences.

'Just – just wanted to say, take as long as you need. I'd like to keep in touch, to check you're OK. And if there's anything we can do...'

I tried to listen, tried to pay attention, but I kept thinking that I had something important to do and this phone conversation was keeping me from it. 'I suppose I should come back to work,' I said, hoping that would shut him up.

'No, you should take more time, really. At least a fortnight. It's all down as compassionate leave, you don't need to worry.'

'Alright,' I said.

'It's fine, Annabel,' he went on. 'We can manage. We need you to come back when you're ready, not before.'

I bit my lip. They'd replaced me, I thought. Drafted in one of the other analysts, maybe even Kate, to do all the work. It was *my* job! They wouldn't have had a clue where to start with it if it hadn't been for my spreadsheet. Well, let them get on with it. It wasn't my problem, now, was it?

'Sure,' I said.

'So you don't need to worry about a thing. We're working our way through it, don't worry.'

'You don't need me,' I said. It was a statement of fact.

'Annabel, we'll be fine. Much as I like to think we can wrap something like this up overnight, it will still be here when you're ready to come back. Alright?'

I hung up and something strange happened. I stood still and waited, and after a few moments I felt calm, the resentment and feeling of frustration draining away. I had this idea that I should be more upset, more concerned about the phone call, but already I could barely remember what he'd been saying. I was too tired to focus on it. And then even thinking about it felt like an exhausting effort.

There was something that I had to do. As I walked towards the shopping precinct and the office of the funeral director, a rainbow sparkled bright against the grey concrete buildings. It felt like a sign, something positive, something to cling to.

Colin

I rang work early and told them I was taking the morning off, and then I went to the precinct as planned, to meet the new one. She was easier than I thought she would be – acquiescent, and ripe, changed greatly since I'd seen her in the supermarket on Tuesday evening. Bereavement, of course. Often it's that. While I was waiting for her I called in at the Co-op, bought a copy of the paper and some milk.

She was waiting for me outside the funeral director's. I thought she'd said she had an appointment but if this was true she'd forgotten all about it. It was an annoyance because I'd been hoping for some time to myself to read the newspaper – but that would have to wait. She told me where she lived and I followed her there, leaving the groceries behind in the car. We talked for a while in her kitchen. The cat was outside, calling and scratching at the door, and for a moment I thought she was going to open it and let the infernal thing in. I told her that there was nothing but silence and peace. Nothing else to concern her. It seemed to do the trick because the cat was ignored. In the end I think it gave up, because when we went upstairs the noise stopped.

I left her an hour or so later and came back home with the shopping. There will be more such conversations ahead of us both before she is ready, but they can wait for now.

I'm shivering with excitement when I open the paper.

There's less information than I thought there would be. Yes, they've found Dana and Eileen, as I knew they would. Yes, they've very sensibly realised that there is more linking the people concerned than depression and a lack of neighbourly concern. But what are they doing about it? Very little, it seems.

But would the *Briarstone Chronicle* be kept up to date with the details of the investigation? It is probably unlikely. I wonder if I've done a very foolish thing, by letting them in on my activities.

By the time I get to work I've worked myself up into a spiral of nervous tension that I can barely contain. I sit at my desk and log on to the computer without speaking to anyone, hoping that spreadsheets and accounting software will gradually calm me down again.

Across the other side of the office, Garth is breathing through his nose. When we moved into this office from the ground floor, a year ago in December, I ended up with the desk directly opposite Garth's. He invariably smelt bad, musty, and he made constant noises: he couldn't even breathe quietly. If he wasn't breathing he was snorting or humming or chuckling to himself or muttering or tapping his front teeth with his pen or running his hand compulsively through his greasy, thinning hair or rasping his finger against the stubble on his cheek or licking his lips or clearing his throat, or leaning back in his chair so that his shirt would tug free of his belt and show me a small patch of hairy white belly.

I lasted a day and a half. I went to see Martha and told her I needed to be near a window as I was claustrophobic. They couldn't persuade Alan to swap desks, so they moved me to a tight space beside the photocopier which had a small window behind it, looking out over the car park. It suits me. I am away from all of them. And although I can still see them and listen to their mindless conversations, I can get on with my work in peace without the discordant percussion of Garth's bodily functions.

This is fine, whilst Garth is in rude good health. If he is unwell, though, as he is today, the noise levels increase to the extent that I can hear him again, across the whole office space separating us. And his odour crosses the room like mustard gas across the trenches. The noises: phlegm, mucus, nose-blowing, the excavation of his nose with his handkerchief; and then the sighs, the moans, the wheezing.

I search through my bag for my iPod, which will at least muffle the sounds of Garth's latest malady, but to my dismay find that I've left it at home.

In the end, I resort to speaking to him. 'Garth,' I say.

He doesn't hear me, as at that very moment he takes out his handkerchief and blows his nose, a wet rumble like a pair of waders being thrown from the roof of a multi-storey car park.

'Garth!'

'What? Can't hear very well,' he calls across from the other side of the room. 'My ears are all blocked up.'

'Would you mind keeping the noise down?' I say loudly, trying to keep the tone of my voice pleasant.

'Sorry, mate. Will do.'

I wince at the familiarity.

'Leave him alone,' Martha says, looking up from her computer screen. 'He's not a well man.'

And then her phone rings before she can say more or I can provide a response, and I'm forced to listen to her chatting away to one of her cronies in Accounts, laughing and joking as though they are at a bar rather than in a professional working environment. Why are they all so incessantly LOUD?

I stare at the spreadsheet but cannot tune them out, and now Garth has started on a productive coughing fit that makes me feel decidedly unwell. I can almost see the germs crossing the room towards me. I stand up, slamming my pen down upon the desk, and go to the kitchen. None of them notices.

In the kitchen, having disinfected the surfaces, filled the kettle with fresh water and washed my hands, I stand at the table waiting for it to boil. Someone has left a copy of the *Briarstone Chronicle* behind, again, and despite the ache of worry that still lingers in my chest I find myself reading the article over.

Twenty-six, it says. Have there really been so many? But then, there will have been some I had nothing at all to do with, and the newspaper and the police wouldn't have been able to tell the difference.

Looking at the pictures, I remember the ones I've known... how delicious the sensation of leaving them behind to transform: the earthy, the filthy disgusting specimens of humanity hovering between the misery of life and the emptiness of death. After I leave them, they have the moment of transition and then everything is good, pure; no decisions remaining for them; everything that follows is as Nature dictates. Their transformations follow immutable laws of decay, rules they cannot deviate from. It has a beauty and a simplicity to it that would have been exactly the same five hundred years ago. Unchanging as the course of the earth. The unnatural processes of the modern world, finally overtaken by the natural, as glorious and unstoppable as life itself.

Annabel

I was lying on my bed looking up at the patterns of the light dancing on the ceiling. It felt as if I had been asleep and had woken up, but I couldn't remember waking up. The sun was bright outside and it was reflecting off something and shining up into my room. It must be daytime. It must be the afternoon, maybe.

I looked at the clock by my bed and registered that it said 12.05. I must have been tired and decided to take a nap, but I had only vague recollection of coming home. This morning I had been... somewhere... in the car. I parked the car, and I saw a rainbow. I remembered that bit, definitely. Frosty had phoned me. I spoke to him and I was in the car park and I was looking at the rainbow. And then... where did I go?

I was talking to someone. I remember talking to a woman, inside somewhere, for a long time – but was that last night or this morning? It had been dark outside – so it must have been last night.

It didn't matter, anyway, did it?

I sat up in bed, slowly, feeling dizziness and a wave of nausea. My stomach was making noises and I thought about going downstairs and making something to eat, but then I had no real need to do it. There was no need for anything like that.

Six o'clock, he said.

For some reason I kept thinking about it. Six o'clock. What was going to happen then? Something I had to remember... something I had to do. At six o'clock. He said I didn't need to worry and I wasn't worried, but I thought I should know something that didn't seem to be there any more. It was gone, whatever it was, fleeting and slippery like a fish darting through silky weeds.

From downstairs I could hear a sound that I recognised, a scratching that was annoying and persistent. A banging, far off, as though someone was trying to get in. Scratching.

It would wait, whatever it was. It could wait until six o'clock and then something was going to happen. I turned the sound of the scratching down in my head, tuned it out. Focused on the rainbow and the angel, my angel.

I watched the clock until nearly six. Then I got out of bed, awake and ready for whatever it was I was supposed to do. I was dressed already but I felt cold. I found my coat hanging over the banister at the top of the stairs and put that on.

I went down to the kitchen and at the back door I could see the shape of a cat through the cat flap. When it saw me it stood up on its hind legs and scratched at the door, throwing itself against it. That was the sound I'd heard. I looked at the cat and wondered why it didn't come through the flap if it wanted to come in.

A phone was ringing. I went into the other room, following the sound. On the sofa was a bag, my bag, and the ringing came from inside it. I looked at the phone. It said 'SAFE'.

I pressed the green button. 'Hello?'

He said some things to me. His voice was quiet and even and soothing, even though I didn't feel worried or upset. I felt so calm. It was like floating on the surface of warm water, letting the waves take me away to somewhere I'd be safe and cosy.

'I need to do something,' I said.

'Remember to plug the phone charger in,' he said. 'I told you about the charger. It is inside your bag. When our phone conversation is finished, you need to plug in the phone straight away. Do you understand?'

'Yes,' I said. 'You told me about the phone.'

'Yes,' he said. 'You can do it when we finish talking.'

'There's something else,' I said. 'I was supposed to do something else...'

'No,' he said. 'Everything is done, Annabel. Everything you do is because you choose to do it. Everything is fine. You are fine. You are safe at home.'

'Yes,' I said. I felt safe.

'I will visit later, but you don't need to worry about that. You can sleep now and I will call tomorrow,' he said. 'At six o'clock. Do you understand?'

'At six o'clock,' I said. 'Yes.'

Then he said goodbye and the phone was silent in my hand. I looked at it for a moment. It wasn't my phone. It was a small black one with a small screen. I looked in my bag for my phone – a big one, bulky, old – but it wasn't there. Instead I found a charger. I took it into the kitchen and plugged it into the spare socket next to the kettle. I put the other end of the cable into the bottom of the phone. The screen lit up and there was a flashing battery and a word that said 'CHARGING'. I put the phone down.

I stood still in the kitchen. There was a noise at the back door but it was a normal noise and I tuned it out. Then I went upstairs and lay down on my bed. My coat was still on. I was warm, and safe, and at home. Everything was fine. I didn't need to do anything. I lay still and waited for six o'clock.

Colin

It strikes me as odd that her house is next door to the one I visited all those months ago. It must be a street full of suicidal people. Misery breeds misery, after all – contagious, the soupy atmosphere of despair. I should really have been holding my breath. And of course she was the one who found Shelley, the one who gave me the fright of my life that evening when I was paying her a visit. I heard the sound of the glass breaking at the back door and took myself off into the hallway, planning to let myself out of the front door, but something made me stay. I feel very protective over my friends, especially when they have not yet completed their transformation, and the thought of Shelley's metamorphosis being interrupted by some thuggish teenage burglar was more than I could bear. And then I heard her call out – something – 'Hello? Anyone there?' – something of that nature, at any rate, and I stopped in the hallway. I knew she would not search the house, whoever she was. She would get as far as the living room and Shelley and no further.

I was intrigued by the thought of observing someone else's reaction to the tableau of Shelley's putrefaction. After all, I know I'm unusual but there is always the possibility of others seeing the same beauty in it that I see, and who knows – I might have found someone to share all this with. Either that, or it would add a new, voyeuristically erotic dimension to the whole process.

She was so beautifully calm. She didn't scream, or vomit, or even turn away. I saw from a crack in the doorway to the hall that she stood there looking at Shelley for a long moment, her face serene, only her rapid breathing giving away the sense of shock.

I hadn't recognised her in the supermarket, of course – out of that context – but it's wonderful to have her as my next subject. I love symmetry in all things. Watching this one go, when she has borne witness to the decay of another, is almost poetic.

Annabel

I opened my eyes and I didn't feel alone.

It was dark in the room but my eyes adjusted and after a while I could hear breathing that wasn't my own.

I lifted my head. It took a lot of effort, as if it was made of iron and my neck was a rubber band.

There was a man sitting on a chair by the door. He was watching me. The light from the window was like an orange glow in the room and it lit up his face. He smiled at me, and I felt safe and comforted because I knew he was my angel and he was here, watching over me.

'Sleep,' he said, his voice just a whisper.

The angels would speak to me in a voice that was just a whisper, a breath. They would hold me in their arms and support me in times of trouble. When I was lonely, or afraid, the angels would be there.

I rested my head back down on the pillow and closed my eyes.

Colin

I went to the house in Newmarket Street first, as soon as it got dark. There was nowhere to park the car, which was annoying. I ended up parking in a residents' only bay in the next street and walking back to the house. I didn't see a single person on the way, and, although I checked behind me before going down the path to the front door, the whole road was silent and empty. I used the spare key she had given me and as I opened the door a shape darted past into the house – her infernal cat, no doubt. I closed the door and listened for a moment. The only sound was the cat, meowing from a room at the back. I went through and found some cat food in a cupboard, and shook the nuggets into the bowl that was on the floor. I would have to let it out again, and maybe put some food outside to keep it quiet.

Upstairs, she was fast asleep on the bed. I found a chair outside on the landing and moved it into the bedroom so I could sit and watch her for a while. She was so silent and still that I could almost imagine, almost pretend that she had already passed into death, that I'd caught her right at the perfect moment, the start of the process – the last breaths, exhaled into the stale atmosphere of the room; the stilling of the heartbeat, the blood cells no longer racing around the body, tension gone from every muscle. Everything peaceful and quiet.

I'm not usually aroused by them until the process of decay has started, but to imagine myself here at the very moment, the precise second she passed from life to death, was thrilling. I shifted in my seat to ease the discomfort, and I was just undoing my trousers when I heard her sigh. The movement must have disturbed her because she lifted her head and opened her eyes and looked at me.

I tried a benevolent, reassuring smile. 'Sleep,' I whispered.

She went back to sleep. That perfect undisturbed moment was gone, and with it my arousal.

Something brushed against my leg and startled me – that bloody cat again. I stood, hooked my hand under its belly and took it down the stairs to the kitchen. By that time it was squirming and fighting in my arms. I unlocked the back door and half-threw, half-dropped it out into the night.

When I got home it took me half an hour to get the cat hair off my trousers using sticky tape. I shan't feed it again.

It's late at night, and I'm at the computer with a tumbler of single malt, exploring the world from the darkness of the study. Shostakovich playing. I'm too peevish for porn tonight: I shall have to turn to my books for inspiration.

Biology first, and this evening's topic of interest – detritivores, a subject approached because of the images I looked at after work. Edward, I think his name was, or rather Eloise, the one who dressed like a woman and indeed fooled me completely until he let me in on the subject of his miserable family. She or he had left the window open upstairs, and of course, because I never interfere in the natural processes, the window had remained open and as a result the detritivores had arrived early, and feasted well.

Often my digital photographs are quite static, but Edward's is a veritable teatime drama.

Detritivores – the vertebrate and invertebrate organisms that feed on decomposing organic matter – are attracted to their sustenance by smell. Different smells are given off as a by-product of the object in question at varying stages of the decomposition process, meaning that the consumption, recycling, destruction (whatever you prefer) of the dead is carried out by a variety of detritivores. In other words, it's not a feeding frenzy. Blowflies like their dinner fresh. Tineid and Pyralid moth larvae will only consume putrid dry remains, and won't appear until after the blowfly larvae have finished. It's a banquet carefully stage-managed by Nature, a series of courses laid out one after the other, the perfect scent – to tempt only those guests who will enjoy each flavour – given off at precisely the right moment.

When I finish indulging in my love of biology, I return the images and the notebooks to their hiding place and move on to the less controversial topic of NLP.

The tutor for the NLP course is called Nigel. He worked in the City, once upon a time, initially without much dramatic success until he discovered NLP and thereafter, if you were to believe everything he says, he became so successful that he managed to retire at the age of thirty-two. He'd decided it was too stressful being a trader and had chosen to turn his hand to a bit of part-time teaching instead. And thus he imparts his knowledge to us.

He is always quite entertaining, to be fair to him. The tutor group sessions start out with an apparent firm structure, descend into amusing anecdotes about Nigel's time in the City – or else one of the other participants' attempts to put into practice the techniques we'd learned – and by the end of the class Nigel will reveal with a dramatic flourish that he has been training us all along, and that what we learned today was actually something quite unexpected.

On one particular occasion, when Nigel had claimed to be teaching us how to lead a conversation away from confrontation and towards resolution, he ended up telling us a story about how he'd used NLP to get a girl he fancied to sleep with him.

There were six of us in the group that night. Lisa wasn't there, for some reason, leaving just Alison and five men. Alison worked in a bank. She'd wanted to attend the class to learn how to increase her confidence when dealing with customers, particularly difficult ones. She wanted to know how to turn a complaint into a sale.

You could tell that Nigel had been saving up this particular topic by the way he relished the telling of it. Alison was shifting in her seat, as was the elderly gent who trotted along to evening classes regularly – he'd already been in three of the courses I'd attended – as a way of escaping from the horrors of having to make conversation with his wife. But the rest of them – the two youngish guys, Roger and Darren, who were hoping for a career in sales, and the music producer who wanted to influence the critics – were hanging on Nigel's every word.

He'd succeeded in his quest with the woman, of course, because Nigel didn't fail at anything, and, if he had, he wouldn't have shared that particular story. The girl he liked had been helpless, powerless to resist his charms. He had slept with her and ended up in a relationship with her that lasted three years. And then she'd moved to the States to pursue a career as an actress and a model. It had ended amicably. And then he'd met his wife, and not used any NLP techniques to woo her, and that, too, had been a success.

And the moral of the story was only partly that all this was immoral. NLP was a powerful tool that should be used with integrity, he said. It worked best when people used it to provide a positive, empowering result for both parties. It was all about honing techniques that every human possessed if only they realised it. It was all about being the best that you could be. If the woman hadn't been attracted to him anyway, Nigel argued, she would never have succumbed to his carefully planned suggestions and influences. It was about maximising opportunities that already existed. Not about faking them, or making people do things against their will. You needed to lead them down a path that they might already have been intending to take. It was about encouraging them to do what they wanted to do, but lacked the courage or the focus or the determination to do on their own.

It was, as Nigel frequently said, win-win.

I tried my hardest, but I couldn't see how anything he said meant that I shouldn't also consider using these techniques to seduce a woman. Surely that would be win-win?

I gave all of it a lot of thought. The idea grew and spread through me like treacle until it was all I could think about. I could find a woman who was reasonably attracted to me, and instead of saying the wrong thing and ruining my chances I could make her warm to me, make her like me. And maybe, yes, make her want to sleep with me. And after that, presumably, if we were compatible and I liked her enough to continue with it, maybe I could actually end up having that most dramatic and unexpected of things, A Relationship. I read voraciously around the topic, every book I could find and every internet page that discussed the Meta Model versus the Milton Model, mirroring, strategies, calibration, everyday trances. I practised at work, even though it felt uncomfortable; I struck up conversations with Martha and some of the others and watched their awkwardness change from wariness to a kind of reserved acceptance. It was undeniably fascinating. It worked, and the more I put into it, the more my confidence grew.

Annabel

When I opened my eyes again he wasn't there. I expected to feel something but there was nothing. I wasn't afraid.

Time was passing because when I opened my eyes the next time it was daylight, and then it was dark again. Six pm had happened twice. I had answered the black phone and listened and spoken, although I couldn't remember what about.

My mouth was dry, sticky, uncomfortable. That was the only thing that bothered me. And then even that passed.

The phone was by the bed. I plugged it in to charge, as he told me to.

I felt as if I was waiting for something.

When it comes I will know it, I thought. *I will greet it, like an old friend.*

Colin

I take my responsibilities very seriously, although I must admit to being distracted since the newspaper article I read on Friday.

I stayed in most of Saturday, only venturing out after dark, and then only making one visit. After Friday's trip to the house in Newmarket Street I resolved to leave her in peace until she transforms properly. It's no fun being interrupted by the living. Instead I made my way to see Maggie. I often think she will be the very last to be found, which is ironic in a way because she was clearly the most wealthy person I've spent time with. You would think her friends and family would show her more respect, when she clearly has a lot to offer them. But as yet, months down the line, she is continuing her transformation uninterrupted. Her house is beautiful, and the rural setting means the scent is unlikely to disturb the neighbours as it often does in the urban areas.

I usually pay her a visit at weekends, and sometimes during the day, because I've never seen a soul down this road and I don't worry quite so much about being seen. You'd think I wouldn't worry about being seen, wouldn't you? But really I'm quite a private person. If you met me in the street I dare say you would not be unduly worried by my presence, and that's as it should be. Nevertheless, I do prefer not to be noticed.

You want to know what I do, on these visits? I thought you might.

I spend time observing the changes that have taken place since my last visit. I make notes, but more frequently this happens at home afterwards. I take pictures with my digital camera, which I then examine further, catalogue, and store when I get home. After a while, when I have noted everything I wish to note, I spend some time just sitting with them, watching them. I am always careful never to disturb anything in the environment, never to leave anything of myself behind.

I have to say with many of them the thrill is not as it once was. The excitement which was once highly erotic has gradually been replaced by a kind of fondness. I would say, even though I've never fully understood the meaning of the word, possibly even by love. After all, sometimes I spend months with them. I get to know them with the affection of a lover. I have seen their most private moments and I know their bodies more intimately than their husbands, partners, mothers. I see things they have never even seen themselves: the moment when the body reveals itself, piece by piece; when it opens like a flower to display the beauty within.

Sometimes I talk to them, although of course they can't hear me. It's a way of reminding myself that they are – or were – human beings, although of course from a purely scientific point of view they are rapidly becoming an object of decay. I think I am more aroused by them when they get to that point – wherever you choose to define it – that they cease to be a person. I wonder what it is in me that finds the idea of sexual intercourse with another human being to be so challenging, and yet can imagine it readily when that point is reached.

What about the smell? I hear you ask. Don't they smell bad? I know you want to know, don't you? That's the first question I'd ask, if I were in your position.

They all smell different, of course, which is part of the charm. Although the smell is pervasive and lingers in the nostrils for a long time after I've left them, I've never found it intolerable. When you've been around them for a long time, you notice how the smell changes and develops as the decomposition progresses. At times it can be like rancid cheese, vomit, spoiled meat, even sweetish, like an exotic dessert you are almost brave enough to try. I object to the smell of decomposing food, of course. It's similar, but has less appeal.

I wear the same clothes when I pay my visits, and wash them often. The scent clings to the fabric, as I imagine the scent of a lover would, and as much as I would enjoy smelling my own clothes I cannot risk others noticing it.

Actually, I haven't told the complete truth there. I said I never found it intolerable, but there was one. Robin, I think he was called. An alcoholic, although I remember him being an intelligent man who would have been a witty and engaging conversationalist were it not for the tragedy of his life. I hadn't realised the depth of his alcoholism until he began to decompose, and the odour that came from his fermented liver was quite unlike anything I've ever smelt. Even I found it difficult to bear. I went back to him less frequently, but each time it was worse, and after a couple of visits I stopped going.

I spent longer with Maggie yesterday evening than I have for a long time. Once I started talking, I found it hard to stop. She's a very good listener.

In the end it was very late when I got home and consequently I slept late this morning.

After lunch I decided on a whim to go and visit my mother in the Larches. I thought it would provide some useful distraction from my worries about the police investigation.

She was asleep in an upright chair in the day room, her head resting at an awkward angle. A number of ladies were watching a football match on the large television, the sound turned up to prohibit conversation. I pulled up a footstool and sat next to my mother, hoping she wouldn't wake up before I'd managed to stay the half-hour I'd decided was a reasonable amount of time. I watched the football, for want of something better to do, but it was unbelievably tedious.

When I next looked up at her she was awake and staring at me, even though she hadn't moved her head at all.

'Hello, Mother,' I said.

She didn't speak but continued to stare, unblinking. Some food was crusted in the corners of her open mouth.

I had a sudden recollection of a moment from my childhood – although my father was already dead, so I must have been a teenager – when she had forced me to eat a saucepan full of cabbage that I had allowed to boil dry. For some reason she believed she'd left me in charge of the dinner while she had gone next door to speak to her friend, and when she came back the kitchen was full of a foul-smelling yellow smoke, and the pan was crackling on the stove top. I was in the study reading a book, oblivious to it.

My dinner was put in front of me at the dining table shortly afterwards, a pan full of cabbage half-stuck to the burned bottom, and a fork with which to prise it loose. When I refused she left me sitting there for an hour, staring miserably at it. After that hour, she scraped a lump of the cabbage from the pan with her claw-like fingernails and pushed it into my mouth, while I struggled and cried and fought for breath.

'You hate me,' I whispered to the ghost of my mother in her wing-backed chair, 'don't you?'

Her eyes glinted back at me.

I left shortly afterwards, calling in at the Matron's office on the way out to make sure she was fully aware of my presence and therefore not likely to phone me again for a few weeks.

It has crossed my mind more than once that my poor dear mother is in need of a merciful release. I can imagine, imprisoned in a body that's now beyond her control, that she would quite possibly rather be dead, especially if, as they seem to suggest, her mind is still sharp. I have no doubt at all from the vile look in her eyes today that she's entirely lucid. And, whilst it is within my powers to assist her with ending her miserable existence – should that be the path she chooses, of course – I find that I'm relishing the thought that I can hold even this back from her. Now the balance of power has shifted to me, and I choose to leave her as she is – humiliated, suffering, trapped.

It gives me immense personal satisfaction.

Back to work tomorrow. I wonder how Vaughn's doing. I think I shall need a pint and some inane conversation by lunchtime.

Another Lonely Death – A Community in Shock

Once again this week Briarstone police officers made a grim discovery when they were called to a house in Blackthorn Row, Swepham following reports of a foul smell in the area. The body of a man, believed to be Edward Langton, 28, was discovered in the bedroom of the property. Mr Langton had not been seen for many months and a source said that the body was found in a badly decomposed state.

At the time of writing, no relatives of the deceased had come forward. The sad death of Mr Langton is just the latest in a shocking number of decomposed bodies found in Briarstone homes in the last few months.

It is not known if the death of Mr Langton has been linked by the police to Dana Viliscevina and Eileen Forbes, who were both found in their homes last week. Investigations are continuing.

Love Your Neighbour Campaign – latest events in your area, pages 34–35.

Eloise

I knew I was in the wrong body when I was much younger, probably before I knew anything else that was a solid fact. I played with girls all the time, my two sisters and all their friends, and until the age of about eight or nine I didn't even really think of myself as different from them, as separate in any way. If it hadn't been for my dad, we might have carried on as we were and my life would have been very different. But my dad was a man's man, a former miner, who wanted me to play rugby and if I couldn't manage that then he would settle for football; he wanted me to stand shoulder to shoulder with him as I grew up. He wanted someone he could take to the pub on a Sunday morning while my mam cooked us both a roast lunch and my sisters chirped and cooed over their babies.

I loved my father and hated him equally; he was never violent towards me when I was growing up, but his displeasure was bad enough. So I learned how to play the game, I learned how to change my voice to suit his conversation and how to sit on my hands and hold my head down.

When I passed my A-levels I was offered a place at art school in London. My father wanted me to study engineering if I was going to 'waste time' instead of going out to get a proper job. We had arguments about it and I thought that I wasn't going to be allowed to go. My mother talked him round, in the end, and he gave in because he loved her and she was the rock upon which his life was built.

At last I set off for the big city. It was like being free when you'd been in prison for most of your life. I studied fashion and design, and every time I drew the female shape and dressed it in gorgeous fabrics and accessories I knew that that was what I was inside, not the lanky lad who everyone thought was obviously gay. By then I had friends, too, whom I loved and trusted. And an older man who taught me how it felt to be loved properly for who I was. I had no money but I started thinking seriously about gender reassignment. I even went so far as to see my GP to ask about the possibility of this being funded by the NHS.

Mam knew all about this, but we'd both agreed that the time wasn't right to talk to my dad. It was something that was going to take a long time for him; acceptance was not going to come overnight. She wanted to tell him that I was gay, but that wasn't the right thing. I wasn't gay, I was a woman who fancied men the same way as my sisters did. My genitals were wrong;

my hormones were wrong. For me it was as simple as having an illness, a physical handicap that meant my bits were malformed and malfunctioning. No different really from having diabetes or hyperthyroidism or any other illness related to the wrong sort of enzyme or hormone.

She didn't tell him, in the end. She left it up to me to tell him at the right time.

Of course, that right time never presented itself until it was all too late. I started going to the gender identity clinic, and after that I started to live as a woman on a permanent basis. This was relatively easy in London, especially in the arty fashion circles I inhabited. Everything felt right for the first time – apart from my relationship with Derek, which faltered. While I wasn't a gay man, he was, and, as much as he loved me, he wasn't looking for a female life partner, after all.

I moved out of his London flat and back in with some friends from college.

On my twenty-first birthday, still drunk from a whole weekend of partying, I found myself on a train home. Our house was near the station and I'd slept on the train, and what on earth I thought I was doing I honestly had no idea. It was mid-morning and on a normal day my dad would have been at work. Except he'd been off for a month with depression, something my mam hadn't told me. And I turned my key in the lock and walked into the living room, expecting Mam to make me a cuppa and present me with a cake she would have made even though she wasn't expecting me to visit, but she wasn't there. Just him. And he was watching the twenty-four-hour news channel, looking up from it to see me in his living room, his third daughter if he'd only realised, but I was still Edward then – and I was wearing a short skirt and platform heels to go with it. He looked me up and down, his mouth open. And the shock of seeing him drowned me like a cold bath and all I could think to say was, 'Hello, Dad.'

He let out a howl of rage and distress, got up from the sofa and launched himself at me. I exited the house as quickly as I'd arrived, tottering up the street back towards the station thinking that he was following me and any minute now he'd strike my head with a massive blow. And when I got to the end of the street I looked back and he was nowhere to be seen.

When I got back to London I phoned Mam. She was home from work by then and had found him. He was alright, she assured me. But of course he wasn't. She tried to shield me from all that, but he hanged himself a week later. It wasn't just down to me, of course, or at least that's what my mam insisted. Maybe she was being kind.

She asked me to wear 'something decent' for the funeral. That hurt me a lot. I felt it acutely, the loss of my dad whom I loved very much. The falseness of my mam's approval of who I was was just another sting. My sisters turned against me then, even though they'd known about me changing and both of them had visited me in London and seen the real me. I wore a tailored trouser suit to the funeral and had my hair done for it. It wasn't my usual look, it was a compromise, but they still didn't recognise it as such.

They never spoke to me again, and I barely spoke to my mam afterwards, either. With my share of the inheritance I got the deposit for a house not far from the one we all grew up in. I wanted to feel close to what was left of my dad, who would have been a different man if he'd grown up a generation later, and close to my mam who was ailing now without anyone left to look after. I wanted to help her but we couldn't be close again, not after all that.

I thought I was starting to recover from it, I thought I was getting my head back above water, but I had a letter from the NHS to say that they would no longer consider funding my surgery because they were aware that I had the private finance to do it. I didn't, of course; I'd spent it on buying the little house. I tried to put the house on the market but by then the bottom had crashed out of it and there were no buyers around. I asked my eldest sister for help but she put the phone down on me, and when I went round there she didn't answer the door, despite the car being on the driveway and the fact that I could hear her kids playing in the back garden.

I didn't realise how easy the solution was, not really. Not until someone showed me. All you have to do is go home and close the door. For some people it's harder – they have to plan, they have to do it gradually. I'd done the hard work all by myself, it was only the little nudge, the little whisper that made me realise the easiest thing to do was to cease to be.

So I went home, and I closed the door, and waited for the black cloud to carry the sun away.

Annabel

'Drink this,' he said.

I opened my mouth and tried to reach for the cup – glass – to hold it but he held on to it and it bumped against my lower lip and teeth.

'I've got it,' he said. 'Drink.'

It was cold and it made me cough. When I'd stopped coughing I opened my eyes and looked and he held up the glass again and this time I drank, two or three gulps, cold water going down my throat. It tasted wrong, made me feel sick.

'Do you recognise me, Annabel?' he asked.

I stared at the face for a moment. There was a name that went with it but I couldn't remember. It was as though the name had been wiped away.

'It's Sam. Sam Everett. Do you remember we met a few times?'

'I don't know,' I said.

'It will be alright,' he said. His voice sounded wrong to me: annoying, discordant, a buzzing – like a fly, or a wasp, somewhere in the room. 'You'll be fine, I promise. I'm going to look after you.'

'Go away,' I said.

'I'm not going,' he said. He sounded sad. 'I'm not going anywhere.' He held the glass up to my lips again but I turned my head. It wasn't the thing to do any more. I wasn't supposed to do this. 'Don't go to sleep, Annabel,' he said. 'Stay with me. Stay awake.'

My eyes were closing. I was tired, and I had to wait until six o'clock.

Colin

I rang Vaughn at eleven o'clock today to ask if he fancied a pint. It feels like a long time since I last saw him – in fact, the last time was when he was scooting out of the pub in search of an engagement ring for Audrey, a whole week ago.

'Colin,' he said cheerfully, when I rang. 'What's this number, then? Your happy little face didn't come up in the caller display.'

I had to think about that for a second, and then I realised my mistake. 'Oh, I'm ringing you from the work mobile. Does it matter? It's still me.'

'Shall I save it in my contacts this time?' he asked. 'I don't always answer if I don't recognise the number. I told you that before, remember.'

'Don't bother,' I said. 'It'll probably be a different one next week. They're supposed to be upgrading them all.'

That seemed to pacify him, anyway. I forgot I'd called him from the wrong phone once before and he'd got all shirty about it.

If I'd hoped that a pint and sandwich with Vaughn would lighten my mood, I would have been sadly disappointed. There's nothing cheering about the place itself, with its brown carpet and wobbly bar stools; nothing to lift the spirits either in Vaughn's countenance or behaviour. He seems almost as miserable as I am.

'How's Audrey?' I ask, when I've ordered my sandwich and sat down opposite him.

'She said no,' he says dismally.

'No? Really? Why?'

'Said she's not ready to settle down.'

'I thought you said she'd been giving off hints.'

'Well, that's what I thought. But turns out I was way off the mark.'

I take a long gulp of the pint of bitter. It tastes faintly, ever so slightly, off. 'What do you mean? What does she want?'

Vaughn sighs heavily. 'You tell me, Colin. I've given up trying to make sense of what women want or expect from us.'

'So,' I say, trying to choose my words carefully and still probably failing, 'she's dumped you?'

He looks aghast. 'No, nothing like that!'

'Well, what, then?'

'She just doesn't want to be engaged, that's all.'

I make a noise that tries to express sympathy for Vaughn, disgust at Audrey and relief that they are still in some kind of relationship. It comes out as a 'Hmmm. Pfft.'

'This pint's off,' I say after a while, and go to tell them to change the barrel.

Vaughn's problems are tiny, pale and uninteresting in comparison to mine, like the runt of a particularly average litter. I've lost one of my subjects – the woman with the satchel. That hasn't happened to me for a long time, since I became choosier about which subjects to engage with.

I called her at six last night, as arranged, and the phone went unanswered. I wondered if she had already expired and begun to transform – but that would have been very quick, even without water. When I drove past the house on my way home, there was an ambulance and a police car parked outside.

However much I try to kid myself that I'm not bothered, I am still pissed off at my own negligence. I've failed her, but, more importantly, I've failed myself; and losing one when the police are already showing an interest in my activities is a big risk.

I lost others, particularly in the beginning. Ones that were unsure, or maybe were less isolated than they first appeared. I thought that sooner or later someone – a family member, perhaps – would put in a complaint about me, or alert the authorities, but nobody ever contacted me with regard to this. As I refined my technique I took steps to guard against discovery. Taking their mobile phones away and leaving them with a replacement for me to keep in touch with them was one particularly genius idea. On more than one occasion I have sent reassuring replies to texts from people who seem a little concerned, and once or twice I have given up on people and not returned to them at all in case they are found.

Each loss is a shame. Some of them were really interesting, too: ones whose transformation I had been looking forward to very much.

All day today I have been trying to reassure myself that they have no way of connecting me with her. And if they do, what of it? I spoke to her. She invited me into her house. She asked me for help, and I provided it. I have done nothing wrong.

Sitting beside the morose Vaughn, I can't help feeling a shiver of arousal at the thought of Audrey's rejection of him. And it is a rejection, no matter what spin he thinks to put upon it. She is not ready to commit to him, which means she might consider playing with someone else. She might consider me…

'Do you want me to have a word with her?' I ask.

Vaughn looks up from his food. I can always tell when he is miserable because he chooses a sausage and egg baguette instead of a ham salad. This makes for a noxious concoction of brown sauce, ketchup and egg yolk which invariably dribbles down his chin (where it will be wiped) or down his sad brown tie (where it will remain).

'Really?' he says, or that's what it sounds like through a mouthful of partially masticated meat-and-dough.

I give him a disgusted look which I hope he takes on board. 'If it might help,' I say. 'You never know.'

His eyebrows furrow. It looks like confusion to me, but I can never quite work this out. Suspicion. Maybe it's suspicion.

'Or – not. It was just a thought.'

He swallows the last of the mouthful and sups some of his pint. Then he clears his throat. 'It's a very kind offer, Colin. Thank you. But...'

'But?'

'Well – it's just that Audrey... she's not very – I don't know – comfortable with you.'

'Comfortable?' Much as it galls me to find myself repeating everything Vaughn says to me, I can think of no better response.

'After the dinner party. She said you were a bit strange. Anyway, sorry. I don't think you'll be able to help. Not this time.'

'Strange? What on earth...' I look at Vaughn and then at the remains of my sandwich, suddenly unappetising and stale. But strange could be a good thing, couldn't it? Maybe she meant strange as in unusual – enigmatic – mysterious.

'I think it was just that evening,' Vaughn says quickly, apparently anxious to avoid offence. 'She was in a funny mood even before you arrived. Hormones, probably.'

I nod and murmur something to indicate assent, but inside I feel my blood churning in my ears. When I leave the pub and go back to the office, I cannot concentrate on anything. I feel the weight of it, the sudden desire to find Audrey and talk to her and ask her what she meant by the word 'strange'. Even Garth and his disgusting ruminatory noises do not distract me. I work on a document for a committee meeting next Monday but Audrey does not leave me, not for a second.

Annabel

In the hospital they put me on a drip and made me see a psychiatrist who prescribed me anti-depressants. The psychiatrist told me I'd experienced some kind of 'episode', which in years gone by might have been described as a breakdown. He said I had been through a lot of stress and I had not been able to process it, so my mind had shut down for reasons of self-preservation.

It all sounded plausible, but there were things about it that felt wrong. My memory of the week before was not just hazy but downright incorrect. It felt as though things had happened which were not available for me to consider. Part of me was desperate to get back home and shut the door and forget all about it, to go back to being on my own, at peace with everything.

When I said this to a nurse it prompted another visit from the psychiatrist, who asked me in a roundabout way, and then more directly, if I felt suicidal. He'd asked me this before, along with a whole load of other questions that I'd tried my best to answer.

'Not really,' was my response.

'Do you feel like it sometimes?'

'I don't think so.' Suicide was an active thing, a doing thing; it would require me to launch into a process that involved activity. No: what I wanted was the absence of activity. I wanted to cease. I wanted to lie still and let the world carry on. Nobody said the word DEATH but it was in my head. It was the same thing as LIFE. For some reason, they were the same thing, linked by an invisible band, the end and the beginning and the end, an endless circle going round and round, a wheel.

If I was not afraid of life, then I was not afraid of death. They were the same.

I think they had been on the verge of discharging me at that point, but instead they moved me from a medical ward to a psychiatric ward.

Colin

You want to know how it all started, don't you? You want to hear how I went from a mind-numbing adult education course in how to make friends and influence people, to steering strangers down a path of self-destruction?

This is what happened.

In the beginning, there were three: Eleanor, Justine, Rachelle.

Eleanor was studying Italian in the room next door at the university, on a Thursday night. I saw her and wanted her. She had long hair that was heavy and dark and looked as though it would feel silky if you touched it. I would go early to the class and hang around in the refectory first, hoping to see her. She was always alone. She didn't sit with others, even the other people from her class. Sometimes she would arrive half an hour before the class started and sit in the refectory with her textbooks, reading through something in them, or looking over a printout of what was probably her latest assignment. I sat at the back and watched her: the way her shoulders hunched, the way she sat, her legs crossed at the ankle under the plastic chair.

And I kept seeing Eleanor, each Thursday evening. Each time I saw her I wanted her a little bit more. The hardest part of the process, of course, was making that initial contact. Having the guts to go up and talk to her. I asked Nigel, making subtle changes to the situation since the whole point of the class was not soliciting for sex but rather for business. So I asked him about cold calling (which I'd cleverly worked out was probably the workplace equivalent).

He told me that people buy from human beings. Make the initial contact personal, open and friendly. Think about how you talk to your friends, Nigel said. Think about the tone of voice, the posture, the way you smile at them.

Easier said than done, of course.

If you don't ask, you don't get, said Nigel. Quitters are never winners. The only thing stopping you is you.

In the end, I just sat down in front of her one Thursday in the refectory. 'My name is Colin,' I said, offering her my hand.

She looked startled, but shook my hand nonetheless. 'Eleanor,' she said.

'What class are you taking?' I asked.

'Italian,' she said. 'Room six.'

Up close, she was even more attractive: dark eyes, a clear, pale complexion. I cleared my throat. 'Is it any good?'

'It's OK.'

It wasn't going particularly well so far. She was holding her coffee cup with both hands, as though she was cold. I mirrored her position, even though I didn't have a drink to hold. I searched around desperately for something to say, something intelligent, something engaging.

'*Il miglior fabbro*,' I said.

'What?'

'Eliot. It's his epigram to Ezra Pound, for *The Waste Land*. "*Il Miglior Fabbro*" – he made it better, he was the better craftsman. I believe that's what it means, in any case.'

'Oh, right,' she said. Then, 'We're still on "Please can you direct me to the railway station?"'

I smiled at her. 'Well, you can keep Eliot in mind for the future, then.'

She seemed to be relaxing, if her posture was anything to go by. She moved one of her hands under the table and I did the same.

'Do you live locally?' I said. It sounded lame. Why was this so bloody difficult?

'Just in town,' she said.

'Will you come for a drink with me, after class?'

The question, so carefully prepared and phrased – no 'I wonder if you'd like to' or 'I don't suppose you're free…' – just a definite, firm, confident question. She could only say no, after all.

She looked startled. I thought she was going to refuse, so I tried again. 'I'll meet you outside, at half-past nine.'

'Yes,' she said. 'Alright, then.'

That was the moment when I knew it was going to work. You can't have doubt when you're trying to bring people around to a particular way of thinking using NLP – you have to at least try to believe what you're saying or else the message will be diluted and might not get through. I knew I had a long way to go and that I needed to refine my technique, but that 'yes' from Eleanor gave me the confidence to work at it. If I could get a woman to agree to meet me, the possibilities that opened up were beautiful and endless, a warm sea lapping against a tropical island.

The classes were due to begin and the refectory was starting to empty, chairs scraping noisily on the tiled floor. We both stood up. What was I supposed to say now? How could I reinforce it?

'Thanks,' I said. 'See you later, then.'

'Sure. See you later.'

Dammit. 'Thanks'? How lame! Still, she went off to her class and I went off to mine, and all through it I could hardly keep still, writing notes in my book about what I would say to her, topics to keep the conversation flowing, and notes in the margin… 'own it'… 'be the message'.

The situation with Eleanor was I believe what they call a good start. It's hard to pinpoint where exactly things went wrong, and I've considered all the possibilities many, many times in the months that followed. I did not rush things with her; I thought about everything I said to her and the implications. If I met her again tonight, I doubt I would do anything differently. I have refined things since then, of course, made adjustments to my technique because of what happened, and I'm certainly much more skilled in adapting my responses as required. Of course, it's worth considering that I did not achieve my desired results with Eleanor because, at that time, I did not fully realise what they were. I had this clumsy, eager desire for an attractive woman to find me cartoonishly irresistible when in fact my calling was an altogether higher one.

Perhaps Eleanor was given to me for just such a purpose. She engaged with me without being interested. She and I connected but we did not kiss or touch or become intimate in any sexual way. Instead she threaded her soul through mine and met with me in a far more intimate place than we could ever have achieved through physical contact.

I suppose what happened was that she was already too far down the path.

I read a lot of Eliot and Rilke after my father's death, attempting to achieve an understanding about this process that we all endure eventually and to which he had been called earlier than might otherwise have been expected. Eliot's perception of birth and death as being essentially one and the same resonated, and I twisted my way through the *Four Quartets* night after night, looking for my father's soul and occasionally feeling I was catching a glimpse of him, his shroud a wisp of smoke behind a door, his scent in the air like a warm current in the sea.

My favourite poem of Rilke's was the one where Orpheus heads off to the underworld to reclaim his lost love Eurydice. He is charged with looking only forward, trusting that his wife and her companion are following behind; when he cannot stand it any more and chances a look at her she has already turned back – what was it he said? 'Her sex was closed, like a young flower in the evening.' Orpheus' So-Beloved was inaccessible, her virginity retrieved through death. She was rooted in death. She was heavy with her great death (birth and death again, inextricable, as with Eliot) – as though she was pregnant with it, pregnant with sweetness and the dark.

And so it was with Eleanor. She was too far gone, rooted in death even as she was still alive, still walking and talking and carrying on with it, day after day, heading towards the end without any desire to turn back.

I recall standing with her in the car park behind the pub. She seemed uncertain, dazed, as though the night spent in conversation with me had dulled her senses and made her oblivious to the world around her. 'I can take you home,' I said to her, my hand gently resting on her arm. It was quite dark, the only light from the windows of the pub. They had a security light that kept coming on and off every few minutes. I thought about what I was doing all the time, listening to her, trying to tune in to her thoughts and hoping that what I was saying was having an effect. She listened to me and heard my instructions but for some reason she was not responding in the way I'd hoped. There was a barrier between us.

I did not want to ruin things. I did not want her to walk away from this without me by her side. I wanted to take her to her house, shut the door behind us and lock it so that we were not interrupted. I wanted to take my time and to explore everything she had to offer – beautiful Eleanor. The girl of my dreams.

There was an element of nerves to be taken into consideration. Maybe I had dulled the message by my hesitancy. One needs to be so careful with this, so sure of oneself and one's intentions. To listen, to observe.

'Home?' she asked, as though she'd never heard the word before.

'Come with me,' I said.

I started to walk back towards the car but she didn't follow. I think this was the moment I lost her.

'I'm not sure,' she said, her voice low so I could hardly hear what she was saying. 'I don't know where home is. I don't know what you mean.'

I knew it was too late. I was agitated, disappointed, and as hard as I tried I wasn't going to be able to stop that coming out in my body language, my posture, my tone. 'Go home,' I said. 'Go home, shut the door and don't come out again.'

'Yes,' she said.

'Fine,' I said.

When I drove past her a few moments later she was still standing there. I spent that evening going over everything I'd said to her, everything she'd said in reply. And I made notes and thought about how I would do it next time.

I didn't intend to cause her death; after all, my plan had been simply to try to find a girlfriend. So it wasn't my fault that she killed herself the day after our date. She had given no indication of her intention when we parted; she was quiet, yes, but this was not so very different from her normal demeanour.

A few weeks later, I saw a news report that Eleanor's body had been found at her home by a concerned relative. The body had been found at the foot of the stairs in a state of decomposition; nevertheless, it was clear that she had hanged herself from the banister. They suggested it had happened at some point between her leaving her evening class on Thursday, and Saturday. I wondered for a while whether anyone would come and interview me; surely people had seen us talking in the refectory – maybe someone had observed us leaving the campus together, or at the pub. But, although I prepared a benign story about considering taking Italian next term, nobody ever troubled me to hear it.

Drinking my third whisky the same evening, lips already numb, cheeks warm, I wondered what might have happened if I had gone to Eleanor's house with her that Thursday night. I wished I had been there when she'd done it, watched her take that final step. Been there as she made that decision. And then I realised with a glow of sudden arousal that I had been there after all – because she'd made the decision that evening, in the pub, when I was with her. At the time, I believed she had listened to my instructions and taken them on board, but that something I'd said had been misinterpreted… when I was telling her she should go home, shut the door and not come out again, she had accepted it. She had not chosen her path at all. I honestly thought that I had taken the pain of the decision away from her. So many tiresome decisions, so much to consider, to think about: and in reality there was only one she needed to make. I thought I had helped her with that. I'd told her to do it – and it was done.

With the benefit of hindsight, of course, I know now that it is highly unlikely that anything I said to her that night made any difference. But either way, the end result was that she followed a path to quick, savage self-destruction. She was dead even as I drove away from her that night. In the car park, breathing, heart beating, but a corpse all the same. The transformation had already begun.

By then, however, I had other matters to attend to – I had moved on to Justine.

Annabel

I wished they would leave me alone.

In the morning they would make me get up and dressed and then they would sit me in a chair. Every time I closed my eyes, someone would come along and wake me up.

At night when they should have left me to sleep I would hear people talking in the corridors, shouts from the others, footsteps walking backwards and forwards.

Maybe this was how they wanted me, permanently in a state of semi-consciousness.

They wanted me to talk to them, but I could not. There were no words left. I had no time or patience for this. I wanted to sleep and be left alone.

Colin

Justine came to me via that most prosaic of meeting places, an internet dating site. It was all made so much simpler after Eleanor's death, when I let go of the idea of a relationship. Why had I aspired to it, for all these years? There was nothing of any value in it for me. No, what I really wanted was sex, with a woman, preferably an attractive one, who would do everything I required of her and would have no expectations of anything further. Having had limited success with Eleanor, I went back to the books and worked out a refinement of my technique, which I thought had the potential to work. And, if it didn't, then having made contact via the internet would facilitate a severance with the minimum of awkwardness.

It took no time at all to find one. I created a fictitious profile, inventing myself as Mark Baxter, an IT consultant, single; spent a frustrating evening working my way through hundreds of female profiles looking for one that might at least be tolerable, and nearly gave up. The next evening I tried again and this time I spotted Justine. She was single, no children, and lived in north London. She said she was looking for 'no-strings fun' and listed various bland characteristics that I neither possessed nor fully understood. What the hell was a good sense of humour, anyway? What was a 'kindred soul'? Her image showed a woman in her early thirties, shoulder-length brown hair, a smile which showed white, even teeth. She was looking at someone to her left, out of the picture. Maybe it was the lack of eye contact that I found particularly appealing.

I sent her a message. Within a few minutes she replied. For half an hour or so we corresponded using the messaging system on the website, and then she asked for my email address so she could send me a picture. I hadn't anticipated this. I messaged her to say my phone was ringing and I would be back shortly, then I went to create a Hotmail account in the name of Mark Baxter.

A couple of minutes later I was back and she was still there, waiting for me. I messaged her the email address and said I was breathless with anticipation.

Hope you like it

When the email came through I was half-expecting a picture of kittens or some awful artwork or something, but it turned out to be Justine, wearing a pale blue bikini, sitting on some rocks, yellow sand between her toes and a foamy wave to the right. I was looking at her belly, tanned, not tight and muscular but a little loose, a small roll of flab just over the top of her bikini pants. Her hair was dry on the top, the wind lifting her fringe, the ends of her hair wet and hanging in rat's tails.

What do you think?
Very nice.
Thats called damming with faint praise
You mean damning.
Whatever
Alright, it's better than very nice.
Hmmmm
Who took the picture?
My sister
You were on holiday somewhere?
Greece, 2 summers ago
Looks as if you were having a good time.
Yes. My sister died six months after
I'm sorry to hear that.
She had cancer

I had no reply. This wasn't the way I needed the conversation to go, and I had no idea how to get from here to asking her for sex, which was, after all, the purpose of this phenomenal waste of a perfectly good evening. As it turned out, though, she managed to surprise me. A few moments later another message came.

You can cheer me up Mark. Do you want to meet?

I met her in a bar in Crouch End. She was three minutes late. I was wearing a black jacket, as agreed, although there were other men in there wearing black jackets I was the only one who was alone and therefore I assumed she would have no trouble recognising me. I had also provided her with a recent picture of my face and shoulders.

She'd aged a lot since the Greece picture, I thought. Her hair was still brown but it had an inch of grey at the roots, and her face was pale, not tanned, and lined around the eyes and mouth. Other than that, she was perfectly acceptable. I shook her hand when she came over.

'So…' she said.

'Shall I get you a drink?' I asked her.

'Dry white wine, please,' she said.

I went to the bar and handed over a ten-pound note in exchange for a small wine and a half of Coke. I would have quite liked a pint with a whisky chaser, but not at these sorts of prices. And besides, if Justine invited me back to her house I would still need to drive home afterwards.

I asked her about herself, avoiding the topic of her sister and her unfortunate demise, and found out that she lived alone, worked part-time for an insurance company in their call centre, went to salsa classes on a Tuesday night and had been single for six months. She had no pets and was on the waiting list for an allotment. She was a vegetarian. She enjoyed meeting new people and, although she wasn't particularly looking for a new relationship, she would be open to it if the right person came along.

It was amazing how simple it was to get someone to share so much personal information without volunteering anything in return. Every time she asked me something I would offer a general answer and then enquire more about her, leaning forward, maintaining eye contact, smiling at her and making a resolute effort to listen to her responses. Within the hour she was leaning towards me, playing with her hair, touching me on the knee.

Half an hour after that we were making our way on foot to her house, a few streets away. She stopped outside a terraced house and on the doorstep she put her hands around my waist, inside my jacket. This sudden contact came as a shock but I recovered quickly and moved closer to her, feeling the warmth of her body. She turned her face up towards mine and I thought she must want me to kiss her, so I did that. Her mouth was dry and her breath smelt of wine. I touched her cheek and she opened her mouth. It was like kissing Helen again. I pulled back from her. 'Shall we go inside?' I asked.

'I'm not sure,' she said, looking at me with her head tilted to one side.

'What are you unsure about?'

'You might be a serial killer,' she said.

I laughed out loud at that and she held me a bit tighter.

Then she smiled. 'You're too sweet to be a serial killer,' she said. She let go of me then and opened the door, turning on the lights in the hallway and leaving the door open for me to follow her inside.

Justine had a greater impact on me than any of the others, even Eleanor. By giving herself to me so freely, she made me realise that the fun was not in the accepting but in the taking; that this wasn't about casual sex, it wasn't something to be taken as a pastime, an amusement; it was a vocation. A calling.

We had sex in her bedroom, in the dark. Her body was somewhere in between angel and whore, I suppose: clean, and slack. She kept trying to kiss me but that always made me think of Helen, so I turned my head away. I'd remembered to take a condom with me and thankfully she applied it. After that it was very quick. I lay next to her in the darkness feeling sated and disappointed at the same time. I had expected so much more. I had expected – what? – a connection.

When she put an arm across my stomach and moved closer against me, I moved away and sat on the edge of the bed, my hands loose between my knees. I could see my penis, hanging flaccid, spent, mocking.

'Are you OK, Mark?' Justine said, from behind me.

'I need to go,' I said.

'Already? Can't you stay for a bit?'

'I've got work in the morning.'

The rest was unspoken. I thought she would ask about seeing me again, but thankfully she did not. She looked sad, but I could do nothing about that. There was nothing wrong with her, other than compliance.

She was irrepressibly, resolutely alive. And that was without doubt a disappointment.

Annabel

Sam came to see me most days. At first when he came I could only stare at the clock on the wall opposite while he asked me questions. Some days I pretended to be asleep. But after a few days I realised I didn't mind him being there, and actually I found myself waiting for him to turn up. I think that was when I must have been getting better, because I began to feel like talking.

'Why are you here?' I asked. 'You should be at work.'

'I can go back in later,' he said. 'How are you feeling?'

I didn't answer that. I had no words to describe it. Or, more accurately, I had no feeling. No sensation of anything other than vague disappointment that I was still here.

'Annabel?'

I looked across to him, aware that it was my name and therefore I should respond to it. 'What?'

'Do you want to know how the investigation's going? Andrew Frost said he'd been to see you. He wanted to keep you updated.'

I tried to remember if anyone else had visited me but it was all just a blur. I looked back at the clock. I waited every day for the line, the perfect straight vertical line that denoted six o'clock, expecting something to happen. Expecting relief, expecting silence, expecting a feeling of peace. But it never came, and by five past six every day the process of waiting had begun all over again.

The clock said twenty past eleven. I felt like going to sleep properly, but soon it would be lunchtime, and in any case every time I tried to sleep during the day someone came by and woke me up. There were rules on this ward, and one of them was that sleeping happened at night. Despite the noises, the shouts and the cries.

'He told me they really need you back, Annabel.'

'I don't know anything,' I said.

'There are so many questions they need to ask you. What happened to your phone? Who gave you the other phone?'

'I don't know.'

'You must have met someone, Annabel. You must have met a person who gave you a mobile and took yours away. Can you remember?'

I tried to concentrate because maybe he would stop asking if I gave him the right answer, but there was nothing there – just a comfortable blackness, a warmth, a space in which everything had been fine until I was ripped out of it and brought to this white, loud, cold place.

'I can't remember anything.'

'Did you go out? Did you meet someone while you were out?'

The nurse came then and interrupted him. He sat quietly and smiled at her while she checked on me. 'You're talking to us today, Annabel? That's really good to hear. Would you like to go outside for a walk?'

'No,' I said.

'Maybe your friend could take you.'

Sam said, quickly, 'Yes – I could take you out for a bit. What do you think?'

'I don't know,' I said.

'It's a lovely day. It would do you good to get some fresh air.'

The nurse put me into a wheelchair even though I could have walked. Maybe she knew that if I'd not been in the chair I would have kept on walking right out of the doors and away.

Sam pushed me out of the fire door and into one of the quadrangles. It was surrounded by buildings; there was no way out even if I could have managed to stand up and run. He sat me in the sunshine and I tipped my head back and felt the warmth of it on my face. A breeze lifted my hair, which was greasy and itchy. The rest of me was clean, though – they'd made me take a shower yesterday and I'd stood there until they came to take me out again.

'There was a rainbow,' I said.

'What?'

'I saw a rainbow. It's the last thing that happened. And the angel.'

'The angel?'

He must know I was talking metaphorically, I thought. The angel was my angel; he wasn't going to appear to anyone else. As far as they were all concerned the angel was a figment of my imagination, only I knew he was real. He was the one who could change everything, who came to me when I most needed him, when I was desperate and lonely and sad. He came to me and showed me the path to take. Sam clearly didn't have an angel and it made me sad for him.

'It's not real,' I said, trying to console him. 'None of it's real. You know that.'

'How do you know it was an angel?' he asked. His voice was calm, quiet.

'He made me feel better. He took all of the bad stuff away.'

'What did he say, do you remember?'

'He said I was fine, that everything was fine. He told me to go home and that I didn't need to worry about anything.'

'Did he give you something to drink, something to eat?'

I started to laugh, which made me cough. 'He wasn't that sort of angel.'

'I'm worried he wasn't a good angel, Annabel.'

I opened my eyes and squinted at him, my eyes adjusting to the bright light until I could focus on his face. It was the first time I'd looked at him properly for a while and I had a sudden recollection of meeting him outside the hospital, how annoyed I'd felt at that intrusion, but how afterwards he'd made me feel better about Mum, about what had happened to her. He had a nice face, and his eyes reminded me of my dad's; how they seemed to be smiling even when he was being serious. He was kind, I thought. Kind to keep visiting me.

'What do you mean?'

He was sitting on a bench and the wheelchair was parked right next to it, so he could reach across and take hold of my hand, which was in my lap. His hand was warm, his grip firm.

'What if he was pretending to help you? What if he was pretending to be an angel?'

The answer came automatically. 'I don't know anything.'

He tried again. 'Do you know where you are, right now?'

I looked around at the buildings surrounding the patch of green. 'It's a hospital,' I said. 'I think it's a hospital.'

'That's right,' he said. 'You're here because you were at home on your own and it looked as if you hadn't eaten any food or drunk any water for four days.'

I could hear the words he was saying but they didn't make any sense. I hadn't felt thirsty, or hungry. I had just wanted to sleep. I had wanted it all to go away, to be left alone. But it was different now, wasn't it? The sun was shining on me.

'They said you were trying to starve yourself to death.'

I shook my head. 'No, that's not right.'

'I said the same thing to them. I said you were busy with the investigation, you had things to do – yes, it had been a rough time for you, with your mum dying, but you didn't want to die. You weren't trying to kill yourself, were you?'

'No,' I said. 'I just wanted to go to sleep.'

'They think you want to kill yourself. That's why you're here.'

'I just wanted to sleep,' I repeated.

I concentrated hard and suddenly something came back to me.

'I remember him visiting,' I said.

'Who? The man?'

I tutted with annoyance. 'No, Frosty. I remember him coming here... sitting by the bed. He wanted to know why I hadn't told him I was depressed.'

252

'He's a kind man, Annabel. He thinks you've had such a hard time of it.'

'I didn't even realise that was what depression felt like.'

He frowned, leaning forward in his seat and looking at the ground. 'There's no shame in it. Lots of people have depression. It's not easy to talk about.'

I watched him closely, wondering why it hadn't crossed my mind during those days I was alone that I would never see Sam again.

'When they discharge you,' he said, 'you can come and stay with me, if you like.'

'No, thanks,' I said automatically.

'I don't think they plan on letting you go home, or at least not for a long time. If you stay at my house they might let you out sooner. We'd love to have you, even if you are grumpy and antagonistic most of the time.'

'Thanks!' I said.

'You're welcome.'

I smiled, despite myself.

'My dad's wife – Irene – she's a good cook. And she's a trained carer, so you couldn't be in safer hands. She's longing to start feeding you up, you know. She needs a project.'

'Is that supposed to be tempting?'

'It was my unsubtle attempt at trying to make you feel comfortable about it. Well, what do you think?'

I didn't reply at first. I tried to imagine going home and locking the door. It felt as though that was the right thing to do, the right path to choose... but there was something about it that made me feel afraid.

He shifted in his seat again. 'Do you remember the people who died, Annabel? You were working on all those bodies that were found decomposed in their homes. Do you remember?'

I nodded, although I hadn't thought about them for a long time.

'You remember Rachelle? Do you remember Shelley, the woman you found in the house next door? And the two who were found just before they started the investigation? Do you remember that I had a phone call from one of the victims, telling me where to find another one?'

I frowned at these specifics, trying to grip the memory and stop it slipping away.

'They're still trying to find the man who's responsible for all this, Annabel. I think he's the man you met. I think he did something to you and you were heading the same way as all those other people.'

'But...' Why was this such a struggle? Why wasn't my brain working; why couldn't I think clearly? 'But I was... happy.'

'You were happy, starving to death?'

'It wasn't like that,' I said, shaking my head. 'It was just like... I don't know... it was like floating away.'

'But you didn't want to die?'

'I don't think so. I wasn't trying to kill myself. I just wanted to sleep.'

'But you would have died if I hadn't found you.'

'You found me?'

'I tried to ring you but your phone was switched off. I sent you a text, and a few hours later there was a really weird reply saying you were thinking of going away and you wanted to be left alone. In the end I went round to your house. The back door was unlocked. Your cat was going mental.'

'Cat?'

'Don't worry. I've been going to your house every day and feeding her. She's a lovely cat. What's her name?'

The cat. I tried to find the other word in my head, searched for it, nearly gave up – and then suddenly it was there.

'Lucy. She's called Lucy.'

'Well, that's better than Puss, which is what Irene came up with.'

The colours were too bright, the green of the grass and the leaves on the tree that were red and gold and brown and every imaginable colour in between. And the sky, so blue, a bright blue that hurt my eyes.

'My mum died,' I said. 'It feels like years.'

'It was just over a fortnight ago,' he said. 'I'm sorry. I know how hard grief is – I went through it too. You need time, and as much support as possible.'

'I should be doing things, shouldn't I?'

'I can help you with it. It's alright. I spoke to the family relations officer at the hospital, so they're keeping your mum safe until you're ready. Nothing to worry about.'

The sun went behind a cloud and the breeze felt suddenly cold. I shivered and folded my arms in front of me.

'Do you want to go inside?'

I looked back over my shoulder at the fire door, at the ward beyond it. 'No. Can I stay a bit longer?'

He smiled then, a big happy smile, and I found I was smiling back at him. 'You're going to be OK,' he said.

'Yes,' I said. 'Of course. There's nothing to worry about.'

He reached across to me and rubbed my arm, then patted my knee.

Colin

Rachelle came into my life a month after Justine.

The time between them was spent on study, whisky and porn. The only class I attended in that period was Nigel's NLP – and every evening, after work, I devoted myself to further study in the subject as well as expanding into such topics as hypnosis, mind control and suggestion. I stayed up until I was too tired to see the computer any more, and at that point I would put a DVD on in the bedroom and watch it to the inevitable conclusion.

I knew now what all this had been leading to. I knew and understood it all with an astonishing clarity – that this was my calling, this was what I had been born to do, and that everything that had happened so far in my life had been leading up to this moment.

I met Rachelle whilst I was walking in the country park in Baysbury one Sunday morning. It was a bright day, cold, sunny – the sort of day you'd expect to find a lot of people in the park, which is why I nearly didn't go. I'd forgotten that there was a big football match on and as a result everyone was at home or in the pub watching the game. Everyone except for Rachelle and me.

I walked past her, sitting on the park bench halfway up the hill, and immediately I was struck by her physique and the fact that she was sitting on the bench wearing jogging pants and trainers, a shapeless hooded top that she seemed to be shrinking into.

She did not pay me any attention and so I felt confident enough to turn back and sit down next to her on the bench.

'Hello,' I said.

She didn't reply but she cast a glance in my direction, a nervous smile. She wasn't used to being spoken to. She wasn't used to attracting attention. She was used to hiding.

'It's a lovely day today,' I said.

'Yeah, I guess,' she said. Her voice sounded wheezy.

'You're out for a run?'

'Yeah.'

'I can do this hill in thirty-five seconds,' I said. I had no idea if such a thing was even possible; it was a random guess at a number that completely did the trick: as if I'd flicked a switch, she engaged.

'Really? Thirty-five? I can only manage sixty. That was last week.'

'You're fit,' I said.

'No,' she said. 'I'm too...'

She'd stopped herself from saying it.

'You're on a journey,' I said. 'Every day is a step towards your goal.'

She looked up at me with astonishment in her eyes, blue eyes that looked too big for her pale, gaunt face.

I put a hand – tentative, but it felt like the right time – on her arm. She winced slightly but did not move away. I could feel the bones under my hand, as though the grey fleece fabric was the only thing between me and her skeleton.

'You're right,' I said. 'Everything you think and feel is right. You're choosing the right path.'

'Yes,' she said.

'You can make the decision,' I said. 'You can choose what happens, how it happens.'

'Can I?' She was wavering.

'You know you're right,' I said, keeping my voice even, keeping the eye contact with her. 'You need to do the right thing at the right time.'

'I need to know it will work,' she said.

'It will work. You can make that choice. If you decide it, it will be. You need to know this.'

A few minutes later she took me to her flat, which was a few streets away. We walked past a pub which was so full of people that some had spilled out onto the street, plastic pint glasses in hand, all focused on the big screens inside. The progress of the game – whatever it was – could be determined by the collective whoops and sighs. As we got to her front door I heard yells of delight from various properties and even, possibly, from the pub.

We had not spoken since she had stood up slowly from the park bench and started walking, but still she stood aside to let me into her flat. She was utterly defeated by life. Complicit with me in every possible way. I helped her to find the path she had already, unconsciously chosen. I helped her to bring her miserable existence to an end, simply by giving her the permission she felt she needed to do it. I helped her to transform.

Annabel

They discharged me, in the end. They hadn't managed to get to the bottom of what had happened to me but since I was clearly recovering they said I could go, as long as I stayed with a friend to begin with. There was talk of a referral for therapy, regular outpatient appointments. I had a letter to give to my GP.

Sam came to collect me and drove me to his house in Keats Road. I remembered looking up at the house from my car, the day my mum was in the hospital and I was giving him a lift home. It felt as if a lifetime had passed since then.

I didn't speak at all. He tried to ask me questions but when I didn't answer I think he gave up. I was afraid of everything, scared of the medicated numbness in my head which meant I couldn't think straight, couldn't focus. The hospital was a bad place but in a way the outside world was worse. *I shouldn't be here*, I kept thinking. *I'm supposed to be dead. Am I a ghost now? Is this what it feels like?*

Sam lived with his dad, Brian, a former serviceman who spent most of his time at the Legion drinking with his friends, and Brian's wife, Irene. She was everything my mum hadn't been: bright, vivacious, full of life. She'd been Sam's mum's carer, once upon a time. They both welcomed me into their home without question, offering up their small spare room – Irene apologising for it just as I expressed my profound gratitude that I'd been let out of the hospital thanks to them.

Sam showed me the room upstairs, a single bed with a floral bedspread on it and a soft toy on the pillow.

'I'll leave you to settle in,' he said. 'Would you like a cup of tea?'

'Maybe later,' I said. 'I'd like to sleep.'

He left the door open when he went downstairs. I pulled it to and lay down on the bed and closed my eyes.

The next day Frosty phoned to ask if I was up to talking to someone. Sam had gone to work, leaving Irene with me. Without him I felt a bit lost, cut adrift.

'I guess so,' I said. 'I don't know anything.'

He came round with a female officer I'd not met before, whose name I forgot the minute she introduced herself. We sat in the living room. Irene made the tea and put a tray with home-made apple cake on the table in front of us, all the while talking about the weather and the roadworks in the town centre and the line-up for this year's *Strictly Come Dancing*. When she finally went and left us with just the ringing in our ears, it felt as if we'd all gone deaf.

'You're looking well, Annabel,' Frosty said then. 'How are you feeling?'

'Fine,' I said automatically.

'You don't need to worry,' the young woman said. She was smiling at me. 'Anything you can remember at this stage is useful.'

'I don't remember anything,' I said.

'Sam told us you said there was a man. An angel. Do you remember that?'

I thought about it, closed my eyes. I wanted to help them. I wanted to remember.

'He was just ordinary. Just a normal man. But he said things that made me feel calm. He was kind.'

'Did he go home with you?'

'No,' I said. 'I drove home. There was a rainbow.'

I wanted to add about the rainbow being a sign from my mum, a sign that I could trust him, that she'd sent him to take care of me, but I kept that bit back. They wouldn't have understood. They would have laughed.

'What happened when you went home?'

'Nothing. I went out again the next morning. I spoke to you on the phone,' I said to Frosty.

'I remember,' he said. 'Where were you, when we spoke on the phone?'

'I was in the car park. I was going to the funeral directors.'

'Do you remember going in to see them?'

'No,' I said. I closed my eyes again, struggling to picture it. 'I remember walking towards the office and he was there waiting for me.'

I looked across to Frosty. He was sitting forward, his hands gripped tightly between his knees. Seeing him like that reminded me of something Sam had told me, on one of his daily hospital visits. He said he'd been out the night before with Ryan Frost. Ryan had told Sam that his dad had been preoccupied, miserable, worrying that he'd missed the signs during the phone conversation he'd had with me that morning, when I'd been standing in the car park at the shopping precinct. Apparently I had sounded 'odd'. He thought he should have done something, come to find me.

'Can you tell us what he looked like?' The woman had taken over asking the questions. I felt embarrassed that I couldn't remember her name.

He was an angel, I thought. *You can't describe angels. And he would have looked different, to everyone else.*

I shook my head. 'No. He was just – ordinary.'

'Was he taller than you?'

'I don't remember.'

Frosty was busy tucking into Irene's apple cake, his mouth full of crumbs. I watched him.

'What did you talk about?' the woman asked.

'I don't remember.'

'Did he ask you to go with him?'

I felt tears starting, then, not at the frustration of not being able to remember, but at her insistent questions. I felt as if I was failing them: failing Frosty, failing Sam and Brian and Irene who had all been so kind to me.

261

'Annabel?'

'I don't remember anything.'

'It's OK,' she said, the woman, whoever she was. I didn't like her. She was giving me a headache with her sympathetic smile and her shiny hair and shiny white teeth.

'I want to go back to sleep,' I said. 'I'm really tired.'

I stood up and left the room. Irene was in the kitchen, standing in the doorway looking awkward and fidgety. I thought she had probably been listening at the door and had jumped back when I'd come out, and hadn't had time to arrange herself into an appropriately innocent activity. I looked at her and went upstairs. I didn't mind if she had been listening; I had nothing to hide from her, except my own pathetic brain and its inability to remember what had happened to me.

I lay on the bed, listening to them talking about me downstairs.

'It's very early days,' Frosty was saying. 'I thought she was doing well, though.'

'She *is* doing well,' Irene said. 'She's had a terrible ordeal. She just needs a bit of time.'

'We have to ask,' the woman was saying. 'We can come again, tomorrow maybe. See if anything's come back to her.'

'No,' Irene said. 'We'll call you if she remembers anything.'

'It's not that,' she said. 'This is a murder investigation, Mrs Everett. We need to gather as much information as we can. We know what we're doing.'

'Not with that poor girl, you don't,' Irene said. 'I won't have you pestering her.'

'Look,' said Frosty then, 'this isn't helping. Thank you very much for your time, and for the cake. Will you give me a call, let me know how she is? She can take as much time as she needs.'

Irene let them out of the front door after that and I heard it bang shut, with force. I wondered if she was angry with me.

Colin

I have been revisiting my biology notebooks in the evenings, comparing the notes I made with the images.

Just occasionally, when I'm in the right frame of mind, I will select an album of images to peruse and put on a slide show in the background whilst engaged in some other activity, chores perhaps. It's peaceful. No sounds.

Shelley decayed quickest, perhaps because her house was warmer. I wonder too whether the medication she was taking had some effect on the chemical composition of the bodily fluids. In either case, the highlight was the loss of the forearm, the tendons which would usually hold the skeletal remains in place long after the flesh has disappeared letting her down, the way her body had let her down in life.

I looked at my notes on taphonomy: the study of the processes that take place to a body, human or animal, after death. Taphonomic processes are not limited to decomposition, of which there are four or five recognised stages depending on which book you read (Fresh, Bloat, Putrefaction – occasionally subdivided into Active or 'Wet' Decay and Advanced Decay – and Putrid Dry Remains) but which may include processes involving external activity. Therefore scavenging, maggot feeding, burning and cannibalism are also described as taphonomic processes.

I've always been fascinated by the role of Nature in all this. Should human activity be separated from the taphonomic processes, since it is an intervention? I mean, I can happily consider animal scavenging for inclusion as a process, since animals have a natural instinct to eat carrion, but what about cannibalism? It would be so much better to observe the process with no human intervention whatsoever, to see Nature at work without hindrance. But then, everything now is subjected to human intervention merely through the state of the world as it is. Even a corpse left undisturbed in a remote location would be subject to human intervention – greenhouse gases, the hole in the ozone layer, acid rain – acting to facilitate the decomposition process along with all the factors that Nature brings to the party. And utterly impossible, then, to separate the 'real' from the artificial.

I wish there were someone I could discuss this with. My father, had he survived, would have been interested. He was endlessly fascinated by Nature and I believe I got my interest in the subject from him. On the long walks that my mother insisted we go on every Sunday while she 'rested', he would entertain and educate me about synchronicity, the beautiful, poetic, creative structures and systems of life and death. Everything has a purpose; everything has a place, a right to exist, a function. Birth, life, death, an endless, echoing cycle, a dance to which all the steps are natural and innate. No confusion, nothing wasted, nothing out of place. Change happens at the right time and for the right reasons.

Vaughn called me at work earlier today to postpone our lunch-time drink. He was ringing from home, having not made it in to work. It seems Audrey has made their separation permanent, and Vaughn is too upset to contemplate anything but the loss of her.

'I just don't understand it,' he moaned over the phone. 'We were getting on so well.'

I was tempted to suggest that the beginning of the end was likely to be the moment he considered Weston-super-Mare as a romantic weekend getaway, but I held my tongue.

I have no particular scruples about the notion of 'stealing' Audrey away from Vaughn, although perhaps the idea of her body and where it has been might be a little distracting if I think about it too much. But the fact that she is now single, and presumably in need of some comfort, or at the very least entertainment, consumes my every waking thought.

I have been here before, remember. There was a time before Justine when I wanted a girlfriend. Is that what I want now? Bored with the dance of death, do I now want to return to the unpredictability and despair of life? Part of me wants to fuck her, yes. Part of me does want that. But there is something else.

In all my dealings with the depressed and the lame and the unhinged, I learned quickly that there was no point trying any of my techniques with those who had not already considered the path and taken some steps along it. It simply didn't work, and no amount of tweaks to my procedure made any difference. That was when I learned how to pick the right people. But now I realise that the reason it has all become so stale is not just that if you've seen one human being decompose you've seen them all, but rather that I have such limited choice in the matter. If I could select people at random, it would all be so much more fun.

So perhaps it isn't about helping people who know what path they have chosen any more. Perhaps it is about giving people a gentle shove in that particular direction.

After I finish the chores, I log on to Facebook for the first time in many months. I've opened accounts under various identities, for various reasons, but today I go straight to my own details. I have not bothered to find or add friends, other than Vaughn, who insisted. He remains my only contact. His page proclaims proudly that he is 'in a relationship with' Audrey Madison. I click on Audrey's profile, which states just as proudly that her relationship status is 'complicated'.

To my surprise and pleasure, Audrey's profile is instantly accessible: under 'info' I discover her email address, a whole list of films that she likes (horror and thrillers, in the main), that her musical tastes can best be described as eclectic (Simon and Garfunkel, Metallica, the Beatles) and that she went to school in Northampton followed by the University of Leicester. Her current interests are listed as cooking and going to the gym.

Unfortunately she has chosen not to complete the employment part of the profile. I move on to her friends list (total three hundred and seventeen) and scan down the list of names.

Ten of the friends show their workplace as Arnold and Partners, Briarstone. I click on the link to the Arnold's page. It's an accountancy firm in the town centre. I go back to Audrey's list of friends and commit the Arnold's employees' names to memory, and then go to Audrey's Wall. And there it is, a Wall post from last Friday:

Cheryl Dann: Hope u have a good weekend hunni. See you Monday at work xxx

An internet search of Arnold and Partners takes me to their home page, which helpfully includes a 'How To Find Us' map and their opening hours.

I go back to Audrey's Wall and read down the various status updates, likes and comments. Yesterday Audrey had written:

Audrey Madison: Can't wait for Adele's bday bash Friday night. Been a long while and am in serious need of a night out.

Below that, some of her friends had commented.

Lara Smith: Will be so good to see you. What time r we getting to Lucianos.

Claire McLeod: Table is booked for 8 Lara

Lara Smith: Thanks. See you there!

Cheryl Dann: Woop woop.

Adele Babycakes Strachan: V excited. Bring it.

I go back to the internet and find that there is a Luciano's in Briarstone – an Italian restaurant right in the town centre. It's in the Market Square, which also contains three bars and one of the biggest nightclubs.

After that, I finally allow myself to click back to Audrey's photos. There are twelve albums, of which three are helpfully labelled to suggest they are images from her summer holidays for the past few years.

I start with the oldest: 'Kos Aug 2009'. I stand up before I go any further, take off my trousers and fold them over a hanger and put them back in my wardrobe. And after that, the rest of the evening is spent wanking over the many delicious images of Audrey in a bikini. And she is no longer Vaughn's. For her, it's 'complicated', but for me it is wonderfully simple.

She is mine.

Body of Former Council Leader Found

Police called to a house in Newton Lane last Saturday evening discovered the decomposed remains of yet another person, an elderly male, believed to be former Briarstone Borough Councillor George Armstrong, 92. A police spokesperson said that neighbours had reported a strong smell coming from the property.

Mr Armstrong served as Councillor for Castle Ward from 1975 to 1988 when he retired. He was Leader of the Council in 1980 and 1985 and was considered to be instrumental in securing the future of hundreds of workers at the Langridge paper factory, who had been threatened with redundancy, in 1980.

A neighbour, who did not wish to be named, revealed that Mr Armstrong had not been seen for some time. 'He used to be always out walking; he'd always say hello. I haven't seen him for a few months. I thought he'd gone into hospital, or into a home.'

Marjorie Baker, of Newton Lane, said she believed Mr Armstrong had gone to live with family in Australia. 'I think it's terrible that in this day and age nobody notices you're gone,' Mrs Baker said. 'People should take more care of each other.'

George

Things were never the same for me after Vilette died. Vi, I called her. She was my sunshine and my light and my joy for fifty-nine years. Vi was the reason I was here, just as I was the reason she was here.

268

We met when I was twenty-two, quite by accident as it turned out. I was on shore leave, only two days, and then I was back to sea. It was February and the lake was frozen over. I was taking a short cut across the park back home, I'd been to the shop to get some cigarettes I think. Some errand for my old mum, anyway. I saw a group of girls by the lake, they were scuffling, laughing, you know, mucking about. I saw something fly up into the air and sail in the wind out on to the surface of the lake, something bright blue, like the wing of an exotic bird. It sailed up into the air and the breeze caught it.

Then the girls ran away, laughing, leaving one of their number behind at the edge of the lake.

The blue thing – a silk scarf, as it turned out, that had been given to her French mother when she had lived in Paris before the war, a scarf that young Vi was forbidden to look at, never mind take out of the house, never mind wear – was lying forlorn in a little blue puddle about ten yards from the edge.

Before I could get to her to help, she'd set one foot on the ice and then another, and was walking with a determined but cautious gait towards the middle of the lake, and the scarf. She was only a slip of a girl, just eighteen, light as a feather and tiny, but even so the ice was thinner than it had been when she'd skated on it the weekend before, thinning by the day thanks to the weak February sunshine.

When I was still a hundred yards away the ice cracked beneath her. I was close enough to see the shock on her face, hear her scream, before it cracked again and gave way. She only fell in up to her chest – thankfully the water wasn't deeper than that – but still she clawed on the edge of the ice and could not get any purchase to pull herself out.

'I'm coming,' I yelled, 'don't worry!' – as though that would make any difference to the terror and the pain of being stuck in an icy lake.

I took off my woollen coat and my jumper that mum knitted for me last Christmas and my shirt too, and tied all the sleeves together. That wasn't long enough, so I ended up taking off my vest too and tying that on the end. All the while I could see her turning blue. After that it was just long enough for her to reach, and I told her to wind the end of it around her hands so that she didn't need to grip, and then I hauled her out.

We were both shivering, her more than me of course. By this time a little crowd had gathered, including my brother Tom, who'd come to see where I'd got to. He gave me the coat off his back, and someone else took off their coat and put it round the young woman.

She was taken to hospital but she was alright after that. She even managed to get the scarf put away back in her mother's closet before it was missed.

The next day I went round to see her before I had to go back to the ship and she told me that I'd saved her life. It didn't feel like all that big a deal to me, after all what was I going to do, leave her in there? But by that time I'd seen her big beautiful grey eyes and how she got dimples in her cheeks when she smiled.

We got married in 1943, which was the next time I put in to port – just a quick wedding, me in my uniform, her in a coat she borrowed from a friend and wearing the beautiful blue scarf, lent by her mother.

Vi died the year before we would have had our diamond wedding. We were planning a big party, with our daughter Susan and all her family coming over from Australia, but by the spring both of us knew she wasn't going to last that long. She fought so hard, but in the end it took her the way we knew it would. She died with me holding her hand on a rainy day in March.

I kissed her goodbye and went home.

You want to know about my story, don't you? Well, my story ended on that day I left my Vi behind in the hospital. Things happened after that but they weren't important. Nothing was important any more.

Susan came over from Australia for the funeral. She stayed two weeks and then went back again. I knew she wouldn't come back to England again until it was my funeral, and maybe not even then – after all, I wasn't to know about it either way, was I?

Annabel

Mum's funeral took place eleven days after I left hospital. Sam had helped with the arrangements. He'd asked for quotes from other funeral directors and then got on with the organising, once I was able to start making decisions again. He hadn't wanted me to go back to the Co-operative Funeralcare on my own once I'd worked out that that was where it had happened… where I'd met him, the angel, whoever he was really.

Irene helped me get ready. She let me borrow a black skirt and a nice cashmere sweater; I didn't think it would fit me, but to my surprise it was quite loose.

'What about a bit of make-up?' she asked me. 'Brighten up that beautiful face of yours? Hmm?'

'I don't usually bother,' I said.

'Come with me.'

I was starting to realise that there was no point arguing with Irene. She took me into the bedroom at the front of the house, sat me on the edge of the double bed and fussed around with my face while I kept my eyes closed.

'Always makes me feel better when I've got my lippy on,' she said.

Whenever I'd worn make-up in the past it had made me feel grubby, but I didn't tell her that. It was easier to just let her do whatever she wanted to.

'You're very kind,' I said, 'taking me in like this. What did you think, when Sam told you I was coming to stay?'

She laughed. 'I wasn't surprised. He talked about you a lot. He was really worried when you were in the hospital, you know.'

'Was he?'

'Of course.'

'I don't understand why he takes such trouble.'

Irene was rattling through her make-up bag. I looked at it curiously – how could one person need so much make-up? What was it all even for?

'I think he sees a lot of himself in you, Annabel. He was very depressed when his mum died, you know. He loved her very much. It took him a long, long time to get over losing her.'

'I thought he just wanted to get to the bottom of the story.'

A frown creased her forehead. She was pretty, I thought. Younger than Brian. I wondered how old she was.

'No, that's not our Sam at all. He's a good journalist but he's also a very moral person. He thinks he can help you, so that's what he's decided he's going to do. He's one in a million, Sam is.'

She moved out of the way and let me see myself in the mirror. I looked very different. Not like me at all. I smiled at myself experimentally.

When I went back into my room I found a small white feather on the floor by the bed. It was from my mum, a message to say that she was there, she was with me. Maybe she even liked the fact that Irene was taking care of me. I felt a sense of relief. There had been moments when I wasn't sure if I still believed in angels, and perhaps I'd been hoping for a sign without expecting it. And here it was.

A couple of people from the Social Club came to the funeral; Len from next door, without his wife. To my surprise Kate came along, and told me that, although Frosty had said he was going to try to make it too, something had come up at the last minute. Sam was there, of course. He'd turned into my shadow, and if it went on for much longer he was going to start to get on my nerves.

Even so, the crematorium was horribly empty. She'd isolated herself so much after Aunty Bet left, there was scarcely anyone who knew her, let alone who would call her a friend.

This came as a nasty shock, and it led to a worse one – the realisation that I was heading in exactly the same direction. If they held my funeral, how many people would be there? Probably not that many more than this. And I was trying, every minute, to come to terms with how close I'd been to that day being right now.

Sam held my hand when the service started in the crematorium, three minutes late. They were meticulous timekeepers but I think they were holding out for a few more people. As it was, there wasn't much to say. I wasn't up to speaking in public – even in front of just a few people – so the celebrant read out the eulogy I'd written, with a lot of help from Sam.

I stared ahead at the coffin while the words faded away, and tried to remember Mum as she had been years ago. How much I'd disrespected her when I was a teenager. She must have hated me then.

They played Jim Reeves. After that Sam got up and read out a poem that he'd found online. He read clearly, his voice strong, although he was blushing. He addressed the clock at the back of the room, above the double doors through which we'd entered.

I tried to think of my mother in a brighter place, as the words of the poem suggested, but all I could think of was how much she would hate it if it was crowded.

When Sam sat down again I whispered to him, 'Thanks.'

He took hold of my hand again and squeezed it by way of a reply. When this was over we were going to go back to the house in Keats Road and have a dinner that Irene was cooking on the unspoken premise that I would need food to cheer me up. In the past few days she'd cooked me healthy, nutritious dinners that I'd done my best to eat. It still felt strange, unnecessary; I think if it had not been for their cautious monitoring of me I wouldn't have bothered to eat at all.

The celebrant brought the service to a close and we all got to our feet. The doors opened at the front of the room and we filed out into the drizzle. We looked at the three floral tributes outside, and after that there was nothing to hang around for. I said thank you to Len, all previous awkwardness between us forgotten, and shook his hand before he turned up his collar against the rain and headed back to the car park, hunched into his coat.

'Annabel? I'm off now.'

It was Kate. I had to focus on her hard to remember who she was, even though I'd sat opposite her every day at work for the past three years.

'Oh, right. Thank you for coming. It was... kind of you.'

'That's alright. I was really glad to get the invite.'

'I didn't do the invitations,' I said automatically. 'That was Sam.'

'Oh! I see. Well...' Her cheeks were flushed.

'I mean – sorry. That was rude. I'm just surprised to see you.'

She frowned at me. 'Why should you be surprised? We've all been worried about you, you know. I know you think – God, this is awkward – it always feels like you don't want to be in the office with us. I wish you'd join in a bit more sometimes.'

Now it was my turn to be shocked. 'Really?'

'Of course.' She smiled at me and for once I was almost sure it wasn't all an act. After all, there was just us. Nobody she was trying to impress, nobody she was showing off for.

'So... who's this Sam?' she asked. 'New boyfriend?'

For a moment I was so taken aback I couldn't reply – how could someone possibly think...? But then she went on, 'He's a cutie. Where did you meet?'

She was looking over my shoulder. I turned to see Sam talking to one of the ladies who had come from the social club. He was smiling at her, his head inclined towards her so she could hear him, dark hair falling over his eyes.

'He's not my boyfriend,' I said, shocked.

'Oh,' she said. 'He seems very nice, anyway.'

'He is – he's lovely.'

'But not…?'

I shook my head. *Not my type*, I thought, not having any clue what my type actually was, nor why Sam wasn't it.

'We miss you at work, you know that,' she said. 'I mean it. They all send their love.'

'I'll be back soon,' I said. 'Maybe Monday.'

'Take as much time as you need,' she said. 'But it would be good to have you back.' She turned to go, but hesitated and came back to me. 'You know Frosty's got a whole pile of billings? He's pretending that he knows what to do with them, but you know…'

'Billings? For the job?'

'Yeah. I mean, I could look at them, but it's your baby, isn't it, this one? I don't want to interfere with it.'

'He never said.'

'He's probably trying not to put you under pressure to come back, but you know – if it was me – I'd want to be involved. You don't mind me telling you?'

'No, of course not. And you're right – I do want to be involved. Thanks, Kate.'

She headed back towards the car park. I watched her go, feeling a buzz of excitement inside. I'd not been looking forward to going back to work, remembering that feeling of isolation, but actually speaking with Kate had made me feel a bit more cheerful about it. She hadn't had to come to the funeral, but she'd made the effort, not just to be there but to speak to me afterwards. Maybe things would be better from now on. And now I had a real purpose, a task to do.

Back at Keats Road, Irene had cooked a roast lunch which I had to force down, even though it was delicious. I'd forgotten what hunger felt like. The atmosphere around the table was subdued, which must have been on my account. Every mealtime since I'd arrived had been conducted to the accompaniment of bright conversation and laughter. Brian was a joker, always starting off long anecdotes about friends, work colleagues, Irene or Sam, with a twinkle in his eye which I'd worked out meant that it was a complete fabrication and at the end of it would be some corny punchline. His method of delivery was always the funniest bit.

'Don't mind him,' Irene had reassured me, the first time this happened. That particular story had taken twenty-three minutes to tell from one end to the other, partly because he'd been distracted part-way through it and had lost track, diverting on to a story about someone's dog that had eaten a prawn sandwich containing a hidden anti-anxiety tablet and had to have its stomach pumped (apparently the stomach contents were also found to contain a mysterious diamond ring that nobody recognised, and a Roman coin), and then eventually picking up the thread of the original story about a friend of his who'd accidentally overdosed on his Valium and ended up asleep for five days. None of which was true. I listened to it all, rapt, mainly because it meant I didn't have to say anything.

Irene and Sam seemed to deal with him by talking between themselves – they'd heard it all before, after all. Every once in a while he'd come up with a new one and then they would both listen with smiles on their faces, waiting for the joke.

When we sat down to eat the roast, Brian started off on a story of a funeral he'd been to, of a colleague whose hobby had been ventriloquism. Irene gave him a look across the table and brought the anecdote to an unexpectedly abrupt halt. After that we sat in silence.

'I'm going to go out for a bit,' I said after we'd eaten.

They all looked at me in surprise.

'I'm coming with you,' said Sam, standing.

'No, it's alright. I just need... um... a bit of fresh air.'

Before they could argue I was out of the door and unlocking my car.

The police station car park was mostly empty, which was unsurprising given that it was nearly four o'clock on a Friday afternoon. They were all in the pub, or on the way home, or playing snooker in the club across the road. I parked in one of the Intel bays.

I made my way up to the Incident Room and did not see anyone on the way, but when I opened the door there were three people in the office – all of them on the phone. I vaguely remembered being introduced to them all on that first day, but none of the names came back to me. I sat down at the desk Frosty had given me and logged on at the workstation. Once the system had granted me access, I opened my email and saw that there were four hundred and twenty-seven new messages. That wasn't bad going. I sorted the emails by sender and concentrated on the ones from Frosty. There were five with the subject headings 'Billings', 'More billings', 'Billings for 872 number', 'Billings for 481' and 'Sorry last lot I promise'.

I sighed with something that might have been pleasure. I'd worked on phone data before; other people might see it as endless lists of numbers, endless spreadsheets with no apparent meaning, but I loved it. It was the knowledge that somewhere, buried deep in tens of thousands of numbers, dates, times and durations, there was a pattern: useful information hidden inside, waiting for me to find it.

I opened the first email. There were several spreadsheets attached to them, identified by mobile phone numbers. The message read:

Annabel

Don't know when you'll get a chance to work on these but if you can sort them out for us it would be great. These are the billings for the phones found at the properties so far. We're still waiting on the others. Rachelle's looks interesting. As you know, we never found the mobile phone that she took with her when she left her parents' house. This one was a basic PAYG. The phone downloads have been authorised and we're waiting for those too.

Andy

I started up a new spreadsheet to record all the information, listing the victims' names, phone number, the date range of all the billings and the phone type. Most of the columns were blank but with a bit of luck I'd be able to fill them in as I went along. I opened all the emails and added the details from the remaining spreadsheets. There were billings for the phones found at all the most recent addresses, as well as a name that gave me a jolt – Shelley Burton.

After an hour or so everyone in the office had left and it was dark outside. It made it easier to concentrate and it wasn't long before the pattern crystallised and began to make more sense.

There were some major differences between the billings of the victims. Judith Bingham, Noel Gardiner, someone I hadn't heard of called George Armstrong who'd been discovered while I was away, some of the others – they all had phone billings that looked normal – they made and received several calls over a prolonged period of time. There were texts, missed calls and voicemails.

As soon as I looked at the others, though, the difference was sudden and acute. Rachelle Hudson's billing was the first. It only had incoming calls, from one number. The calls started about two months before she was found and were regular – one call every evening, lasting a couple of minutes only. No texts. The last three lines of data showed unanswered calls on consecutive evenings towards the end of March. Rachelle had been found on April 21st.

I ran a search on the databases for the number that had called Rachelle's mobile, but it was unknown.

I went back to the billings for Judith, Noel and George and searched for the unknown number in their calls, but it did not feature in any of them. I looked for a different number that showed a similar calling pattern, regular incoming calls each evening, but there was nothing like that. I was beginning to feel more certain that these three were not part of the series.

After that I looked at the billings for the two victims found immediately after the phone call that had been made to Sam, and the next discovery after them, someone called Edward Langton, and each showed exactly the same pattern as Rachelle's billing – incoming calls only. One each evening, short in duration. For each set, the calls were made at slightly different times. Dana's phone was called at 18.46, 18.42, 18.44… around a quarter to seven each night. The last two calls went unanswered, and then stopped. That was in August.

Eileen's regular incoming calls were earlier – 18.31, 18.30, 18.27, 18.30… and then, one isolated outgoing call, the night before she was found – a local landline. It must be the call that Sam had received. Momentarily distracted, I put the number into the search facility on the database. That was right – it came back as being the newsdesk at the *Briarstone Chronicle*.

I looked at the billing for the phone found at the last address – the one for Edward Langton. And again, the same pattern. Incoming calls only, this time they were all around six o'clock. Sometimes a minute or two earlier, sometimes later, but always around six. There was something about the timings that bothered me. I frowned and scratched around in my head for what it was, but it wouldn't come. Maybe it was the regularity of it, the boldness, the sense that this was something that was being organised, planned. I went back to the spreadsheets, and the phones found at Robin Downley's address, and, finally, Shelley Burton's. Each set of billings showed the same defined pattern – regular, incoming calls at the same time each evening – then two unanswered calls – and then no further contacts. It was difficult to believe that they were not linked – but in each case the mobile number which was making the calls was different.

I used the internal address book to find Andy Frost's mobile number, reached for the phone and dialled it. The phone rang once and then went to voicemail. I tried to think about it rationally but the excitement of how easy it might be to unravel the case kept me fidgeting on my chair.

The sensible thing to do would be to document everything, finish recording the summary of the data on my spreadsheet, and then complete a report with recommendations for them all to peruse on Monday.

I stared at the screen, then back to the phone, then I rang his voicemail back and this time I left a message. 'Hello, it's Annabel. I'm in the office. Can you give me a ring urgently, please?'

I looked at the black windows and listened to the unusual silence that I hadn't been aware of until that moment: no tannoy, no rattling of coffee cups in the kitchen, no laughter and chatter, no phones ringing. It was as though I was the only one left in the whole building. That wasn't the case, I knew – custody would be just warming up for its busiest period of the week, Friday night, and night duty staff would be coming in and changing over with the late-turn ones down in the patrol office. But up here... the MIR was asleep.

I started typing up the report and before many minutes had passed I was engrossed in it, so focused that I didn't even hear the door opening behind me.

'Hello,' said a voice. 'What are you doing here so late?'

It was DCI Paul Moscrop, but I had been so absorbed in the spreadsheets that for a moment I couldn't think of his name. 'I just wanted to get this finished, sir,' I said.

'I didn't know you were back, Annabel. How have you been?'

He was leaning against the door, tie loosened, sleeves rolled up. The Friday afternoon look, except it was Friday evening and he should have been at home by now.

'Alright,' I said. 'Thanks for asking. I just wanted to get back to being busy, I think.'

'Sure,' he said. 'Well, it's good to see you.' He gave me a warm smile and turned to go. 'Don't stay too late, will you?'

'Sir,' I said, 'can you hold on a minute?'

He turned in the doorway and, although he smiled and said 'Sure!' again, his posture said he'd had enough and wanted to go home. But dutifully he leaned over and looked at my spreadsheet. I explained that the similarities between the billings for Rachelle Hudson's phone and the other five linked them – and that the rest seemed unlikely to be part of the group of victims.

'Unless there was another phone that they were using, which either wasn't found, or was removed before the bodies were discovered,' I said. 'But, even so, their call patterns varied and some of them were receiving calls from more than one number – friends and family, I suppose – until a few weeks before they were found. So I think we can rule them out.'

Paul Moscrop pointed at something on the screen. 'What's that?'

'The list of numbers used to contact Rachelle and the others. A different one for each of them.'

'But the pattern's the same?'

'Yes.'

'Very interesting. Have you requested billings for these numbers – the ones that are calling the victims?'

'No, sir. I've never done the requests myself before. But we need to get them urgently, I think.'

'Right,' he said. He took his mobile phone out of his trouser pocket and dialled a number. To me, he said, 'Can you put all that in an email to me, or something?'

'I'm doing a report – ' I started to say.

'Keith? You still on the station? … Can you? That would be good. I need you to come up to the MIR when you get here, there's been a development… No, nothing like that. I need you to sort out some more phone billings – can you do that?'

There was a pause. Presumably Keith, whoever he was, was not quite so keen on turning out again for a 'development' that involved filling in online forms.

'I wouldn't be ringing you if it wasn't important. And you are on call.' The DCI's tone had taken on a distinct chill. Finally, 'Thanks. Can you ring me when it's done? Cheers. Have a good weekend. Bye.'

He disconnected the call and looked at the handset, shaking his head slightly, distracted. Then he looked back at me.

'Keith should be here in ten minutes or so. He's on call, so don't let him bloody complain about it, right? Tell him what needs doing and get him to email them to me for authorisation. With a bit of luck we should get the billings back quite quickly. Make sure he does them on Priority. Is that OK?'

'Thanks,' I said. 'Any idea how long before they come back?'

'Depends on the service provider – hopefully less than twenty-four hours. Maybe quicker than that. How do you feel about a bit of overtime this weekend?'

'That would be great.'

'Are you sure you're alright doing this, Annabel? You've had a tough few weeks.'

'I know. I need to stay busy. But thank you.'

He was hovering. I sensed his sudden awkwardness, waited for whatever was going to come next.

'They interviewed you, didn't they?'

'Yes.'

'You've not remembered anything else? About what happened?'

'I've been trying not to think about it, sir. I know that's not very helpful.'

'It's alright. It's not about being helpful. I just didn't want you to think you can't come and talk to us, you know. If you think of anything else.'

What did he think I was going to do, suddenly recall everything the angel said to me and then keep it to myself, just for a laugh? I shook my head.

He made sure I had his mobile number and then he went, leaving me in the big silent office on my own waiting for Keith. I went back to the report.

Colin

The *Chronicle*'s campaign continues. Three weeks ago, there was a brief paragraph in their usual proselytisation about a woman who had been found in a 'state of distress' and taken to hospital. Mr Sam Everett used his column to put out an appeal asking for anyone who knew the person responsible to make contact with him. Responsible for what, exactly? Helping people escape from interfering well-wishers who don't understand that sometimes the most blissful state of being is to be left in peace?

There is nothing on the front page today, just the one article inside about maintaining contact with friends and loved ones wherever in the world they happen to live. And a brief interview with the man in charge of the investigation. Detective Chief Inspector Paul Moscrop. He looks like one of those Americans they describe as a 'go-getter' – all even white teeth and management hair. He says the investigation is progressing well and that anyone with any information should come forward.

Reading that, I feel momentarily like coming forward myself, emerging, blinking, from the crowd and surprising all of them. As it is, the brief moment of recognition in the newspaper gave me a kick, and now I want another one. The thought of them getting bored with the story already – already! – when I have other surprises for them, other treats in store, makes me grit my teeth with frustration. They should be proud of me, of my achievements. They should recognise what I am doing and praise me for it – not push it aside and call it a crime as though I'd graffitied a wall or stolen a joint of meat from the supermarket.

If they are bored, I'll have to give them something to wake them up a bit. I'll have to show them exactly what I am capable of.

Even though there are others out there, still alone, still undisturbed, transforming in the privacy of their own homes, I can feel I'm losing interest. I've observed so many of them now. And despite the differences, the variations in the process, there is little that happens which is truly surprising. So I need to introduce some variables, something new, that will reignite the spark.

In other words, the delectable Audrey.

I got into the town centre half an hour ago, at six-thirty, while it was still crowded with people making their way home and I could blend in with the masses. Directly opposite the Italian restaurant called Luciano's is a fast food place with further seating upstairs. I bought a coffee at the till and took it upstairs with me. I should probably have ordered food as well but I am not willing to corrupt my digestive system with it or waste money by purchasing it. So it was just a coffee, and even that is scarcely drinkable.

Nevertheless, sitting by the window overlooking the square, it gives me a perfect vantage point from which I can watch the restaurant and the various pubs and clubs. I can even see the taxi rank if I stand up and lean over a little.

I see Audrey arrive with a female companion, at five past seven. She is wearing a short dress in a dark, silky fabric that clings to her thighs. Her high heels make her walk across the cobbled square look particularly hazardous. And yet, her thighs... I can't tear my gaze away from them. I've been concentrating on them, gazing at various photos from her Facebook profile since Wednesday night, yet seeing them here, moving, rubbing against each other, the muscles under the skin and the flesh moving as she walks – the way her arse moves, visible through the outline of the tight, silky skirt – and the temptation to go out there and grab her, force her round to face me, and instead of speaking (for there is

285

nothing, really, to say) to just run my hand up her thigh and push the fabric away...

They go into Luciano's and shut the door.

I sip a lukewarm coffee that might as well be gravy, and wait.

Annabel

Keith Topping turned up about half an hour after the DCI had gone. He seemed nice enough when he finally turned up – but I got the distinct impression that despite being on call he didn't consider applying for phone billings to be reason enough to come back into the office on a Friday night, however urgent they were. In the end he showed me how to apply myself – not something that was technically supposed to happen, but it would save everyone a lot of time in the long run, he said.

'Won't they need some sort of authorisation? I thought you had to put in passwords and stuff,' I asked.

'Usually you do. Not for something like this, though. As long as you use the Op Name – there, look,' he answered, leaning over me and granting me a whiff of his armpit, 'you put in the DCI's Force Number there. Right? Think you can manage that?'

I was non-committal. I wasn't planning on doing his job for him. I had enough work of my own as it was.

'So...' he said, as I started to write a list of queries for him to complete... 'how have you been?'

'Alright,' I said.

'We've all been really worried about you,' he replied.

I looked up in surprise. 'You don't even know me,' I said, before I could stop myself.

He looked a bit embarrassed. 'Well – you know. You're one of the team. We look after our own.'

Really? I thought.

'We got the CCTV back. That's when it all went a bit mental. I don't think any of us really believed there was someone behind it all until then.'

'What CCTV?'

'Of you. In the shopping centre.'

'I didn't know there was CCTV.'

Probably, if he'd thought about it for a bit longer, he wouldn't have shown me, or even mentioned it in the first place. But he showed me where the file was saved on the Operation's drive on the network, and before I knew it I was launching Media Player and waiting for the file to buffer.

The footage from the shopping centre wasn't very good. The camera was facing into bright sunlight so there was a glare that obscured much of the image, leaving the rest dark and indistinct. Despite this, I saw a person standing outside the glass window of a shop, and after a moment of thinking that I had a coat like that I realised with a jolt that it was me. Seeing yourself on film was always a bit strange, but this was worse – I didn't recognise myself, not just because of the shadow but because the way I was standing was just so odd. I looked hunched into my coat, the slope of my shoulders and my bent head making me appear utterly defeated. Lost.

As I watched, I realised that there was a second figure standing next to me, slightly to my right, and I saw myself nod, and then again – although I had no memory of any of it. He was talking to me. He had his back to the camera and the top half of him was obscured by the glare from the sun, so all anyone could really make out was that it was a man, wearing a short jacket of some dark colour, dark trousers and proper shoes, not white trainers.

And then the man turned slowly away, and a few seconds later, without lifting her head at all, the figure that was me moved and then followed him, not exactly with reluctance but just with an attitude of utter dejection.

'I can't believe that's me,' I said at last.

'I know,' he said. 'Weird, isn't it?'

'Was there any more CCTV? Did they look at ANPR?' This was the car numberplate recognition system used for tracing vehicles.

'No,' he said. 'We did check. There's no ANPR at the shopping centre; the nearest is on the ring road. But we had nothing to compare the data to, since we don't know when or where he met any of the others. And it's impossible to ID him from those images. Which is why we were all hoping you'd remember him.'

'I don't remember anything,' I said, mystified. 'It's like looking at someone else. I don't remember being there and talking to someone at all.'

He patted me on the shoulder, which made me flinch slightly. 'Ah, well,' he said. 'We'll get him, Annabel. You know we're throwing everything we've got at this, don't you?'

Until the next job comes along, I thought, but I didn't say it. I went back to my list of phone billing queries, thinking that it would probably be easier and quicker to give in and do them myself.

Colin

A long evening spent sitting on a custard-yellow plastic seat that was fixed to the floor has been rewarded, eventually. I have had to watch people coming and going for hours on end. I've seen fights, disagreements, five separate women falling over – a cocktail of alcohol, high heels and the Market Square cobbles – and the police, turning up in the riot van and taking people away, wandering through the square in their fluorescent jackets, moving people on, helping drunk women get to their feet again.

But at last I see Audrey and her friends leaving Luciano's. It is ten to midnight – not especially late, but late enough. My arse is almost completely numb. And I can still taste that filthy coffee.

I leave the restaurant promising myself I will never set foot inside it again, and step outside into the freezing air. I twist my muffler around my throat and over the lower part of my face, and pull the black thermal wool hat over my head to keep it warm, as well as for the benefit of the CCTV cameras that are by now paying very close attention to the masses thronging the square.

Audrey and a friend are making for the taxi rank and the inevitable queue.

I head towards the multi-storey where I left the car, and spend a few moments affixing the numberplates I unscrewed from Garth's Volvo in the street behind the office yesterday. Just in case things don't go according to plan.

I drive slowly around the corner towards the taxi rank just in time to see Audrey parting company from the blonde woman. Audrey isn't going to wait in the queue for a taxi.

Audrey is going to walk. I feel a little tremor of excitement. Everything is going so well, so perfectly. I could not have planned it better. I take a left turn and park in a side street. The arousal and the thought of what might happen later are making it hard to concentrate, so I stare at the clock in the car and make myself wait exactly five minutes. Then I start the engine again and drive back to the main road. It is still busy, the street-lights illuminating her path. She must feel safe, walking home, with cars and people passing her every few seconds. She does not feel alone. She does not feel threatened, not in the slightest – which is all good. Very good.

I pull alongside her and open the window on the passenger side.

'Audrey!'

She stops walking and looks at me, at the car. Her face registers drunken confusion. She is more pissed than I'd thought. This, too, is good.

'Colin?' She comes over to the car and leans in a little, through the passenger window.

'You need a lift?' I ask.

The car is warm and I can feel the freezing air flooding in through the open window. As she bends towards me, her cleavage is on full display. I force myself back to the eye contact, back to the reassuring smile.

'Oh, that's kind of you. I'm nearly home, though.'

'Come on, I'll drive you the rest of the way. Get in.'

It's the confidence, the easy friendliness that does it. The lack of explanation. Don't beg. Keep it simple. Assume assent. And besides all that, her shoes are hurting her and it's bitterly cold and what could happen with someone she knows, less than a mile from her front door?

She smells of wine and the remnants of a citrus perfume and drying sweat, and I inhale her as subtly as I can while trying to keep up a reassuring conversation.

'So how are things with Vaughn?'

'We've split up,' she says.

'Really? Oh, I am sorry. He didn't say anything.'

'No, he's in denial.'

'So what happened?'

She looks out of the window as we slow for the traffic lights.

'He's just – not the right person for me. It's nothing he's done wrong. He's a decent bloke.'

'But it's time to move on?'

This time she smiles at me and for a second – just a second – I falter. Is this the right thing to do? I could still choose a different path here. I could drop her off at home, give her my phone number, wish her a pleasant weekend and ask if she'd like to come out with me some time. That's what they do, isn't it? The sorts of things people say?

'Yes,' she says. 'Time to move on.'

I put my hand across and touch her knee. Just her knee – no higher – but still she makes a clumsy grab for it and pushes it away.

'What do you think you're doing, Colin?' Her voice has lifted an octave. 'I know I'm a bit drunk but that doesn't mean you can start taking advantage, alright?'

I feel the anger and the bile rise in my oesophagus. *Audrey, how could you? Ruining everything, so quickly?*

'I wasn't,' I say coldly. The traffic lights are on red. They shine into the car and make everything inside it red, too.

She softens, then. 'Alright. Sorry if I overreacted. I'm a bit jumpy at the moment. It's the next turning on the left – just up there at the top of the hill.'

I look across to her, inhaling her scent again. It's the turning point, right here, right now. I could drop her off at home still, no harm done. No risk. Or I could take her now and move my life forward down this journey. And her attitude, the defiance in her eyes, makes me want her more than ever. She would put up a fight, no doubt about it. But taking the fight out of her would be so much better; so much more of a kick than watching people die who have no fight in them at all.

She stares back at me, drunk but challenging, almost daring me to try it.

The lights change to green and I ease the car up the hill.

Annabel

I woke up early on Sunday and got dressed in my work clothes, and went downstairs. Irene was in the kitchen cooking a fried breakfast. The cat, who'd settled in far more readily than I would ever have expected, wound herself around my legs affectionately.

'Don't mind her, she's been fed,' Irene said when I came in. 'Scrambled egg and bacon?'

It smelt good, but I wasn't hungry. However, experience had taught me already that Irene had trouble hearing the word 'no' and so it was easier just to give in. 'Thanks. Maybe just a little bit?'

There was tea in the pot on the table and I poured a mugful and tasted it. It was black, stewed, but it would do me.

They'd let me out of hospital on the understanding that I had someone to keep an eye on me, and Sam had taken it upon himself to be that person. It had only been supposed to be for a few days, but then we'd gone back to my house to get some clothes and my spare key was missing. I kept it on the bookcase and it was definitely not there. After that I hadn't really felt like going back home, even after we'd got the locks changed at vast expense. As things stood, it looked as if I was going to be staying with the Everetts for a while.

'You were late getting back on Friday night,' she said. 'I didn't hear you come in.'

'I was at work,' I said.

'Till that late? Are you sure that's a good idea, Annabel?'

'I was fine. I needed to get some things finished, that's all. And they're giving me some overtime so I'm going to go in this morning as well.'

Irene made a noise that might have been disapproval. 'Better get a good breakfast inside you, then,' she said, and loaded my plate with eggs and bacon. The cat started kneading my socked feet, keeping her claws tactfully retracted. She was purring wetly and probably dribbling on me too. I reached down under the table and she nestled her head in my cupped hand.

'Where's Sam?' I asked. At that moment the back door opened and Sam came in, wiping his trainers on the mat and breathing hard. 'I didn't know you ran,' I said.

'First one... for ages... really hard,' he said. 'Any tea in there?'

I poured him a cup and he sat opposite me at the kitchen table. Irene shovelled food on to his plate too and he added a squirt of ketchup to it.

'Sort of defeats the object,' he said, around a mouthful of food, 'going for a run and then stuffing my face afterwards.'

'I guess so.'

The cat had transferred her affections smoothly to Sam, tiptoeing around his legs, her tail twisted into a flirtatious question mark. He paused to slip her a covert morsel of bacon when Irene had turned back to the sink.

'I think that cat's forgotten we used to live together,' I said.

'Don't be silly,' Sam said. 'She's happy because she knows you're OK here, that you feel safe and you're getting better, that's all.'

She's happy as long as someone gives her bacon and a scratch round the ear, I thought. But who could blame her for being cross with me? I'd ignored her for days. She must have felt completely abandoned. It was a wonder she'd stayed around at all.

'So where are you off to?'

Nice as it was to have somewhere to stay, with kind people who cared about where I was and what time I got in, cooked me meals and made me drink tea, I was starting to feel like a teenager.

'Just work,' I said, eating some bacon to try to bypass the need for conversation.

'Oh?' Sam's posture had gone from slouched to alert in a second, scenting a story above the salty tang of breakfast-with-ketchup. 'You're going to work on a Sunday?'

I took a deep breath in. How could I make this sound less exciting? 'Not really. Just overtime. Updating some spreadsheets. Catching up with things. As I'll be going back in a bit.'

'If they're giving you overtime, something's definitely going on. I know for a fact that they have no money for overtime at all. What's happened? Is it the investigation? Have they found another one?'

'Sam,' Irene said, 'stop pestering her. Annabel, tell him to mind his own business if he's bothering you.'

'He's a journalist,' I said. 'My business is his business. Unfortunately.'

'I'll drive you in,' he said. 'And you can ring me when you're done. I'm going into town anyway.'

'I might be ages,' I said, not wanting the responsibility of him sitting waiting for me. 'I can drive myself.'

But he was quick finishing his breakfast and by the time I'd collected my bag and coat he had showered and was downstairs, fully dressed, his dark hair slicked back from his face. He looked so eager and excited that I gave up and followed him out to his car.

To my surprise, the office was not empty, as it had been on Friday night. Three of the desks were occupied and Paul Moscrop was in his glass cubicle in the corner. All of them were talking on the phone and another phone was ringing on one of the other desks. I thought briefly about answering it but decided not to. I slipped into my chair and turned on the workstation. A further surprise. The billing results for the phones I'd identified were back, forwarded on from the DCI who had been sent them by Keith Topping.

Paul came out of his office as I was opening up the attachments. 'Ah! Annabel,' he said. 'Really good to see you. Have you seen the results?'

'Just looking at them now, sir,' I said.

'You can drop the "sir",' he said. 'It's Paul. Alright?'

'Right. Thanks.'

'We did subscriber checks too, but they're all pre-pay and unregistered. No surprise there. But the billings are very interesting.'

I waited for him to tell me all about it, wondering if he'd done all the analysis before I'd got here.

He had a wry grin on his face. 'Have a look, and then come and tell me what you think,' he said.

I worked through the attachments one by one, and he was right: the results were interesting. Each set of the phone billings was the mirror image of those we'd obtained from the victims' phones. In other words, the offender was only using one SIM card per victim, and not contacting any other numbers. After each victim died, presumably he'd discarded the SIM and moved on to another. The phone numbers were not sequential, suggesting he bought them at different times and locations rather than as a bulk lot. And because the call traffic was so low, it was unlikely that the Pay As You Go account had been topped up with credit before it was discarded – he was just using the 'free' credit that came with the SIM – and that was probably more than enough for his purposes.

The cellsite data for all the phones showed locations around the town centre of Briarstone – not from a residential area. Unless he lived right in the town centre, he was only using the phone when he was in town.

He was methodical. And clever, too. But then I saw it, and took in a sharp breath that made me cough. Surely – surely he couldn't have missed something so obvious?

I got up on legs that were surprisingly shaky and went through to Paul's office. He'd left the door open and this time the wry grin was a great big beaming smile. 'Got it?'

'I can't believe he could be so clever and so careless at the same time,' I said. 'He's swapping the SIMs over, but he's only used one handset.'

'It's not a case of being careless,' he said, 'to be fair to the poor bastard. People don't use cheap phones these days. They use smartphones, iPhones, BlackBerries. They're not as disposable, or rather they're too expensive and people don't want to throw them away. They think disposing of the SIM card when you've done with it makes you untraceable, but of course we know better.'

'So have you applied for data for his other numbers? The other SIMs he's used in that phone?'

'First thing this morning. We're waiting for the results, but in the meantime we got a subscriber check done on his one and only handset.'

'And?' I was holding my breath.

'The phone comes back to a Mr Colin Friedland. Address in Briarstone.'

'He registered the phone?'

'He's had an account with the service provider for five years. Clearly a fine upstanding citizen, Mr Friedland. I like him already.'

If he'd registered the phone, he was either stupid, or completely innocent, or truly believed he had nothing to hide. Or maybe when he'd registered it he hadn't intended his current activities – maybe it was a recent thing. I wondered if he even realised that having an account with the service provider meant that all his efforts in swapping the SIMs were pointless.

The DCI rubbed his hands together. 'I think we deserve a cup of tea, don't you? I'll make it. What are you having?'

He didn't make it, of course. There was no milk. He took me up to the canteen that was usually busy, but which on a Sunday was home only to a few members of the patrol team enjoying their bacon sandwiches before heading back out into the town centre. We got coffees from the machine and sat with them in a slightly awkward silence.

'I can't help thinking about Eileen Forbes,' he said.

'Eileen? Why?'

'It was just a matter of hours, that's all. If we'd taken it seriously – if we'd been a bit quicker with the trace... I wonder if we could have saved her.'

I shook my head. 'I doubt it,' I said. 'I think she must have passed that point a long time earlier. And he obviously had some kind of control over her mind from the moment she met him. You couldn't have changed that.'

'We saved you,' he said.

I didn't answer. I thought of Sam, wondered if that was what he thought, too.

'How's it been, at home?' he asked eventually.

'Fine,' I said, not wishing to embark on a lengthy explanation of how I'd ended up living with a reporter from the *Chronicle* I'd only met for the first time a few weeks ago. And his parents. And my cat.

I could see him fishing around for another question to ask me, holding them up to the light for scrutiny and discarding them – boyfriend? No, too personal... family coping? She might start crying... Children, pets? Ditto...

'Rain seems to be holding off,' I said.

'Yes,' he said, with obvious relief. 'Shame to be stuck in here, really.'

His phone rang then, loud enough to make me jump.

'They've got him,' Paul said, when he ended the call. 'He's on his way in now.'

Until that moment I'd felt nothing other than the excitement of being involved in a job at the arrest phase, something I'd never done before. But now, there was something else – relief? The feeling that it was over, that I was waking up from a long sleep and that my life could begin again.

We took our coffees with us back up to the MIR.

After that, the phones rang constantly. Now the case was unravelling, senior officers were ringing Paul with offers of help, trying to find ways in which they could snaffle a bit of the credit for a job that was potentially going to be high-profile. There was a lot to be gained from it. Every time Paul put the phone down again we had a bit of a laugh about how nobody had been particularly interested and now suddenly our job was the most important thing going on in Briarstone. I didn't mention that I'd been working on the case for a while before anyone had shown any interest at all – including him.

'So what happens now?' I asked.

'He'll be put in a cell while we get a search team inside his house with the PACE clock ticking down. Keith and Simon will be doing the initial interview. When they get back up here we'll have a meeting to talk about the interview strategy.'

'Is there anything I can do?'

'Yes,' he said. 'You can go home.'

'What?'

'Annabel. You've been absolutely pivotal to this whole investigation, you know that. But you're also a victim. You shouldn't really have come back in here after you were off. That's Frosty's fault, really. He didn't know what to do with all those billings and he told Kate and she decided to mention it to you.'

'I'm glad she told me. I'm glad of it.' I felt choked, suddenly, as though I was being dumped.

'We couldn't have done this without you,' he said gently. 'But we need to separate you from the investigation now, or else having you on the team could threaten any prosecution. If we get past the CPS, you're going to be a key witness. Do you see what I'm getting at?'

He was right. I knew he was right. But it still felt like being punched in the gut. *Well done, Annabel, thank you for solving the whole sodding case for us, now piss off back to the civvies' office where you belong.*

'You're not going to be able to tell me anything about the interviews? What he says?'

He shook his head. 'I'm so sorry. This has to be it. You can see that, can't you?'

'Yes,' I said. I felt tears starting and I pushed myself up from my chair before he could see them. 'Thanks, though. And good luck.'

He started to say something else but I couldn't wait. I logged myself out of the system while I was putting on my coat. By the time I'd done that he was on the phone again and I could give him a happy little wave through the glass partition, then down to the corridor to the Ladies', where the sobs began.

Colin

When the knock at the door came, I was half-inclined not to open it. On a Sunday? It was likely to be some sort of evangelist, or, worse, someone trying to get me to change my energy supplier. I framed my face into a polite but assertive smile, ready to get rid of whoever it was quickly.

And of course the smile died on my face when I opened the door.

'Colin Friedland? My name is DC Keith Topping; this is my colleague DC Simon Lewis. Can we come in, please?'

'It's not convenient,' I said, eyeing them up and down. The younger one – Lewis? – was taller than me and twice as wide – a rugby player if ever I'd seen one. I wanted to ask him if he was front row or back but thought better of it.

'Oh?' said Lewis. 'Why's that?'

'I was just preparing dinner,' I said.

'I'm afraid it's rather urgent,' Topping said.

What a name. Keith Topping? I'll bet he was bullied at school; what would they have called him? Dream Topping? Tip-Top?

After a brief discussion in the house they arrested me and took me out to the police car that was parked just out of sight at the end of the drive. It's funny that my first thought on their introduction was not that something must have happened to my mother, in her nursing home – I knew immediately why they were there. And it felt like the start of an exciting new chapter. A new game for me to play, with new rules. In the back of the car, my hands uncomfortably cuffed behind me, I was smiling with a delicious anticipation of what was going to happen next.

Dumb and dumber, these two. The same two who arrested me. The skinny one now sitting on a comfy chair in the corner and the one built like a prop sitting on a plastic chair, too small for his fat arse, across the table from where I'm sitting, awaiting the best they can do.

'Colin Friedland, you're aware that you are still under arrest for the murders of Rachelle Hudson, Robin Downley, Shelley Burton, Edward Langton, Dana Viliscevina and Eileen Forbes. You do not have to say anything but it may harm your defence if you do not mention when questioned something you later rely on in court. Anything you do say may be given in evidence.'

I say nothing.

'You have the right to legal representation, as I mentioned before. You've said you don't want a solicitor to be present but I just want to remind you here that you can change your mind about that at any stage. Do you understand?'

'Yes,' I say. 'I don't need a solicitor.'

'This interview is being recorded on DVD, Colin. Do you understand everything I've said to you so far?'

'Yes, of course,' I say.

'Right, then. Let's make a start, shall we? Can you tell me when you first met Rachelle Hudson?'

I genuinely have to think about that one. They think I'm going to be difficult, I can tell. They're settled in for the long haul, braced for it like fishermen heading for the North Atlantic. 'I think it was just after the beginning of February. I don't recall the exact date.'

I was expecting them to exchange glances; I can almost feel the surprise like an electric shock between them. They didn't think it was going to be this easy, did they? And yet they still have no idea of any of it, not really.

'How did you meet?'

'In the country park in Baysbury. She was running. No, actually, she was sitting on a bench – but she had been running. We fell into conversation.'

'What about?'

'I could tell she was unhappy. I was trying to make her feel better about herself.'

'Did you ever visit Rachelle Hudson's home?'

'Yes,' I say. 'She invited me in.'

'Just that time, or did you go back there again?'

'I visited her once she had died.'

There is a brief silence broken only by the electric hum of the DVD recorder. Both of them are staring at me.

'Colin, did you kill Rachelle Hudson?'

I smile at them. 'No, of course not. She did that all by herself. I was just there to comfort her, to ensure that she was happy with the decisions she made.'

There's another pause while they digest this information and clearly thrash about in their collective tiny minds for a new type of interview strategy, since the direction this one is taking evidently wasn't in their plan.

'Did you help her to take her own life?'

'No,' I say.

'Did you touch her in any way?'

I think about this for a moment, trying to remember. 'No, I don't think so. I might have touched her arm or something. I was never violent or anything like that.'

'Did she talk to you about wanting to take her own life?'

'Oh, yes.'

'What did she say?'

'I think she said she felt sometimes that she would be happier if she ceased to exist.'

'Did you suggest she seek help? Talk to someone about how she felt?'

'She was talking to me about how she felt.'

'But you didn't think you should try and stop her from ending her life?'

'No. That was her decision. She was a grown adult.'

'And you didn't report her death?'

'No.'

'Why not?'

'Surely that sort of thing should be up to one's next of kin, shouldn't it?' I give Lewis a cheerful smile which he does not return.

'Did you say anything to try to dissuade Rachelle from taking her own life?'

'Not at all. Once she had made the decision to die, she was much happier. That was a good thing, don't you think?'

Lewis does not answer the question. Instead, he looks across at Topping for the first time since the interview started. He's way out of his depth already and we've only been talking for five minutes or so. I almost feel sorry for him.

After that brief wobble, he comes back from another angle. 'Did you give Rachelle a mobile phone?'

'Yes, I did.'

'Why did you do that?'

'So I could keep in touch with her.'

'Did she ever call you using the phone?'

'No. I called her on that number a few times.'

'And did you take Rachelle's own mobile phone away from her?'

'Yes, I did. She wanted to cease all contact with her family. She didn't need the phone any more.'

'You took it without her permission?'

'No, she gave me permission to take the phone away.'

'What did you do with the phone?'

'I got rid of it.'

'How did you do that?'

'I can't remember exactly. I might have put it in a dustbin somewhere.'

Lewis sighs heavily and consults his notes. Then he says, 'Going back to the mobile phone you left at Rachelle's house. You said you called her on it a number of times. What did you say to her when you called?'

'I don't remember exactly. I was calling to check if she was alright, if she needed anything.'

'Did you know she was starving to death?'

'Yes.'

They look at each other again and I smile. This is such a lot of fun. I wish I'd owned up to it all months ago.

'Did you not think, then, that she might have needed food?'

'No. That was the way she had decided to die. If I'd brought her food I would have been going against her wishes. She'd already chosen that path. That was her right.'

Lewis raises his voice slightly for the first time. '"She'd chosen her path"?'

'Yes, indeed,' I say cheerfully. 'We all choose our own paths, DC Simon Lewis. You've chosen your path, too, haven't you? And you, DC Keith Topping. It's only when we've chosen our path and taken steps towards it that we can realise what it means to be truly happy. Don't you agree?'

Annabel

Sam's car pulled into the side entrance to the police station car park and swung round so that it was facing back to the main road. I opened the passenger door and got in.

'Everything OK?' he asked.

He hadn't been expecting me to finish so early, judging by the surprised tone of his voice when I'd called his mobile. I had considered getting the bus or a taxi back to my house and sending him a text to say I'd gone home, but he would only have turned up there. Shutting the door and leaving the world behind me was no longer an option.

'Yes and no. I'm off the case. Apparently I shouldn't have been allowed back in the MIR after that man made me into a victim.'

'Is that the good news or the bad news?'

'The good news is that they've made an arrest and he'll be interviewed, probably later this afternoon.'

'Really? Who is he?'

'Sam, I can't talk about it.'

'What do you think I'm going to do? I can't name him if he hasn't been charged, you know that. Tomorrow's issue's already gone to press. There's bound to be an official announcement about the arrest on tomorrow's local news. By Tuesday morning everyone and his uncle will know all about it.'

'Alright, then, I don't *want* to talk about it. Is that better?'

He went quiet and I felt bad. It wasn't his fault; none of it was his fault. The car windscreen was speckled with rain and when he used the wipers they squealed across the glass. I tried to think of a way to change the subject and cheer things up a little bit. 'Did you get anything nice in town?'

'Not really,' he said.

'You're not sulking, are you?'

'Of course not.'

'You are.'

He didn't reply, which meant I was right. I couldn't stand sulkers. 'Look,' I said, 'how about if I buy us all a takeaway for tonight? I'd like to say thanks to you and your parents for putting up with me for so long.'

'You'd better clear it with Irene,' he said. 'You can't go interrupting her cooking schedule. She plans it like a military operation.'

'I'd like to say thank you anyway,' I said. 'I'll get all my stuff together later. Maybe I could stay one more night, what do you think?'

'What do you mean?' he said. 'You're leaving?'

He stopped at the lights and turned his body towards me. I looked at him. If I'd suggested sawing off my own leg he couldn't have looked more horrified.

'You don't need to look after me any more, Sam. He's locked up. I'll be safe at home.'

'It's not just him,' he said. 'I don't like to think of you on your own. You've been through a very difficult time. You need friends around you.'

'You've been very kind. But really, I'm going to have to go home sooner or later. It's better that I do it now, I think.'

He stared at me for so long that the car behind us beeped its horn. The lights had changed. He shook his head and drove off. 'What about the cat? She's just settled in.'

'What – you want custody of my cat now?'

'Don't be like that.'

'I was joking.'

'Well, I'm not laughing. I don't want you to be in a house on your own. It's not good when you were just in hospital less than two weeks ago. What if something happens?'

We carried on like this all the way to Keats Road. In the end he was almost placated by my promising to stay in almost constant phone contact with him, to keep the door locked and not open it to anyone I didn't know. If I wanted to go into town he was going to volunteer to drive me around, presumably for the rest of my life. It was ridiculous. The more he went on about it, the more I wanted to escape the nagging.

I needed to go home.

Colin

The interviews have continued intermittently throughout the day. In between interviews I was taken back to the cell that I am already starting to think of as mine. At lunch I was given a tray containing something that might have been shepherd's pie, peas that were khaki in colour and had probably come out of a tin, and a plastic cup of water. I ate some of the shepherd's pie and regretted it straight away. The taste will be coming back to me for several hours to come.

They have asked me again if I want a solicitor, I have a right to one, which of course I know, and they will find me a duty solicitor if I do not have one of my own. I told them – again – that I wasn't bothered.

I'm not bothered about any of it, much, but I do object to the prospect of having to sleep on a plastic-covered mattress in a concrete cell, and I asked them politely how long they were likely to be detaining me. The custody sergeant told me it was likely to be at least another eighteen hours. Eighteen hours! Still, there's plenty to entertain me. The cells adjacent to mine appear to be empty, but beyond that I can hear shouted expletives as the drunks start to roll in. They expect me to be worried, I can tell. But I have nothing to lose, nothing at all – whereas they are in a very tricky position. Especially with regard to the media coverage the case has gained so far.

The only slight concern I have is their question about whether I reported Rachelle's death to anyone. Is it an offence to fail to report a death? I have a vague memory of reading a news article about a woman who'd been found to have kept the bodies of her stillborn babies in the attic of her house – and she'd been arrested, of course. She hadn't killed them,

310

though. But surely reporting the death is the responsibility of the family, the next of kin – not some random stranger who happens to be there at the time.

By the time it got dark we were on to the fourth interview. Topping and Lewis again, the comedy double-act. This time they brought a cardboard box with them that Lewis stowed away under his side of the table. Maybe it contained sandwiches. I could only hope.

We'd been through the list of names already, and I was pleasantly surprised to find that they were short of quite a few. Some of mine still haven't been found. I like that thought. No matter what happens here, my legacy is still out there, like buried jewels waiting for an archaeologist to unearth them.

With each interview, I could feel their confidence waning and their doubt increasing. If they couldn't charge me with failing to report a death, what else was there? I had harmed no one. Other than the odd gentle touch on an arm, maybe, I had not laid a finger on them. And if they wanted to have a go at charging me with assisting a suicide, well – how could they prove it?

'Colin,' Lewis said. His voice seemed to be brighter this time. Maybe he had indulged in a strong cup of coffee in the interval. I sniffed the air, but could smell only body odour, and possibly something that might have been cheese and onion.

'Detective Constable Lewis,' I replied.

He frowned a little but clearly was not going to let my sport spoil his surprise.

'I'd like to ask you about the mobile phones.'

'Yes,' I said.

'You provided a mobile phone for each of the individuals we discussed in the last interview. That is...' he searched in his notes for the list we'd agreed and then ran a finger down it as he recited the names aloud '... Rachelle Hudson, Robin Downley, Shelley Burton, Edward Langton, Dana Viliscevina, and Eileen Forbes. Is that correct?'

311

'Yes.'

'When these individuals were deceased, did you then remove the mobile phones from their properties?'

'Sometimes. Usually I just left them behind.'

'Why did you do that?'

'I had no need of them. They were cheap phones anyway.'

'And how did you make contact with these people, while they were alive? Using your own personal mobile phone?'

'That's correct.'

'We have data showing that each of the mobile phones you left with the victims was called by a different telephone number. What can you tell us about that?'

'They're not victims, Detective Constable Lewis. They are innocent members of the public who chose to end their own lives. Nothing more.'

'You're aware that we have seized your mobile phone, Colin?'

'Yes.'

'We are in the process of conducting a forensic examination of that phone, which will confirm that you used a different SIM card in it for each of the victims. Is that what happened?'

I found myself wondering briefly where they were heading with this. So what if they knew I was using different SIM cards for them all? Did it matter? Did any of it really make any difference at all?

'I did, yes,' I said.

'Why is that?'

I didn't answer the question, feeling as if I was being led away from the point that I needed to get across. Their stupidity and insolence, and the overpowering smell of their tired, sweaty bodies in their day-old clothes, crumpled and frayed, made me angry. At home my dinner was waiting for me, prepared but uncooked: the vegetables sitting in a pan of cold water on the stove, the neatly filleted salmon marinating in lime and white wine in the refrigerator. They had not achieved anything by their interviews yet and we had been here all day. *All day!*

'To be fair, gentlemen,' I said, 'I can see why you are confused. Neither of you has ever met anyone like me before, have you? I know of nobody else who is as comfortable with the concept of death as I am. All these people, so many of them out there, who are tired and ill and depressed... and what do we do with them? We pay for extensive, invasive courses of medical treatment at vast expense to those of us who take care of our bodies and remain fit and healthy. Or we put them into care homes, at even higher cost, where they no longer have the option to end things for themselves. We are treating our neighbours appallingly. We are allowing them to linger in misery for months, years even, when all they need is someone to tell them that it's alright – that, if they want to go, they can go. That it's easy and simple and it can be pain-free. They can choose that path if they want to – and God knows many of them do, given the alternatives they face! All I have done is to show them that they can choose the path. They could have chosen a different one if they'd so desired. But they did not. They chose to die. And I did not "help" them, I just spoke to them and provided comfort and reassurance when they had no one else to do it. And where were you when they needed your help? You never even knew they existed, did you? Because you're here to force people to perform and behave and react in a certain way. Even, it seems, when no law has been broken at all.'

They were staring at me. I took a drink from the plastic cup of water on the table in front of me.

'Finished?' said Lewis.

I didn't answer. The anger was still there.

'This is an interview, Colin. While we appreciate your contribution, it would be very helpful if you could stick to the questions we're asking. Do you think you could do that?'

'If I must.'

Lewis took a deep breath in, leaned forward slightly across the table towards me.

'How do you do it?'

I stared at him.

'Come on, Colin, you've developed what must be a genius technique for getting people to kill themselves. How do you do it?'

I raised my chin in defiance. 'It has taken me a number of years of detailed study, Detective Constable Lewis. Explaining it would take longer than either of us has.'

'Maybe you could give us a summary,' he said.

'You wouldn't understand.'

'Indulge me.'

I breathed in, a long, deep breath through my nose, wondering how to start, wondering if I could phrase it in words the plod could understand.

'They all wanted to end their lives. You must understand that: if they weren't ready for death, whatever my "technique", as you call it, it would not have worked.'

'So you're not responsible for their deaths?'

'Absolutely not. They took their own lives, every one of them.'

'But you... helped them?'

'I helped them with their resolve. My "technique" is something I tailor to meet individual needs. Some of them were afraid of pain, so my discussions with them concentrated on pain relief, or the blocking-out of those feelings, and also on the removal of fear. Because, as I'm sure you are aware, fear makes pain more acute. If we have no fear, pain is easier to bear. So I helped each of them with their specific requirements.'

'Doesn't hunger override all of this?' Topping said abruptly. 'I mean, surely the human body needs food and water...'

'Voluntary Refusal of Food and Fluid is surprisingly common, you know,' I said. 'I suggest you research it on the internet. It's also called Voluntary Death by Dehydration, or VDD. Or I've seen it referred to as Terminal Dehydration. Once you pass a certain point, the body starts to shut down, and from then on it's quite a simple matter. It doesn't take long, and if you've dealt with fear, and the limited amount of pain, it's quite a pleasant way to die. Depending on how fit you are,

314

and whether there is any underlying medical condition, five to seven days is the average length of time, for most of which the subject is asleep, resting. It's not at all violent; in fact it's very peaceful. You just slip away in your sleep.'

They were both staring at me.

'If any of them had changed their minds about dying, they could have got themselves a drink of water. They were in their own homes. Some of them still had food in the fridge, in the cupboards. They could have changed their minds at any point. But they had chosen their path. All I did was make it easier for them to continue.'

'Were you there when they all died?'

'No. It was a private moment for them. Usually once they lost consciousness I left them alone.'

'But you went back?'

'I went back to make sure they had achieved their goals.'

They looked at each other. I waited for them to ask if I went back again after that, because if they had asked that question I would probably have responded with an untruth. But, fortunately for me and my dedication to the truth, the notion of someone voluntarily spending time with decomposing human flesh was one that was beyond their comprehension.

'Let's go back to the phones you used, Colin. You have admitted that you used different SIM cards for each of the – er – people you met.'

'I suppose so.'

'You suppose so?'

'Alright, then, yes.'

'Why did you do that?'

'It was a way of keeping track of everyone I'd met.'

'Seems a complicated way to go about it. Why didn't you just save their numbers in the contact list on your phone?'

'I don't keep contacts in my phone. You may have noticed.'

'Why's that?'

'I just prefer to keep things separate, that's all.'

Lewis sighed, something I recognised as heralding an imminent change of direction.

'Your phone has also been linked with – ' he consulted his notes ' – a further twenty-seven SIM cards, in addition to the ones we have already discussed. What can you tell us about that?'

'I have no comment.'

'Come on, Colin. Another twenty-seven SIM cards! It must be a right pain, having to fish them out and change them all the time, isn't that the case?'

'Not really. I used the different SIM cards over a long period of time.'

'And were they all used for the same purpose?'

'To keep in contact with people, yes.'

'Am I right in thinking there are another twenty-seven people out there who have yet to be located?'

I smiled at him. 'It does sound rather a lot, doesn't it? Clearly you're not so good at taking care of your communities as you think you are.'

'Are any of them still alive, Colin?'

'I wondered when you were going to ask me that.'

'And? Are there any people out there still alive?'

They both looked at me. Motionless in their seats, breathless. At last they'd asked me something interesting, something that might make a difference. And the time had come for me to lie to them for the first time.

'No.'

They both breathed out in a sigh. It was almost comical. And it felt as though they believed me, or maybe they just wanted to believe me so badly that their tiny minds could not compute any possible alternative.

'You're sure about that?'

'There was one lady a few weeks ago, but I believe someone intervened before she had enough time.'

There was a pause, paper shuffling. Under the table, Lewis kicked the cardboard box. 'Right, so, going back to the phones.

Have you always used this method to keep in touch?'

'Yes.'

'With your friends, as well as with those you – er – "helped to choose the right path"?'

'I don't have friends, Detective Constable Lewis.'

'I'm not surprised. You spend too much time meddling in other people's lives, don't you?'

'Is that an actual question?'

'Why do you do it, Colin?'

He was trying to be friendly with me now, trying to break down the barriers that he perceived existed between us. The only barrier was the table. He'd constructed all these issues when in reality it was all beautifully, serenely simple.

'Come on, Colin. Why do you do it?'

'I've already explained. I'm saving the taxpayer a fortune, and making people feel happier about themselves.'

'And that makes you feel good, does it?'

'Why wouldn't it?'

'Do you become sexually aroused when you're dealing with these people, Colin?'

I was too shocked to answer, just for a moment. I stared at him, my face hot with rage at his insolence. The change of topic had been sudden and, this time, unexpected.

'How dare you?' I said, my voice low, calm. Disguising the fury as best I could.

'You see – our search teams found this in your house, Colin.'

From the cardboard box under the table Lewis brought forth a plastic bag, sealed at the top, covered with printed writing but transparent. Inside was an old copy of the *Briarstone Chronicle*, the centre spread showing all the pictures of them. The happy smiling pictures.

'Do you know what this is?'

'It's a copy of the newspaper,' I said, my tone even.

'We retrieved it, as I said, from your house. Specifically, from your bedroom. More specifically, from underneath your bed.'

'Quite.'

'It's covered in semen, Colin. Is it yours?'

My face flushed again and I could not bring forth any words that would sufficiently express my indignation and discomfort. Damn the man!

Eventually I hissed through gritted teeth, 'No comment.'

'Did you masturbate over the newspaper, Colin?'

'No comment!'

'Did it turn you on, knowing you'd caused these people to die?'

'No comment!'

They both sat staring at me for several seconds. I was breathing hard, my hands clenching and unclenching at the rudeness of it, the terrible intrusion into my private life. *How dare they?* I thought. *Do they have no idea who I am, what I could do?*

'What?' I said. 'Is it a bloody crime to masturbate, now? Are you going to charge me with desecrating a fucking newspaper?'

'Please don't swear, Colin.'

'I'd prefer it if you called me Mr Friedland, Detective Constable Lewis.'

'Whatever,' Lewis said with a sigh. 'We'll stop there, for now. I'll ask the custody sergeant to take you back to your cell.'

Now that I have finally calmed down, lying on my narrow bunk back in my cell, I realise something that makes me smile. The newspaper is their best weapon. Which means they haven't found my notebooks or the images. If they don't find those, they have nothing at all.

Maggie

I wasn't always like this. Alone, I mean. I had a husband and a family, two boys. When they grew up and left home it was just back to Leonard and me, and that was fine with me. I worked two days a week at a tea shop in the village, and that was only for fun really. Leonard was quite senior in his organisation when he retired, and with the boys gone it left us with quite a bit of money. Stephen said we should sell the house, buy something smaller, but that would just give us more money sitting in the bank earning next to no interest, and what were we supposed to spend it on? We had holidays, of course; a cruise, usually, and a month or more in the sunshine during the cold, dark days of winter. But even when we were away I was always looking forward to coming home.

Our house was large, on a quiet lane outside the village, with a garden extending right down to the river, trees hundreds of years old which groaned and sighed when the wind was strong. This house had nurtured us, looked after us, kept us safe and grown my boys into tall, proud men. Why would I want to live anywhere else?

Stephen got married to a Norwegian girl called Ina. They settled in north London and had two daughters. I saw them regularly, at least once a month. They would come for Sunday lunch. My younger son, Adrian, met a girl and went travelling with her. They ended up settling in Australia because she had family there, and a year after that they had a boy. They never got married. Of course I didn't see them nearly as often as I saw Stephen and Ina. Adrian and Diane came home for Christmas, once. They came for my sixtieth birthday. And then they came back for the trial.

They came for him early on a Tuesday morning. He was still in bed, fast asleep. I was up because in those days I had trouble sleeping past five. I'd made a cup of tea and I was sitting at the kitchen table reading yesterday's newspaper, waiting for it to get properly light so I could go outside and do a bit more of the weeding that I'd abandoned when the daylight faded the evening before.

There was a knock at the door. I thought, 'The postman's early today,' but of course it wasn't the postman. It was two detectives, a man and a woman.

'What is it? Is it the boys? What's happened?' I demanded.

'We need to speak to your husband, Mrs Newman. Is he in?'

I took the ID the man offered me, shut the door and studied it in the hallway, and then I opened the door and let them in.

'Where is your husband?' the woman asked, once they were in the hallway. 'Where is Leonard?'

'He's in bed, of course, it's half-past six. What's all this about?'

The male detective went upstairs and I waited in the kitchen with the female. It was all very quiet, upstairs. There was no shouting, no crashing and thumping. A few minutes later Leonard came down the stairs with the police officer, dressed in the clothes he would wear to do the gardening: jeans, a sweater over an old shirt. His hair was standing up away from his head because he hadn't brushed it. He was by the door with the man, putting his shoes on, and I thought for one dreadful moment he wasn't going to acknowledge me at all, so I called out, 'Leonard!'

He spoke to the man for a moment and then came through to the kitchen. The look on his face was terrible, as though he'd just received the most appalling news.

'What is it, Leonard? What on earth's happened?'

He didn't move towards me, or try to touch me. He just said three words: 'I'm so sorry.'

He didn't even use my name.

When they'd taken him away I called his solicitor, who promised to get to the police station as soon as he could. My house was full of people; in the end I had no idea who they all were. I made them cups of tea and some of them looked at me with pity. Some of them with other expressions that I couldn't interpret.

They practically dismantled Leonard's office. They took his computer away in plastic bags, and the laptop, all the mobile phones, including mine.

I used the landline to call Stephen. I couldn't seem to get through to him how serious this was. He was about to leave for work, and until I started to cry and get hysterical he was fully intending to go to work and call me in the evening. But when I broke down he said he would come right away. Then I tried to ring Adrian in Australia, but there was no answer.

I thought he'd been caught fiddling his taxes. That was my first thought and for a long time after that I didn't consider any possible alternative. It seemed the most likely problem, and explained why they were concentrating on his office rather than anything else in the house.

Stephen went to the police station in the afternoon, while I stayed at home to tidy up and clean the house, but he was back soon afterwards. They wouldn't tell him anything. His father was still being interviewed. He was unlikely to be released before tomorrow morning. I sent Stephen back with a bag containing pyjamas, a dressing gown, his washbag. A clean shirt.

'He's not staying in a fucking hotel, mother,' Stephen said.

'I don't care,' I replied. 'And don't swear at me.'

He did as he was told, but when he came back he wanted something else. He'd not been allowed to see his father but a request had come through. He needed a suit.

'What for?' I asked.

'He's going to the Magistrates' in the morning,' Stephen said. 'He wants to wear a suit. Like it will help.'

'Of course it will help,' I said. I went upstairs and found his best suit, the tailored one he wore at the board meetings.

A new shirt, a silk tie in a deep blue to bring out the colour of his eyes.

He was charged the next morning with possession of child abuse images. The shock was immense. I think they thought I was in denial – in fact Stephen said as much – but I wasn't. I knew it wasn't possible, there was no way such a thing was true. There were very few people I could confide in, but one of them was my sister Janet, who lived about twenty miles away. I went to stay at her house for a few days at Stephen's insistence. I think he thought the press might get wind of it and he didn't want them taking pictures of me in the garden, or standing at the window like a lost soul.

'I can't believe it,' I said to Janet. I must have said this to her five times already. 'I just can't believe any of it's true. I mean, we still have a good sex life! Surely he wouldn't…'

She looked at me over her mug of coffee and let me get it all off my chest. Trouble was, it didn't help. It made things worse, talking about it, because the disbelief didn't go away. It was as though somebody had made all this up, just to spite us. I tried to think who could hate us enough to do this, to tear us all apart.

He got bailed in the end and he came home, but by that time the press had worked out who he was and what he was charged with, and there were TV camera vans parked at the bottom of the driveway.

We moved out. Leonard wasn't allowed out of the country so we had to cancel our holiday that had been booked and paid for. Our insurance didn't cover the loss; apparently being arrested, even for something you haven't done, doesn't qualify as being enough of a disaster to warrant a payout. He tried to insist I should go without him, but I could not. What if they came again, and took him away without me knowing? And besides, if the worst should happen – I wanted to spend every moment I could with him.

He tried so hard to act as though nothing was wrong. We tried to live a normal life, in the little house owned by friends of ours who were living overseas. Only close family knew where we were, and of course the police. Leonard only left the house once a week to sign his bail document at the police station. When he came out again we drove for miles and miles to make sure we weren't followed back to the house.

Eventually the press moved on to other matters, but I was still too afraid to go home.

My sister Janet asked me what he'd had to say about it all, what his excuse was. In truth I never talked to him about it. I never even asked him if he was guilty of the crimes he had been accused of, such was my faith in him. He was my husband and I'd vowed to stand by him no matter what, for better, for worse, and this was about as 'worse' as it was possible to get. So I made the decision that he was innocent, that it was a mistake, or someone else's malicious accusation, that had caused all this.

But, as hard as he tried to act normally, things were not really the same. Leonard hid himself away for hours at a time, working on possible lines of defence. Late in the evening I would hear him weeping after I'd gone to bed. Despite his efforts, reading over legal documents the solicitor brought, to give him something to do, his demeanour faltered and it felt as though he'd given up already.

I hadn't given up, not by a long shot.

The trial changed everything. It was not quite a year since that Tuesday morning that they'd come and arrested him. We were all prepared for it, briefed by the solicitor as to what to expect, but even so the boys suffered terribly. Seeing Adrian and Diane and my grandson Joshy who was five by then and quite a handful… it was so good in many ways but so bad in others. Diane stayed for a week with us and then when the trial started she took Joshy to stay with her parents in Scotland. Adrian stayed with Stephen and me.

I was there every day, apart from the second day of the trial when they showed the images that they'd found on his computer. They had been well hidden, which made me feel convinced that someone had put them there without Leonard's knowledge. He was an executive of one of the largest computer hardware firms in the world, but he had no idea of how these things actually worked. He bought and sold assets, he dealt with the shareholders and organised trade; he didn't know how to encrypt a hard drive, or whatever it was they said he'd done.

In any case, I had no wish to see them.

But Stephen did, and Adrian did. Even Janet was there. In her younger days she'd worked at a centre for abused women, so she claimed she was unshockable; there was little she'd not already had to deal with. But it seemed this wasn't quite true.

They came home that day quiet. I'd made them a big joint of roast beef, Yorkshire puddings, roast potatoes, parsnip, spring cabbage, carrots, gravy, even home-made horseradish sauce. All of this was mainly to keep myself occupied for the hours that the house was empty. But when they got home, none of them wanted to eat. The three of them sat at the kitchen table talking, trying to make sense of it, while I carved and dished up. It was as though someone had turned their positivity off at the mains. They were no longer talking about what they could do to help the legal team that Leonard had put together. They were talking about how they could come to terms with what they'd seen.

I tried to understand them. I tried to buoy them up again, tell them that this moping around wasn't going to do Leonard any good. I tried to tell them that they should eat something, that it would help, it would make them all feel better.

Stephen shouted something at me, something about how I couldn't make it alright, not this. That a roast dinner wasn't going to suddenly make everything better.

Janet's husband came to collect her. He was supposed to be coming for dinner, but they both left straight away and went home. The boys sat in the kitchen and I sat in the dining room on my own, at the table laid for six (I laid Leonard's place at the head of the table every day, whether he was here to eat or not). The beef was cooked to perfection and every mouthful tasted of anger. Fury at their failure to support their father in his hour of greatest need; resentment at their refusal to eat the meal I'd spent the whole day cooking for them.

When I'd finished I went back through to the kitchen. They'd been talking, but they fell silent when I came in.

'What about pudding?' I said, as cheerily as I could manage. 'I made a trifle, would you like some of that?'

Stephen stood up abruptly, his chair scraping noisily against the terracotta tiles. He pushed past without even looking at me and left the room.

'What about you, Adrian? Could you manage some trifle?'

'No, Mum,' he said.

I sat down next to him and put my hand over his. There were tears running down his cheeks. The sight of my grown son in tears affected me more than any of it.

'It's alright,' I said, moving my hand to his shoulder. 'It'll be alright, my darling! They'll see that it's all been a horrible mistake and then they'll let him come home. And we can all get back to how we were.'

'You don't understand,' he said. 'Those pictures…'

'I know, I know. They must have been dreadful for you to see. But they were hidden on his computer, and…'

'He was *in* them, Mum. Dad was in some of the pictures.'

'But they can do things with pictures now, can't they? They can do airbrushing, or whatever it's called. They can manipulate – '

'It was him, Mum. If you'd seen it…'

I still didn't believe it.

They didn't go back to the court after that. I was there on my own the next day, and for the remaining two days of the trial. I imagined the press were reporting on every aspect of the case, given Leonard's position, but I deliberately avoided the newspapers; I didn't turn on the television when I came home.

When he was convicted, I stood up in the court and shouted 'NO!' as loudly as I could. I was asked to leave. The next day he was sentenced.

The trial was very costly for me. It destroyed my marriage, because, even though I'd stood by him at every stage, once he was convicted Leonard refused to see me. He didn't send me a visiting order and even when I applied directly to the prison I was told that the prisoner was under no obligation to see anyone he did not wish to.

Stephen didn't come round any more. I spoke to Ina on the phone once or twice, but they never came round for Sunday dinner after that. I phoned up and asked if I could see the girls, if I could take them out somewhere. Ina made excuses. When I pressed her, she said that Stephen did not want the girls to see me until they were much older. I didn't understand this at all. It was Leonard who was accused of those terrible things, not I. But Stephen said I must have known. That I had covered up for him.

I knew no such thing. I still didn't believe it could be true. They had all denied him, all abandoned him.

Adrian took Diane and Joshy back to Australia and, although he phoned me once in a while, when I rang them there was never a reply. His calls grew less frequent as the months and years passed.

Things had also changed between Janet and me. I called her every so often for a chat, and it was an unspoken rule between us that we would not discuss Leonard. We talked about the children, about politics. But even those calls grew less frequent. She was cold towards me, as though my cheeriness disgusted her.

I went out, although less frequently. I found I could not trust my friends, after one of them gave an 'exclusive' interview with a daily newspaper and suddenly the whole thing was brought up again.

I went occasionally to the university to do a yoga class, but when the block of sessions I'd booked came to an end I didn't renew. There was no point. I'd reached the end. And so I went back to the house, the wonderful house that had nurtured us, kept us all safe, seen my children grow into strong men and protected me in those lonely months when the wolves were at the door, and I shut myself in and closed my eyes, and I waited.

Annabel

Sam was supposed to be giving me a lift to work when his mobile rang. I was already about half an hour late, but instead of asking me to answer it, he pulled over into a bus stop and accepted the call. 'Hello? … No worries, what's happened?' There was a long pause during which I could hear a muffled voice ranting about something in Sam's ear.

It was Monday, and it was raining, and despite myself I was still living at Keats Road. I had gone home with Sam briefly yesterday evening, the cat in a basket. The house had been stale and hostile, as though it was pissed off that I'd left. I stood in the living room and looked around, while Sam undid the cat basket. She'd leapt out, bolted for the kitchen and shot straight through the door, which he'd opened to let in some fresh air.

We went outside to look for her. We shook a box of cat biscuits and called her. After that I started to get a bit worried.

Sam made cups of peppermint tea for us both, since I didn't have any milk. We sat at the kitchen table with the back door open in the hope that the cat would come in of her own accord once she realised she was home.

'I wish you'd think again about this,' Sam said.

'What?' I asked.

'About being here, on your own.'

I sipped my tea, even though it was scalding hot. 'I just think it's a bit weird, moving in with a family of complete strangers. Don't you think it's weird?'

He looked at me with a surprised expression, then looked away. 'No, I don't think it's weird.'

'Really?'

'We're just helping out, that's all.'

'Don't get me wrong, I'm very grateful... but it's just... I've been so rude to you. Haven't I?' I gave up, then, feeling awkward.

'You haven't been rude. Not that I've noticed.'

'I mean in the hospital when my mum was ill. I know you were trying to help. I just thought it was a bit strange that you turned up. It was like you were stalking me.'

He coughed over his tea. 'I did explain, I was there because of that body.'

'Not the second time.'

'No, but you can hardly call it stalking when I came to find you *once* to check you were OK.'

'Once, and then you came to my house because I wasn't answering my phone.'

He didn't reply, and I remembered I was trying to apologise and had instead accused him of being a weirdo and a stalker. I backtracked. 'Although... you did kind of save my life...'

'Yep,' he said, his tone of voice suggesting he was starting to wish he hadn't bothered.

'And I am grateful. Really. For everything. And sorry, for being such a... pain.'

He was quiet again. He wasn't about to deny it.

'What was your mum like?' I asked Sam, doing my usual trick of changing the subject to avoid awkwardness and instantly making everything a hundred times worse.

'She was lovely,' he said. 'I still miss her.'

'Was it hard for you, when your dad started a relationship with Irene?'

He smiled over his tea, the discomfort of our previous exchange apparently forgotten.

'No, it wasn't like that. I think me and Mum engineered it, to be honest.'

'What do you mean?'

'She didn't like any of the carers she had until I found Irene. She wasn't especially fond of Irene either – too bossy, she said –

but she let her stay. I think she chose her not because she liked her as a carer, but because she could see that she got on with Dad. And with me.'

'I like her. She's been so kind.'

I watched Sam drinking his tea, wondering why he looked so sad. 'Did I say something wrong?' I asked.

'No. I was just remembering my mum. That's all. I miss her. You must miss your mum, too…'

'Yes,' I said.

I missed being a daughter, I thought, more than anything. I missed being useful to someone. Being important.

An hour later, while we were sitting discussing the man they'd arrested, and what he might be like, Sam's phone had beeped with a text message. It was Irene, to let us know that the cat had just turned up back at Keats Road. After that, with the heavy weight of inevitability resting on my shoulders, I'd picked up my untouched holdall full of the clothes that Irene had washed and ironed, even though I'd insisted I'd be fine to do it myself, and we'd gone back to the car. Clearly the cat and I weren't quite ready to go home after all.

Sam was still talking, parked in the bus stop. When he was finally able to interrupt the tinny voice I could just hear from his phone, he said, 'That's really interesting. Have you got the address?'

He pulled a ballpoint pen from the driver's side door pocket and selected a parking receipt from the pile in the central console, scribbling something on the back of it while the muffled voice continued.

'Right,' he said. 'I'm on it. I'll let you know. Ring you later. OK. Bye.'

He turned to me, his eyes sparkling again. 'Guess what?'

I was still a bit pissed off with him for making me even later for work, however reluctant I was to go back to looking at criminal damage and sex offenders, but now I was curious with it.

'No idea. What?'

'One of my contacts tells me that a woman phoned in just now to report that her housemate went into town with friends from work on Friday night and hasn't been seen since.'

I frowned at him. 'And?'

'The woman's name is Audrey Madison.'

'Is that name supposed to mean something to me?'

'You obviously haven't been rooting around Facebook, have you?'

'I'm not on Facebook.'

'You should be,' he said, pulling the car round in a wide U-turn and heading back towards the town centre. 'It's a fantastic research tool. Audrey Madison is the former girlfriend of one Vaughn Bradstock. Still not ringing any bells?'

I shook my head. His cryptic delayed reveal was getting on my nerves.

'He has a few friends on Facebook, unlike Mr Colin Friedland, who has only one: Vaughn Bradstock. In other words, the ex-girlfriend of Colin's one and only mate has gone missing.'

I stared at him.

'Colin's your man, isn't he? The one you identified by phone records?'

'How the hell did you know that?'

He smiled.

'I keep telling you you're not my only source of information, Annabel. In fact, you're the crappest source I've ever had, to tell you the truth.'

'Here he is,' Sam said, as the black cab stopped outside Colin Friedland's address.

The house was large, detached, set back from the road a little and on a slope above it. It was an old house, Edwardian by the look of it, likely to be worth a fortune. The search teams would have been through it from top to bottom, and, if they'd found anything at all, Colin would not have been released.

We'd come here by car and waited, parked about a hundred and fifty yards away from the big house in which, according to the edited electoral register, Colin lived all by himself.

'I still don't know what you're hoping to achieve by this,' I said.

'I don't know either,' he said. 'I just don't trust him. Do you?'

'I need to get to work, Sam,' I said. I'd been trying to call Frosty, trying to call the DCI, trying every number I could think of and leaving voicemail messages all over the place, but I hadn't managed to get hold of anyone yet. The thought of Audrey Madison – whoever she was – missing for the whole weekend was developing an uncomfortable bubble of urgency inside my chest.

Down the street, a figure got out of the taxi and leaned in through the window to pay. He looked as if he was counting out coins.

'Is that him?' Sam asked.

'Yes.'

The man who had been my angel turned away from the cab and towards us, seemed to look straight at us. Then he went towards the big villa, opened the gate and went up the path and out of our line of sight.

They'd let him go.

Colin

The house is cold, the vegetables in the pan smelling faintly rotten. I tip the water out of the saucepan and throw the vegetables in the bin. The refrigerator smells worse, and to my intense disappointment I have to throw away the salmon as well. And then of course I have to take the bag outside to the wheelie bin to dispose of it properly.

They've been in here, although nothing appears to be out of place. The whole house smells of them and their boots, trampling over my carpets and disturbing the ghosts. I will make sure I get some sort of compensation when all this is finished with. They didn't interview me – they went for humiliation and disrespect. I deserve better than that. I deserve their thanks.

I spend several minutes walking from room to room, inspecting the house as though I've been away from it for weeks, not just a few hours.

It takes a while for me to relax in here, but when that feeling comes it feels good. They have nothing they can charge me with, despite their best efforts, despite their crass need to try to humiliate me into saying something incriminating. I couldn't incriminate myself even if I wanted to, because I've done nothing – NOTHING – wrong. I know it and they know it. It is deeply satisfying, this warm thrill of vindication spreading through my whole body. I sit down in my favourite armchair and let myself daydream, picturing the beauty of the transformations I've observed and loving them, loving them all.

Annabel

'Sod it,' Sam said, after half an hour of sitting in the car with nothing at all happening. He turned on the engine.

'Thank goodness. Can we go to the police station now, please?'

He looked at me closely. 'Are you OK? I'm sorry, I didn't think – seeing him again...'

'It's not that,' I said, quickly, although I'd just about had a heart attack when Colin had looked up the road directly to where we were sitting. 'I need to get back to work...'

'I told you,' he said, heading back towards the main road, 'they won't be expecting you; you're still supposed to be on compassionate leave. And besides, we need to catch up with someone far more important.'

As it turned out, Lindsay Brown lived just a bit further down the hill towards the town centre from Colin. It was a fairly substantial house that had been divided into flats. Lindsay and Audrey shared the bottom floor.

'Oh,' she said, opening the door before we'd even had a chance to knock.

'Lindsay?' asked Sam. 'I'm from the *Chronicle*. You spoke to one of my colleagues, I believe?'

'Yeah, um... I'm just on my way to work.'

'Oh, sorry,' he said, looking genuinely apologetic. 'I thought I'd be able to catch you before you left.'

She hesitated, one hand on the door, looking from Sam to me and back again. 'Well, you're here now. I can spare five minutes. You want to come in?'

The living room was neat, all the furniture old and mismatched but cosy nonetheless, the kitchen through a big arch. Last night's washing-up in the sink. 'Do you want a drink?' she asked. 'Tea, or something?'

'That would be wonderful, thank you. Do you mind if I use your loo?'

'At the back,' she said, filling the kettle, and Sam scuttled off down the corridor. I sat awkwardly perched on the edge of a sunken sofa. 'You go around in pairs, do you?' she asked me, over the noise of the water boiling.

'Oh, um – no. I'm just – er – shadowing him.'

She looked baffled. 'What – like work experience?'

'Kind of.'

Clearly I looked far too old to be doing work experience on a newspaper, but to tell her the truth would take far too long.

By the time Sam came back Lindsay had placed three mugs of tea on the table, along with a bowl of sugar and some spoons. I was ravenous all of a sudden and was on the verge of asking if she had any biscuits.

'Do you mind if I...?' As well as the notebook and pen he'd fished out from his canvas bag, Sam waved his phone at Lindsay. 'I'm just really bad at taking notes, I always miss things...'

'Go ahead.'

'Thanks.'

He found the voice recorder function on the phone and put it on the coffee table in front of her.

'Have you and Audrey shared the flat for long?'

She cradled her mug of tea and, looking at how relaxed she was, I could have easily predicted her answer.

'No, just a few months. My last flatmate went travelling. Audrey answered an ad – in the *Chronicle*, in fact. Must have been... erm... February? March?'

'Did you get on well?'

'Yeah, I guess. I didn't see much of her, to be honest.'

'She went out a lot?'

'She was round at her boyfriend's, most of the time. She didn't sleep over there that often, but I was usually in bed by the time she got in.'

'That would be Vaughn Bradstock?'

'Yes. Funny old thing, he was. But they seemed to get on, until last week, that is.'

'They had a row?' Sam shifted in his seat, took a gulp of tea.

'They split up. I think it was all her idea.'

'Do you know why she finished it?' I asked.

Sam shot me a look of surprise – it was his interview, after all – but I felt like a spare part and, besides, I was curious.

'She said he was just a bit dull. She liked him a lot, but I think she was looking for a bit more – excitement? He collects stamps, for God's sake. Who collects stamps in this day and age?'

'Was she really upset by it all?' I asked. 'I mean – do you think she was depressed?'

'I wouldn't go that far. She had a bit of a cry and then started planning a night out with her friends.'

I frowned at this.

'So when did you last see her?' Sam said then, getting back to his list of questions.

'Friday. She was going out after work – someone's birthday, I think. She was quite excited about it. She wanted to go out on the pull.'

'You saw her go?'

'Yeah. She was all dressed up; she looked gorgeous. I remember thinking she was quite likely to pull looking like that.'

'But she didn't come home?'

'I went away for the weekend, to see some friends in York. When I came back on Sunday evening I knew straight away she hadn't been back. The clothes she'd tried on before going out on Friday were all over the bed still.'

'And you rang the police?'

'I sent her a text and tried to call her, but her phone was switched off. I thought about ringing Vaughn but then I thought, maybe she was with some other bloke. I didn't want to involve him.' Lindsay put her empty mug down on the table and looked pointedly at her watch.

'Sorry,' Sam said. 'Just one more question – so when did you report her missing?'

'I rang her at work first thing this morning. At Arnold's – that's where she works. I wanted to just check she was OK; after all, she hadn't taken any clothes with her... or anything like that. And they said she hadn't come in – she's always very punctual. The girl I spoke to was really worried when I said I hadn't seen her. So after that I phoned the police.'

'Do you know who that was? The girl you spoke to?'

'Cheryl, I think she said. I seem to remember Audrey talking about her, I think they got on well. Cheryl said she'd last seen her walking up the hill on Friday night. She didn't want to wait around for a taxi. She was walking up the hill on her own.'

'Can we please go to the station now?' I said, when we were back in the car.

Sam was sitting in the driver's seat. He hadn't turned on the engine; he was staring straight ahead with his hands on the steering wheel.

'Sam?'

'Don't you want to go and talk to Cheryl?' he asked. His eyes were bright with excitement. I hadn't seen him like this before. Had he been like this when we'd sat and had coffee in town, the first time we'd met? I'd been so full of suspicion then – maybe he'd toned it down.

'I want to go and make sure they're looking for Audrey,' I said.

'Try ringing them again,' he said, turning on the engine at last. 'If there's anyone there, I'll drop you off on the way.'

There was still no bloody answer, of course, from anyone. They were all in the morning meeting, which was where I should be by now. I wondered what would happen if I failed to turn up for work. Would they even notice?

Arnold and Partners took up the whole of the second floor of a building behind the Market Square, overlooking the back of the bingo hall that had been a cinema when I'd been a teenager. We found a space in the Pay and Display car park and walked across to the building.

'Is this what you do all day?' I asked. 'You wander around and pester people?'

'I'm not pestering anyone,' he said. 'Am I?'

'Hmm.' I had my arms crossed over my chest. At the bottom of the hill I could see the roof of the police station, covered in aerials and antennae, all Sixties grey concrete and pebbledash.

'If anything I should be in the editorial meeting,' he said. 'But technically it's my day off, so they won't miss me.'

'Why are we doing this on your day off?'

He stopped, then, and turned to face me. 'I'm starting to wish I'd just dropped you off at the station first thing.'

'So am I!'

We stared at each other.

'Don't you want to help find Audrey?' he asked.

'It's not our job to find Audrey!' I exploded. 'Why don't you trust the police to do it?'

'I'm willing to bet they haven't got as far with this as I have,' he said, still perfectly calm.

'They can only work with intelligence received,' I said. 'And at the moment I've got crucial stuff to tell them, and I'm farting around outside an accountants' with Nancy Drew.'

I could tell by his expression that he didn't know who Nancy Drew was. 'Or the Hardy Boys, or whatever they were called,' I said, lamely.

'You don't have to come in with me,' he said. 'I'll pick you up later if you want. Just send me a text. Or... whatever.'

'Fine,' I said, giving him a backward wave and stomping off down the hill, trying to look purposeful.

The morning meeting was just finishing when I arrived. Trigger and Kate piled back into the office talking and laughing without even registering that I was sitting at my desk. 'Did I miss much?' I said, in the end, as much to remind myself that I was alive and breathing as anything else.

'Nah,' said Trigger. 'The DI's got his knickers in a twist because the Chief might put in an appearance this afternoon. Clear desk policy and ties on, you know. Welcome back, by the way. Are you – er – alright?'

As if I'd been off with the flu or something.

'Thanks,' I answered. 'I'm much better now.'

Kate had gone next door, presumably to round up her mates for a coffee break.

I found the incident log, by searching for Lindsay Brown and the address where Sam and I had had tea this morning.

CALLER IS REPORTING THAT HER FRIEND HASN'T COME HOME THIS WEEKEND
*

FRIEND IS AUDREY MADISON AGED 36 DARK BROWN HAIR BLUE EYES F507 TEL MOBILE NUMBER 07670 212 212
*

AUDREY WENT OUT WITH FRIENDS ON FRIDAY NIGHT AND HASN'T BEEN SEEN SINCE – WORK SAYS SHE HASN'T TURNED UP THIS MORNING
*

MOBILE PHONE IS SWITCHED OFF
*

AUDREYS BOYFRIEND CORREX EX BOYFRIEND IS VORN BRADSTOCK LIVES IN BRIARSTONE TEL NO 07672 392 913
*

REPORT TO INTEL MAJ CRIME – ADVICE GIVEN TO CALLER

That was it. That was literally it. Nothing further on the report. It didn't mean nothing was happening, of course, just that the log hadn't been updated since – I looked at it again – 9.15 this morning.

Something else was bothering me, too. Keith Topping had said they hadn't got very far with the Automatic Number Plate Recognition database because there weren't cameras in the right places, and the time window was just too big to provide a useful dataset. But this window of time was much smaller... and there was an ANPR camera on the main road heading away from the Market Square.

I opened the ANPR software and started filling in a query. The field for the vehicle registration number I left blank. I isolated the cameras to be included down to just one – Baysbury Road, northbound. And the time – what time had Cheryl Dann said goodbye to her?

I pulled out my mobile phone and sent a text to Sam.

Ask Cheryl what time she left Audrey and where. Urgent. A.

While I was waiting for a response I put in an experimental time period for the search just to see what came back: 11pm to 12 midnight. Just one hour, one camera, and the system reacted as if I was forcing it to do manual labour. The processor on the workstation started whirring alarmingly. I opened up the Police National Computer in another window and performed a search for vehicles linked to Mr Colin Friedland of Briarstone, giving DI Frost as my authorising officer.

It seemed he had a Fiesta, blue in colour.

A minute and a half after I'd started the ANPR query, it came back with 1,759 hits. I put the registration number of Colin's Fiesta into the search results box.

No results.

My phone bleeped with a response from Sam.

Midnight, she was walking up Baysbury Rd. Why? S.

I didn't bother to reply. I felt cross that Colin's car hadn't been on the Baysbury Road that night when I'd fully expected it to be. And yet... there was something else. I felt so close to it, the thrill of being right and the possibility of finding something that might be useful. Something that might make a difference...

I went back to the query and changed the time parameters to ten minutes either side of midnight.

This time the data came back quite quickly: 259 results. Still a lot, but the likelihood was that, if Audrey had got into a car after leaving her friend, it would have gone past that camera.

I added a filter to the results for vehicles that had any alerts on them. This was unlikely to bring up anything interesting, after all, but the alternative would be to look through each of the 259 vehicles one by one in the hope of coming up with something. Fifteen alerts. I scrolled through them: No Insurance... No MOT... No Tax... several were flagged by the main office, so were likely to be linked to known offenders. Some of them probably with a curfew that meant they shouldn't have been out at that time of night and were therefore most likely up to no good.

Theft of Number Plate.

I clicked on the crime report number and to access the details. The owner was identified as Mr Garth Pendlebury, and the theft had taken place in Wright's Way, the road that ran behind County Hall. Mr Pendlebury worked at the council, and had noticed the theft when he returned to his car after finishing work on Thursday evening. No suspects. No other vehicles targeted in the area. The vehicle was identified as a white Volvo V40 estate.

I went back to the ANPR results and clicked on the link to the image from the camera. The car relating to the alert had passed the camera heading north, at 00:07. I waited for the picture to load, knowing that it would be dark and impossible to tell much from it.

But I was wrong. The camera was under a street-light and just for a change you could see quite a lot of the car.

It wasn't white, it was very definitely dark in colour, even allowing for the effects of the street-light. But, more importantly, it certainly wasn't an estate. It was much smaller. I couldn't tell exactly what the car was, but it looked a lot like a Fiesta.

I put the screen lock on the computer and stood up, walking past Kate and out of the office, heading upstairs to the MIR.

I knocked on the door and then opened it and went in. The room was full of people, busy, on the phone, but they all ignored me. The DCI's office was empty, and there was no sign of Frosty either. I felt panic starting in my chest.

'You OK there?' a woman asked me.

'Do you know where DI Frost is?' I asked. 'Or the DCI?'

'The DCI's gone to a meeting at HQ,' she said. 'I don't know about Frosty. Have you tried his office?'

'I've been ringing him and leaving messages. It's really urgent.'

'Anything I can help with?'

I looked at her, then, for the first time: jeans, a pale blue shirt over a white T-shirt, long brownish hair tied in a loose knot on the back of her head. Her ID badge told me she was DC Jenna Jackson. She looked young. But she'd asked, and for want of anyone else she would do. She would do just fine.

'I'm the analyst,' I said. 'I was working on this job until recently.'

'I know,' she said. 'You're Annabel. You got us to Colin Friedland through the phone data. I read your report.'

'Did you?'

'Come and sit down,' she said, pointing to her desk in the corner.

She'd obviously drawn the short straw, or perhaps been the last one at the briefing this morning. The desks were all shared ones, but hers was the smallest and piled with other people's crap.

'I shouldn't be in here,' I said. 'They made me come off the case.'

'Yeah. Heard about that. You want a coffee?'

'Oh. That would be good.'

'How do you take it?'

'Um, whatever's easiest? Black. Thanks.'

The single advantage to her desk was that she was next to the fridge, on top of which was a dirty tray toppling over with stacks of mugs of various sizes and states of cleanliness. Spoons that were dark brown with tannins and encrusted with sugar. Coffee and tea spilled and dried. A brown glass mug of the type that used to be given away with petrol, half-full of some liquid, which was already growing a cushion of mould. I was willing to bet this same still life was repeated in almost every office in every police station in the county.

'Now,' Jenna said. 'Tell me.'

'Do you know about Audrey Madison?'

'Who's Audrey Madison?'

I told her about Audrey and Vaughn and the links back to Colin, and then she started to take notes. I told her about seeing Lindsay this morning, and about Cheryl at the office where Audrey worked. I told her about the small dark-coloured car that might have been a Fiesta driving on the Baysbury Road at seven minutes past midnight, with stolen numberplates. I drank the coffee. It was reassuringly foul.

'I just want to make sure that they are investigating,' I said, when I got to the end.

'I'm sure they are,' she said, comfortingly.

'You don't understand,' I said. 'If Colin took her on Friday night, the chances are she's been without food or water since then. He will be waiting for her to die. I mean, is he under surveillance? Surely he wouldn't just be released without being put under obs?'

She looked uncomfortable.

'As far as I'm aware, he was supposed to be under observation but then something kicked off in North Division and both teams were deployed to that.'

'They think he's low-risk,' I said.

'He seemed to be quite compliant,' she said. 'It's always more of a concern when they're unstable. He came across in interview as being alarmingly rational.'

'Don't you think that's even more concerning, given what he's been doing?'

She shrugged, managed a smile.

'That's not my call.'

'But they don't know about Audrey,' I said.

'Annabel,' she said, 'leave it with me, OK?'

I left it with her. I drank half the coffee and left the rest, then I went back to the main office.

I couldn't believe they weren't watching him, and at the same time, given the appalling lack of resources and the usual bureaucratic wrangle involved in deploying what little they had, I wasn't surprised at all. Colin could have been doing anything. I was more certain than ever that he had taken Audrey.

Trigger and Kate had disappeared, which suited me fine. If I was going to try to break the rules, I didn't need an audience. I logged on to the system, into Windows Explorer. They'd granted me access to the Major Crime drive where all the documents were stored – Drive L. Surely they wouldn't be efficient enough to have removed my access already? But they had. I only had the Intel drives again. They'd shut me out.

I put my head in my hands, the sense of urgency building, growing, thumping inside my chest and my head like a pain.

I opened my email, thinking that I would send emails marked urgent to the DCI, the DI and anyone else, just as a last resort. Two hundred new emails. I scanned through them, and, finding four from Frosty, I gave a sudden yelp of delight.

Four emails, sent first thing this morning – after the DCI had taken me off the case, but clearly before he'd told Frosty about it. And he hadn't bothered to retract and delete them. They all had the subject line 'phone data' and they all had attachments. Fidgeting with anticipation, I opened the first one. There were five Excel spreadsheets attached. The message read 'A – here's the first batch of data for Colin's phone. More to come.' The second email – the message just said 'More data for you'. Another six Excel spreadsheets.

The third and fourth emails didn't even have messages attached, just more spreadsheets. Shit, shit. It was going to take me weeks to go through it all properly, time I didn't have. I opened all the spreadsheets and saved them to my personal drive, so it would take them a while to find them – if they ever even looked. I opened my spreadsheet that had listed all the numbers for everyone I'd identified so far, and started adding to it – each number that Colin had used, in other words each SIM card that he'd slotted into his phone, and the dates for the data that Frosty had obtained for me, so that I had a reference list to go to when it all got confusing.

I matched up the phone records with the existing ones – so now I had the rest of Colin's call records, for all his other SIM cards.

And very quickly I spotted what I'd hoped to find.

As well as the outgoing calls from Colin's SIMs to the phones the police had found with the bodies, there were other numbers, with the same calling pattern, going back to the earliest date of the billings. More people out there, then, that we hadn't found. I started jotting them down. How many were out there still? I made another note to apply for earlier data, too. He'd been doing this a long time.

And then I noticed something else – the outgoing calls to the victims weren't the only calls he made. There was a landline that featured on three sets of the billings, and when I put it into an internet search it revealed itself to be the number for the Rising Sun Chinese Takeaway, Stafford Road, Briarstone. Another landline, with one outgoing call, turned out to be a number for the Larches Residential Home in Baysbury. There was a mobile number, too – the same number came up in two different billings, with outgoing calls. The fact that the number featured on more than one set of billings was relevant. Whoever owned the phone was a real, live person whom Colin was prepared to speak to. And the latest phone contact was on a Wednesday lunchtime. Whoever they were, they were probably still alive.

I put the number into the internet search first, and drew a blank. Then I put it into the crime database and came up with nothing. Finally, only half paying attention because I'd already decided that this wasn't going anywhere and I still had twelve sets of billings to look at, I fed the number into the incident database.

There was a match. Incident log 13-0189, dated today. The number looked familiar, and when I clicked on the link I knew instantly why:

AUDREYS BOYFRIEND CORREX EX BOYFRIEND IS VORN BRADSTOCK LIVES IN BRIARSTONE TEL NO 07672 392 913

It was Vaughn's number. Colin had been so officious about swapping his SIMs, but he couldn't be bothered to do it all the time. He'd used his phone to call Vaughn.

I started a log for all my searches and queries. It was true I wasn't on the case any more, but if I was ever going to be asked to justify my behaviour I wanted a record of my thought processes to be able to hand over to someone. I wasn't doing this out of idle curiosity, or for any sort of personal gain. I was doing it because of Audrey. Despite this justification, my heart was still banging in my chest as I logged on to the telephone enquiry page of the intranet, keeping my fingers crossed. The operation was still in my list of queries – they hadn't removed my authorisation here, at least! Thank goodness. I went to the list of results and checked that there hadn't been any more since Frosty had emailed them to me.

Nothing. I'd been hoping for the forensic report on Colin's phone, the actual handset which would have been seized when he'd been taken into custody, but if they'd ordered a report it wasn't back yet. Sometimes these took weeks, depending on the backlog of cases and the level of urgency. And, as Colin had been released without charge, the likelihood of this one being a priority was low.

The call data for Colin's own number, the one he'd provided when they'd booked him in to the Custody Suite, was sparse. On that Wednesday lunchtime, after a brief outgoing call to Vaughn's number, he'd made a call to an 0845 number which turned out to be a Customer Care line for a supermarket. Then, on Saturday – after Audrey went missing – three incoming calls that were not answered – from the number that I'd noted as belonging to the Larches Residential Home. After each one, an incoming text from Colin's voicemail server. Each of these contacts registered a cellsite location – the first two calls and texts were shown as #WATER TOWER GRAYSWOOD LANE and the last call and text were #CAPSTAN HILL NR BLACKTHORNS.

I opened up the mapping software. I knew many of the cellsite locations, but these were unfamiliar. Grayswood Lane turned out to be about six miles outside of town, the other side of Baysbury, and Capstan Hill was a long, straight road heading through Baysbury village, where it would eventually form a junction with the main road to Briarstone.

The first two calls were three hours apart – at 11:05 and 14:18. Colin had been there – wherever it was – for a long time. And the last one was two hours later, at 16:33; it looked as if he might have been heading home.

I had a closer look at Grayswood Lane. It really was the middle of nowhere, starting at the junction with Capstan Hill and then winding through farmland for a few miles, ending abruptly with what looked like a track and a few buildings. I zoomed in on the buildings, which the software identified as Grayswood Farm. There were just a few houses dotted along the length of the lane, the aerial images showing the telltale bright blue rectangles of swimming pools. Halfway along the stretch between the farm at one end and Capstan Hill on the other was a circular structure in a woodland clearing. The water tower, I assumed. Of course, the cellsite location was hardly what you'd call exact – Colin's precise location when those calls came in and were ignored could have been anywhere within several hundred metres of the water tower. But the likelihood was that the phone had been somewhere on Grayswood Lane, because where else would he have been? In the middle of a field?

I did a search on the intelligence database for Grayswood Lane. There had been a burglary at the farm in June – a tractor had been stolen. A call about nuisance motorbikes riding off-road through the woods had come in from a house called Three Pines, Grayswood Lane, in May. A patrol had been sent, but by the time they got there the bikes had gone.

The voters' register showed that there were five houses in addition to the farm at the end. They all had names: Three Pines, Newlands Barn, The Old Manor, Woodbank and Pond House. I went through them one by one, looking at the names of the residents, in case something jumped out. Nothing did. They all showed at least two people resident at each address. This was starting to feel like a dead end.

I updated my log with all the searches and what I'd found, and made a note that I could draw no conclusions from it. Only that Colin's phone had been in the vicinity of Grayswood Lane, probably for several hours, on the day after Audrey had gone missing. There was nothing whatsoever to implicate him in her disappearance. There was little else I could do. The priority emails I'd sent to the DCI and the DI had still not been opened. I tried both their mobile numbers one last time, just to be sure, and left another voicemail.

Just before I shut down the workstation, I emailed my log, and my notes, and the list of additional numbers – to Frosty. Just in case. I grabbed my coat and left the police station by the back exit, dialling Sam's number on my phone as I did so.

Half an hour later we were parked in the road a few doors up from Colin's house, obscured by the slight bend in the road and out of the direct line of sight of the windows.

'I shouldn't really be here,' I said. 'I was in so late as it is.'

'Never mind that,' Sam said. 'Call it a late lunch if that makes you happier. And as I keep telling you, you're still on compassionate leave, or sick leave, or something. You shouldn't have gone in at all.'

'It's not that simple. I have to record all my hours, you know.'

Sam had been telling me all about Cheryl, Audrey's friend. She'd been reluctant to talk, having only just been interviewed by someone from Major Crime – which was a great comfort to me. It meant they were taking Audrey's disappearance seriously, at least. She had left Audrey around midnight in the town centre. Audrey lived just up the hill, about a mile away, and she hadn't wanted to wait to share Cheryl's taxi. So she had taken herself off up the Baysbury Road, protesting that she always walked home, it wasn't far, and what was going to happen on a brightly lit main road? And that was the last time Cheryl had seen her.

In return, I told him about the ANPR results. I should have kept quiet about it, probably.

'You know Colin works for the council?' Sam said.

'I didn't know that.'

'I guess it might have been a convenient place for him to steal numberplates.'

We sat in silence for a moment. My head was starting to ache.

'Did Audrey seem OK, when Cheryl said goodbye to her?' I asked at last.

'Apparently. She was a bit drunk, but they all were. Not staggering, Cheryl said. A bit tipsy. Anyway, after that I went to see Audrey's ex.'

'You went to see Vaughn Bradstock?' I asked. 'And?'

'He wasn't there. The receptionist told me your lot came and asked him a load of questions, and after that he was all upset and went home. I went to his house but there was no answer. No car outside.'

We stared in silence at the road ahead, a mother with a pushchair and a toddler making slow progress past Colin's house and towards the town.

'He's got her,' I said.

'Who? Vaughn?'

'No. Colin.'

'We don't know that for certain,' he replied.

'I just feel it,' I said. 'And you know he won't be giving her access to any food or water. How long do you think she'll last, Sam?'

He looked at me. This wasn't exciting any more. 'She wasn't depressed, or lonely. You heard her friend, this morning. She was happy, looking forward to going on a night out. He's only ever gone for – well. You know.'

'I just think the fact that he knew her is too much of a coincidence, don't you? I think he's got her somewhere. He's waiting for her to die.'

I'd been thinking about telling Sam what I'd found out this morning, about Colin's apparent visit to Grayswood Lane on Saturday, but that would have been crossing a whole new line beyond the one I'd already crossed by performing unauthorised searches on the system. Besides that, Sam had just given me an idea. Audrey wasn't depressed, not the way I had been – without even fully realising that I was that bad, without even giving it that name. It had been the shock, really, but also the loneliness and the frustration at work and the feeling that I was slipping away, beginning to disappear. It had been like evaporating, as though I was going to cease to exist and nobody would even notice. And seeing Colin, outside his house, had brought back memories of things he had said to me. The words he'd used – *release* – *choice* – *acceptance*. It had been my decision. He'd not made me do anything I hadn't already considered, already wanted to do. I had wanted it all to go away, and he had said that was alright, it was a decision I could make. He gave me the guts to do it, I think. Permission, if such a thing was needed. And he told me it wouldn't hurt; it would be peaceful, quiet, on my terms. He told me I could sleep and wait for it to happen and that I would not be afraid.

If anything, Sam had been the one in the wrong. He'd hauled me back from a place I'd gone to willingly. But now, of course, I knew he'd been right to do it. There were still moments, though, when I thought of being alone, of closing the door, and waiting for the quiet and the stillness and the word he used a lot – *transformation*. Becoming something better, more beautiful, with no striving or effort. Just peace.

It still crossed my mind that maybe he was an angel after all.

The only thing that really made a difference was the thought of all those other people he'd done it to. They couldn't all have been suicidal. And, by the sound of it, Audrey wasn't – she hadn't chosen his path, had she? He'd taken it upon himself to shove her down it, for whatever private gratification he was going to get. And how had he felt, when he'd realised I hadn't transformed at all? When there hadn't been a news report about me? When he'd realised that I'd escaped? Had he been pissed off, cross, upset?

And how would he feel if he saw me again? Would he even recognise me?

'If he comes out…' I said out loud, and then didn't finish my sentence.

'If he comes out what?'

'I want to talk to him.'

Sam looked at me, alarmed. 'What? No. I don't think so.'

I turned to him, trying to make sure I had his full attention. 'I've got an idea, Sam. I know how we can find Audrey.'

'How?'

'He can take me to her.'

'What? What do you mean?'

I hesitated, wondering whether to tell him, what he would say if I did. And in that moment's hesitation the chance passed, because Colin Friedland came out of his house and shut the front door firmly behind him. He got into a dark blue Fiesta which was parked on the driveway and reversed out into the road.

Sam had already started the engine. He waited until the Fiesta got to the end of the road and helpfully indicated left towards the town centre, and pulled out to follow.

'Don't start,' he said, even though I'd said nothing. 'I just want to see where he goes. Alright?'

'That's fine,' I said.

'Really?'

Once we were on the main road, a white van was between us and the Fiesta. We slowed down at the lights and I could just about see the side of the car, and Colin's wing mirror.

'Don't lose him, whatever you do,' I said.

'I won't,' Sam said, with a sigh that suggested I was starting to get on his nerves.

We were both privately hoping that he was going to lead us to Audrey, but a few moments later he pulled in to the Co-op's car park. Sam drove straight past, up to the roundabout and back again.

By the time we drove in, Colin had parked and was walking towards the supermarket. He was carrying a reusable Co-op carrier bag.

Sam reversed into a space in the row behind the Fiesta and cut the engine. I undid my seatbelt.

'Where are you going?' he asked. 'We can just wait for him to come back…'

'No,' I said. 'I'm going to talk to him.'

'*What?*' Sam said. It was the closest I'd ever come to hearing him shout.

I was rooting through my handbag for my mobile phone, just a cheap Pay As You Go one that Irene had given me – an old one of hers, I think – because the one Colin had taken from me was still in some evidence bag somewhere. I had considered buying a nice new one, but now I was glad I hadn't – this would be ideal. It was small and lightweight. I found it at the bottom of the bag and to Sam's surprise I undid the top three buttons of my shirt and pushed the phone inside my bra.

'What the fuck?'

'Look,' I said. 'I'm going to sit outside the Co-op, and when he comes out he might recognise me. You know? He might want to – have another try.'

'Are you actually fucking mad?' Sam's eyes were wide. I'd never heard him swear once, never mind twice. 'He was trying to kill you, Annabel. And you want to let him have another go?'

'Not really, no. But things are different now, aren't they? I know who he is, what he is. I'm not vulnerable now. I know what I'm doing. But he doesn't know that, does he? That gives me an advantage.'

Sam was frowning now.

'You are mad. Seriously. What the hell are you thinking? And in any case, surely your lot will have him under surveillance or something?'

'They're all deployed to other jobs. I asked someone. Look, we don't have much time,' I said, 'he might only have gone in to buy a paper. I don't even know if this will work – he might not see me, he might avoid me. But if he has got Audrey, it's not at her house or his house, is it? So where is she? He might take me to the same place, wherever it is.'

I opened the car door and Sam went to grab my arm, missed, and got out his side instead. It was raining, a dull soft drizzle that made everything look out of focus. The clouds overhead were dark grey, the wind picking up and cold.

'Wait. Just wait a second,' he said, standing in my way. 'What if I can't follow you? What if we get separated?'

'I've got my phone. You hold on to my bag. I don't think he'll search me, or anything. If he does take me somewhere, it won't be far. Get hold of DI Frost and tell him. When I get a chance, I'll send texts, so they should be able to find me.'

'And what if they can't find you? What if you can't get a signal? What if he kills you straight away? Annabel, this is insane...'

'He won't kill me,' I said, cheerfully, setting off across the car park, through the puddles, in the direction that Colin had taken. And I was a little bit mad, I thought to myself. But Sam knew that all along, didn't he?

I glanced back at him. He was following me, jogging to catch up.

'Annabel,' he said, breathless, 'just hold on a sec. Stop.'

I stopped. We were on the ramp leading up to the arcade of shops, the entrance to the Co-op around the corner. I had already spotted a bench outside where I could sit and wait.

'I'm going to look in the Co-op and just make sure he's in there,' he said. 'After that I'll come out and wait in one of the other shops where I can see you. Just in case he takes you somewhere on foot. Alright?'

'Yes,' I said, surprised at the wave of relief. 'Thanks. Don't...'

'What?'

'Just don't interfere.'

I left him then and plonked myself down on the bench. It was tempting to watch Sam to see where he went, but now I was in full view of the Co-op and if – just if – Colin had caught sight of me, I didn't want to ruin this enterprise before it had even started. I kept my head bent low but chanced a brief glimpse up, at the door.

For this to work, I had to look right. The rain was helping a good deal, soaking my hair already and plastering it to the sides of my head. I'd left my coat in Sam's car and I was sitting on the bench in my blouse and cardigan. I looked down at the wool and saw the rain settling on the fibres, tiny droplets that sparkled in the light from the shop window. I closed my eyes slowly and opened them again, and when I raised my eyes I saw the automatic exit doors of the supermarket slide open, and the figure I recognised as Sam coming through. He walked past me and if he acknowledged me I didn't see it, just his legs, his stride purposeful. He went out of my line of vision. I thought of the CCTV footage, of the camera that was positioned somewhere behind me and to my left, no doubt pointing in another direction. I thought of the way I'd looked. I let my shoulders sag.

I listened to the people, the conversations going on, snatches of voices. I could smell the fish and chip shop. My face still, my eyes opening and closing slowly. Waiting. Even this, even this feeling, trying to fake it now but actually it was easy to do: the loneliness, people all around me but even so I might as well not exist. Sitting here on a wet wooden bench in the rain wearing my cardigan, the rain soaking my hair and my clothes, and nobody looked at me, nobody stopped. Feet walking past. Schoolkids laughing and pushing each other around. I didn't look at them. I didn't look up. It was this – inertia – this waiting, waiting for something to happen, for something to act upon me so that I didn't need to act myself.

I remembered then how it felt, waiting for him.

After a while I almost forgot to look up. It was such a strange feeling. Quiet, cold, waiting.

I saw a pair of feet walking directly towards me and I almost thought to myself, at last, someone is going to ask me if I'm alright, and I nearly raised my head. Then I remembered what I was doing, and why, and I kept still, my eyes looking down at my knees.

He stood directly in front of me. I found myself looking at a pair of brown brogues, obviously coated in some kind of water-repellent suede protector spray, because there were small bubbles of water on them that hadn't soaked in. Dark blue jeans, with a crease down the shin where they'd been ironed.

'Annabel?'

I recognised the voice and for a moment I was afraid, a shuddering fear that was oddly accompanied by the same jolt of relief I'd felt when I'd thought he was an angel. His voice was so calm, quiet; so soothing.

'Annabel?' he said again, and this time I looked up, slowly, raising my head and blinking as though I wasn't sure of anything, where I was, what I was doing.

He was looking at me with concern. And then he looked left and right, as though he was worried someone might be playing some kind of cruel trick on him. He looked at the bench and brushed the raindrops off it with his hand, shooting the water off and on to my feet, down my legs. Then he sat down next to me.

I lowered my head again. What was I supposed to say? This was difficult – I could get this wrong, so wrong...

'You're – you are... Ed?'

'That's right,' he said, his tone even. 'You remember.' He was leaning towards me, and as I thought about what to say next he touched me on the arm, a light touch.

'How are you, Annabel?' he asked.

I shook my head in reply, slowly, and then faster so that my wet hair swung in rats' tails around my cheeks. I pulled a face. Was it working? I had no idea. At the same time as trying to create these feelings – whatever they were that had attracted him to me in the first place: desolation, grief, confusion, despair – I realised they were still inside me, somewhere.

'You said I could go,' I said then. 'You said it would all go away and I'd be alright.'

'Yes,' he said. 'I'm sorry.'

'It didn't work,' I said. 'I'm still here. I'm still in hell.'

He paused then and took his arm away and I had the terrible feeling that I'd said the wrong thing without knowing it; that I'd somehow given myself away. The phone, small as it was, felt like a brick against my skin, sticky and warm. My blouse was damp and clinging to me, and I pulled the wet cardigan around me just in case he could see the outline of the phone.

'Help me,' I said.

'You can help yourself, Annabel,' he said.

'How?' I said. 'Tell me what to do. Please tell me.'

'You can go home,' he said, 'and shut the door...'

I was shaking my head before he'd finished. 'No, they'll find me again. They put me in the hospital. They watch me all the time. I just want to be alone. There's nowhere I can be alone.'

I looked up at him then, even though it would have been better to keep my head down. I wanted to check his face, to see if he looked suspicious. The rain was running down my face like tears and I didn't brush it away. He didn't look suspicious. He looked sad, sorrowful, but his eyes were bright.

I thought he was going to say 'I can't help you'. I could picture him saying it and standing again and going back to his Fiesta and driving away. And if he had done that, I would have found Sam and we would have probably gone back to his house and dried off and everything would have been fine. We would have lost nothing – other than the chance to find Audrey.

But he smiled, and stood up, and held out a hand to help me to my feet. I'd got stiff sitting there in the rain and the awkwardness in standing up was completely genuine.

'You can come with me,' he said.

I didn't smile back. I just kept my head down, out of the rain, and followed his feet back to the car park, my steps measured, docile, compliant. He had a bag with him, a reusable canvas bag, swinging against his legs, full of shopping. My stomach grumbled and I wished I'd thought to eat something before launching myself into this crazy plan.

He stopped next to the Fiesta and opened the passenger door for me.

I think I hesitated, just for a moment. What was I doing? What was I getting myself into?

'Get in, then,' he said.

I got in and sat down. Colin shut the door and a few moments later opened up the boot, putting the shopping inside and slamming it shut again. The windscreen had started to mist up almost straight away, but I could see Sam across the car park, walking towards his car, hunched into his jacket. I hadn't been afraid until then, not really, but something in me made me want to launch myself at the door and open it and run towards Sam.

And then the driver's door opened and he got inside. I didn't look at him. I looked at my hands in my lap.

'You put your seatbelt on,' he said.

It had been habit, I hadn't even thought about it. His tone – curious. Suspicious?

'Yes,' I said simply, and went back to sitting with my hands in my lap, head low.

This seemed to satisfy him and he reversed out of the parking space and drove through the exit, then turned left on to the main road. We were heading up the hill towards his home. Surely he wasn't going to take me there? I wanted to look behind to check whether Sam was following but I didn't move. I was sitting as still as I could but now, for the first time, I felt the panic rising inside me like a swell of salty water, and I had to concentrate to keep my breathing steady. I could hear my heart above the noise of the car, the blood rushing through my ears. And I was picturing the DCI asking what the hell I thought I was doing, jeopardising a case that I'd been specifically told I was not involved in.

This was not a good idea. It was insane. A wave of terror hit me. And it was far too late to back out of it now.

We drove straight past Colin's road and onwards, through the leafy suburbs, past the business park and the council dump, and then right down a lane that took us out of town completely and past fields. The windscreen wipers squealed back and forth like fingernails down a blackboard.

'Where are we going?' I said quietly, unable to keep silent any longer.

'I have a house where you will be safe,' he said. 'You can make your own choice, your own decision. Whatever you want to do.'

His voice was jerky, odd, a staccato rattle, and I realised that he was jumpy too, whether through nerves or excitement I couldn't tell. I didn't want to look up at him. Not just because I was afraid, but also because it didn't feel like the right thing to do. I kept my head down.

'We can talk things through, again, like we did before.'

'I just want to go to sleep,' I said.

'Good,' he said. 'That's good. You can sleep soon. We're nearly there.'

We took a left turn down another lane. If there was a sign, I missed it. As we turned, I glanced out of the window at the thick bushes in case there was a road sign. There wasn't. I tried to think which way we'd come out of town, which villages we should have passed, but I'd never been that way before. *Think, Annabel,* I told myself. *Focus. Concentrate. You're here to do a job.*

If we'd come out of Briarstone towards the east, we should have hit Baysbury. But we hadn't been through a village – just fields and trees – so we must have skirted it somehow. We'd been driving for about five minutes, so that meant – how far had we come? Thinking about it was making my head hurt. About four miles, maybe five?

I looked up, through the windscreen, determined to try to get my bearings even if it did make him wonder. Did he really think I was still under his influence, hypnotised or whatever it was he'd done to me? He wasn't trying to hypnotise me again, anyway, was he? Unless he was saving that for when he could give me his full attention. He wanted to talk things through. That was his plan – he was going to do it again, whatever he'd done. The thought of it made me afraid, and just for a moment I thought I'd made a big mistake. I wasn't this brave person. This wasn't me.

Sam wasn't following us. I didn't know this for sure; I just felt it, as though there was a cold wind behind me, an emptiness. There was something about the narrow lane, the bushes high on either side, blocking out what little daylight remained under the leaky clouds, closing in on us. If he'd been following us, Colin would have noticed. He would have said something.

We reached a T-junction and Colin turned left again. The road opened out and for the first time since we'd left the town other cars passed us in the opposite direction: a brown removals van, a pickup truck from a local builder's merchant. I could see houses up ahead and wondered if this was Baysbury, but before we got there I heard the tick-tick of the indicators and we turned right into another narrow country lane. This time I saw the sign, on its back, half-buried in the undergrowth as though someone had taken the bend too quickly and knocked it over: Grayswood Lane.

I felt a shot of triumph, just a brief one. I'd been right. And the log I'd sent to Frosty would tell them where to look.

The car slowed and turned into a driveway. I heard the tyres on the gravel and then we stopped. I looked up, at last. It was a big house, old, with a limestone portico. I sat where I was until he opened the door and then when I got out I could take it in properly. The front garden, which must once have been beautiful, was overgrown. The gravel driveway, spotted with weeds, swept in an elegant turning circle around a stone fountain which was dry, the bowl of it coloured with a dried green slime that might once have been algae, the outside of it pitted with lichen. The grass lawn that edged the driveway was waist-high, and beyond it the yew hedge that hid the house from the road, and which must once have been trimmed to neat angles, was bushy and losing its shape.

'Come on,' he said impatiently.

'Is this your house?' I asked, following him up the steps to the front door.

He paused, fishing out a single key from his pocket. 'Yes.'

The door opened and the smell hit me at once. Food gone rotten, rooms that hadn't seen fresh air for a long time, damp fabric, mould, must. But above it, overpowering, a smell I recognised from Shelley's house. Someone in here had died.

I put my hand over my nose and mouth. Perhaps I should have been unconcerned, but I couldn't help it. I felt my stomach, empty, heaving.

'Sorry. The smell – I forget,' he said. 'Come on. It's not so bad upstairs.'

The hallway was dark, quiet, the deep red carpet that ran up the wooden staircase dull with a film of dust. Beside the front door was a pile of newspapers, takeaway menus and unopened post. I glanced at it, tried to see if I could see a name, but he was waiting for me at the bottom of the stairs.

'Annabel, come with me.'

I followed, watching his back as he climbed the stairs. The fear, which had abated a little with the triumph of realising that my analysis had been spot on, was coming back.

Last time we'd met, I'd been in a very bad place. Lack of sleep, grief, shock, the horror at losing my mum so suddenly – and he'd appeared. Whatever it was he'd said to me, whatever he'd done, I didn't remember it at all. I remembered his appearance, an ordinary-looking man, not old, not unattractive, his head shaved to hide the receding hairline, green eyes, unsmiling but not threatening in any way. His clothes had been unremarkable. I could have passed him any number of times on the street and not looked at him twice. But, in that crazy few minutes when my heart was shattered and my head spinning, I had looked at him and listened to what he said and I had genuinely believed he was an angel, and that he was there to take care of me.

And what he was doing now amounted to the same thing, didn't it? He hadn't hurt me, and, even though I was jumpy and afraid and felt as if I'd taken a stupid risk, I didn't think he was going to hurt me now. He'd just done exactly what I'd asked him to do – taken me somewhere where I could be alone. Was that not what he'd done to all the others? Helped them achieve what they could not do alone? Answered their prayers?

At the top of the stairs a hallway stretched down to an arched stained-glass window at the end; behind it the branches of a tree created dancing patterns, rattling against the glass, scratching against it like clawing fingers. All the doors on either side of the hallway were closed. I followed him down towards the window, to the last door on the left, which he opened.

It must have been a guest bedroom once. The double bed was covered with a pink satin counterpane, but the divan underneath it was bare. The carpet was peach with swirling patterns, grey with dust. The curtains, heavy, frilled, were closed against the greyness outside, leaving the room gloomy. Built-in wardrobes lined one wall, the doors closed. A dressing table was set into the wardrobe with a stool tucked underneath, the seat a dark green velvet, a gold-coloured satin twist fringe coming away from one corner and hanging forlornly underneath. The walls were painted a pastel pink, two faded landscape prints hanging from the walls in pink plastic frames either side of the bed. A single bedside table held a lamp with a shade tipped to a drunken angle, an old-fashioned alarm clock with two bells and a hammer, no tick.

I didn't know if I was getting used to the smell or if it was just fainter up here, but the odour coming from the room was not unpleasant, merely musty, the smell of a room with no fresh air – a faint sweetish floral scent to it. On the dressing table I noticed a porcelain bowl filled with a brown pile of dried flowers and a single pine cone, all of which were coated in grey dust. Nothing said 'guest bedroom' quite as loudly as a bowl of pot pourri.

Colin stood to one side of the open door, watching me with interest. I could feel his eyes on me as I looked into the room.

'You can stay here,' he said.

'Yes,' I said. I walked into the room and stood still, waiting for whatever came next. I didn't hear him shut the door or leave, so I sat down on the edge of the bed. He was filling the doorway, watching me, and the glance I had of him made me alarmed. In that one glimpse I could see how alive he looked, how animated – excited, even.

He paused for a moment, and then he said, 'I will come back in a little while to check you're alright. We can talk some more then, if you want.'

Then he closed the door, without waiting for me to reply. A second later, I heard the key turn in the lock. He was locking me in! Why? Surely he had no need to do that? But of course I kept quiet, and then I heard muffled footsteps receding as he went down the hallway.

I waited for ten beats, thinking that he might come back straight away, might have forgotten something. The room was silent. I could hear nothing, not even the wind, or the rattling of the branches on the window in the hallway.

I reached inside my blouse for the mobile phone. There was almost no signal here. Hadn't Sam been going on about that? But of course it was rural – it was quite possible that I wouldn't be able to connect to the network. I checked again that the phone was on silent – it wouldn't be good to give myself away now. Then I sent a text to Sam.

Am in big house on Grayswood Lane. Am alone now. He has locked me in a room. Did u follow? A

A few moments, then a message illuminated the screen.

Error – Unable to send text. Retrying

I stood up and went to the cupboards, opened them one by one. They held piles of linens, towels, curtains, bed sheets, everything folded neatly. Clouds of dust rose from everything. I wanted something solid, something I could use to lever the door open, or even just to use as a weapon if I needed it. In the second wardrobe on the top shelf was a suitcase, a brown one with leather straps around it. I thought about getting it down but it might make a noise. Better to wait until I was sure he was gone.

The floorboards under the thick carpet creaked faintly as I crossed the room and for a moment I held my breath, hoping that, wherever he was, he hadn't heard. Nothing. I carried on to the window and pulled the curtain to one side a fraction so I could see out. The room was at the rear of the house. I'd already worked that one out. I wasn't going to be able to see if the Fiesta drove away, but if I could open a window I might be able to hear it.

The window was a sash one, heavy-looking, and the catch hadn't been opened in years. I could see a garden, a long slope of overgrown grass leading down to a tall brick wall with a gate in an arch at the middle of it. The trees bordering the garden were immense, and moving soundlessly in the wind.

From somewhere in the house, I heard a bang. I stood still, in case he was coming back, but there was just empty silence. Had that been the front door? Had he gone?

I went to the door, trying the handle gently. The door stayed firmly shut. I bent down and looked through the keyhole, which showed me a tiny patch of flock wallpaper on the opposite side of the hallway. He had taken the key with him.

I went back to the bed and took out the phone again. The message was still showing as pending. I tried to dial Sam's number but all I got was a disconnection bleep. I took the phone over to the window to see if there was any signal there, but it was no better. Would they still be able to trace the phone, if there was no signal? I tried various places in the room, with no result. After that I went to the door and pulled at the handle again, turning it and tugging at the door. It gave a little, just a little, but the lock held firm.

A noise again.

I stopped dead and listened, my ear pressed to the door. Silence. And then, very faint, from somewhere – I heard a short high-pitched sound, like a cry.

I banged on the door, hard. 'Hello?' I shouted. 'Hello? Is anyone there?'

I listened to the silence, and more silence, and then suddenly footsteps outside, fast, rustling, the key in the lock, and I leapt backwards, stumbling, over to the bed, my breath coming in gasps. I just had time to shove the phone back into my bra.

The door opened and he stood there watching me. I noticed he was as breathless as I was, as though he'd run up the stairs.

'What are you doing?' he said, his voice measured and steady even though he was clearly upset.

'I don't want to be locked in,' I said. 'Why did you lock me in?'

He frowned. 'I wanted you to be safe. You need to be safe.' He stepped towards me, into the room, and at that moment I wondered if I would have enough strength to overpower him. He was taller than me, but I was probably heavier. If I rushed at him, I could probably knock him over – but then what? Where would I go?

'I'm scared of being locked in,' I said. 'I can't sleep. I can't sleep if I'm locked in.'

Maybe I could get away with this, I thought. Maybe there were some instincts that overrode his influence – some primal fears that were more insistent than the desire to fade away. And it occurred to me that he didn't entirely trust me. He didn't fully believe that I was ready to just lie down and die, after all – or else why had he locked me in?

'You're safe. You're safe with the door locked,' he said.

He was close enough now to touch me, and, although my eyes were level with his chest and I did not want to look up, he touched my upper arm – and the touch was soothing, comforting and I felt my heaving heart start to calm, felt the hollow thumping in my chest lessen. He said some other things. I did not hear them.

'You should sleep,' he said. 'It will be easier when you're asleep. You can sleep, Annabel.'

I sat down on the bed. 'Will you be here, in the house?'

'For a while,' he said.

'I am sleepy.'

'That's good. Why don't you lie down?'

I lay back on the bed that smelt of damp and dust. I felt the phone move a little and, worried that it would be visible through the fabric of the blouse, I turned on to my side, away from the door, away from him.

No sounds for a moment, other than his breathing and mine. I wondered what he thought of me, lying on this strange bed in this strange house that probably held one dead body and another one that was probably on the boundary between death and life. I'd heard her cry out. That was the noise I'd heard – which meant she was alive, and she was somewhere in the house.

My heart was beating fast, the dust in my throat making me want to cough. I had my eyes closed and a tear leaked through the corner of my eye and rolled down my temple, dripping off on to the bedspread. *Help me,* I thought. *Mum, please, help me.*

And then, just as I thought he was going to stay with me, I heard his steps retreating and the door shutting behind him. I waited for the sound of the key in the lock, but it didn't come.

I lay still on the bed for a while, not quite trusting that he wouldn't be waiting for me to do something. I pulled the phone out of its hiding place and tried again for a signal. Nothing. I wrote another message to Sam just in case at some point it would send.

Please hurry up. A

I waited a good ten minutes, playing with the useless phone, and then I stood up again. As I did so I heard another noise in the house – and then another bang. I went to the door and turned the handle carefully so it didn't make a noise, opened it a crack, half-expecting him to be standing in the hall watching the door.

A little wider. The hallway was empty, all the other doors closed just as before. I trod carefully on the carpet, wary of creaking floorboards, but everything felt muffled, silent, as though a carpet of snow had fallen on the place rather than dust. There were flies everywhere, I noticed now – dead ones, mainly, on the carpet. A couple buzzing lazily in the fusty air.

At the top of the stairs I stopped and looked around the corner. No sign of him. The house waited for me to move.

By the time I got to the bottom of the stairs I was fairly certain that he'd left. The windows either side of the front door, filthy as they were, gave me a good view of the front driveway and I could see it was empty. The Fiesta was gone. I tried the front door, but, predictably, it was locked. I checked my phone again and this time there was a signal, just two bars but it was probably enough. I dialled Sam's number. It rang and rang and then he answered.

'Hello?' I said, my voice an urgent whisper.

There was no answer though, just a crackle and hiss. 'Sam, can you hear me?'

The phone beeped and the call disconnected. I sent another text.

Am in big house on Grayswood Lane. Yew hedge.
He has gone but is coming back. Hurry. A

Downstairs, the smell was much worse. I didn't want to explore, but at the same time I needed to find a way out. He would be back soon, and I didn't want to be here when that happened.

Behind me there was a noise, the same as before – a moan, rising into a wail. It sounded nearer, but still a long way off. All the doors were closed, but I tried the nearest one and found myself in a large kitchen, a wooden farmhouse table at the far end and beyond them patio doors on to the large back garden. The kitchen was tidy but not clean, and the smell had ramped up a notch. I was getting closer.

'Audrey?' I said, and then a little louder, 'Audrey! Can you hear me?'

I waited, listened. Nothing. My shoes crunched on the bodies of the dead flies – so many more of them, in here. The kitchen widened at the far end into a conservatory that went in an L shape around the corner, opening out on to the main living area. It had its own door on to the hallway, I noticed, thinking that someone must have knocked a wall down and at the same moment wondering what on earth I was doing creeping around this house thinking about home improvement.

Then I saw the body.

Lying on the sofa this time rather than sitting in a chair, as Shelley Burton had been: what remained of the person was black, hollow-looking, still wearing clothes that were stained and slack against what remained. Patches of greying hair clung to what was left of the head, skull-like but still with shreds of skin clinging to the bone. Around the sofa, apart from the flies, everything was normal – but, on the sofa, what had once been a human being, with emotions and intelligence and a sense of humour, had effectively liquefied and melted into a reeking mess of decay.

I looked at the body for a long moment, without moving closer, my hand over my nose and mouth as though that would stop the smell, as though it would keep my scream and my sobs of fear and horror tight inside me. I didn't want to do this any more. I didn't want to be here, in this mad place, where people were dead and nobody noticed.

Enough. Stop it, Annabel. Get a grip.

I walked carefully, my back to the bright windows which gave out on to the tangled foliage beyond, to another door at the far side of the room. Some kind of utility room by the look of it, and another smell in here – not death this time, but something even worse. There were Wellington boots lined up under a coat rack, a long work surface with Tupperware on it, a tennis racket, cleaning materials in a bucket, a tray containing small pots for cuttings, twine, a watering can, wasp spray, a pair of gardening gloves, a broken drawer, a pile of old net curtains. I could see the back door, bolted at the top and bottom. I undid the bolts, easing them jerkily back and forth until they gave. The key wasn't in the lock and I already knew the door would be locked. But, when I pushed it, it moved a little. I looked around for the key, thinking that they would leave it somewhere close by, whoever it was who had lived here, and there it was – on a hook, hanging on a rusty nail amidst cobwebs on the window frame.

I seized it and tried it in the lock. It was stiff, but this time the door opened and I pushed against the wood, warped from the rain and lack of use. Outside, the weeds were monstrous and once the door was open I could not close it again. But the fresh air, sudden after so long without it, was delicious.

Having secured my escape route, I went back into the utility room. There was another door, and when I opened it what I found behind it was, as I'd expected, a pantry: food tins lined up on shelves, jars of pasta sauce, and, on the wider shelves below, catering-sized pots and pans, wide serving platters, packs of paper napkins. Perhaps because the doors had remained shut, there was no dust in here – just a wafting smell of something bad, rotten, like the smell of the sewage outlet I'd found on a lonely beach as a young girl. A sudden assault on the senses.

There was a noise again, this time much closer, as though she was inside this space with me.

'Audrey?' I said. 'Hello? Is there someone there?'

To my left, between two shelves, was a light switch. I had been expecting the electricity to be disconnected, but to my surprise when I flicked the switch a single bulb overhead came on, and illuminated a long, narrow space lined with shelves. And at the back – right at the back – another door.

It was locked, of course. And although I fumbled on all the shelves, my hands shaking, there was no sign of a key.

I went back out into the utility room and started searching in all the drawers, pulling them out quickly and slamming them shut again, and then the cupboards underneath. In the very last one I tried, there it was: an old metal toolbox, of the type that opened like a concertina at the top. I pulled it out of the cupboard, clattering it on to the terracotta tiles, tugging the creaking hinges to open it. The tools were old, rusted, but here was exactly what I needed – a big, flat-headed screwdriver. I went back to the pantry and the door at the end, inserted the screwdriver into the space beside the lock and levered it. I was expecting the door to pop open, but of course what happened was that the wood splintered and cracked, and from behind the door somewhere I heard wailing and crying, and finally a single, wailing, desperate word rising to a shriek: 'No!'

I worked at the door, digging away at the wood, until finally the screwdriver came up against metal, and I dug beneath it and levered, and with a sudden shudder and a bang the door opened.

Beyond it, darkness, and a staircase leading down.

'Audrey?' I said.

A pause, and then a hushed, throaty voice: 'Who are you?'

I looked for a light switch – surely there must be one? And then there it was, under a shelf loaded with tubs of dishwasher tablets. I flicked the switch and the staircase illuminated, and from below another shriek.

I went down the steps, gripping the screwdriver firmly in front of me in case Colin was going to appear from nowhere.

It was a small room, whitewashed brick, with a window high up on the left wall. The darkness it looked on to suggested that it was buried beneath weeds. There was a table, and an old divan with a mattress, a tea chest, empty boxes – and on the bed, curled into a ball, her face covered with both her hands, a dark-haired girl wearing a short satin skirt.

I felt a surge of relief. It was her; it was definitely her.

The room stank.

'My name's Annabel,' I said. 'I've come to get you out. Are you OK?'

'Water,' she said.

I went back up the stairs to the utility room. There was a butler sink in the utility room and when I ran the tap it rumbled for a second and then cold water splashed into the sink. I left it running and looked for something to hold water. In the pantry, finally, a ceramic vase. It would have to do. I filled it and turned off the tap.

As I did so, I heard a noise, a sudden bang from the front of the house.

I froze for a second, then ran back to the pantry, turning off the light, then to the door to the cellar, turning that light off too and coming down the steps blind. He would see the open doors. I'd opened them all over the house, and the one to the cellar was broken open. My only hope was that he'd think we'd escaped already through the back door.

'We've got to hide,' I whispered, my heart already thudding from the exertion of running up and down the steps. I took hold of her upper arm but she shrank away from me, curling into a tight ball.

'I've got water,' I said, 'come, you've got to come!' I put the vase down by the bottom step, felt for her again in the darkness and half-dragged, half-lifted her down off the bed and into the corner next to the steps. She was whimpering. There was nowhere to hide down here, not really. My only chance was that, if Colin looked down here and didn't spot us, he would assume we'd gone...

'Shhh,' I whispered, trying to get her to look at me. 'You've got to be quiet. Please be quiet.'

There was silence for a moment, broken only by my breathing and Audrey's. She sounded wheezy. If she coughed, she would give us away.

Then from upstairs, footsteps and a sudden roar. 'NO!'

Colin came crashing through the pantry to the door at the top of the stairs, the light went on and the room flooded with light. I closed my eyes tight at the sudden brightness, and even though Audrey whimpered again I realised he'd turned away almost immediately and a few moments later I could hear him calling from what must have been outside, 'Where are you? Audrey! Come back!'

Now what? I couldn't think straight. Try to get Audrey up the stairs? Try to get through the front door, assuming he hadn't locked it? He would be back long before then. If he had any sense, he would get himself away from this place quickly.

I reached for the vase and held it up to Audrey's face. In the light, despite her eyes still being screwed shut, I could see that she was pretty. Her face was dirty, streaked with grime and tears, her eyes hollow and her skin pale.

'Here,' I said, 'drink this – slowly.' She gulped at it, and I had to hold it away from her, her fingers clutching, fumbling for the vase. 'No, slowly – you'll make yourself sick. Just little sips.'

It was too late to move now: he was back inside. I heard more banging and crashing upstairs, then the floorboards creaking over our heads as he moved through the house. I could hear noises as though he was throwing things about, knocking things over.

Audrey's face creased with panic. I felt her fear, her panic.

'Don't be scared,' I said. 'I'm here. I'll protect you.'

On the divan lay the flat-handled screwdriver. Had he seen it? I leaned Audrey against the wall and put the vase on the floor, then ran to get the tool.

'What have you done?'

From the top of the stairs, the sound of Colin's voice, so calm, so unexpected, made me freeze where I was. I hid the screwdriver in my hand, palming the handle up inside my cardigan. Maybe he hadn't seen it.

'What have *I* done?' I replied, surprising myself. 'What have *you* done? You were keeping her prisoner!'

'Where is she?' he said, and to my surprise he sounded so sad, so distraught that I realised he hadn't seen her. But she gave herself away, reaching for the vase, knocking it over on to the stone floor with clumsy fingers and crying out as the water spread out around her.

'Audrey!' He came down the stairs two at a time and went to her, as though he was going to hold her, embrace her, and then stopped short as she shrank away from him. He seemed to recover himself then and he stood upright, turning to me.

'Yes, well… she's been through a lot. She needs time.'

'Without food or water? You were waiting for her to die?'

'I wouldn't hurt a fly, Annabel. You know that.'

He took a step towards me, then, and I stepped back and my calves hit the edge of the divan. I looked up the stairs and wondered if I could make it quicker than he could.

'Let us go,' I said, trying to summon up a tone of voice that suggested confidence and authority.

'You've tried to make a fool of me.' He sounded angry now, frustrated. He took another step forward.

'Don't come any closer!' I said.

He laughed, he actually laughed then. 'What, you think I'm scared of you, Annabel? Why should I be? All I've done is try to help. That's all I've ever done.' He was close enough now to touch me, and he put his hands on my upper arms as though he was going to shake me, or embrace me, or push me over. His touch was firm, his hands warm through my cardigan which was still slightly damp from the rain.

'Don't touch me,' I said, but quietly.

'You need to take some deep breaths, Annabel,' he said. 'Calm yourself down.'

Behind him, Audrey was trying to pull herself up to a standing position. He glanced round at her, and laughed then at her efforts as she fell to one side, grunting with the strain of it. In her hand, gripped at tight as she could manage, was the ceramic vase.

'You planning to hit me with that, are you?' he jeered. 'Poor Maggie. That might be her favourite vase.'

I forgot about the screwdriver and when I moved it fell out of my sleeve and on to the floor. Something took over. I twisted out of his grip and leaned back and brought my fist up and round and hit him as hard as I could on the side of his head. With it came a roar of rage and indignation, fuelled by terror at what he might do next if I gave him long enough to think about it.

He let out a noise of surprise, almost a yelp, as he spun backwards and lost his footing, falling to his hands and knees, then holding his cheek with one hand. 'Ow!' he said. 'What did you do that for?'

I clearly hadn't managed to knock him unconscious.

Audrey held up the vase. She was sobbing, her arm over her head and flailing as though the vase weighed ten times what it did. Colin was looking up at me reproachfully and she let her arm fall. The vase hit him across the temple and in the same moment I was thinking *She hasn't got the strength, what's she going to do, tickle him with it?* – he went down like a stone. Flat on his back, head to one side.

Audrey gasped, then laughed breathlessly. She sounded hysterical.

'Christ,' I said. 'I didn't think you'd hit him that hard.'

She was sobbing now, slumped back on her heels, and I stepped over Colin and went over to her and put a hand on her shoulder to provide some comfort. Then I sat down next to her and we held each other, both of us crying.

'We need to get out,' I said. 'Can you walk, do you think?' I tried to get her to her feet, her legs wobbling underneath her.

Using the wall for support, I half-dragged her up the steps and into the daylight outside the pantry. There was a man outside the back door, a member of a search team by the look of the uniform. When he caught sight of us his eyes widened and he shouted something I didn't catch, and then more people came and they took Audrey from me and someone I didn't recognise started asking me questions.

I said, 'He's down there,' and then I couldn't say anything else because I was sobbing with it, the retrospective fear. What had I done? What had I even thought I was doing, coming here with him in his car?

They walked me round through the weeds to the front of the house. There was an ambulance and several police cars and unmarked cars, as well as Colin's Fiesta, parked outside the door. And, right at the back, Sam's car.

As I went towards him I tripped over a loose slab on the pathway and fell forwards on to my hands and knees. Strong arms either side lifted me up as I said, 'Sorry, sorry,' as though it was my fault, and my knees were scraped and bleeding. I wiped the grit off my hands on to my cardigan, still damp from the rain earlier. My palms were stinging.

'Are you alright?' Sam said, when he got to me. He took my hands in his, looked at the palms and blew on them gently.

'I just tripped,' I said.

He laughed. 'I didn't mean that. I meant... God, I'm just so glad to see you.'

He put his arm around me and we moved into an awkward hug. He was patting my shoulder. I stepped away, conscious of my grubby clothes, my still-damp cardigan covered in dirt and dust.

'I tried to get here as fast as I could,' he said. 'I lost you on the main road. And then I got hold of DI Frost and after that it all happened really quickly.'

'Thanks,' I said.

'He was having kittens. I've never heard him like that. He'd just read your email. When I told him you'd gone off with Friedland it sounded like all hell broke loose.'

'Where is he?'

'He's on his way. Look, can you please not do anything like this in future? I've never been so bloody scared in my whole life.'

'You weren't the one in the car with him,' I said. 'Why the hell were *you* scared?'

'I thought he was going to kill you.'

I thought about the body on the sofa, wondered how long she had been there. How long Colin had been visiting her.

'There's another body,' I said. 'I think she's been in there a long time. He called her Maggie.'

Annabel

'I don't want to make things difficult for you, Annabel, in the circumstances – but you do realise you put the whole investigation at risk?'

I looked at Paul Moscrop's fingers, both of his hands flat on the desk in front of him, spread out as though he were trying some sort of supernatural table-tipping experiment.

The table didn't move.

'That wasn't my intention, sir.'

'Not to mention your own life.'

'Well, I thought you'd have had him under surveillance.'

He had no reply to that, of course. The teams had, as Jenna Jackson had told me, been deployed to another division.

'Of course, without your analysis we might not have found Audrey Madison in time. But nevertheless, you are not a trained investigator. You're not even working in Major Crime. You put yourself in a position of grave danger and I can't even begin to think of what might have happened if you'd got things badly wrong.'

'I know.'

I looked up briefly at Bill, who was pretending to read the top sheet of the folder open on the desk in front of him. His cheeks were red, whether from embarrassment or the warmth of the room it was difficult to tell. It being early December, the heating in all the police stations across the county was at full blast. It was stifling in here.

'The CPS have been trying to decide whether what you did constitutes entrapment.'

'You can tell them I went temporarily insane if it will help,' I offered.

'I don't really want to be here, you know, Annabel,' he said then. 'If it were up to me I'd be giving you a medal. What you did was incredibly brave, and very, very stupid.'

'I won't do it again,' I said.

'Good.' He even managed a tiny hint of a smile. 'I think we should finish there – everyone in agreement?'

Bill looked relieved and nodded; the woman from HR who had a face that could turn milk gave me a glare but nodded her assent to the DCI. The union rep looked pleased with herself. I was hoping that was a good sign.

Sam was waiting for me in the café where we'd had our first meeting, which felt like years ago but was only just over two months.

'How did it go?' he asked, when I put my bag and coat over the chair opposite him.

'It was all over in twenty minutes. I thought it would be longer than that.'

'What did they say?'

I kept him in suspense for a little while longer while I went to the counter and got us both another drink.

'They're going to phone me when they've reached their decision,' I said, sitting down.

'They should be giving you some sort of good citizen award, Annabel, not putting you through all this stress. How's Audrey?'

Audrey was staying at her parents' house for the time being. To my surprise, as well as hers, probably, we'd become quite good friends. Physically she had recovered well, but she was not sleeping and was suffering from regular panic attacks. Not having to worry about going to work while I was suspended pending the disciplinary investigation, I had been visiting her every day. Sam had come with me once or twice, but we could both tell that Audrey wasn't comfortable with him being there.

'Vaughn phoned while I was there.'

'Oh?'

'He wants to go and see her. She's not having any of it.'

'I guess she probably blames him, somehow. Poor bloke. Bad at choosing his friends.'

This morning she had been dressed, in jeans and a T-shirt that was too big for her, but it was still a step up from the grubby dressing gown. She'd washed her hair.

'Wow,' I'd said. 'We going out somewhere?'

She'd looked briefly panic-stricken, and then she'd smiled at me. When she smiled, she looked so different. She was the sort of girl who would have been way too cool to associate with me at school, or at work, for that matter. She would have been friends with Kate and the rest of them, and would never have paid me any attention. When I'd thought about that, I'd asked her mum if she really thought Audrey wanted me to come round and visit, or if she just felt sorry for me.

'Oh, no,' she'd replied. 'Please don't stop coming. Audrey's completely in awe of you. She says you're the bravest and strongest person she knows.'

'Audrey's not too bad,' I said to Sam. 'She was even dressed today. I'm hoping she'll want to come out of the house soon.'

'That's good news. Has she said any more about what happened?'

She had told me some of it. I knew Sam wouldn't print anything about it unless he had permission to do so, although he was desperate to do it. It was almost as though he wanted to take his revenge on Colin using the best method at his disposal. But he was silenced by his own moral code, and by the fact that printing the details of Audrey's captivity would prejudice a future trial.

'She's getting there. She needs time.'

He had tried to do whatever it was he did to me – hypnotise her, brainwash her, whatever it was – but it hadn't worked, he'd had no mental control over her and so he had kept her locked up. She'd felt as though she was being disposed of. She had been afraid of closing her eyes and sleeping, in case she woke up to find him there. Or in case she never woke up at all.

Sam drank his cappuccino, recognising that I wasn't going to say more. 'So, when they ring you, is that the end of it?'

'I guess so. Either I get the boot, or I go back to work.'

'Well, at least it means you can come on holiday with us. If you're back at work tomorrow you can put in a leave request, can't you?'

He'd been pressing me on this for the last fortnight. They were going to stay in a cottage in Devon for a week over the Christmas period, booked last year. Only two bedrooms, but Sam was going to sleep on the sofa if I came along. I needed a holiday, Irene insisted.

What I need is to go home and start sorting out my life, I thought.

'I really don't think I can come with you,' I said. 'It's a very kind offer. But I have so much I need to do. And I can't leave Audrey.'

'As you said, she's getting better. One week won't make a difference. Everything you need to do will all still be here when we get back.'

We needed to have that conversation, the one that had been hanging over us ever since he'd arranged my move into the spare room. I'd been putting it off and hoping the problem would go away, but it was getting worse.

'Sam,' I began. God, this was awkward. 'I don't really understand. I just don't know... what it is you want from me?'

'I don't want anything,' he said, cheerfully.

'I mean – I don't know. We're friends, right?'

'Yes, of course.'

'Nothing else? I just – it feels weird that I moved into your house. And now going on holiday with you. I'm no good at all this stuff; I never really understand people's motives. And I'd really hate for you to be... you know... expecting...'

'I'm not expecting anything, he said. 'And it's not weird that you moved in. We invited you, didn't we? It's what friends do – help each other out.'

'I'm sorry,' I said. I was feeling hot all of a sudden. The fact that he was so disarmingly relaxed was making it far more difficult even than I'd imagined it might be.

'You don't need to be,' he said.

'Are you gay?' I said quickly. 'I mean, not that you have to be gay not to be interested in me, far from it, I mean why would you be interested in me, after all? I'm twelve years older than you at least and... well...' I looked down at myself as though that made the point.

Sam's gulp of coffee had gone down the wrong way. When he recovered, he stared into the dregs of his cup intently, as though the answer lay in the foam.

'I'm not gay.' He was smiling, trying not to laugh. 'I'm just happily single right now, is that OK?'

There was a momentary pause. I sipped my tea. This wasn't going very well. I was just working up to another apology when he surprised me.

'It's not that you're not attractive. I think you're lovely, and of course you're clever and very interesting to talk to, even though you don't seem to realise it. But...' He took a deep breath in. 'Can we just be friends?'

'Yes,' I said, with relief. 'That sounds great.'

'And that means we can go on holiday?'

I couldn't very well refuse now, could I? 'Alright, then,' I said. 'As friends.'

In my bag, my phone started ringing. The caller display showed a withheld number – which meant it was probably Police HQ. I took a deep breath and answered it.

Colin

I've always taken pride in making the best of any given situation. Even if I do whinge and complain from time to time, I see that as being a healthy expression of indignation, pertaining to any infringement of my basic rights.

In this case, my right to liberty.

The solicitor (invariably they seem to send the junior out to me, a young man in an ill-fitting suit with a pustular outbreak around his hairline – but he seems efficient enough) has been unable to tell me exactly how long I might be here. They have me on remand, charged with abduction and assault, which is horrific enough but not beyond the limits of my endurance. I have achieved a certain notoriety already, and, as for those of my fellow jailbirds who choose not to take me seriously, I only have to look at them in a certain way and mumble a few incantations and they back off immediately. It's really rather comical, and it passes the time.

The downside to my notoriety is that this is the third remand centre I've been shipped to since my second arrest. Every time a suicide takes place in whatever institution I'm in, they decide I must be responsible for it and move me elsewhere.

It's utterly ridiculous, of course, as I've told them many times – I have no interest in death itself. Why would I even bother? Being moved around like this is a hideous inconvenience. I don't know why they don't just put me in some sort of solitary confinement; that would be infinitely more agreeable to me. I might suggest it if I get moved again.

I am also getting letters from people in the most appalling circumstances – people paralysed following accidents, suffering terminal illnesses, those who want to 'die with dignity' but can't afford to take themselves off to Switzerland and don't want their loved ones to take any blame.

I can't help them, of course. Well, perhaps I could – and in response to one particularly touching letter I did reply suggesting they research voluntary refusal of food on the internet – but why the hell should I? There is nothing for me following their death, after all. There will be no process to observe.

I've given up reading the newspapers. I was in an almost constant state of outrage. The debate about euthanasia that has been provoked by my activity was quite intriguing to follow, but once the 'bereaved families' formed themselves into a mutual support group I had to stop reading. *Bereaved families*, indeed. Where were they when their so-called 'loved ones' were suffering? What support did they provide to the lonely, the depressed, the suicidal? None at all. And now they want some sort of justice. I despair of this country and the depths to which it has sunk.

As part of the preparation for the court case, they arranged for a psychological evaluation of me, which was most entertaining. In fact it remains so because the process seems to be never-ending – once one of them has finished with me, they send someone else, so I am clearly an intriguing case for them. Are they trying to decide if I'm sane?

After a particularly interesting discussion with one of the psychologists regarding guilt and blame, I wrote to Audrey to apologise formally. What happened with her was a dreadful misunderstanding, of course, and I do regret it deeply. Whether they passed the letter on is a matter for them.

Vaughn, on the other hand, can go to hell as far as I'm concerned. I have no desire for further communication with him.

I sometimes think about all the others – and there are still more – who remain in peace at home. I think about what might be left. I have wondered about Leah, too – where she might be now and whether she has continued down her path without my encouragement. I had thought her still unsure, but who knows what has happened to her and her unfortunate married lover since then. If she has turned back from that particular Underworld, followed the path behind her apathetic Orpheus back to life, it may be that she has memories of our meeting and may come forward. Would she speak for me, I wonder, or against me? It all depends on her frame of mind. They all know I did nothing of harm to them. They all know I was on their side.

There has been no mention of the images and my accompanying notes, and I presume from this that they remain safely hidden. I have no doubt that if they came to light it would prejudice my trial, if it ever takes place, even though they show nothing other than decay. There is no further crime they could charge me with, but if the prosecution showed the pictures in court I can imagine the jury would take it the wrong way. Without them, it may be possible that this whole sorry farce will result in a very brief custodial sentence, probably a suspended one in recognition of time spent on remand.

I could be free quite soon, in fact.

I've asked for books to be brought from home, but instead they limit me to the library here, which is insufficient for my needs but, as they say, better than nothing. However, unfortunately several of the requests I have submitted have been declined without reason. It's enough to make me wish they would hurry up and convict me of whatever it is they think I've done, just so that I can get back to studying something more interesting than the state of the canteen assistants' fingernails and the endless pile of letters I've been receiving, including some from women who suddenly, and ironically, seem to find me irresistible. I re-read these for my own amusement, since there is precious little else to do. Sometimes I correct the spelling and grammar – 'you didn't need to do them things you done, you could of had me' – dear

God, I ask you – and sometimes I spend a while picturing the females who take the time to write to me. Easier, of course, when they have enclosed a photograph. One last week was even wearing a bikini, but that was unfortunate and with the best will in the world the sight of her was not enough to provoke even a flicker of arousal.

There is one, however…

Her name is Nancy Heppelthwaite and she is twenty-nine years old. She studied at Oxford and enjoys art, music and literature. She paints. She dances, sometimes, but she has never met anyone she likes to dance with. She has yet to send a photograph even though I have replied and requested one – but in a way I'm glad she remains faceless, as I can impose any number of wonderful thoughts upon her, in those restless hours after lights-out when all you can hear are the shouts and moans of the insane ones who shouldn't be on remand at all, the sobs of the lonely and the homesick, and the grunts of all the others like me who fill the dark hours with harmless acts of self-abuse. They use posters ripped from the pages of *Nuts* and *FHM*, or disturbing pictures of their wives in their underwear. I use Nancy's letter.

Ahead of me lie several paths, and, although limited by the restrictions of the British Criminal Justice System (may it rest in peace), I can still choose my own destiny. I want – oh, I dearly want – to experiment with letters to Nancy, to see what may come of this blossoming attraction between us. And, of course, it may yet be possible to extend my influence to her through prison visits (a privilege to which I am entitled, but have yet to avail myself of) or even, simply, through writing.

Leaving Nancy reluctantly aside, there remains the greatest adventure of all. I have within me the power to change. They would not leave me to transform naturally, of course, but I can leave a will and express the desire for burial over cremation – which would mean the process would take place much as my father's did. It would not be a gentle transformation in the privacy of my own home, which would be the best of all, but it would be acceptable to me, I think.

For now, though, I am not ready. I am at the very beginning of enlightenment, the very source of knowledge. There is so much still to do.

Acknowledgements

I would like to thank everyone in the extended Myriad Editions family, not just for this book, but for the love and support you have all shown to me over the past few years. It might seem simplistic to describe Myriad as a family, but that's how it feels: everyone connected with the organisation, and their families too, are a part of the enterprise. There is a real sense of belonging, and I am incredibly fortunate to be in on it. Thank you all. There are two members of the Myriad family, however, whom I would like to thank in particular: my wonderful editor, Vicky Blunden, and my genius copy-editor, Linda McQueen. They made this book so much better. Thank you.

Many individuals provided me with very specific help and advice with particular aspects of *Human Remains*, and so I would like to express my thanks to: Caroline Luxford-Noyes, for a long conversation in which she described to me how a person's life might end in hospital; Dean Edwards, for the details surrounding a disciplinary investigation; Freddie Elspass-Collins for his expertise concerning the Coroner's Office; Fi Gutsell for insight into the life of a reporter on a local newspaper, and Sarah Hockley for putting us in touch in the first place; Niki Baier, David Baier and Liz Dyer for assistance with regard to funeral arrangements; David Holmes, Ernie Pratt, Paul Pope and Wayne Totterdell who generously shared their experiences of attending scenes; and Mike Silverman, whose description of decomposition odours over a CWA lunch in Brighton proved too tempting to resist.

In particular I would like to thank Mitch Humphrys and Lisa Cutts, for checking the entire manuscript for procedural issues, and for being so kind and supportive with your comments all the way through the writing and editing process.

As well as Mitch and Lisa, I would like to thank those who also read early drafts of *Human Remains* and provided me with fresh perspectives, pointed out crucial omissions and inconsistencies, and yet still managed to make me feel that I'd written something quite good: Alison Arnold from Text Publishing, Rob Hope, and my genius husband David who has developed a real knack for spotting opportunities I've missed. Thank you.

Many of my friends kindly provided listening ears and I'm sorry not to mention you all – but in particular, thanks are due to Samantha Bowles and Katie Totterdell who had to endure every last whinge. Bless you both.

I would also like to thank Paul Moscrop and Lindsay Brown, for allowing me to use their names, and for not being too concerned about how they were used!

Over the past year I've been lucky to have met a number of book groups, as part of the Big Book Group tour, via Skype, and by having been invited into people's homes. I wanted to say thank you very much to everyone I've met, for your enthusiasm, and your kindness in making me feel so welcome and special.

Last and best thanks and love to those who have put up with the most – my family. I love you all.

A F T E R W O R D :

What was the starting point for Human Remains?
As an analyst working for Kent Police, I did receive a copy of the Chief Constable's report every morning, and with some degree of regularity this would include bodies found in a state of decomposition. There was never (to my knowledge) an alarming increase in the numbers, but I found myself wondering what I would do if I did notice something like this – and who or what might be the cause. The thought of that made me shiver, which is always the best sort of starting point for a novel.

How much did you draw on your own experience working as a police analyst in the writing of this book?
I've always felt the role of analysts within law enforcement has been sadly overlooked by fiction writers, and I thought it was time to redress the balance. However, it's harder than it might seem to convey the excitement that we analysts sometimes feel over a particularly enlightening spreadsheet – it makes us sound really geeky and dull. But I've always found beauty in patterns, and it's the perfect sort of puzzle, where something random and nebulous suddenly clears, the various pieces slide into focus and you realise that what you have is evidence about the circumstances of a crime. Everyone in law enforcement knows that thrill, when you realise you've found something nobody has spotted yet. I hope I've managed to convey something of that.

The novel is told from the perspectives of both Colin and Annabel and, movingly, the dead. What made you decide to structure it in this way?
I wanted to experiment a little more with narrative voice, having used a past-present narrative structure in both *Into the Darkest Corner* and *Revenge of the Tide*. I also liked the idea of the roles of predator/prey and hunter/hunted and I thought it was interesting that Annabel and Colin take both roles at different points in the story. Having researched articles, stories and films about those who decide to withdraw from society

390

and end up dying alone, I wanted to explore the potential reasons why people make this choice – and to consider our responsibility as a society to find that balance between caring for our neighbours, and recognising our right to make adult decisions for ourselves as individuals. It's difficult to know whether dying in your own home, alone, and at a time of your choosing, is something that should be seen as a tragedy or as a basic human right.

Did you enjoy conjuring up Colin's voice? Do you think he has any redeeming qualities?

It was without doubt a challenge for me to write a male voice, and more specifically one that is so unusual. Without wishing to sound unhinged myself, it took me a long time to persuade Colin to 'open up' and let me write his story. It was particularly daunting because he's clearly far more intelligent than I am and I'm sure he wouldn't consider me to be equal to the task. Despite his idiosyncrasies, I find his unrelenting confidence in his own importance quite funny.

How did you come up with his particular technique?

There are elements of many different therapies or systems at play in Colin's technique, all of which are fundamentally designed to be therapeutic or empowering. What Colin does is subtly twist things so that what people actually want – to die without pain or fear – is accomplished in such a way that he can also benefit. One of the principles underpinning neuro-linguistic programming is that it needs to benefit both the practitioner and the individual with whom rapport is built – in other words, win-win. Despite his unusual desires, and his undeniable lack of integrity, Colin's technique still achieves this to a certain degree.

Do you think it could be possible in reality for someone like Colin to use benign therapies for evil intent?

NLP is a powerful way to approach communication, and at its best can be empowering, helping people to change their lives for the better, to encourage them to take control of their own destinies and realise their goals. Whether a combination of NLP, hypnosis and mind control could achieve what Colin does in my story is another matter. Colin's technique is only successful with those who have already chosen a particular path, after all.

Do you think there is such a thing as an untraceable murder?
No, but it's endlessly intriguing to try and imagine one. Everything leaves a trace – the trick is knowing where to look.

This is your third novel; how does it differ from *Into the Darkest Corner* and *Revenge of the Tide*?
The first two books are fundamentally about relationships, so I wanted to write a book about the absence of them, about people existing in the world and revolving around the wider society like satellites – living as part of the system but not connecting with it. I am intrigued by the idea of loneliness – or, more accurately, aloneness – as a lifestyle choice.

How did you decide on the structure for *Into the Darkest Corner*?
I wanted to write a dual narrative to explore the story of the same character four years apart, to show the difference in her life before and after a traumatic event. In *Into the Darkest Corner* we meet Catherine as a carefree and outgoing twenty-something, living her life to the full, but we also see her four years later, clearly suffering from crippling OCD and terrified for her safety. Running the two strands of her story in parallel allowed the contrast to unfold, from how she copes with Christmas, for example, to more essential themes such as her opinion of herself; her courage, her fears, her self-esteem. And the structure provided the perfect way to build suspense, since the reader is waiting to find out what happened to Catherine in between those times, and whether her fears in the present are justified after all.

When we meet Genevieve in *Revenge of the Tide* she's living on a houseboat on the River Medway. What made you choose this setting for the novel?

I've always been intrigued by the idea of living on a boat, and as I live quite close to Rochester and the River Medway I thought it would be a great place to write about. I really enjoyed threading Genevieve's adventure through locations that are familiar to me; it made the whole story much more real. The river can be so beautiful in the sunshine, with Rochester Castle standing guard over it, but at night time, on a foggy night in November, it can be quite chilling too. For Genevieve, at the start of the novel, living on a houseboat is a long-held dream, but it rapidly turns into a nightmare when a body washes up against the side of her boat, and she recognises the victim. The story of how she came to escape her double-life in London – office worker by day and pole dancer by night – is revealed as her sense of security in her new life unravels, and the boatyard that initially felt like such a safe haven can't hide her secrets forever.

How has your life changed since the publication of your first novel, *Into the Darkest Corner*?

It's all gone a bit mad, really. I have to keep pinching myself, since the life I'm living now is pretty close to the writerly fantasies I had as a teenager. I did think I'd rather like to live in a converted lighthouse on a clifftop, but for now I'm quite happy with my writing shed. I particularly enjoy meeting book groups, in person or via Skype. It's a real privilege to get feedback from readers and I'm always amazed and chuffed to bits when people take the time to email to let me know what they thought. I still can't quite believe that I am a writer and I struggle to call myself that if anyone asks what I do for a living. I can manage to think of myself as a novelist – as is everyone who successfully completes National Novel Writing Month! – but being a proper writer somehow still seems a little unreal, as though the day I take that on board will be the day it all ends. For now, though, I'm going to enjoy everything while I can.

If you have enjoyed *Human Remains*, you might also like Elizabeth Haynes' bestselling second novel *Revenge of the Tide*

For an exclusive extract, read on...

One

It was there when I opened my eyes, that vague feeling of discomfort, the rocking of the boat signalling the receding tide and the wind from the south, blowing upriver, straight into the side of the *Revenge of the Tide*.

For a long while I lay in bed, the sound of the waves slapping against the hull next to my head, echoing through the steel and dulled by the wooden cladding. The duvet was warm and it was easy to stay there, the rectangle of the skylight directly above showing the blackness turning to dark blue, and grey, and then I could see the clouds scudding overhead, giving the odd impression of moving at speed – the boat moving rather than the clouds. And then, that discomfort again.

It wasn't seasickness, or river-sickness, come to that: I was used to it now, nearly five months after I had left London. Five months living aboard. There was still a momentary shock when my feet hit the solid ground of the path to the car park, a few wobbly steps, but it was never long before I felt steady again.

It was a grey sort of a day – not ideal for the get-together later, but that was my own fault for planning a party in September. 'Back to school' weather, the wind whistling across the deck when I got up and put my head out of the wheelhouse.

No, it wasn't the tide, or the thought of the mismatched group of people who would be descending on my boat later today. There was something else. I felt as though someone had rubbed my fur the wrong way.

The plan for the day: finish the last bit of timber cladding for the second room, the room that was going to be a guest bedroom at some point in the future. Clear away all the carpentry tools and store them in the bow. Sweep out the boat, clean up a bit. Then see if I could cadge a lift to the cash-and-carry for party food and beer.

There was one wall left to do, an odd shape, which was why I had left it till last. The room was full of sawdust and offcuts of wood, bits of edging and sandpaper. I'd done the measurements last night but now, frowning at the bit of paper, I decided to recheck it all just to be on the safe side. When I had clad the galley I'd ended up wasting a load of wood because I misread my own measurements.

I put the radio on, turned up loud even though I still couldn't hear it above the mitre saw, and got to work.

At nine, I stopped and went back through to the galley for a coffee. I filled the kettle and put it on to the gas burner. The boat was a mess. It was only occasionally that I noticed it. Glancing around, I scanned last night's takeaway containers hurriedly shoved into a carrier bag ready to go out to the main bins. Dirty dishes in the sink. Pans and other items in boxes sitting on one of the dinette seats waiting to be put away, now I had finally fitted cupboard doors in the galley. A black plastic sack of fabrics and netting that would one day be curtains and cushion covers. None of it mattered when I was the only one in here, but in a few hours' time this boat would be full of people, and I had promised them that the renovations were almost complete.

Almost complete? That was stretching the truth a little thin. I had finished the bedroom, and the living room wasn't bad. The galley was done too, but needed cleaning and tidying. The bathroom was – well, the kindest thing that could be said about it was that it was functional. As for the rest of it – the vast space in the bow that would one day be a bigger bathroom with a bath instead of a hose for a shower, a wide conservatory area with a sliding glass roof (an ambitious plan, but I'd seen one in a magazine and it looked so brilliant that it was the one project I was determined to complete), and maybe a snug or an office or another unnamed room that would be wonderful and cosy and magical – for the moment, it worked as storage.

The kettle started a low whistle, and I rinsed a mug under the tap and spooned in some instant coffee, two spoons: I needed the caffeine.

A pair of boots crossed my field of vision through the porthole, level with the pontoon outside, shortly followed by a call from the deck. 'Genevieve?'

'Down here. Kettle's just boiled, want a drink?'

Moments later Joanna trotted down the steps and into the main cabin. She was dressed in a miniskirt, with thick socks and heavy boots, with the laces trailing, on the ends of her skinny legs. The top half of her was counterbalanced by one of Liam's jumpers, a navy blue one, flecked with bits of sawdust and twig and cat hair. Her hair was a tangle of curls and waves of various colours.

'No, thanks – we're off out in a minute. I just came to ask what time we should come over later, and do you want us to bring a lasagne as well as the cheesecake? And Liam says he's got some beers left over from the barbecue, he'll be bringing those.'

She had a bruise on her cheek. Joanna didn't wear make-up, wouldn't have known what to do with it, so there it was – livid and purplish, about the size of a fifty pence piece, under her left eye.

'What happened to your face?'

'Oh, don't you start. I had a fight with my sister.'

'Blimey.'

'Come up on deck, I need a smoke.'

The wind was still whipping, so we sat on the bench by the wheelhouse. The sun was trying to make its way through the scudding clouds but failing. Across the other side of the marina I could see Liam loading boxes and carrier bags into the back of their battered Transit van.

Joanna fished around in the pocket of her skirt and brought forth a pouch of tobacco. 'The way I see it,' she said, 'she should keep her fucking nose out of my business.'

'Your sister?'

'She thinks she's all clever because she's got herself a mortgage at the age of twenty-two.'

'Mortgages aren't all they're cracked up to be.'

'Exactly!' Joanna said with emphasis. 'That's what I said to her. I've got everything she's got without the burden of debt. And I don't have to mow any lawn.'

'So that's what you were fighting about?'

Joanna was quiet for a moment, her eyes wandering over to the car park where Liam stood, hands on his hips, before pointedly looking at his wristwatch and climbing into the driver's seat. Above the sounds of the marina – drilling coming from the workshop, the sound of the radio down in the cabin, the distant roar of the traffic from the motorway bridge – the van's diesel rattle started up.

'Fuck it, I'd better go,' she said. She shoved the pouch back into her pocket and lit the skinny cigarette she'd just managed to fill. 'About seven? Eight? What?'

I shrugged. 'I don't know. Sevenish? Lasagne sounds lovely, but don't go to any trouble.'

'It's no trouble. Liam's made it.'

With a backward wave, Joanna took one quick hop-step down the gangplank and on to the pontoon, running despite the boots across the grassy bank and up to the car park. The Transit was taking little jumps forward as though it couldn't wait to be gone.

At four, the cabin was finally finished. A bare shell, but at least now it was a bare wooden shell. The walls were clad, and the berth built along the far wall, under the porthole. Where the mattress would sit, two trapdoors with round finger-holes in the board gave access to the storage compartment underneath. The rest of it was pale wood in neat panelling, carved pine edging covering the joins and corners. It would look less like a sauna once it had had a lick of paint, I thought. By next weekend it would be entirely different.

Clearing away the debris of my most recent foray into carpentry took longer than I thought it would. I had crates for the tools. I hadn't bothered to put them away since I'd started work on the bedroom, months ago.

I lugged them forward into the bow, through a hatch and into the cavernous space below. Three steps down, watching my head on the low ceiling, stowing the crates away at the side.

It was only when I made the last trip, carrying the black plastic sack of fabric from the dinette and throwing it into the front compartment, that I found myself looking into the darkest of the spaces to see if the box was still there. I could just about see it in the gloomy light from the cabin above; on the side of it was written, in thick black marker: KITCHEN STUFF.

I had a sudden urge to look, to check that the box still had its contents. Of course it did, I told myself. Of course it was still there. *Nobody's been down here since you put it there.*

Stooping, I crossed the three wooden pallets that served as a floor, braced myself against the sides of the hull, and crouched next to the box. KITCHEN STUFF. The top two-thirds of the box was full of rubbish I'd brought from the London flat – spatulas, wooden spoons, a Denby teapot with a crack in the lid, a whisk, a blender that didn't work, an ice cream scoop and various cake tins nested inside each other. Below that was a sheet of cardboard that might, to the casual observer, look sufficiently like the bottom of the box to deter further investigation.

I folded the cardboard top of the box back down and tucked the other flap underneath it.

From the back pocket of my jeans, I took out a mobile phone. I found the address book and the only number that was saved there: GARLAND. That was all it said. It wasn't even his name. It would be so easy to press the little green button now and call him. What would I say? Maybe I could just ask him if he wanted to come tonight. '*Come to my party, Dylan. It's just a few close friends. I'd love to see you.*'

What would he say? He'd be angry, shocked that I'd used the phone when he'd expressly told me not to. It was only there for one purpose, he'd told me. It was only for him to ring me, and only when he was ready to make the collection. Not before. If I ever had a call on it from another number, I wasn't to answer.

I closed my eyes for a moment, for a brief second allowing myself the indulgence of remembering him. Then I put the screen lock back on the phone so it didn't accidentally dial any numbers, least of all his, and I shoved it in my pocket and made my way back to the cabin.

**To read on, buy your copy
of *Revenge of the Tide*
from any good bookseller**

MORE FROM MYRIAD EDITIONS

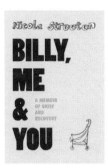

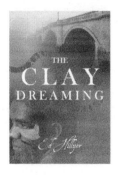

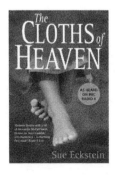
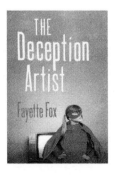

MORE FROM MYRIAD EDITIONS

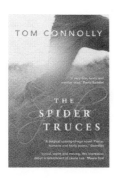

www.myriadeditions.com